The Soulmate Theory

SARAH A. BAILEY

Cover Design and Illustration by Gemma Rakia

Editing by Jacelyn Schley

For my Bubs,
Thank you for believing my mind was capable of creating art worth sharing with the world.

And for inspiring all my soulmate theories, too.

Playlist

Summertime Sadness | Lana Del Rey

Homesick | Noah Kahan

Can't Fight This Feeling | REO Speedwagon

Surf | Mac Miller

10,000 Emerald Pools| BØRNS

It's Nice To Have A Friend | Taylor Swift

Until I Found You | Stephen Sanchez

Take Me To Church | Hozier

Past Lives | BØRNS

Hey Girl | Stephen Sanchez

Astronomy | Conan Gray

This Love | Taylor Swift

Author's Note

Please be advised that there is content within this story that may be sensitive for some readers. You can find a comprehensive list of content warnings on my website:
sarahabaileyauthor.com
With love,
S.A.B

Five Years Ago

Carter

I can't decide if the Universe loves me or hates me.

Maybe it loves to hate me. Maybe it's mischievous. Maybe this is all karma. Karma for what, I couldn't be sure, but I've done something to catch the Universe's attention and I think it's definitely fucking with me. Because I'm in love. I'm madly, deeply, painfully in love with a girl that I know I'll never have. Because the heavens created arguably the most perfect creature in their repertoire, dangled her in front of me for my entire life, and chose to rip her away before I had the chance to tell her how I felt.

There is no other reasonable explanation for the series of events. Fate sucks.

I always thought falling in love would feel like flying, soaring, swimming through clouds. But being in love with her feels more like a punch to the stomach. A karate chop to the throat. A wipe out on a surfboard. The way she looks in that green dress. Pretty much anything that can knock the wind right out of you and make you forget how to breathe. It's confusing and excruciating, an overall aching in your chest cavity. Living for the slight hope that maybe it's all worth it because she can't breathe either. Moments like that do exist, sometimes. Rare moments where I'm sure she feels the same way. Well, maybe not so madly, deeply, painfully; but maybe something's there. When she looks at me in a certain light, or when she laughs at my jokes. When she smiles that smile that's just for me.

I didn't notice it at first– *that* smile. I watched her smile at everyone she knows. Her smiles were a little different with each of them, her special way of making everyone around her feel special too. We were nine years old when I found a penny on the ground and I gave it to her. I thought she needed luck more than I did because I felt lucky just to know her. That was the first time she gave me the smile that was just mine. A smile unique in itself, something she doesn't give anyone else. That day felt like flying. Soaring. Swimming through clouds.

"You have to make a move," Dom whispered in my ear. I rolled my eyes at my best friend.

I didn't want a joint graduation party at first. Our parents insisted because that's what would be easiest for them. They were best friends, after all. It made sense to celebrate the high school graduation of both Penelope and I at the same time.

Except, Penelope was going to the University of Oxford. *That* Oxford.

I was going to Hawaii. Not to be confused with the University of Hawaii.

No, I was just going to the state of Hawaii. Not for anything in particular but just because my mother lived there and I had no idea what I wanted to do with my life. I thought I'd rather figure it out on the beach than in the rain of the Pacific Northwest. My plan was to have no plan at all, much to the disappointment of my father. The last thing I needed was all of his friends from the country club telling Penelope how impressive she is while patting me on the back in pity.

I watched it happen now as a group of her father's doctor friends gathered around her asking her about her plans. When was she leaving? Where would she be staying? What did she plan to study? She looked uncomfortable, and I wished there was a way I could save her from this moment of unwanted attention, but unfortunately, I'm not the true Guest of Honor at this party.

She looked beautiful, though. Her thick auburn hair and the way it flowed down her back in waves, tapering out towards the bottom. Her skin looked like a painting, without a flaw. Little freckles sprinkled like cinnamon across her bare arms and the bridge of her nose. Her cheeks flushed slightly with embarrassment, but it tended to make her glow as her emerald eyes glistened in the evening sun. The most debilitating of her features was, without a doubt, her lips, resting in a perfect pout as she nodded her head in conversation. I was entranced as her tongue snaked out across her bottom lip. She pulled it down under her teeth, the way she does when she's asked a question she doesn't know how to respond to. I used to watch her do that in the middle of math, much to my distraction. She somehow always made math my favorite subject of them all. Most likely because it was her worst, and she spent a frequent amount of time biting down on her lip.

"Now is your last chance," Dom said. He was right, but he was also wrong. Tomorrow Penelope would be boarding a flight across one ocean, and in two weeks I'd be boarding a flight across another. Oxford, England and Honolulu, Hawaii may very well be the farthest destinations we could possibly get from each other on this planet. So, he was wrong. My last chance passed a long time ago because that ship had sailed and I was not on it.

Penelope and I had always seemed to be on two separate planets, always orbiting each other but never making contact. We were neighbors, our parents were best friends. Most of our childhood was spent in-between the back doors of each house, coming and going as we pleased. We had joint family vacations, holidays, and parties– obviously. All of the situations that should force two people into something that would make us feel like siblings.

And while we were friends, it was never like that for us. I fell too early, too hard. I'd never be able to see her in the light I was supposed to see her in. But it was never quite like that for her, of that I was certain. I used to hope someday our planets would end up colliding either destroying us, or welding us into something completely new. I grew too afraid of either outcome, so I kept to my planet and she kept to hers.

"No, I can't," I said. Dom moved to stand in front of me, pity in his brown eyes. He was the only person on earth that knew how deep my feelings for her truly ran.

"Actually, I think you can. I think you *should*. What is the worst that can happen? She leaves tomorrow. So, tell her how you feel, and if she tells you she doesn't feel the same and things get awk-ward– well, you'll never have to see her again."

"I don't want to never see her again." We may have been on different planets but she was always a part of my solar system, and I could convince myself that was enough. My stomach tied in knots thinking about the fact that I would wake up tomorrow morning without her being just across the street from me.

"You don't really have a choice in that, bud. She's leaving whether she knows how you feel or not. You may run into each other from time to time, but she's not going to be part of your everyday life anymore. You might as well get it all out there," he said as he shrugged.

I began to think there may be a certain relief that may come with putting it all on the table, knowing there would be no real consequences. Except that it may break my heart. Rupture my soul. Punch me in the stomach, karate chop my throat, wipe me out.

Maybe that was exactly what I needed. The absolute certainty that would come with her rejection would allow me to move on. No more fear of collision, but an absence of her entirely. With that thought, my chest dropped to my knees.

"She's going inside. Go." Dom shoved me towards the doors that led from my backyard, where the party was being held, into my house. There'd hardly be anyone inside. Penelope slipped through the doors, likely needing a quiet respite from the chaos of a few dozen people wanting to know all the details of her future. That made me feel guilty because I was about to offer her no respite at all. Dom was right, though. It was now or never, and I wasn't sure I wanted to go on with never telling her how I felt. I looked around to make sure nobody was watching her before slipping through the door myself. I had a feeling I knew exactly where to find her.

Our house held a sunroom off the entrance. It was a small space paneled with windows giving an abundance of light. Our family didn't use it much other than my stepmother, Marlena, who kept her house plants there. Penelope would come over sometimes with her mother, who was an artist, and they would paint together. The sunroom gave off the best possible lighting. I knew it was her favorite place between both houses, except maybe the ledge of the roof outside her bedroom window. Sure enough, as I made it to the sunroom, I found her. Her back was turned to me and she was staring at a canvas of her mother's.

"Pep?" I asked.

She turned around as if slightly startled, before shaking her head and letting out a breath. "Hey."

"Are you okay?"

She shrugged. "You know, it's just a lot. Everyone asking about our entire life plan and whatnot."

I laughed. "Nobody is asking me."

"Isn't your whole vibe to like, not have a plan?"

"I guess," I chuckled. I found myself rubbing my arm against the back of my neck, unsure of how to go about things. She was right. I rarely had a plan. I kind of winged life, and most of the time I liked it that way. Except now, I hated it because I didn't know how to wing this– telling Penelope that I was in love with her.

After a moment of awkward silence, she smiled softly and said, "We should probably get back to the party, Carter." I started to follow her, fully prepared not to say another word. Prepared to let this go. *I should let this go.* I felt a pang in my chest, a reminder of the dull ache inside my heart. She was clearly overwhelmed already. It would be inconsiderate of me to dump my guts on her just to make myself feel better.

Against my better judgment, I strode up behind her and grabbed her hand. She whipped to face me with a puzzled expression. I looked around quickly, unsure of what I was even doing. The kitchen pantry was on my right, so I yanked the door open and pulled her inside, shutting it behind us. The pantry was small, causing us to be pressed up against each other chest to chest. She leaned back as far as she could and I could tell, even in the dark, her eyes were wide in shock and confusion.

"Carter–" she began to protest but I cut her off.

"I don't know if I'll be able to live with myself if I don't do this, and now may be my last chance," I said through bated breaths, my face closer to hers than it had ever been.

"Okay," she whispered, to my surprise. She said okay.

She said okay.

I didn't know what I was expecting her to say, but it wasn't that. As my eyes adjusted to the darkness, I began to make out her features. Her eyes were still wide, now with anticipation rather than shock. Her perfect lips parted just slightly, feeling like an invitation.

There were so many words that should've been coming from my mouth. So many things I was supposed to be telling her. Yet, I found them lodged in my throat because it felt as if there were not enough words to be said. No words to describe the intensity that I felt in that proximity to her. My hand cupped her face and I rubbed my thumb across her cheek. She shivered at my touch but didn't flinch or recoil. Time seemed to suspend itself as my hand moved down her cheek and behind her neck. I leaned into her, bringing my face so close that I could feel her breath against my lips. I stopped, waiting for her to tell me no. Waiting for her to pull away. She didn't say no, though. She didn't pull away, either. She didn't hesitate when *she* closed the gap between us.

Her lips felt as soft, as warm, and as perfect as I always thought they would. It was gentle in a way I would've always expected. Almost timid, the way her hand found itself on my chest. I didn't just want to kiss Penelope anymore. I *needed* to kiss her. I never needed something more.

Her head tilted to the side, opening her mouth to me. A small moan escaped her throat and I thought I may very well lose myself right in that moment. I tangled my fingers into her hair, deepening the kiss. My other hand came around her back and dug into her hips. I kissed her with everything in me. All the words I couldn't say, all the emotions floating in my head. I kissed her with all the fervor in my body and all of the force inside my soul. I traced my tongue across her lip, groaning as I tasted her for the very first time. She tasted like strawberries and wine.

So, so sweet and harmfully intoxicating. I was fully drunk on her. Head foggy by her lips, body flaming by her touch. If her kisses were the new alcohol, then my heart must surely be the new liver, because this would ruin me beyond repair.

I pushed those thoughts aside, unconcerned with the aftermath. I brought my hand away from her head and slowly slid down her neck, over her shoulder, my fingers snaking across her collar bone.

God, I love her collar bones.

A body part that should be entirely inconsequential, but on her, utterly alluring. I explored her body slowly and with care, touching only the places I think she'd allow. Something in the way she pressed against me told me she'd be okay with any of it, but I knew the moment may be the only of its kind, and I dared not do anything that would jeopardize it. I moved down her waist and back to her hips, feeling the way they flared out in contrast. I brought my hand around to her backside, hoping she'd allow me to take my exploration to the next level because I wasn't sure I could constrain it any longer.

"Penelope," I groaned against her lips as she nipped on mine. Her name tasted like candy, her body feeling like heaven itself inside my arms. She hummed against me but didn't let up, devouring my mouth once more. Her breath was labored, and I could feel her heartbeat mix with mine, creating a drumming as our chests pressed together.

"Penelope!" Her name echoed in my mind. She paused suddenly and I realized that her name was not ringing inside my head but through my house. Someone was looking for her. She pulled back, her eyes fluttering open in slow motion as she floated back to reality. I was in space with her, also needing a moment to come back down to earth. Her eyes were hooded, dopey. I could tell her head was swimming with passion.

Her name rang out again and she blinked rapidly a few times as she adapted to her surroundings. I cupped her face, knowing the moment was just about to be over. All the words previously logged in my throat were now on the tip of my tongue and I was ready. I tilted her head to face mine. Her eyes, devastating through her long lashes, looked at me.

"Penelope, I–" *I'm in love with you.*

"I can't do this," she whispered. Her voice broke in a heart wrenching resonance. She sighed and dropped her eyes before glancing back at me briefly. The look lasted only a fraction of a second but within it I saw everything she couldn't say. For the first time ever, I knew that Penelope Mason felt exactly the way that I did.

And there wasn't a damn thing either of us could do about it.

She slipped out of the pantry quickly, shutting the door behind her. I stayed behind, letting her return to the outside world alone so it wouldn't be obvious we'd been together. I leaned my forehead against the wall, lightly pounding my fist on the door. The words I never got to say still hung off my tongue:

Penelope, I'm in love with you.

I know you're leaving tomorrow but I can't let you go without telling you.

Chapter One

"Before you find your soulmate, you must first discover your soul."

-Charles F. Glassman

Penelope

"I think we got lucky here. I'd almost call it a twist of fate."

I blinked, the words flowing into my ears and requiring an extra second to comprehend. "What?" I asked, realizing I hadn't been paying attention. I'd felt uneasy since Mr. Collins found me in the hall this morning and asked if I could meet with him in his office during my prep period. He'd never asked to meet with me one-on-one before, and if his reputation served him right, these types of meetings were *never* a good thing.

It certainly must not have been helping that I had entirely zoned out since the meeting started. He blinked back at me. "Well, I suppose I should just get to the point then, shouldn't I?" He laughed awkwardly. "At the most recent School Board meeting, I explained that we have been unable to find a substitute to cover Mrs. Carlson's leave of absence due to the extraordinary shortage in available teachers, and we discussed canceling art classes for the rest of the year."

What on earth does that have to do with me?

"That's too bad," I said. I almost added: *art used to my favorite class in school* but decided against it. I was, after all, aiding for a history teacher. History probably should've been my favorite subject.

Collins nodded. "Yes. However, Mr. Edwards provided an alternative solution that was approved by the school district, and that is where I am hoping you'll come in." He glanced down at his desk and that back up at me, like whatever was going to come next was going to be uncomfortable for him to say. "Mr. Edwards said you may be wary of agreeing to this, so I want to preface my request by saying that this would be hugely beneficial to the school and the students here." He paused, swallowing again. "Tom mentioned that you are a talented artist yourself and–"

I snorted, "I'm not an artist."

He looked at me pointedly. "I would be inclined to disagree. I had the opportunity to view some of your work."

"How?" I asked even though I knew the answer. If Tom had asked my dad for one of my old sketchbooks, my dad gladly would have recovered one from the boxes in the garage. I'd bet that he was in on it the entire time. My parents had asked me recently why I quit drawing, and I didn't have the heart to tell them that there wasn't a reason why. It just didn't bring me joy anymore.

"I wanted to see your work for myself before I agreed to move forward with his proposed solution." I hate the way he said *your work*, as if it was anything other than old sketchbooks that I used to fill with doodles when I was a teenager.

I nodded and attempted an appreciative smile.

"Miss Mason, we'd like you to cover Mrs. Carlson's art classes for the remainder of the school year. As you know, the spring semester will be starting next week, and we are hoping you'll agree to teach her classes so we don't have to reassign the students who've already registered for them." He paused, but I made no motion to respond. I became hyper fixated on the fluorescent lights of his office and the way they shone atop his bald head, how he had both smile and frown lines, but the frown lines were more apparent. I wondered how much of his life he spent frowning versus smiling. I was pulled into his ice blue eyes, which seemed to be swirling with growing frustration. "It would overwhelm the elective teachers as well, including Miss Cunningham, if we had to relocate those students into other courses. It would be a significant relief not to have to cancel those art classes."

He's using Macie against me. He singled her out as an elective teacher hoping that it'd sway me in the right direction because he knew we were friends. *Well played, asshole,* I thought to myself. "I completely understand, Mr. Collins. However, I don't have a degree in teaching. I'm really not qualified," I said as sympathetically as I could manage.

He smiled in a cynical way, though he attempted to mask it with something more genuine. "Actually, all you need is special permission from the School Board. Which you received."

Fuck. I forced my lips to tilt upwards. "Wow, I'm so flattered," I said, falling flat.

His mouth twitched. "I'm sure. So, here's the deal, we'd have you take over the three general art elective courses. Mrs. Carlson already has the projects and coursework outlined for the entire semester. You'd just need to supervise the classes, grade projects, and offer support to the students, of course. Mrs. Arnold has still requested partial access to your aide, so you'd continue working with her two class periods a day."

I chewed on my lip. He was making a damn point. There was no way I was getting out of this. I knew that Katie Carlsen also taught photography classes, and though Collins hadn't mentioned them, I was afraid there may be an expectation for me to take them on if I agreed to do this. "What about her photography class?" I asked. "Yearbook club?"

Collins smile grew as he realized I was on the verge of giving in. "Yes, well I understand you are not an experienced photographer, and because we will be splitting your duties between Mrs. Carlson's coverage and Mrs. Arnold's aide, we had to find an alternative solution for those classes. Mr. Edwards, luckily, had another reference for a substitute role. He's a very accomplished photographer, in fact. Though, you two will need to share the art studio as well as Mrs. Carlson's office." I shrugged. I hardly believed sharing an office with a stranger would disrupt my life too heavily. Plus, I already shared Christine's office with her. If the guy was really that bad, I'd have a place to run away to. "Mr. Edwards did mention the two of you know each other, so I'm hoping sharing close quarters won't be an issue."

We know each other? I don't know any photograph–

A knock sounded on the door before it squeaked open. Collins' secretary, Margorie, peeked her head in. "Apologies, Mr. Collins. Mr. Edwards has arrived." I glanced between the two of them, eyes wide, wondering what the hell Tom was doing here in the middle of a Thursday.

Collins turned to me and smiled. "Sounds like your office mate has arrived."

Tom isn't the Mr. Edwards he's referring to.

I'd never describe my mind as a pleasant breeze. If anything, it was a whipping wind. In the last fifteen minutes, it'd become closer to a thunderstorm. In the last ten seconds, though, it'd become an entire tornado. Shredding apart the inner walls of my brain, destroying all ability to speak, or think, or act. Everything ceased to exist except the panic-inducing, inconceivable, agonizing realization of who was just about to walk through the door in front of me.

My heart stalled briefly in my chest and I struggled to breathe, hoping it wasn't obvious. My mind was playing tricks on me as it did sometimes in my dreams. Sometimes not even when I was dreaming, but when I was lying in bed at night unable to fall asleep. I imagined this very moment in my head, but it had never been like this. Everything moved in slow motion as he stepped through the door. My eyes desperately searched the space around us for some kind of glimmer, a glitch in the matrix– anything to prove that this isn't real. Inside my imagination, I always recognize him immediately, unchanged from the eighteen-year-old boy I had once known. I never thought to imagine him as a man. Unfortunate for me, because I am much less prepared for this moment than I should be, considering how many times I've thought it through.

It's not him. It's not. It can't be.

Then, he laughed.

That laugh. I know that laugh.

Fireworks explode throughout my mind. It's him. *Oh God, it's him.*

I squinted my eyes as I studied his face again, now looking for all the familiarities I should be seeing. He'd grown into his features. His jaw was more defined, and his body seemed to take up the entirety of the door frame he was standing in. His hair was lighter, but his skin was darker than I remembered. Both seemed to be kissed by the sun. Little hints of blond peeked through the otherwise caramel color of his hair, like rays of sunlight that got caught inside the strands. My eyes fell to his lips, the way his bottom lip was fuller than his upper, but his upper lip formed a perfect cupid's bow.

I've touched those lips before. It was so long ago, in another lifetime it seems, but I know those lips. My eyes were still watching his mouth when I noticed it tilt up on one side, somewhere between a smirk and a grin. His way of saying '*I got you.*' I'd spent my entire childhood memorizing that grin, staring back at it, because he always had me.

Instinctively, I shot up from my chair to step closer to him because I still wasn't convinced that he was the person standing in front of me. It would seem more likely I'd gone deliriously crazy and was now having full blown hallucinations. He stepped closer too, positioning himself right in front of the window that overlooked the courtyard in the center of the school. All my doubts about the person staring back at me diminished when his hazel eyes reflected in the light. Green, yellow, and brown all fighting a war inside them. Someone new seemed to be winning at any given time. Gold highlights speckled throughout, just like the sunshine caught in his hair. His eyes reminded me of a jungle I'd never seen, with the sun setting somewhere in the distance, reflecting on the flora and fauna in a perfect moment. *It's really him.* I took a step back and let out a breath.

"Penelope?" he asked, sounding as shocked as I felt.

I nodded as he smiled wider. His arms extended and he moved to close the gap between us. I knew I should've stepped into him too. I should've opened my arms wide to embrace an old friend.

That's what we were, right?

I remained frozen, though. His arms wrapped around me and I finally returned the hug after a moment of stillness that lasted far too long. He was so much bigger than I remembered him. I knew the hug was innocent but I couldn't help but to breathe in his smell and take note of the way his arms felt around my waist. He laughed effortlessly and I felt his chest rumble with it, like thunder against my own.

If I was a whipping wind, he was a sea breeze.

I should respond. I know I should respond. I should tell him it's good to see him and ask how he is. Reference the cold and cloudy weather and ask why on earth he'd leave Hawaii for it. I couldn't seem to get the words through my esophagus and out of my mouth, though.

I wasn't *that* happy to see him. Truth be told, he picked the worst possible time to walk into my workplace. Based on the shock in his voice when he said my name, he had no clue I worked here either.

Any other time I'd be able to shake off old feelings and exchange pleasantries. But now I'm twenty-three, I'd been withdrawn from the greatest University on earth, rejected from their grad program. *Living with my parents.* Working a job that I only got because *his* dad set it up for me. The list could go on. I knew if I opened my mouth, he may ask me questions that would require me to disclose how my life was really going, and I couldn't stomach that in addition to just seeing him here in the flesh.

Mr. Collins cleared his throat, a silent reminder that public displays of affection of any kind are not permitted on school premises, even if you're running into someone you haven't seen in five years, apparently. Carter and I both stepped back from each other, "See? Like I said, a twist of fate." I struggled to pull my eyes away from Carter's stare to look at Collins. He seemed to read my expression. "I just mean– You know, what are the odds that you both are so talented in your respective fields *and* that you two are already friends? It's a perfect combination."

I hated that he used the word *fields* because art was *not* my *field*. Art was not even something I did for fun. Not something I thought about. Once upon a time, I liked to draw when I was bored. That was it. But my mother had been an artist all her life and given that neither of my siblings ever took it up, she hung tightly onto that future for me. While I used to find it therapeutic and relaxing, it was never a career path for me.

"We grew up together." My eyes shot up to Carter's face, catching him as he smiled at Collins. To anyone else the smile seemed easy, genuine. It was fake. Carter's real smiles would stand a room to attention. Would knock the wind out of any poor, unsuspecting woman who found herself on the other end of it. I would know. I'd been said poor, unsuspecting woman a time or two.

"Yes, your father mentioned that. Now, if you'll both follow me; I'd like to show you the art room, let you take a look around." Collins stood and led us out of his office and into the courtyard at the center of the school, and I realized I had never officially agreed. As Collins walked down the lengthy hallway that led towards the art studio, he said, "Miss Mason, I'd like to ask if you'd be Mr. Edwards's guide on his first few weeks at the school. Ensure he gets acquainted with other staff, knows where to find the things he needs, and that he's comfortable."

"Of course," I found myself blurting out. I tried not to look at Carter as I said it, but my eyes moved on their own, just as my mouth had. I no longer had control of my body. He smiled, fake again. He dipped his head slightly in gratitude.

We stepped into the studio. It was a large, open room with paneled windows looking out over the parking lot. Tables scattered throughout the middle of the room, while the perimeter held countertops overflowing with art supplies. To the right of the door was another door that led to a small office, hardly large enough for one person, let alone two.

I tried to ignore the intensity of his presence as I watched Collins open the cabinets and closets, explaining where we'd find all the supplies we needed. He handed us each a packet with a syllabus and detailed lesson plan for the semester. He promised we'd each get to shadow Katie for the remainder of the week to learn the ropes.

Normally, I'd be extremely overwhelmed by the thought of teaching classes all my own. I didn't even want to be a teacher. I don't even like kids that much. Yet, I didn't have it in me to care right now. All the fear inside my body was fixated on the presence of the man standing next to me. Every emotion in my body, actually. I discreetly (maybe not so discreetly) glanced at him just in time to watch him lick his lips. *Dammit.* Why does he look so good?

"I'll leave the two of you to look around, get acclimated with the space. Miss Mason, I told Mrs. Arnold you'd be back by next period to assist her with the last class of the day," Collins said. I pretended to sort through a basket of paint, nodding absently. "Mr. Edwards, Mrs. Carlson has already left for the day since her classes have finished. Why don't you just shadow Miss Mason next period so she has a chance to introduce you to the other school staff?"

"Sure," he said. I felt his eyes on me but refused to look up from the box of paint. My brain rapidly tried to think of a question, a comment, a concern. Anything to stall Collins from walking out of that room. The tornado in my mind returned to its reign of terror as the clicking of Mr. Collins' loafers faded down the hallway.

We were alone.

Against my internal pleas, my mind thought back to the last time I was alone in a room with Carter. My stomach twisted in knots beneath me, my breath became shallow and rapid. Feeling the need to separate my body from my mind, I quickly stepped back from the counter I was facing. So quickly that I knocked a bottle of red paint from the counter, watching it fall to the floor and break open. The bottle was old, mostly empty and dried out, but there was just enough paint left inside to splatter onto the floor after the lid popped off.

Some of the paint sprayed across my foot, seeping into the fabric of my shoe. My *white* shoe. It almost kind of looked like a flower, one of those abstract ones where the artist just splatters the paint onto the canvas but it still ends up pretty when they're done. I watched the paint as it rolled over millimeter after millimeter of the fabric, sucking in all the white and coating it in red. Thick, red liquid.

I felt the contents of my stomach spin inside me as the scene set in. *It looks like blood.* My chest began to tighten, and I felt lightheaded as I squat down behind the counter and examined my foot. I moved my hand forward to wipe it off, but my body jerked and stopped before my fingers could reach it, so I grabbed the bottle of paint from the floor instead. I breathed through my nose and out my mouth. I did it again. *It's just paint. It's not blood. Just paint.*

The bell rang, signaling the end of the class period. I shot up from the floor in a flurry and slammed my hip against the side of the chair, causing it to slide across the tiled floor. Carter, who'd been facing away from me and looking through a box of digital cameras provided by the district, spun around at the sound of the screeching chair. He raised a brow and opened his mouth as if to ask me something when the classroom door flew open.

"Holy shit. I ran straight in here the minute my prep started." She paused for not even half a second. "Well, that's not true. I ran straight to Christine, who then informed me I'd find you here. Which begs the question, why are you here? What happened with your meeting with Collins? Did you get fired? Well, of course not. Right? If you'd been fired you wouldn't be here, in the art room, and–" Macie stopped. Her mouth was already speed boating before she'd fully entered the room, not long enough to allow her to take in her surroundings. By the time she had, she'd lost her words as she stared, mouth gaping, at Carter. "Hi," she said, finally.

"Hello," he replied, his most charming grin rising from the corner of his mouth.

"Do you work for the school district?" she asked.

"I do not." He smiled.

"Board of education? The State of Oregon?"

He shook his head.

"Are you in any way involved with any organization or person who may be able to fire me from my job?"

"Not that I'm aware of."

She grinned. Whipping around to face me. "Penny, can you please explain to me what is going on? Why were you called into a private meeting with Collins today? Why are you now in the art studio, instead of your classroom, with some random, stupidly hot, man?"

"Macie, this is Carter. He was my neighbor growing up. Our parents are friends. Tom Edwards, from the school board, is Carter's dad." I sighed. "Evidently, the district couldn't find a substitute for Katie's maternity leave, so Carter will be teaching her photography courses, I guess. And apparently, I will be teaching her art courses." I dropped my head, rubbing my temples.

"Why on earth–" Macie started.

Carter cut her off, "Pep is a great artist."

My heart skipped a beat as he said that nickname I hadn't heard in so long. When I was adopted and Maddie was only two, she couldn't say Penelope. She'd somehow taught herself to say 'Pep' instead. Throughout our childhood, my siblings and friends called me that, but as we grew up my full name took its place.

Macie looked at me. "I didn't know *Pep* was an artist."

"I'm not. I used to doodle in high school. That's all."

She hmphed at me. Carter looked like he was about to say more, but I shot him a look that begged him to stop, hoping he was still capable of reading my features. "Okay, so you're *not* an artist. Please explain how you ended up in this situation, then."

"Pretty sure our dads set me up." I craned my neck toward Carter.

"So, you must be a photographer, then?" Macie asked Carter. I leaned in, desperate for his answer, yet hoping it didn't show. I need something– some kind of inkling as to what his life had been like before showing up in Collins' office today.

"Yeah," he paused, "and thank you. For the hot part, not the stupid part." He then winked. *Winked.* At Macie. She was practically panting, and I suppressed an eye roll. "I'd been wanting to get out of Hawaii for a while. I guess the school was having trouble finding a substitute for the teacher here who's going on leave." Looking down at his feet he timidly added, "I didn't know you were working here too. I thought you were still in England."

My stomach twisted. Would he not have accepted the job if he knew he'd be working with me? Would I have accepted if I knew I'd be working with him? Likely not. If he thought I'd still be in England, then his dad must've not told him about my... *situation.*

I wasn't sure what to think of that.

"Anyway, after my feature in *Travel + Leisure* my dad pitched me as the substitute, and the school board approved it."

I stared after him in shock. "I– I'm sorry. Did you say *Travel + Leisure*? You're like, legit?"

He chuckled, "Yeah, I guess. Mostly landscape. I was shooting Hawaiian locations for tourist publications. I'm hoping to get into some other stuff now that I'm out here. Focus more on the creative and artistic side of it."

"Very cool. Very hot," Macie said. I shot her a look that could melt her face. She snorted. "I've got class soon. It was nice meeting you Mr. Carter. I'll see you later, Penny." She blew me a kiss as she headed toward the door. I knew she'd have a million and a half questions for me later. I also knew her prep period just started, meaning she did *not* have class soon. For whatever reason, she'd decided she wanted to leave me alone for the first time ever.

After she was gone, Carter looked at me and raised a brow. "I thought only your dad was allowed to call you Penny."

"He is, but you'll soon find that Macie doesn't give a shit about rules." He laughed. I'd found that I had mindlessly placed all the paint I'd pulled out of the box back into it, just as mindlessly as I'd pulled it out. "Speaking of class, I need to get back to mine," I said.

He pulled his hands from the box of cameras he'd been inspecting. I wondered if he was also doing so mindlessly, or if he'd actually had a purpose for what he was doing. He rubbed them together. "Totally. Let's go."

"So, what are you doing in Brighton Bay?" he asked as we exited the studio. "You know, since you're clearly not still in England."

"Am I not in England? I hadn't noticed." He caught up to me and turned around, walking backward down the hallway, raising a brow at me. "I live here," I answered finally.

He huffed. "I mean, when did you get back?" I didn't answer, as he continued walking down the hallway backward, staring at me. I let him continue walking, even though he was going straight when we should've turned left down another hall. Once he'd passed the entryway to the forked off hall, I cut down it. His footsteps stopped, and then sped up until he was racing up behind me. My mouth twitched upward.

"I moved back in September," I said, unwilling to divulge additional information.

"From Oxford?"

I nodded.

"You graduated?"

"Yep. Archaeology." I hoped he wouldn't pry further into my past than he already was.

"Wow," he breathed, shaking his head. "Pep, that is incredible."

A twinge of gratitude escaped me as we continued down the hall, even though his praises were hollow. Yes, I had graduated from Oxford, but it wasn't as if I was using the degree that cost my parents thousands upon thousands of dollars. It wasn't as if I was following the dreams I had since I was a child, the dreams that led me across the Atlantic.

"Penelope." His tone had me skid to a halt. I turned back to face him. "Is there blood on your shoe?"

I forgot about the paint. I stared down at it and my stomach flipped. I threw my head back and groaned. I pressed my hands to my eyelids, breathing deeply before glancing back down at my feet. Why am I so scared of paint? *Fucking paint.*

"It's paint."

"Oh, okay. Do you want to go clean them off? Before it stains?"

"It looks like blood," was all I could respond with. I closed my eyes. "It's fine. I'll throw them out when I get home."

"Throw them out? Why don't you just–" He stopped, then he sighed. "You're still afraid of blood."

I cleared my throat, still staring down at my feet. "I guess."

"Come with me." He spun on his heel and began walking the opposite direction, not checking if I was following. My feet stayed firmly planted as I stared after him. "Come on, Pep," he repeated. I looked down at my feet, and then back to him, and down at my feet once again. With an exasperated sigh, I followed him. We returned back to the art room and he began to open cabinets and drawers searching for something. After a few moments, he managed to pry open a locked closet and hummed, indicating he'd located whatever it was he'd been looking for.

He backed out of the closet with a jug of bleach in his hand and walked over to the back of the studio where a deep sink stood. He motioned for me to join him and patted the counter next to the sink. "Hop up," he ordered. I obliged, taking off my shoes and handing them to him, trying not to look at them too closely. He set my shoes in the sink and flipped on the water, scrubbing away the paint with bleach and an old rag.

"Thank you," I said timidly after a moment of silence.

He laughed. "Anytime, Pep. You know that."

"I think it's really cool you're a photographer," I said, attempting to sound genuine. It wasn't that I didn't really feel that way. I did think it was cool, and I thought it fit him perfectly. I forced the sincerity in my voice because I was disgustingly jealous. Jealous he had found his *thing*. Jealous that he was good at it. Jealous that he found success in it. Jealous that he seemed *happy.* He never even tried. He was so... carefree. All the time. About everything. I used to get frustrated by it. The way he would shrug off failed tests in school. How he never stressed about his future. Or how he never cared what people thought about him. I swore to myself that someday it would all blow up in his face. Meanwhile, I cared too much about everything. My grades, college, the future. All things that had come crashing down on top of me, no matter how hard I tried to control them.

After a few more silent minutes, he shut the faucet off and patted off the last of the moisture on my shoe before moving to stand in front of me. I took notice of how tall he's gotten. His shoulders are so much broader too. His button up was rolled up to his elbows, and it looked as if his arms could shred the fabric if he only flexed hard enough, and the way his torso tapered down to his hips...my breathing became a bit labored as I leaned back, away from my own thoughts.

If I leaned forward right now, my head would fall right against his chest, and if I tilted it up, my lips could graze his neck. A chill shot through me at the thought of my lips anywhere on his body. He looked down at me, as if he had felt my response, and a small smile formed on his mouth. His familiar scent washed over me. He smelled like rain and saltwater breeze. I've never been much of a fan of rain, but I do enjoy the way it smells on wet pavement, or within the leaves of the evergreen trees.

He spread my legs slightly with his knee, and my entire body tensed. He slowly bent down and squatted to the floor before grabbing my shoes and placing them back onto my feet. When he stood back up, his hands stayed wrapped around my ankles, slowly sliding up my legs as he stood. His hands never made it above the knee before they left my body and landed back onto my hips. He lifted me slightly before my feet hit the ground and I was standing again. I leaned back against the counter as our chests pressed together– reminiscent of a moment in another dark room. In another life. His hands lingered on my hips briefly before he let go and stepped back.

We both found ourselves breathless. Stunned at the intensity of the moment.

No, no, no, no, no.

Emotional vomit built in the back of my throat. It had been about twelve seconds since he'd been back in my life and I was already feeling... *things.* Things I had absolutely prohibited myself from ever feeling again. From ever thinking about again.

I allowed my eyes to roam across him. To take in every dimple, every freckle, every inch of his golden skin. I allowed myself to momentarily get lost inside his brindled eyes. I watched him lick his lips, the slow roll of his throat as he swallowed. For one brief moment, I'd give myself the allowance to drink him in. To imagine his mouth, his hands, and his body.

I, forcibly and painfully, pulled myself from that moment after it turned from just one into several. As I pulled back, I examined his face and realized that he might have been looking at me exactly the way I was looking at him. I fought the urge to ask him if he'd tell me every single thought running through his mind.

He cleared his throat. "They're not brand new but should be wearable." I glanced down at my feet and could now only see a faint outline of faded pink across the top of the sneaker. "It doesn't look like blood anymore."

"Thank you," I said again as we made our way back down the hall to my classroom. I knew he was supposed to be staying with me for the rest of the day, but something felt strange. Like this was the last moment I'd be able to say anything for a while. The last time I could. Once we stepped through the threshold of that door, whatever feelings I'd felt in the art room would be shoved deep, deep down—locked away—as they'd been for the previous five years. As they'd need to be forever.

I shut the metaphorical door on Carter the moment I stepped on that plane to England all those years ago. I padlocked it. Built a cement wall around it. Painted it red and let it fade into the dullness of my heart. I'd come to terms with the fact that he, among other things from my past, were meant to be suppressed until they were forgotten, no matter how long that'd take.

My trembling hand reached for the door handle.

"Penelope?" he breathed from behind me. He wasn't inappropriately close, but I could feel his breath blow across the nape of my neck, sending a shiver up my spine.

"Yeah?" I whispered.

"It's really good to see you again."

Chapter Two

"Oceans separate lands, not souls."

-Munia Khan

Carter

I can't believe she's standing there. *Right there.*

Bent over a table with her back to me, her hair a crimson curtain draping her face. I think my mind may still be frozen in shock, because I feel almost as if I'm outside my body, looking on from somewhere else. I'm watching this scenario play out between two different people, feeling pity for them both.

I'd thought about it before, what it may be like to run into her again. At first, I thought it would be some grand reunion, a collision of all the lost feelings we never had the chance to express. As the years passed and we continued to miss each other, I started to think that it may never happen at all. Or that it would, at some point in the far-off future where both of us were married, happy, and fulfilled, and it would just be a funny little water mark on our adolescence. But five years is nothing compared to the number of years I spent in her presence. It may have only been one kiss, but I spent my whole childhood falling in love with her. The first time I noticed a person in *that* sort of way. The first lips I dreamt about at night. Every single fantasy between that dream and the day I actually kissed her. She was never actually any of my firsts, of course. Not the physical kind, anyway. But even then, she was who I wished they could've been. No, five years certainly was not enough time to recover from the way she wrecked my world.

Now, she's standing right in front of me. She's helping walk a group of students through the guidelines of their group project on ancient Greece, and I can't help but wonder if she felt it too. The palpable tension that floated in the air around us. Five years couldn't have been enough time for her to forget the drumming of our hearts and the fire in our bodies. Where the moment in the past was a tidal wave, the moment in the art room today was rapid. I heard her gasp, the acceleration of her heartbeat. The way she shivered when I touched her hips.

She remembers.

I'd spent these years replacing her lips with so many others, all in an attempt to heal the scars she left on mine. Nothing thus far has been comparable to that moment in the dark pantry of my parent's kitchen. That is, until I found myself alone with her again.

Penelope was helping her students by outlining a rough draft of a map they were supposed to draw. I remembered when very few people knew her creative side. She was an artist at heart, and I considered myself one of the privileged ones who'd seen her art before. Although, I'm probably not anymore. But by the sound of it, she doesn't draw these days. She doesn't talk about it with her friends, assuming that girl—Macie—was her friend.

I used to glance at Penelope's notebooks in class, all the drawings sprawled across them. I would wonder how she could be so distracted, creating drawings so detailed and beautiful, and yet still have the highest grade-point average in our school. She left her sketchbook on the kitchen table in her house once, and I looked at it when nobody was around. The doodles in her notebooks were no comparison to the drawings sprawled across the pages of her sketchbooks, unlike anything I'd ever seen before.

I had so many questions for her. How her life has been and what it has become. Why did she end up back here when I had known her to desire living anywhere else? I wanted to know every detail of what her life has been like since the last time I saw her. I wanted to ask her about the last time I saw her. How she felt about it then, how she feels about it now. I wanted to ask her if she has a boyfriend.

I should not want to ask her if she has a boyfriend.

I suddenly realized I was staring far too intensely at her while she was bent over a table and her back was facing me. She was wearing a pair of deep purple jeans that hugged every curve in the just the right way and drew my eyes to all the places they should not be going. I struggled to pull my gaze away from her ass and glance around the classroom. I wouldn't lie to myself and pretend I wasn't excited to see Penelope again, but at this moment it felt strange. I did, as much as I could manage, try to shadow Penelope and the other teacher, Christine, as they worked with their students. I tried to understand the way they interacted, the way they critiqued, and how they listened. Penelope, of course, was a natural.

Starting next week, I'd be taking over three photography classes, a study hall, and the Yearbook Club. I only knew how to take photos. I had no clue how to teach other people to take photos. I had no clue how to interact with students, but the contract was a solid income and gave me an excuse to live with my parents rent free for the next few months. I couldn't turn it down.

After the last bell had rung and the class had cleared, both Penelope and Christine remained. They split a stack of assignments that Christine slipped into her bag to grade at home later. She packed up her things, but Penelope seemed as if she'd be staying for a while. I wasn't sure if I should stay too.

"You sure you don't mind tidying up?" Christine asked.

"Not at all! I was actually part of the carpool this morning, so I'll be waiting on Macie anyway." Penelope smiled a smile I'd never seen before, and I realized it must be the one she created specifically for Christine. I wonder how many of her other smiles have been created in the last five years that I haven't witnessed yet.

Christine thanked her again and smiled at me softly before leaving the classroom, her heels clicking down the hall in echoes. Penelope went back to what she had been doing before, stacking books in corners and picking scraps of paper off the ground. I began doing the same.

"You don't have to wait for me," she chuckled. The tone in her voice was light, as if she didn't care either way if I stayed or went. That bothered me because I had no idea what I should do. I tried removing the connotations of our past and considered how I would act as a professional, simply in this situation with a coworker of mine and not... well, not *her*. My eyes wandered about the room, and everything seemed to look like it was in the place it was meant to be.

Except for myself, of course.

I assumed she's just diddling until she meets her friend to leave for the day. "Okay, sure. I'll take off then," I replied blithely. She was kneeled on the ground, sorting through a box of books. I knew she was attempting to make herself appear busy as a way of dissolving the awkward tension between us.

"Okay, have a good night." She reached her hand back to wave but didn't turn around. I tightened my lips in frustration. I had no way of knowing how much she's changed but one thing about her that certainly has not; she remains reticent. Pushing down all emotions until she feels she's in control. I used to do the same when it came to her, mimicking her movements because I wanted to do what made her feel comfortable. The constant game we played when we were young. The both of us too afraid to convey the way we feel.

"Pep, we should talk about this." I found myself saying it before my brain could tell my mouth to stop, frustrated with everything I'd pent up for so long.

She was silent as she slowly stood up and straightened out her jeans, kicking the box of books back into the corner of the room. She sighed. "Talk about what?"

"Come on, Penelope." I was exasperated. "You know exactly what–" I was cut off by the sound of approaching footsteps and laughter. She turned around to face me just before I turned around to face the door, but I noticed her close her eyes and let out a breath of relief at our interruption. I rolled mine.

The woman that flurried into the art room earlier, the one who (more than once) referred to me as hot, strode into the classroom, her tight blonde curls bouncing with her laughter. Close behind her was an incredibly tall man, and another man entered behind him, shorter with a wormy face. They all stopped abruptly as they entered the room, like they thought they may be interrupting something. Macie smiled at me kindly. The tall man stood close to her and smiled as well. His hair was red, like Penelope's, except his was ginger where hers was cherry. He stood close enough to Macie that I assumed they may be involved. The shorter man with a stocky build and a wormy face held my gaze with narrow eyes and a judgmental expression.

"Hi, Penny," Macie said slowly. "Are you ready to go? We don't want to be late for Thursday night trivia."

"I'm ready." Penelope had a hint of annoyance in her tone. "Carter, will you be able to find the parking lot on your own? We normally park in the teacher lot in the back."

I chewed my lip. She clearly wanted me to leave, but I realized I could use the excuse of pretending I didn't know where to go so she'd have to show me. She'd probably just send one of her friends to show me instead and that would be even more awkward. "Yeah, I'm sure I'll manage." She tilted her head in a brief nod and reached around her desk to grab her bag.

Macie cleared her throat. "Mr. Carter, this is Jeremy and Marshall. Jeremy teaches math and Marshall teaches health and PE."

She pointed at each of them, Jeremy being the redhead and Marshall having the wormy face. I shook both their hands. "Oh, and you can call them Mr. Bridges and Mr. Ross when students are around."

"The name thing is all so confusing." I smiled as genuinely as I could. "Nice to meet you both." Jeremy smiled back at me in a dopey yet honest way. Marshall seemed much more reserved, almost impertinent as he greeted me.

"Carter will be covering for Katie while she's out on maternity leave. He'll be taking over her photography classes and Yearbook," Penelope explained as she floated past me and the rest of us filed out the door behind her. We all walked together on the first stretch of the long hallway where I'd cut off towards the right and they would all cut off towards the left once we reached the end of it.

"Who's taking over her other art classes?" Jeremy asked.

Pep sighed. "Me."

The wormy guy, Marshall, cackled. "They must be desperate."

I looked at Penelope, expecting her to be offended. She just shrugged and nodded as if she agreed. Marshall continued, nodding towards me, "Since Penelope, clearly, isn't *really* an art teacher. Are you *really* a photographer?"

"Yes, I am *really* a photographer." I tried, and failed, not to grind my teeth.

He frowned, shrugging, and then shook his head with a condescending snort.

Penelope's eyes flashed to me with a look that was almost apologetic, but mostly blank. It was silent for a few beats before Macie rang out, "Oh, and I already called dibs on the front seat!"

"You can't just call dibs when I'm not there. It doesn't count unless all parties are present," Penelope argued. They stopped walking and stared at each other. Only a fraction of a second could've passed before the realization dawned on them both.

"Dibs!" They yelled at the exact same time.

"I said it first–" Macie started.

"No, I said it first!" Penelope exclaimed.

"Macie definitely said it first," Marshall chimed in with a sinful smile on his face.

"I know you're only saying that so you can sit in the back seat with Penny, but I won't argue with you." Macie laughed.

I tried not to make a face at Macie's observation.

Penelope straightened up, no longer glimmering with the shiny expression she held when she was joking with Macie. "The driver decides who gets shotgun whenever the declaration of dibs is too close of a call to tell who said it first," Penelope said seriously, like she was reading off a contract.

All eyes turned to Jeremy, including mine. I probably should've stepped around them and continued on my way, but I somehow got pulled into their strange dynamic and wanted to see what happened.

"I think Macie was a hair quicker," Jeremy said. Macie cheered and wrapped her arm around his waist as they walked away. Marshall threw his arm around Penelope's shoulder, and I thought I may have caught her stiffening slightly. He moved off behind the other two, pulling her along with him. Once they made it to the fork in the hallway, Jeremy and Macie absent mindedly turned left, with Marshall following right behind. Penelope glanced back at me with a soft expression.

"I'll see you tomorrow," she said just above a whisper.

"See ya, Mr. Carter!" Macie yelled without turning around at all.

"I'm so confused, is his first name Carter, or his last name?" I heard Jeremy ask her as they disappeared through a set of doors.

I chuckled briefly at that because I had no idea why Macie decided to call me by my first name with a suffix in front of it. Their laughter and conversation faded into nothing, and I found myself standing alone in the middle of the hall, staring after the living, breathing ghost who'd been haunting me all this time.

I thought my heart had healed from the soul splitting anguish she'd cause me. As I watched her disappear from sight, another man's arm around her, I wondered if I'd ever had a stitch in it at all.

Chapter Three

"There is no such thing as soulmates. And who would want there to be? I don't want half a shared soul. I want my own damn soul."

-Rachel Cohn

Penelope

"A little heads up would've been appreciated," I said, shutting the front door behind me. I'd hardly made it through trivia last night as I found myself reliving every dreaded moment of yesterday afternoon. By the time I made it home my parents were in bed, and when I woke up this morning my dad had already left for work. I hadn't had the chance to confront him about his potential involvement in the scheme to appoint me Seaside Middle's newest art teacher, or maybe worse, Carter Edwards's new office mate.

Regardless, I wasn't sure I wanted to confront him about it. Wasn't sure I could. The last year had been rough for my parents and me. The moment I stepped out of the terminal at PDX, my father forced a smile that said: *I'm so disappointed in you right now but I'm still trying to love you.* More than anything else in the last year, maybe more than anything else in my entire life, that look on his face broke me. I'd failed the man who never failed me. The man who saved me.

The drive home from Portland to my hometown of Brighton Bay was silent. We got home late, and my mother hadn't stayed up to greet me. My father went straight to bed. I collapsed onto the floor of my childhood bedroom and sobbed. Sometime later, my sister silently opened my door, pulled me onto my bed, and slept with me. We've never talked about that night. My parents didn't tell Maddie the full extent of my experience at Oxford, but I did. None of us speak of it now.

That was nine months ago, and I've been walking on eggshells every moment since. I knew that I'd disappointed them. They were trying to be supportive, trying to mask that disappointment, but I could see through it.

"They're not pretending to forgive you, Penelope. They were upset, yes, but they're over it. They love you. Of course they expect a lot from you, they expect a lot from all three of us, but you put all this pressure on yourself to be perfect. I promise you, Mom and Dad do not expect perfection. They just want to make sure you're happy," my sister had told me a couple of weeks after I returned home. What she didn't understand was that while my parents may not expect perfection from me, I did. I owed it to them in a way she never would. I was adopted– I was a fucked up little kid and they took me in. I'll always owe them a debt that can't be repaid. The least I could do was not be a failure and an embarrassment. And my parents could pretend all they wanted, but they were embarrassed. I'd failed them and failed myself.

After I returned from England, I immediately began applying to graduate programs within the United States, the west coast specifically. I wanted to remain as far away from England as I could reasonably get.

My parents begged me to take a gap year, saying diving back into school too soon would do more harm than good. I think they just wanted to keep me under their roof until they could ensure I wouldn't fuck up again. Regardless, I continued applying, but once I'd been rejected from the first two programs, I began to give up hope. By August, my father had enough pity on me to ask Tom to get me a job with the school district. Preferably something with history, I believe he expressed. Something that would make me feel like it wasn't all a waste. The day that Tom offered me the teaching aide job was the first day I'd allowed myself to think about Carter.

I had wondered if news of my situation would reach his side of the ocean.

We'd always missed each other before I moved back. I'd visit at Christmas, and he'd come for Thanksgiving. I came home in the summer, but he'd visit in the spring. I knew the probability that I'd end up running into him would grow the longer I stayed in Brighton, but when I missed him at Thanksgiving last year, I thought I may make it out of here before it happened.

But I didn't. Thanks in part to my father. I wanted to be angry with him, but only in the last couple of months had I stopped feeling like I was walking on eggshells. I still felt like I was walking on a creaky, dilapidated, splintered wooden floor. One wrong step, one wrong sound, and I'd remind them of what I did– why I was here. It *had* gotten better, though. He now asked me how my days were and made eye contact with me as we spoke around the dinner table.

I continued doing everything I could to prove to them I was the daughter they deserved. I had started applying to graduate programs again. I volunteered at a local history museum some weekends. I chauffeured my sister and her friends around. I'd even taken some classes at the local community college. That's what my life had become: to prove to my parents that I'm not a failure, work, and think about a future where I no longer felt this way.

No, I decided I couldn't confront my dad about his meddling, but I could vent to Maddie about it. Maddie and I kicked off our shoes and threw our bags by the door before moving towards the kitchen. It was an old routine of ours back when she was about twelve, and I was about eighteen. I'd pick her up after school, then we'd come home and watch trashy reality tv shows while we ate potato chips directly from the bag.

While not my most shining moment, it was a routine that I didn't mind falling back into.

My parents had dinner with the Edwards' most Friday evenings. I assumed my dad would already be over there with Tom. My mother's car wasn't in the driveway, so I figured she wasn't home yet. Meaning Maddie and I had the house to ourselves to watch our trash tv and eat our trash snacks. And talk about how upset I still am with my parents even though I couldn't say anything to them directly. Maddie will eventually join them for dinner so she could see Charlie, Carter's sister and her best friend. I stopped attending family dinners a long time ago.

"He knew I wouldn't have agreed to do that. He knows I have no desire to teach art. I don't even know how." I flipped on the dim light that illuminated the long hallway leading from the entry to the kitchen. "And what about Carter? I'm sure he knew about that too. I can't believe he didn't think to mention that he was moving home, that we'd be working together. You don't think that would've been something to, I don't know, mention casually around the dinner table?

'*Hey Penelope, remember our neighbor? The one you had a* huge *crush on in high school? I know you haven't spoken to him in half a decade, but we've decided you two should work together, against your will, obviously. You'll share an office and everything. It'll be great!*'"

Maddie had been walking a few paces in front of me when she stopped dead in the kitchen entryway. "Penelope, you should stop talking," she said. She was staring straight ahead but I couldn't yet see what she could. It was a calm warning. Something deep in my gut had me dreading the turn of the corner. *Shit, is Dad home after all?*

Nobody knew the extent of my history with Carter. Maddie knew I'd crushed on him when I was younger, but I think both sides of the family always saw us as more of siblings, regardless of how messed up that sounded to me. Maddie only knew because she found *Mrs. Penelope Edwards* scribbled into my diary when I was eleven. She made fun of me for years. Right up until the point

Carter began looking like the *Baywatch* version of Jason Momoa. After that, she couldn't make fun of me because I'm pretty sure she had a crush on him too.

I rounded the corner into the kitchen, expecting my father's kind, deep, brown eyes to come into my line of view. They weren't the first set of eyes I fell on. The first eyes—the only eyes I saw—were a blazing hazel. His eyebrows came together at the center of his forehead. The right side of his mouth tilted slightly from chewing on his inner cheek. My stomach bottomed out as I froze at the corner of the kitchen counter.

It felt as if I could see the world as it spun around me, but my feet planted themselves at the center of it, refusing to move anywhere. Not a single thought existed inside of my brain. Nothing except for the spinning of the room, my planted feet, and those hazel eyes. They crinkled, drawing my eyes to his mouth, which was now showing that grin.

I got you.

My cheeks flooded with pure humiliation. My sister leaned against the counter watching us like we were the trash reality tv shows we enjoyed. My feet still refused to move but my breathing had returned, anger rising with the air bellowing out my throat.

"Why are you in my house?" I asked, my tone unintentionally cruel. Yet, I didn't waiver. I didn't allow my face to soften, or my arms to become uncrossed from my chest.

I had a bad habit of sticking to a reaction once I had it. Even if it was unwarranted, I didn't want to give up control of my emotions for even a second. So even though I'd snapped at him in a state of shock, I'd continue to pretend he offended me for some inexplicable reason.

He frowned. "Sorry." I chewed on the inside of my lip, feeling guilty. "Dinner is at my parents' house tonight. Lena is cooking. She needed olive oil, and your dad asked me to come grab some." I nodded at his perfectly reasonable explanation. "He also asked me to let you both know to be over by seven." His tone was flat, even for someone like him. Someone who was normally sunshine trapped inside a human body.

He side-stepped me, keeping as much distance between us as possible. Nodding curtly at Maddie, he turned the corner and out of my sight. "Let Dad know we'll *both* be there!" Maddie chimed as the front door opened and shut again. She turned to face me. "You're kind of an asshole, Penelope."

I sighed. "Yeah, I know."

I sat at my desk, blankly staring at the digital clock that rested atop my nightstand.

The minutes ticked by slowly as I waited (dreaded) for the time to reach seven o'clock. I didn't even argue with Maddie when she specified that we'd both attend dinner tonight. I knew that Tom would want to talk to me about my new position, anyway. I, however, did not expect Carter to overhear the conversation I had with my sister earlier, so I was looking forward to this dinner less than I already had been.

The sun slowly faded beyond the heavy clouds outside my window as it set on the early March evening. The last twenty-four hours had me feeling as if I was in the Twilight Zone. I kept searching for glimpses of proof that I was.

Maybe the sun won't come up tomorrow morning.

Maybe I died and this is purgatory.

Being stuck in my parents' house, no future to speak of, had kind of felt like a year of purgatory. Throwing Carter in the mix made it feel more real. I wouldn't be surprised, I suppose. A religious person would certainly believe I had more than a few sins to atone for.

Logically, I knew Carter hadn't done anything wrong. He had just as much—if not more—of a right to work for the school district in which his father was a Board Member. Dwelling on the last twenty-four hours had made me realize that being around him was more than my brain was capable of handling right now. I ignored him entirely at work, and when I found him standing in my kitchen, something snapped. I realized there'd be no escape.

It felt as if every teenage raging hormone I thought I'd outgrown came rushing back when I was in his presence. My stomach would flutter, my hands would get clammy, I'd start to sweat a little. My mouth would either move on its own volition, or not move at all. My body did the same. I'd either run away entirely or I couldn't move, period. When I tried playing adult in England, it blew up in my face. I spent months trapped in this adolescent purgatory, crawling my way out of it, only for Carter to return and seemingly kick me back down.

I wanted him all my life. As long as I knew what it felt like to want someone. I was fucking in love with him. In love with him in the most desperate, tragic, cheesy kind of way. It was almost humiliating how much I dreamed about him when I was younger. He was so close, and so out of reach. So far out of my league I wouldn't voice my feelings to anyone. I could hardly even allow myself to acknowledge them.

Until that very brief moment five years ago in his parents' kitchen. He finally looked at me the way I always dreamed he would. And, *oh my God*. I knew then. I knew at that moment that he felt, at least a little, of what I felt. That was the first—the only time—I let myself fully give into what I felt for him. Walking away from that nearly killed me. He'd made me no promises, and he confessed nothing. Words were never said. There was only the pounding of our hearts as our bodies pressed against each other in the dark. Only the ferocity of our mouths as we soaked each other in, knowing it'd be the only time. His mouth, his hands—his soul—had left their prints all over me.

At first, since it was exactly the second kiss of my entire life, I tried to convince myself it was just that. That I had never experienced something so intense before, and that someday it'd fade away as I replaced his lips with others. I quickly discovered that wasn't true. It doesn't matter how far you go with someone, how much of yourself you give to them. Some people will leave heavier imprints than others. I'd only given Carter my lips, but he'd left them forever branded.

Even after five years apart, I wasn't sure I could be forced into his proximity without stumbling back in love and undoubtedly wounding myself in the process. In support of the idea that I was stuck in adolescent purgatory, being around him again had given me an intense feeling of déjà vu. My body's reaction to him certainly had not changed, if anything, it'd grown stronger. I now knew what the warmth of bare skin felt like against my own, I knew what it felt like to strip away the layers between myself and someone else. Those instinctive, carnal feelings had been dormant in me for a while, and he'd awoken them all. There were a lot of reasons that feeling wasn't okay, the primary one being that if I had him, I'm not sure I'd be able to let go.

I was almost positive he wasn't experiencing the same thing. This was all me. I think that's why I'd been acting distant, even a little cold, toward him. I knew it was a reaction coated in pure self-preservation. I knew I had to stay away because I had to escape this purgatory, and my only way out was grad school. I had to move on at some point, and if I had him, I didn't think I'd have the strength to leave again.

My mother called me down for dinner. My stomach tied in knots as I descended our staircase. I was hoping the walk to the Edwards's would feel longer, but it took less than thirty seconds.

We entered through the back gate and directly into the backyard. It was one of those phases of Oregon spring that gave us four or five days of glorious sunshine before coating us in rain again for two straight weeks. Our families had always made an effort to enjoy the sunshine days, and that often meant meals outside. Marlena was standing inside the oversized kitchen window that looked out over their yard. Our fathers were nowhere to be found– probably in the garage. Maddie and Charlie had taken to setting the table, and my mother walked straight inside to assist Lena. Carter was bringing food out from the kitchen.

"Penelope, can you help Carter bring the food out, please?" my mother asked.

Carter paused as he set a salad bowl down at the center of the dining table. He glanced up at me, a vacant smile that didn't quite reach his eyes complimented his features. He craned his head toward the door, beckoning me to follow him. We made our way into the kitchen. Lena was standing over the stove when she looked up at us and smiled.

"Well, there's a sight I haven't seen in a while."

Carter and I looked at each other and then at her, confusion plastered across both of our faces. The door that led from the garage to the kitchen swung open as both of our dads came inside. "Hi, Penny," my dad said, coming around the counter and kissing the top of my head.

"I was just telling them that I haven't seen them together in a while," Lena said as Tom came up behind her and wrapped his arms around her waist lovingly.

"You're right," my dad agreed. "When was the last time you two saw each other?" I bit down on my lip. I wondered if it felt this awkward for everyone or if it was just me.

"This morning at work," Carter chirped.

Our parents looked at each other awkwardly before shooing us all outside. We each took our place at the table, our fathers on either end and our mothers next to them. Charlie and Maddie insisted on sitting next to each other, which left me in between my mom and Lena and Carter in between Charlie and his dad. At least we weren't across from or next to each other. Even so, I could almost feel the heat radiating off his body as I watched him sip from his glass. My eyes dragged down his throat as he swallowed, then found themselves back at his mouth as he licked his lips. His gaze found me then. I looked down at my lap, hoping I wouldn't blush. My appetite was suddenly gone.

Once everyone had piled food on their plate, Tom asked, "Penelope, are you excited for your promotion?"

I looked sidelong between him and my father, forcing a smile. "Is it considered a promotion?" I asked in a joking tone. *It didn't come with a pay raise*, I wanted to add.

Tom barked a loud, throaty laugh. "I'd say so. Wouldn't you, Carter?"

"I'd always consider sharing an office with me to be a step up for someone." He shrugged, drawing the laughter of the entire table. I tried (and failed) not to roll my eyes.

"If you plan on keeping our office as organized as you used to keep your bedroom, I'd beg to differ," I muttered. His bedroom was always a pigsty when we were kids.

"It *was* organized for me. It didn't seem that way to you due to your OCD tendencies, but I always knew exactly where my things were."

"Except the time I let you borrow my geometry textbook and you lost it inside the blackhole that was your closet."

"And I paid to get you a new one!" Carter exclaimed. He was trying to keep his face serious, but it lightened just enough for one small chuckle to bust out of him. The sound of his laugh had me smiling, if not also laughing myself.

No, no, no. Don't smile at him. Don't let him make you laugh. I shook the feelings away. I looked away. Out to the pool. The pine trees that lined the back of their property. Anything but him.

"Actually, *I* paid to get her a new one," Tom chimed in. The table erupted.

"Oh gosh, I missed this," Lena said. "When was the last time you two saw each other before you started working together?"

Carter narrowed his eyes, like he was trying to remember. I blinked a few times as if I was doing the same, even though we both knew exactly. "The graduation party," we mumbled simultaneously.

"That long?" my dad asked.

"No, that can't be right," my mom added. All of our family members zoned out as their eyes circled, adding up the math of the last time they remembered seeing Carter and I in the same room. Eventually, they all settled on the realization that it had, in fact, been five years. "Wow," Mom said finally.

"Yeah. We had quite the reintroduction in Mr. Collins office, considering none of you told us," Carter said. He didn't have to specify what they had failed to inform us about. It was clear. Nobody had told Carter that I had moved home. Nobody had told me that he was also.

"Well, that wasn't entirely our fault." My dad nodded toward our sisters.

They looked at each other and giggled. Charlie and Maddie looked more like sisters than Maddie and I did. I, of course, was adopted, so it wouldn't have been expected that I resembled her. Although, she and Charlie weren't related either.

Despite the contrast of my mother's dark brunette hair to my auburn, people often thought I more closely resembled her than Maddie did. We both had light colored eyes and fawn, freckled skin, where Maddie's were a honey brown, like my dad's, and her hair was black as onyx. My brother had my mother's eyes, except where hers were ocean, his were ice. Almost silver. Easton also had my father's chestnut brown hair. Charlie and Maddie had the same skin tone and brown eyes, but Charlie's were amber like her mother's.

Neither of Tom's children resembled him (luckily for them if I'm being honest). Tom was a good man. He was proof that beauty was only skin deep, because I don't think he could ever be described as beautiful. He was short, rounded. Aged by years of stress and overworking. His eyes were so dark they were almost black, small, and beady. They'd been overtaken by the wrinkles that sagged against his skin. He kept his head shaved, because the only hair that grew there was at the nape of his neck; coarse, and curly, and gray. I knew, even as he aged, Carter would never look like that. Not just because he lived so carefree and stress-free. I doubted he'd ever wrinkle. He also had a thing about sunscreen—specifically the reef-friendly kind, of course—always telling everyone that they needed to put it on, even if it was cloudy. But Carter looked like his mom. I'd only met Laila a handful of times, but Carter had always been the spitting image of her. Not just in the coloring of their golden skin or hazel, almond shaped eyes; but in their wide set noses, full lips, and thick brows. They smiled the same, too. Where Carter's curls were short, tousled on top of his head, his mother's were long and cascading waves. His mother was the kind of beautiful you didn't think was real until you saw it up close, just like him.

"What did you two do?" Carter asked our sisters.

Bouts of laughter evaporated between them. "We convinced everyone to keep it a secret. We thought it would be funny if you both just randomly ran into each other," Charlie squeaked.

"You guys supported this?" I asked all our parents at once. "Meddlesome, insane family," I muttered under my breath. I was almost convinced nobody heard me, but Carter's eyes met mine through his lashes. They were glistening playfully.

My dad shrugged. "It didn't seem like a big deal. I didn't realize you two hadn't seen each other in so long. I thought you saw each other at Thanksgiving."

"I didn't come home for Thanksgiving last year," Carter said.

"Right. I forgot," Dad said through a mouth full of enchilada.

"Well, we also thought if we told you, Penelope, you might ask why. We didn't want you to know about the proposal to have you become Seaside's art teacher yet, because we thought you'd say no," Tom said as he shrugged.

I snickered, "I probably would have."

He straightened up. "Well, I'm glad you didn't. You're doing a good thing for those kids, for the district. It'll look great on your resume, too."

I nodded.

"We got this," Carter said. His tone was quiet, as if the words were meant just for me. I looked up at him, all my will dissolving. I'd done a good job at avoiding eye contact until that moment, but the tone in his voice made it impossible not to stare directly into his kaleidoscope eyes. He smiled at me. It was some variation of *that* grin. Instead of saying '*I got you*' as in, I've caught you staring at me, or you're the brunt of my joke; it said, '*I've got you*' as in, I've got your back, as if we're in all of this together.

I wanted to smile at him, but I forced it down. Deep, deep down and away from us both. If I allowed so much as one smile, it may be enough to demolish the wall I'd so carefully built around my heart.

The wall I built to keep him out.

Chapter Four

"Soulmates arent the ones who make you happiest, no. Theyre instead the ones who make you feel the most. Burning edges and scars and stars...They hurl you into the abyss. They taste like hope."

-Victoria Erickson

Carter

I arrived over an hour before the first bell would ring, my nerves not allowing me to sleep a moment longer this morning. I'd never had a job like this. I'd never worked somewhere that required pants, even. My first job was at a surf rental shop in Waikiki. Then, I picked up photography and began getting published. I've been freelancing ever since.

I was mostly nervous about the job. I had no idea what it took to be a teacher. I didn't know how to work with kids. I used to teach surf lessons to hotel tourists, and even though I knew it would be different, I hoped there were aspects of teaching children how to surf that would translate to teaching adolescents how to take photos. Luckily, for the entirety of the first week the students would be creating photo collages from old magazines to create mood boards for the type of things they'd be interested in photographing throughout the course of the semester. So, for this week I would be doing less teaching and more observing.

I was also nervous about being around Penelope. I hadn't seen her since dinner Friday night, and to say that went badly would've been an understatement. First, she snapped at me for standing inside her house. Then, she wouldn't so much as look in my direction during dinner. When I smiled at her, she scowled and looked away. When I tried speaking with her, she abruptly changed the subject and spoke to someone else. It was as if she was trying to block out my existence entirely. Her behavior was frigid, so unlike the person

I thought I knew. Penelope had always been a little timid and quiet, except for certain moments where she felt entirely comfortable with not only herself, but those around her. I'd only seen her like that a handful of times. Even so, Penelope was never callous.

She never rejected my presence, never made me feel unwanted or unwelcome. I used to always think she'd treated me like somewhat of a comfort blanket. As if she'd always known I would never judge her, never do her wrong. I'd always thought if she didn't love me the way I wanted her to, she at least trusted me. In some ways, I'd thought that was more important. I should've assumed she'd have changed in our years apart, but never to the point of coldness.

I begged to know if it was something I had done. If, after that day in the pantry, I had broken that trust that was so important to us both, even if unspoken. If I had, as I feared, misread things at that moment. If I had confused her wide eyes and her heaving chest for passion when it was really fear. She had kissed me back, sure. But what if she had just gotten caught up in the moment, and when it all came down, she realized that she wasn't okay with it? What if she had carried those feelings around all these years?

Regardless of how much it may hurt, even after all this time, I needed to know.

If I had hurt her, I needed to make it right.

Except, she was all but refusing to speak to me. One thing that hadn't changed about her, she was stubborn as hell. She had a hard exterior shell. I'd seen more than a few people try to break through that and fail miserably. I'd always believed I was exempt, though. That I had been around since before the shell had been created so I got to live on the inside, I didn't have to break through it. Dinner Friday night had made me realize that maybe that wasn't the case anymore. Maybe it was my turn to break the shell. The question wasn't just whether or not she'd let me in, but whether or not I even wanted to try.

Somehow, I knew I'd always try for her.

As I inched closer to our classroom, I could hear the shuffling of feet and the low bass of music playing. I should've assumed she'd already be there as well. If I was nervous about something, she'd be a full-blown wreck.

"Good morning," I said quietly as I opened the classroom door.

"Shit!" She jumped around to face me, startled anyway. "Dammit, Carter. You scared me."

"Sorry," I muttered.

"You're here early."

"Nervous." I shrugged. She nodded as if she agreed.

I ducked into our office and set my things down on the desk. It truly was a small space. One desk shoved against the far wall, a filing cabinet next to it. There was a small table set up behind the door with two chairs on either side. There was no way we'd both fit comfortably at the same time. After I'd set my things down and stepped back out of the cramped office, I found Penelope leaned back against the counter with a stack of papers in her hands. She held an arm out to me.

"What's this?" I asked.

"Our schedules," she said matter-of-factly. "I've outlined when each of us have our classes and our prep periods. When we'll each need to use the room and the office. We have separate prep periods but the same lunch. I normally eat with Macie or Christine anyway, so that shouldn't be a problem." There was an edge in her voice that wracked me to my core. "Anyway, my prep period is during your study hall, but that's fine. I'll use Christine's office during that period so you can use ours."

"You don't have to do that, Pep–"

"Really, it's fine. I'd rather have the space."

I didn't say anything else as I took the schedule from her. Looking it over, I realized she had organized things to the point that would cause us to have almost zero interaction with each other. She wanted to be as far away from me as possible.

"I've organized the classroom," she continued. She pointed to one side of the room. "All of my supplies are in those cabinets, and they're organized so don't touch them." She then pointed at a set of two more full-sized cabinets in the corner of the room. "Those are yours. I haven't touched anything, but all the cameras are in there." Lastly, she pointed at the closet next to our office. "I think there are some things in there you could use so I took out anything I'll need. You can do what you want with that space."

"Er– Thank you," was all I could get out.

She nodded. "I know you've got class first. I'll be heading to Christine's room shortly to get out of your hair. I'm just finishing up some things."

"You're not *in my hair*, Penelope," I said, my own tone turning chilly.

She stiffened and inhaled through her nose but didn't turn to look at me, nor did she respond. I began working around her, setting out the things I'd need. We moved in silence, only the quiet sound of the music she had been playing floating around us.

Not more than twenty minutes before class was set to start, Macie and the ginger-haired man, Jeremy, entered the room. Macie kind of looked like how I would imagine Tinker Bell looked if she was a real person. She couldn't be taller than five-foot-two, her hair was dishwater blonde and highlighted. She had tight curls that she'd pulled into a bun on top of her head. She was wearing ballet slippers, and she walked with a graceful skip in her step that almost made it seem like she was floating. She was bubbly, charming– almost like she glittered. I could tell she loves attention, too.

I hadn't had a single conversation with Jeremy since I'd met him, other than greetings and farewells. He watched Macie intently, seeming to fade into the shadows behind her. I wasn't sure if that was good or bad. Sometimes when she made a particularly outrageous comment, he'd cringe like he was embarrassed. Sometimes he'd squeeze her arm to get her to stop speaking. There were moments when I couldn't disagree with him, because Macie seemed to have no filter at all. But other times, it seemed like Jeremy was trying to dull the sparkle that existed beneath Macie's skin. I didn't know Macie well, but that bothered me. Penelope might not always sparkle, but she glowed. Like the moon. The thought of someone trying to dampen it– I hated that.

I kept to my corner of the classroom as Macie floated through the room to Penelope. Jeremy nodded at me but lingered beside the door. "I thought I'd find you here," she said as she pulled Penelope in for a hug. I noticed Penelope roll her eyes, but a smile hinted at her cheeks. "It looks so good! Are you excited?"

Penelope's only response was a shrug.

Macie laughed musically. "You'll be great. Or, well, I think you will. It's not like you've shown me your artwork or anything." She nudged Penelope with her elbow.

"You or anyone else," Penelope muttered. "And it wasn't even art. It was just something I did because I was bored. And I haven't touched a sketchbook in years. It's really not anything worth seeing, I promise. The school was just desperate."

"I've seen your sketches," I found myself saying. "They're incredible. There was that one you did of the Mayan Ruins in Mexico. I mean, *God Penelope*, it felt like I was standing right there! And–" She leveled me a raised brow, a silent demand to change the subject. "And," I continued, "insinuating the school was desperate and would hire *just anyone* is kind of an insult, y'know? This is my profession." I tried to add a glimmer to the last part of my sentence, but I was only half-kidding.

I knew she'd likely never seen my work. It wasn't as if my father was keen to show me off, but even if she had, I wouldn't have been insulted by her. I just wanted her to realize that whether or not she took it seriously, she was talented. She should be proud.

Macie nodded at me. "Suppose you have no issues showing off your work, then?"

I smiled. "Not at all."

I popped into the office and grabbed my laptop off the desk before carrying back out to one of the tables. I pulled up my portfolio website before sliding the screen around to face Macie. Penelope was attempting to look uninterested, but her eyes kept darting to the screen as Macie scrolled through.

I made most of my money selling my work to stock-image websites. I also worked with freelance writers to provide accompanying photos to their articles, particularly travel writers. I tried my hand at photographing a few surf competitions also, but I'd quickly found that shooting action—people in general—was not something I was interested in. I'd been picked up by a couple of resorts and travel agencies in Oahu to provide photos for their brochures and websites. That had been easy in Hawaii. There was a never-ending landscape to photograph, and a never-ending line-up of people to buy them to market their tourist attractions. I knew it'd be harder here. I'd have to work more, trek deeper, and produce images more unique, and more creative than anything I'd done before. But I'd been looking forward to the challenge.

I could see the reflection of my images in Macie's wide, dark eyes. The sprawling cliffs, crashing waves. All the green, blue, and gold. Photos of turtles, the reefs, the waterfalls. The crest of a wave within the setting sun. The shadows of palm trees dotted along the sand beneath the morning sunrise. "I've never wanted to go on vacation more than I do right now," she said.

I laughed. "Yeah, that's pretty much the point of it."

Penelope's eyes were softer than I'd seen them since I'd found her back in my life. "How do you do it?" she asked. "The photos, I mean. How do you make them look so good?"

"Well, the camera does a lot of the work. I've taken more than a few photoshop classes also. Otherwise, though, it's about timing, lighting, and calculations." I pulled the computer back and scrolled up to the first photo I'd ever sold. A cresting wave, in the second before it'd crash. The sun was directly underneath it, just falling behind the horizon. "Patience, too. I was in the water for *hours* trying to get this shot. When I came out, I was so pruned I could hardly walk." I pointed at the sun. "I had to wait until the sun was in the perfect spot on the horizon. Then, I had to wade in and out of the waves until I found the best spot for the sun to fit inside. After that, it was all about waiting for the perfect wave to come. Taking a million photographs until I caught just the right angle, just the right light, and just the right second for the sun to dip beneath the crest of the wave like that," I said. "I took over a thousand photos that day. This was the only one I kept."

Macie and Jeremy were both staring, nodding. I was only looking at Penelope. Her green eyes pulsated. She nodded, and then her cheeks began to redden. She looked away suddenly. "It's...beautiful," she said. "You should make a slideshow of your best work to show the students. It'll make them take you more seriously."

"That's not a bad idea," Jeremy agreed.

"Yeah, little fuckers are vultures," Macie muttered, bringing the attention back to her.

We all laughed before I said, "Then maybe you should bring some of your old sketchbooks to show them, Pep."

Her face slackened into a hard line. "Not likely."

The first bell rang, indicating there were ten minutes left before class started. A couple of students began to mosey inside through the door and sit down. I found my stomach developing knots. I shut my laptop and placed it back inside the office. I found myself somehow thankful for the distraction the three of them had provided me this morning. I hadn't the time to overthink how I would start class or what I'd say to the students. At this point, I had no choice but to just wing it.

"I've got to get to class. Christine is probably wondering where I am," Penelope said.

"Yeah, me too," Macie agreed. "But I wanted to catch you this morning because I'm trying to finalize the volunteer list for the dance next Saturday. You're chaperoning, right?"

"Yep, I'll be there," Penelope confirmed.

"And you'll be there early to help me set up?" Macie grinned.

"Yes, I'll be there too. Whatever you need, Mace. I am your slave."

Macie raised her brows. "Don't get me excited." She turned to me. "Mr. Carter, do you want to volunteer for the Spring Fling dance next weekend we're putting on for the students? It's Saturday–"

"I'm sure Carter is busy," Penelope interrupted. My eyes darted back and forth between the two of them, my mind completely void of a response.

Macie rolled her eyes and tsked at Penelope. "Anyway, the single teachers normally chaperone the dance so that the teacher's with families can take the night off." She looked me up and down. "I assume you're single."

I chuckled, "Am I that transparent?"

Her eyes flickered between Penelope and I. "I'd say so."

I followed her gaze to Penelope. She was chewing on her lip and looking down at her feet, arms crossed. Something about her stance irked me. She clearly didn't want me attending that dance. She didn't want me to associate with her friends. Invading her life. I couldn't understand it.

My instincts wanted to cater to what she wanted. Even if that wasn't me. But I didn't want to be the one asshole who refused to volunteer for a school function. It'd be a bad first impression. Plus, if she didn't want me around her friends, I'd need the opportunity to make some of my own.

"I'll clear my *very busy* schedule and make sure I'm available to help. Just let me know what time I need to be here," I said.

Macie's smile was positively feline. She said a quick goodbye and skirted out the door with Jeremy in tow. Penelope grabbed her bag from our office and gave me a strenuously fake smile before heading out the door.

The next week continued exactly like that. We circled each other briefly in the transition of our classes with tight lipped, insincere smiles and shallow nods. I wasn't even sure I could describe what we were doing as orbiting each other. It didn't feel as if we were on two different planets anymore, but on two different realms, merely acknowledging the existence of each other when required.

Even before, when it had felt like orbiting, there was something more. There was a level of comfort and acceptance that came with the relationship we held. It was, at times, friendship. But often, it was something deeper, something softer, something unspoken. Before, I was her atmosphere– her protector. She was my shooting star.

Now, it felt as if I was nothing to her at all. A void that roamed within her space.

To me, she felt like stardust.

Chapter Five

"Love is seldom. Soulmates are endangered."

-C. Joybell C.

Penelope

I can't remember a lot about my life before the age of about nine.

A therapist once told me that it's a trauma response. When I think about it hard, I see flashes of memories. Sometimes they're things I want to remember, and sometimes they're moments I'd rather forget. I don't want to see the bad moments, so I find myself often avoiding memories from my childhood entirely.

I remember meeting Carter, though.

I can't remember that day hardly at all– the events of it, anyway. I don't remember the car ride over to what would become my home, I can't remember seeing my room for the first time. I can't remember meeting my parents or my siblings. I can't really remember meeting Carter. I don't know the first word he said to me, or I to him. What I remember is the way I *felt* when I met him. I felt nothing. That nothing was the first time in days that I was *allowed* to feel nothing at all. I was supposed to feel sad. I was supposed to be thankful for my foster (who would someday become my adoptive) family. I was *supposed* to feel so many things. When all I really felt was pressure. *Pressure* to love my parents, and love my siblings; because if I didn't, then I might lose them. And even though I didn't know them, I *wanted* to love them because I wanted—needed—to feel loved. Those types of feelings, the supposed-tos, and the wants, and needs, were a lot for a little girl to process.

When I looked at Carter, there was no expectation there. He wasn't family, he wasn't a friend, so I had no obligations to him. I didn't need his love the way I needed the love of the family I was joining. I was allowed not to like him, or to like him. I was allowed to feel however I wanted about him.

I found comfort in that realization. The first smidge of comfort I'd felt since my mom died.

From then on, that's what I felt with Carter: comfortable. I think he caught onto that, and being the person that he is, he took it upon himself to help me. I don't know how many of the details he knew about me before I was adopted, but I imagine that Easton had spilled most of them. We've never talked about it, but I could always tell. To whatever extent, he knew. So, he always protected me in whatever way he could. However coy, however hidden, he protected me. From kids at school, from things he thought might trigger me (he would always change the channel when Marlena left *Law and Order* playing so I wouldn't accidentally see a bloody, dead body), he even took my side in every argument I had with my brother. Sometimes I think that's part of the reason they grew apart.

He protected me. He comforted me. Always.

As we got older, I wasn't sure what it all meant. I don't think he did either. It was an unexplainable yet delicate balance, he and I. Kind of like the way gravity, pressure, and heat work together to give us stars. And when the heat gives out, so does the pressure, then gravity takes over and it collapses in on itself, creating a black-hole. Nobody knows what happens after that.

I think that's what happened when he kissed me.

We accidentally created a supernova. We collapsed into a black-hole.

As he's standing in front of me now, I realize that I don't know what happens in the aftermath.

"Alright, you want to tell me what this weirdness is with you and Mr. Carter?" Macie asked from the other side of the table, pulling me out of my thoughts. I looked down at the half-eaten croissant in front of me and shook my head. "The moment he walked through that door you became worthless for conversation," she muttered. "He walks into a room and you go all Han Solo on me."

I lifted my head and blinked at her. "Han Solo?"

"Yeah, frozen." She fluttered her hands as if I should know what she's talking about.

"I don't understand the reference."

She groaned, "Han Solo gets frozen in carbonite at the end of *The Empire Strikes Back*. God, Penelope, I've been telling you to watch these movies for years."

"I've only known you for six months," I snorted.

"Feels like years," she murmured. "Anyway, I need to understand the history here." She waved her finger between me and Carter, who was standing on the far side of the coffee shop. He hadn't greeted me when he walked in, but I knew he saw me. "You've never mentioned anybody named Carter to me before. Then, a couple of weeks ago, this guy—very, very hot guy, might I add—comes walking into your classroom saying you're old friends? Except, you must not be because after that you've hardly said a word to him, and you become a literal glacier every time he's within your vicinity. There is tea here and I am going to need you to serve it." Her rapid speech had her panting by the time she had finished.

I dropped my head in my hand. "Can you wait until he leaves?" I peeked at him through my fingers and saw him standing at the to-go counter waiting for his coffee, meaning he likely wasn't staying inside. It had been two whole weeks since he showed back up, crashing head first into my life.

He is a bull, and my life is a china shop.

I'm honestly surprised Macie let it go this long without interrogating me about it, because the weirdness had been intense each time I was around him at work. I had a feeling this conversation was coming though, since we always met up for coffee on Wednesday mornings. The school district had classes delayed by an hour every Wednesday to accommodate budget cuts, meaning we had time to catch up during the week.

The barista called out Carter's order and we both looked up at him. He glanced at me as he headed out the door and nodded. *Of course, he'd be here*. But I supposed that was the thing about living in a small town, there was only one good coffee shop in it.

I let out all the breath I had been holding in. "Okay," I started. I explained to Macie my history with Carter. She already knew I had been adopted, but I explained how I had been adopted when I was seven. How my father and Carter's were neighbors and friends, and how when we were little kids Carter and Easton were also friends. The day I was brought home, Carter was sitting on our front porch with Easton. How from that day forward he was always there. We were never best friends, but we were never *not* friends, either. We just were whatever it was that we were.

"Then, around, I don't know, twelve, I started having a crush on him. He's always been tall, but he used to be skinny too. When he started hitting puberty, it was like the rest of his body caught up with him. His parents have a pool we spent a lot of time at in the summer and I had seen him a million times without a shirt on, but one day he walked outside and just looked different. After that, I noticed him in different ways. He is actually really funny. He's smart too but doesn't like people to know it. He's got this easy demeanor that kind of makes everyone fall in love with him, but it's more cute than it is annoying. He's protective. Thoughtful–" I looked at Macie and noticed her grinning at me. I blushed. "Anyway, I just started having this big crush on him but I was way too timid and afraid to say anything. I knew he never felt the same way

I did and that embarrassed me, so I kept it to myself." She raised a brow at me but nodded. "Then, at our high school graduation party he just... he pulled me into a closet and kissed me."

Macie's eyes bugged. "He just casually pulled you into a closet and kissed you? And then what? Walked away?"

I chewed on the inside of my cheek. "No, more like I ran away."

Macie laughed. "That sounds like you. What happened after that?"

I shrugged. "Nothing. I left for England the next morning. I didn't see him again until last Thursday." I ran my fingers through my hair. I noticed Macie hadn't responded so I glanced up at her to find her mouth gaping open at me.

"I'm sorry, let me get this straight. You crushed on this kid for, like, your whole life pretty much. One day he randomly kissed you, knowing you were moving across the planet the next morning, and then you guys just didn't speak again for years?"

"That about sums it up," I murmured.

"Was it, like, a predatory thing?" she asked.

"What?" I gasped.

"Well, you said he pulled you into a dark closet and kissed you. It doesn't sound like it was consensual." She gave me a look that read a little confusion and a little concern.

"Oh, no. No, no. It wasn't like that. I mean, yes, he pulled me into the closet, but at first he tried to just talk to me. He told me there was something he needed to do before I left, or he wouldn't be able to live with himself–"

Macie gaped, "Oh my."

I nodded. "I was pretty sure, once he said that, that he was going to kiss me. I said okay, so I gave him permission. Even after I said it, he paused. Like he thought I was confused, or he was surprised at my reaction. He seemed really timid, which was so unlike him. And actually, now that I think about it, I was the one who kissed him." I blushed again. "Carter would never do something that would make me uncomfortable."

Macie smiled knowingly. "After that, though, you had no idea what he was up to this entire time? No run-ins? No Facebook updates?" She asked.

"He doesn't use social media." I rolled my eyes. "The only time I heard about him were brief updates I got from his parents when I would visit at Christmas."

"You never saw him at Christmas?"

I shook my head. "I think he would come at Thanksgiving. He always celebrated Christmas with his mom, even when we were kids. She lives in Hawaii."

She nodded. "Damn. Well, it's starting to make sense now. Was it good?"

"Was what good?" I countered.

"The kiss?" She cocked her head.

I looked out the window and watched the rain fall onto the ground, the puddles jumping across the parking lot. I had never told anyone this information before, so naturally I had never been asked this question. The answer was yes, of course. It's easy to say that the kiss was good. A lot of kisses are good. How was I supposed to explain to her that it was the kind of kiss that kept me up at night for years on end? The kind of kiss that made my skin feel like pinpricks whenever I thought about it, even now. The kind of kiss I've been wanting to replicate since the day it happened but have yet to experience anything that even comes close.

"If it's still causing me this much distress five years later, it must've been good, right?"

"Yeah, I guess so," she cackled. "So, what are you going to do about it?"

"There is nothing to do about it," I muttered defensively.

She was quiet for a moment while she sipped her coffee and watched me inquisitively.

"Are you still attracted to him?" I was the one now raising my brow at her. She blew out her nose, shaking her head. "Right, obviously."

"It doesn't matter, though. I feel like a completely different person than I was before I moved to England. I'm sure he's different too. I don't think we're compatible now. I'm not sure we ever were to begin with. Plus, hopefully I'll get into a grad program somewhere. Which means I'll be moving away, and I'd rather spare myself the déjà vu."

A sullen look crossed her face, a seriousness I rarely ever saw with her. "I'm sorry," she said softly. I nodded and sipped my coffee, looking back out at the rain. "Maybe you guys should talk about it, though. Clear the air, y'know? It'll probably lift a little weight off your chest."

I nodded again but offered no response. I already knew she was right.

I kicked open the front door with my foot, to the irritated gasp of my mother on the other side. *Shit.* I stood straight up and stepped inside hesitantly.

She closed her eyes slowly and let out a breath of annoyance. "Penelope, please don't kick the front door."

"My hands are full," I mumbled, referencing the stack of papers in my arms.

"You could've knocked and I would've opened it for you."

I darted to the right and began climbing the stairs. "Alright, sorry. I'll keep that in mind next time." I had no time to argue with my mother considering I have at least three hours of grading to do this evening. I normally got my grading for Christine done during slow times throughout the day. Splitting my time between her classes and my art classes now left little free time during the weekday, though.

"You can make it up to me by running across the street and grabbing your father for dinner!" My mother's voice rang throughout the house.

No, no I really don't want to do that.

"Mom, I have a lot of work I need to get done and–"

"I can't hear you!" she lied playfully, chiming from downstairs. I glowered before kicking open my bedroom door with my foot. I threw my bag down on my bed and the stack of papers at my desk. I retreated down the stairs and across the narrow residential road. I walked through the Edwards's front door without knocking, hoping I could relay the message to my father and get out quickly.

I slipped through their door and meant to beeline for the kitchen but was stopped at the doorway to the sunroom. I noticed several of my mother's canvases set up in there with half completed paintings. I always wondered how she could do that. Start something and not see it through to completion. I was never able to work on two things at once, I had to finish something entirely before jumping into something else.

"Have the classes you've been teaching inspired you?" Carter's soft voice came from behind me.

I snorted, "No, definitely not. I was never a painter anyway."

"Right, you like to draw." I could hear the smile in his tone.

"Liked," I corrected, turning to face him. "Have you seen my dad?"

He frowned. A second later, his face relaxed into his typical boyish grin. Something about it felt forced. "Yeah, they're outside. I passed them on my way in."

We both made our way through the living room and into the kitchen, headed towards the backyard. Marlena was standing over the stove when she looked up at us and smiled. "Look at our two teachers!"

I rolled my eyes, catching a glimpse of Carter doing the same. The matching expressions on our faces made it difficult for me not to smile. I wondered if he'd been having the same experience with his students that I had. The only word I felt capable of using to describe mine was... challenging. It almost seemed as if having one short class period per day wasn't enough time to get out their creative energy. Knowing they'd have to pack it into just forty-five minutes made them wild and restless. At least I could throw paint at them and let them do what they wanted with it, for the most part. Carter had described photography as being calculated, requiring patience. Two things, I'm sure, were next to impossible to teach middle schoolers.

The door that led to the backyard opened, both of our fathers stepping through. "Hi, Penny. What're you doing here?" my dad asked.

"I was saying, look at our two teachers. Aren't you so proud of them?" Lena beamed. I'd always admired the way she loved Carter as if he was her own. I imagined it wasn't hard– loving him. She'd been with Tom since Carter was five, but even so, it was clear she'd taken over a mother role for him simply because she wanted to. There was no obligation in the way she looked at him, the way she hugged him. He was her son. "Can you get me the pasta out of the pantry, Carter?" she asked.

Carter stiffened briefly before nodding. A blush creeped up my neck. Suddenly the room felt like it was closing in around me. The Edwards's kitchen was big enough to prepare food for an army, but it seemed entirely too small at that moment. "Mom wanted me to run over and let you know she needs you to come home for dinner, but I actually have a bunch of grading I need to get to so I'm going to head back," I said, suddenly remembering why I'd come over in the first place.

I circled the island counter and made my way through the open doorway that led back to the front of the house when Carter's voice startled me. "Penelope." There was a slight irritation to his tone that caught the attention of our parents too. He handed Lena the box of pasta and walked towards me. "I need to talk to you about that... project you were working on for class."

I gulped audibly. The tension that had existed between just the two of us was now floating all around the room, visible to our parents too. I nodded slowly before continuing out of the house, Carter at my heels.

"Do you want me to quit this job?" he asked once we had made it past the front door.

My face contorted with confusion. "Why would you ask that?"

"You can't seem to stand being in the same room as me. It's as if the initial shock wore off from learning we'd be working together, and now you get irritated by my presence. Like I'm not good enough to breathe the same air as you. It's honestly quite insulting. Would you prefer that I quit my job so we don't have to be around each other?"

I opened my mouth and clamped it shut, then opened it again. "No, of course not," I said, finally.

He closed his eyes and breathed deeply through his nose. "Then I'm going to need you to cut the shit with the cold shoulder, Penelope. You're making it hard for me to feel comfortable at work, and now inside my parents' house too. That's not fair to me. I told you I wanted to talk about it, and you weren't willing. So, if there is something you want to say to me, say it. If there isn't, then act right. What you're doing right now is immature and a little cruel, even."

I bit down on my lip, hard. My body was vibrating with emotion. I wanted to get defensive, but I couldn't. He was completely right, and I knew it. Except, he'd never spoken to me like that before. He had always handled me so carefully, like he thought I'd break. I kind of expected him to do the same now. "I'm sorry."

He stepped back like he was surprised by my reaction. Running his hand through his hair, he stared down at his feet. I took the opportunity to look at him since he wasn't looking at me. He had on dark gray sweatpants that hung low on his hips, and a black t-shirt that fit him too well. I could just make out a tattoo on his bicep, peeking out from his shirt sleeve. Not enough to tell what it could be, but enough to know it was there. It made me curious.

"It's fine, Pep. I'm sorry, I shouldn't have spoken to you like that. It's just... I don't know what I did."

"You didn't do anything, Carter. You haven't done anything wrong. It's me," I whispered, realizing I had only considered what pushing him away was doing for me but hadn't considered how it must've been making him feel.

"Is it... were you...upset? After it happened? Have you been walking around pissed off at me for half of a decade?"

I shook my head. "No, I wasn't upset." I thought back to what Macie had said earlier. I knew she was right. It was time to clear the air between us, and Carter's honesty had made me feel brave. "But I never moved on from it. It happened rapidly, and then it was over. It feels like the two of us stood frozen in time, but the rest of our lives kept going. I don't know what to do now."

"Me either," he said. We both stared after each other for several long moments.

"I'm sorry," I repeated.

"I'm sorry too." Just like that, the air was cleared. It had always been that easy with him. "But just because we don't know how to move forward doesn't mean we need to shut each other out. We're going to be around each other for at least the next couple of months. We might as well try and make the best of it, right?"

Ever the optimist.

I wanted to agree with him. I wanted to be cordial. I wanted to be able to work together. I even wanted to be his friend, maybe. I wasn't sure I could. I wasn't sure I could breathe him in, watch him laugh. I was afraid that any relationship I had with him would have me falling once again. I was terrified of falling for him and not being caught; but even more, I was terrified of him catching me and dropping me later. Once he realized I was no longer the person he thought he knew.

Yet, watching his face fall every time I iced him out didn't feel much better. It appeared that regardless of the route I took, it'd likely end in my own heartbreak. So, for the first time in a long time, I decided not to be selfish. I'd give him the best of the situation he was seeking, I'd give him friendship, even. And I'd expect nothing in return.

"Yeah, we should," I found myself saying.

"You know, despite your barbarous demeanor, you're still one of my favorite people in the world." He smiled at me, teeth gleaming.

The way his skin sparkled in the sun made me feel things that I shouldn't be feeling. Things that would most definitely hurt me later. "Yeah, yeah, you too," I muttered with a grin.

Surprisingly, it wasn't too hard to smile like that with him.

"C'mon." He walked past me and waved behind him. "I'll walk you home."

"Carter, it's like fifteen feet. I can manage."

He stopped, now in the middle of the road. "Hey, we're trying this friend's thing now, okay? Friends do nice things for each other. Like, walking each other home. Accept my politeness."

I rolled my eyes but followed. "And it's two hundred and ninety paces, by the way."

"Oh God, you counted."

Once we'd reached my parent's front door, he leaned next to it and crossed his arms. "Well, you're welcome, Pep." He winked.

"Why'd you kiss me?" I blurted. As soon as the words left my lips, I regretted them. My mouth was doing that thing again, where it moves on its own. It's the way he smiles, the way he says my nickname. The insisting on walking me home, and how his biceps flex beneath the sleeve of his t-shirt. I needed to know how someone like him could've wanted someone like me.

I needed to know whether it had been a fluke.

He laughed in a soul-stopping, thunderous kind of tone. "Are we doing this, then?"

I shrugged, too afraid to open my mouth for fear of what may come out of it.

He shook his head, still smiling. Staring down at his feet, he inhaled like he was bracing himself. "I didn't mean to kiss you. I initially followed you into the house because I just wanted to talk to you. It didn't feel right, you moving to England, without telling you how I felt. I just wanted to get it off my chest. I couldn't stand the fact that you were never into me and if I at least told you... if I had to watch you reject me, it would hurt less to see you leave..." He paused and rubbed the back of his neck. "The words aren't coming out the right way."

My head was reeling. My mind moved a thousand miles a minute as I took in what he was saying. I forcefully clamped my mouth shut, still feeling as if I had no control over the things I may say. I could feel my pulse fluttering inside my head, like a drum beating his name.

After a moment, he continued, "And then we were in the pantry, and it was dark, and we were standing so close. I just had to go for it. I waited for you to say no, or to push me away, but you didn't. At that time, I thought that it would be easier to express the way I felt physically than with words, which I apparently failed at. All though, clearly, I'm no good at talking either–"

"You liked me?" I interrupted. I needed him to spell it out. I needed to hear it bad enough that I actually allowed my mouth to open.

He snorted. "Yes, Pep. I liked you. Was it not obvious?"

I shook my head.

He laughed again. "I think it was. I think you were just oblivious."

I felt my heart become a pretzel as I thought about all our missed chances because the two of us were simply too afraid to speak our minds. It had always been easy with him, except for where my heart was concerned. We'd both made that harder than we ever needed to. What a disappointment that turned out to be, because only now am I able to realize there was so much more hiding behind his jungle eyes.

"So, did I just make things more awkward?" he asked.

Things were definitely going to be more awkward– for me, at least. The way my stomach dropped when he spoke, and the way my chest fluttered when he smiled were already difficult enough to deal with. The pretzel my heart had been tied into tightened when I thought about the fact that, at one point, I had made him feel the same way. It squeezed just a bit more when I thought about the fact that he couldn't possibly feel that way still. Not with the energy I had been giving off lately. Not with the person I'd become.

There was no reason to subject him to the mess that was my life any more than I already had, though. "Nah, it's all water under the bridge." I smiled as genuinely as I could manage. As chaotic as my mind was at the moment, his face made things a little easier.

"Good," he said, dazzling.

"Good," I agreed with an unbelievably bright tone, dull on the inside.

"There are two kinds of feeling—one from our body, another from our soul. Love, it is the affection of soul to soul."

-Silenus Poetry

Carter

My hands tapped against the steering wheel as I pulled into the parking lot of the school. I pretended they were tapping along to the music I was playing, but they weren't. They were tapping in an attempt at controlling my anxious nerves. I wasn't entirely sure why. The remainder of the week had gone well. Penelope and I still moved around each other, but rather than shallow nods and unconvincing smiles, our interactions were real. We held brief conversations about our lesson plans, our students, or our families.

Everything was proper, cordial, if not a little awkward after our conversation Wednesday night. Things between us were better than they had been before, but I still wasn't sure I'd call us friends. I wasn't even sure I wanted to be friends with her. I wasn't sure if I could.

Maybe that's why I was nervous. Macie asked me to arrive at the school *four hours* before the dance to help her, Penelope, Marshall, and Jeremy set up. As far as I knew, there wouldn't be any other faculty or students there for at least a few more hours. The four of them were friends, and I was not. Maybe I was afraid of being a fifth wheel of sorts. Maybe I was afraid of Penelope feeling like I was interfering with her life too much and shutting me out again. Maybe I was afraid I'd fall in with them seamlessly and make connections with them all, bringing me closer to Penelope in a way I wasn't sure I could handle.

One thing I knew for certain. I was absolutely afraid of Macie.

Ultimately, the reason I'd decided to show up so early to help is because she'd been running around frantically all week to prepare for the dance. She'd spent nearly all her free time in our classroom, borrowing hordes of art supplies without asking, making messes of signs and decorations (and not cleaning them up). She was irritable and touchy all week. She'd snapped at Jeremy more than a few times. I'd made the unfortunate decision of asking her why it was so important. She snapped at me then too.

She explained that it was the only dance they got all year. When Penelope and I attended school here, we had two. We had a winter-themed dance during Christmas break, and another dance at the end of the school year. Due to budget, that was cut down to just one a few years ago. Macie explained that she had attended an all-girls catholic school that didn't have any dances at all (and no boys, she had added) and that it was a miserable experience she never wanted her students to have. She said when she started working here three years ago, she asked to take over the planning of it, and she's been doing it ever since. Jeremy explained to me that she often began planning at the beginning of the school year, and even set personal savings aside to afford extra entertainment that would be outside of the school's budget.

So, when she had demanded that I arrive as early as the rest of her friends because, *I know for a fact you've got nothing else going on and Penelope won't be at home for you to drool at anyway,* I hastily agreed. Along with the added eye roll and secret thanks for making the comment when Penelope wasn't around.

The parking lot was empty, apart from about six cars, one of which I recognized as Penelope's black Kia. Once I made my way inside the gym, I saw the space had been transformed into the colors of spring, making the gym nearly unrecognizable. Green tapestries hung across the ceiling, balloons that looked like flowers were plastered up along the walls with orange and yellow streamers coating the bleachers. Twinkle lights draped the perimeter of the entire gym and a large wall of greenery with multi-colored flowers sprinkled throughout it stood in the corner. A neon sign that read: *Spring Fling* hung in the middle of the wall.

Macie stood on top of a forklift that was fully extended as she tried to hang a disco ball in the center of the gym. Jeremy stood at the foot of it, directing her from below. Mesmerized by all the work Macie had already done, and naturally, being drawn to the spectacle that was her on a forklift, I hadn't yet spotted Penelope. That was, until a cackle of her laughter echoed throughout the gym. I found her in the corner opposite the wall of greenery. Her cherry-colored hair was thrown into a knot on the top of her head. Her white t-shirt was oversized and hanging off her shoulders as they bounced with her giggles. In a squatting position, she slowly wrapped a ball of streamers around Marshall's body.

He stood—pin straight, legs together, arms tucked at his sides—watching her. He let her wrap him up completely as she rose slowly, binding him in with each round she made of his body. His eyes held only desire and shameless hunger. He was smirking at her as she worked up on him. As if making her giggle was a competition, and she was the prize he believed he won. Once she got to his neck, she wrapped the streamer tightly around him three more times, reaching his jaw and covering his mouth. She tore the streamer from the ball and tucked it in behind his head.

"Talk about my ass again, and I'll cover your nose." She had been laughing before, but her tone now was a vicious, simple warning. Marshall's eyebrows rose in amusement.

I frowned.

Claps thundered. "No fucking around!" Macie yelled.

Penelope twirled around to face her, but her eyes fell on me instead. Her mouth gaped, and then snapped shut. She looked as if she may flush. "Hi," she said. "I didn't realize you were here."

I craned my neck toward Marshall. "I didn't want to interrupt."

Marshall was already tearing off the decorations. He stepped out of the pile of streamers that pooled at his feet. "No worries, we've got all night for foreplay, don't we, Penelope?" He winked as he passed her, brushing against her shoulder.

My gut plummeted.

"Pig," she seethed.

I suppressed the kindred words that I wanted to throw at him myself, but I could feel them burning inside my throat. My face must've been giving me away because a pressure on my forearm broke my gaze. I looked down to find a set of large green eyes blinking back at me.

"He was just messing around," she said. Not defensive, or justifying, but reassuring.

I had to assume there was some kind of understanding, some kind of relationship between them that would cause such intense banter in such a casual manner. Unless Marshall was truly just that brazen. I hoped and hoped, even knowing I shouldn't care, that their banter was not, in fact, some sort of foreplay.

I hoped and hoped that Penelope knew she deserved better than him.

We followed behind Marshall and back towards Macie as she finally lowered down the forklift. A sparkling sphere now hung in the center of the gym. She glanced around the space, crossing her arms. "Okay, we're still waiting for the DJ to get here and set up, and I'm waiting for some more tables and chairs to be delivered."

"What do we do until then?" Marshall asked.

Penelope had wandered away toward a lone table that was set up by the door. I assumed it was for some kind of check-in process. She pulled a bag out from under it and pulled a book out of that bag. I tried to ignore the patter in my chest as I realized the book she was holding was my favorite one. Plopping down in the chair, she began to read. Everyone else followed her, Marshall immediately taking the only other chair in the area and draping his arm over the back of hers. I leaned back against a set of bleachers nearby while Macie and Jeremy took to the floor in front of the table, leaning against the door.

"Until then, we will practice for next week's trivia night."

Everyone groaned.

"Oh, shut up," Macie muttered.

"Are we at least going to be quizzed on something interesting next week?" Penelope asked without looking up from her book. Marshall must've caught my confused expression because he said, "Penelope only participates when the week's topic is something she's an expert on. When it's not, she pretends she's not interested, but it's really because she doesn't want to be outsmarted by one of us." He winked at her.

Penelope rolled her eyes.

"What is next week's topic?" I asked Macie.

"Early 2000's sitcoms." Macie's brows lifted. "Do you watch any early 2000's sitcoms, Mr. Carter?" I shrugged in response.

Macie's eyes met Penelope's and widened, almost imperceptibly. Penelope shrugged slightly as if they were having an unspoken conversation. Penelope pretended to keep her face straight, casually turning over the page of her book. "I don't watch that garbage."

"Oh, right. We can't forget that pretty little European princess over here hates American television." Marshall craned his neck toward Penelope.

Macie nodded. "She does this every time trivia night is pop culture themed."

Penelope let her book fall shut and closed her eyes. "I just think it's a waste of time. And for the record, I was *very* active on *Game of Thrones* night."

"Exactly. That's not an American show," Marshall quipped.

I hated the way he looked at her.

"Okay, so you're proving my point." Penelope smiled back at him. I hated it just as much.

"What are the odds that Penelope finds some excuse not to come next week? She'd hate for us to see her lose."

"*If* I felt like going, I'd still beat the rest of you. I can easily brush up on all the crappy tv shows."

"I'll bet on that." Marshall held his hand out to her.

She raised a brow at him. "And if I win, what do I get?"

"A date with me." He smiled widely. My insides cringed. She rolled her eyes and went back to her book. "I'll buy you lunch for a month," he countered.

Her eyes brightened and she returned the handshake. "Okay."

Marshall's hand paused right before making contact and he added, "But, for every question you get wrong, you have to take a sip of your drink." He was giving her that same sinful smile I'd seen before. She hesitated for a moment, and I was sure she would say no. She shook his hand anyway.

I glanced at Macie to find her matching my frown. She cleared her throat. "Carter, you should come with us."

I glanced at Penelope, trying to see some sort of reaction on her face. Permission or denial. Marshall's face certainly spelt denial but I didn't care. Penelope smiled softly again, the type of smile that existed just for me.

Only if you want to, she mouthed at me.

Ignoring Marshall's eye roll, I turned to Macie and smiled. "Okay."

By hour three of setting up, I was a sweaty mess. We'd succeeded in transforming the gym into a springtime wonderland, though. The DJ had been set up, and the catering had arrived, so the five of us all went home to shower and change. A handful of other teachers were helping to chaperone the dance itself. I was pleasantly surprised to find that Mr. Collins was not among the other chaperones and that he'd handed the reins of the dance over entirely to Macie.

Once I arrived back at the school, the gym's transformation had been completed. All the lights were off, the DJ was now playing, and kids were starting to pile in. I got back before anyone else, apart from Macie. Once I located her, I asked her where to station me. "I'm going to need you and Penelope to watch the drink table. I don't want anything getting spiked."

"You really think middle schoolers would spike the punch at a school dance?"

"Yes." She said it in a way that made me question if it was something she'd experienced before. I held up my hands as if not to argue and marched over to the drink table.

I tinkered with the cups even though they were already lined up. I stirred the punch even though it didn't need it and picked at the tablecloth. Growing boredom overcame me and I wondered where Penelope was. The dance had officially started, but she still hadn't returned.

"Hi," she said, finally reaching me. Her voice was a hollow echo. "Sorry I'm late."

I glanced down at her. Her hair was slicked back into a tight bun that complimented the shape of her face and the sharp angles of her cheek bones. She had on a knee length black dress that fit snugly around her curves. Sheer, netted sleeves hung off her shoulders and down her arms, black polka-dots sprinkled among the sleeves. "You look beautiful," I blurted. I didn't mean to say it out loud, but I found the words rolling off my tongue anyway.

"Oh. Th– thank you," she stuttered, glancing upward to meet my eyes.

Hers were a glowing green, rimmed with red, as if she may have been crying. "Are you okay?"

"Yes," she said too quickly. "Yes, I'm fine."

I bowed my head. "Pep."

"I just got my admission letter from Stanford. I was too afraid to open it. My parents tried to convince me to do it before I left but I was too scared. And now I know I'm going to be thinking about it all night."

"Penelope, come on. Of course you're going to get accepted," I chuckled. Being that I didn't go to college, I didn't know a lot about the admissions process. But as far as I knew, Oxford was *the* college. You couldn't get any more prestigious than that. I would've thought that a degree from Oxford would've guaranteed admission to anywhere else.

She shook her head. "No. I've already been rejected from a few other schools."

I tried not to show the surprise on my face because I could tell by hers that the sentence had been tough to get out. She put all her value on her accomplishments. Not getting accepted into a college would've been difficult for her. "I'm sorry, Pep."

She shrugged.

"You'll get in. I know you will. If there was anyone in this world I'd bet on getting into college, it'd be you."

She blew out a breath that kind of sounded like a laugh. "Thanks."

I glanced around the darkened gym, watching the students dancing, feeling a bit of déjà vu. I wondered if she remembered. Regardless, I knew she needed a distraction.

"I'll be right back," I said. I sauntered off toward the bathroom, and once I was sure she wasn't looking at me, I circled back around and walked over to the DJ.

When I reached our table once again, I asked, "Do you remember our eighth-grade dance?"

"No, I absolutely do not."

"Liar."

She rolled her eyes. In a mock tone she asked, "Why are you asking?"

"I'm just wondering if you'd run away from me if I tried to dance with you again."

She looked at me with an expression that seemed like a challenge. "I guess that would depend on whether or not you'd be asking out of pity."

I narrowed my eyes. "I did not ask you to dance with me out of pity, Penelope."

Penelope had attended our eighth-grade school dance with a group of friends. I intended to ask her, but Easton made it apparent to me that she was off limits. Then, before I could convince him otherwise, I was asked by another girl. I didn't want to say no and look like an asshole. During the dance itself, the DJ played one slow song, and all of Penelope's friends either danced with other boys or with each other. Penelope stood at the corner of the gym by herself. It wasn't that I pitied her, though. She had no issue with being alone in the corner of the room. I think that is sometimes where she preferred to be. She wasn't embarrassed about it or feeling insecure that nobody had asked her to dance. They would have– other boys. They would have. But the no-limits rule set by Easton applied to more than just me. Plus, I called dibs on Penelope when we were nine, and I made sure every boy our age knew it too.

When I'd seen her standing alone, and my hands were on the hips of another girl, I realized there was nobody else in the world I wanted to dance with except for Penelope. So, I stepped away from my date, and left her standing in the middle of the dance floor as I walked straight for Penelope. I asked her to dance with me. And she ran away. She looked at me for not more than a fraction of a second, and then took off. An hour later, Lena picked us up and drove us home in a silent and painful car ride. A week later, school ended and I spent the summer in Hawaii with my mom. We never talked about it again.

"Penelope, look at me," I demanded. "I did not ask you to dance with me because I pitied you."

She scoffed, "You came with a date."

"Who I left standing in the middle of the dance floor by herself so I could ask you. Because once the music started playing, I realized you were the only girl I cared to dance with. It had nothing to do with you being alone. If you had been with another boy, I would've interrupted that too."

Heat bloomed across her face. "You left Becca Whitten in the middle of the dance floor, *alone*?"

"Yes. And she slapped me for it. Which I deserved. But I would've done it again."

She burst into vivid, heart-filled laughter.

As if the DJ had been waiting for us, listening to our conversation, he answered my previous request and the beginning chimes of REO Speedwagon's *Can't Fight This Feeling* began to echo through the gym.

"You did not," she gasped.

"I have no idea what you're talking about, Penelope. This is the most cliche middle school dance song of all time. Of course they'd play it." It also happened to the song that was playing during our own dance. The song that was playing when she ran from me.

She pointed out to the dance floor in front of us. Kids were blinking around at each other in confusion. The adult chaperones were laughing. "Not a single kid in here knows this song."

I let a moment pass before I responded. The students looked around the room as if they weren't sure if it was supposed to be a slow song or not. Yet, couples began to pair up. Arms on shoulders, hands on waists, and the swaying began. "Well, they seem to be getting the gist of it." I held out my hand to her. "Dance with me, Pep? Absolutely no pity here."

She snorted, "No way. Not in front of the students. We're teachers, Carter."

I waved her off. "They're not even looking at us."

She just shook her head.

I waited for the music to swell, but she'd looked away from me by that point. I leaned into her, just above her ear. "*Even as I wander, I'm keepin' you in sight...*"

Her eyes bugged out of her head.

"*You're a candle in the window on a cold, dark winter's night.*"

"Sto–"

"*And I'm getting closer than I ever thought I mi–*"

Her hand flew to my face, clamping itself over my mouth. A wheeze erupted from her throat. Her fingers were warm, her hands were soft. I tried to ignore the way they felt against my skin. Tried to fight the childish urge to lick her palm. "Please stop singing," she requested. Hesitantly, slowly, she began to move her hand away from my mouth.

"*.... Fight this feelin' any mooooore. I've forgotten what I–*"

It slapped back over my face. "Carter." She was attempting to sound serious, but her eyes glistened with pure glee. She held her own mouth shut in a failed effort to keep from laughing.

"*What I started fightin' fooooor,*" I sang into her hand, the sounds muffled.

She sighed, removing her hand. "If I dance with you, will you stop singing?"

I smiled. "What's wrong with my singing?" She threw me a pointed look. "I've been told I'm a rather talented singer."

"Whatever your mom told you doesn't count."

"Actually, *your* mom told me that. After our fourth-grade choir concert," I shot back.

"She also told Easton his football skills were good enough to go pro, and we all know how incredibly untrue that was."

I shrugged. "At least your mother is an optimist."

She snorted, "Yeah, well, I'm a realist. I am telling you that you *really* suck at singing."

"I suppose you'd better dance with me, then."

Her lips clustered together to hide her smirk as she shook her head at me. I held out my hand once more and she took it, finally. I walked around the drink table to the far end of the dance floor. Out of sight for anyone who wasn't looking for us specifically.

I turned around and let her walk into me, searching her face for confirmation of permission to touch her. She brought her shoulder to her neck and gave just a hint of a nod. I softly, slowly, wrapped both arms around her waist. She glanced down to the place where our chests pressed together, inhaling sharply. She stretched her shoulders as if she was shaking something off. I loosened my grip to let her go, but her arms came around the back of my neck, pulling us tighter together. We began to sway.

The air around us buzzed with energy. I fought to keep my breathing even, afraid of her feeling the change in my breaths or in the rate of my heart. Her fingers lightly caressed the nape of my neck, and I fought the chills her touch sent down my spine, too. Her expression was unreadable, her jewel-colored eyes taking up her entire face. The freckles across her nose glittering in the reflection of the disco ball. As I matched her gaze, every thought was lost in my mind. I could only feel my fingers on the fabric of her dress, the heat of her back beckoning me from beneath it. The way her chest constricted against mine in time with the silent breath leaving her perfect lips. The vibration of the music beneath our feet. I'd lost all ability to use words, all ability to think about anything except touching her.

She made me feel truly prepubescent. As if I'd never touched a woman before.

"Macie isn't going to be happy about us abandoning the drink table," she said just above a whisper. So quiet I almost couldn't make it out.

Coming back to the reality of where I was, I scanned the crowded gym for sight of the petite, curly blonde. "I'd say she doesn't seem to mind," I said, craning my head in Macie's direction.

Penelope followed me with her eyes. Macie was on the other side of the gym speaking with a few of the other chaperones, positively beaming at us.

Pep smiled. "She likes you, you know." I raised a brow. Her eyes did a somersault. "Oh, don't get ahead of yourself. I just mean, she thinks you're... good. A good guy." She paused, then scoffed, "Although, she does find you disturbingly attractive."

"And what about you?"

"I've always thought you were good, Carter." The sincerity in her voice made my heartbeat twice as fast.

"I meant, do you also find me disturbingly attractive?"

"Meh." She shrugged. The blush in her cheeks said otherwise.

I grinned. "The tall, dark, and handsome thing doesn't do it for you, huh?"

She frowned at me, her eyes narrowing. "Those with narcissism may be characterized as having a grandiose sense of self and–"

"What?"

"Oh, nothing. I was just thinking out loud." Her smile was playful in a way I hadn't seen since I moved home. I removed my hand from her waist and stepped back, lifting my arm and her hand inside mine into the air above our heads. I twirled her around, and as she came back to face me, I flicked her nose.

"You ass," she gasped. I was sure she was joking, I hardly touched her. But I put both hands on her hips and pulled her a little tighter so she wouldn't run away. Her hands lazily clasped behind my neck, and she laughed.

Where her giggles with Marshall were mischievous and revengeful, the one she gave me was enthralling. It was a song, a melody. And I felt triumphant.

REO Speedwagon began to fade behind us, but I wouldn't let go yet. I'd hold on until the very last second. I'd savor it all. I wasn't sure how I felt about Jeremy yet, and I wasn't crazy about Marshall. But I liked Macie. And Macie liked me. And Penelope, she outshines them all. I realized that I was fine falling in with this group. I was fine with anything that brought me closer to her.

I'd welcome her friendship– anything at all that she was willing to give me. As long as I didn't have to let go of her ever again. I lived more of my life with her in it than not. After living in the not for the last five years, I realized I never wanted to live there again.

Chapter Seven

"I'd believe your soulmate was somebody who had all the things you didn't, that needed all the things you had. Not somebody who's suffering from the same stuff you are."

-Taylor Jenkins Reid

Penelope

I always ran.

My entire life when it came to facing things I couldn't, I ran. I'd learned to run the night my mom died, and sometimes it felt like I never stopped. There were moments when I knew that running was the wrong choice. When I knew running made me a coward. But other moments made me think that leaving a toxic situation, walking away from something that can only hurt, was the best decision. Sometimes running away from something just meant procrastination. A delay of the inevitable. The key to it all, the thing that I never learned, was when you were supposed to run from something and when you stood your ground.

When I was fourteen and a boy asked me to dance for the first time, I ran away. I learned tonight that it had been the wrong choice– the cowardly one. So, when that same man asked me to dance again at twenty-three, I said yes. Because I had already run away tonight. I had run away from my admissions letter, one of only four I had left to receive. I was quickly running out of options for my future. Staring down at the unopened letter on my kitchen counter, it was too much to endure at that moment. So, I ran. I think that might have been a cowardly choice, or maybe it had just been a way to delay the inevitable.

Regardless, when I ran to Carter, he didn't stop me. He just took my hand and ran with me. He knew exactly what he had been doing when he was making me forget about all my worries for a moment. While we were dancing, and I was trying to think of anything other than the way his hands felt against me, I thought maybe the two of us hadn't changed so much after all. Of course, things were different. As they should be. Nobody should be the same person at twenty-three that they were at eighteen. But maybe, when you know someone to the depths of their soul, things didn't change as much as they do when you only know them on the surface. I think, maybe, Carter and I knew each other like that.

After we danced, we resumed our places at the drink table. Carter made a comment about the way Marshall had been watching us. I almost told him that Marshall was the farthest person on my mind. That Marshall was nothing and no one to me. That he was Jeremy's roommate, and if Jeremy and Macie weren't together, if Macie wasn't my best friend, I'd not even know Marshall's name. Except, I kind of liked the look on Carter's face when I could tell he was a little jealous, so I held my tongue. Then, he asked me about life in England, all the things I'd seen and done in Europe. I asked about his mother, his life in Hawaii. I didn't think about the potential rejection letter waiting for me at home.

Not until I reached my car. As I drove home, I thought about it. I knew my parents would be in bed, and Maddie was likely with her friends. It would be the best time to read the letter so that I could face my rejection alone. I could feel it stirring inside my bones. I'd been rejected by Stanford. I couldn't bear to see the look on my parents' face when I received the rejection from any school, but especially Stanford. The school my father had attended.

The headlights of Carter's 1975, Kentucky blue Bronco blinded me as he followed me onto our road. I pulled to the right into my parents' driveway, and he pulled left into his. I shut off the engine to my car and stepped outside into the chilled night. He was already outside his truck, leaning against the door with his arms crossed, smirking at me. I could tell he had some sort of smartass comment hidden in his breath, but I spoke before he could.

"I know what you were doing tonight."

His smirk grew. "And what was that, Pep?"

"You were distracting me. From thinking about my admission letter."

He pushed off his door and took a step forward. "Did it work?"

I smiled. "Yes." Then added, "Thank you."

He inclined his head. "Are you going to open it right now?"

"Yep."

"Do you want company while you do it?"

I pretended I was contemplating it. "Thank you, but no. I actually specifically waited to do it now so that I would be alone."

And even though it was dark, I thought I may have noticed his face drop. "Okay." He started to turn towards the house but paused. "Do you still have the same phone number you've always had?" I nodded. I couldn't tell him that I had deleted his number the day I landed in England. "Well, if you change your mind, let me know."

He turned completely and walked through the gate that led to the backyard of his parent's house. I wondered why. "Goodnight!" I called back to him just as the gate shut.

I stepped inside the quiet house. My mom had left the lamp next to the front door turned on, but the house was otherwise dark. I took off the heels I'd worn to the dance and loosened the tight bun I held my hair in, which was now giving me a headache. I tip-toed into the kitchen, my letter from Stanford still sitting on the counter next to the fridge. I remembered applying to Stanford back in high school. I'd been nervous about the admission then too. I remembered my father telling me it didn't matter whether I'd gotten in or not. He was proud of me regardless of where I attended school. No such words of encouragement existed this time around.

I knew I likely received the decision through email as well. Probably a few days ago. But I'd been avoiding checking. Something about the mailed letter felt more definitive. I flipped on the dining room light and sat down at the table with the letter in hand.

Dear Penelope,

It is with great regret that I write to inform you that we are unable to offer you admission to Stanford Uni–

I crumbled the letter into a ball. Standing up from the table, I threw it in the kitchen trash before turning out the lights and walking upstairs. My phone buzzed in my hand. I had a text message from an unknown number: **If you need someone to share the news with, good or bad, I'm at your beck and call.**

I didn't respond.

When I woke up Sunday morning, the kitchen trash had been taken out, with the letter inside of it. My parents didn't ask me about it, and I didn't tell them. I assumed they found the crumpled letter and read it themselves. On Monday morning, Carter beat me to school. An iced coffee sat on our desk, written on the lid was: *I'm not sure if this is a congratulations coffee or a condolences coffee, but you deserve it either way.* I laughed and tried not to cry.

He must've inferred my rejection because Tuesday morning there was another coffee on our desk. That time it read: *definitely a condolence coffee.* I thanked him, and again, said nothing. My rejection letter from Berkeley came on Wednesday morning, Macie bought my breakfast then. I imagine, if my life continues to unravel around me, I'll never have to buy my own coffee again. There were only two schools I had yet to hear from: Pepperdine, and UCLA. If I received rejections from both schools, I'd likely end up spending another year in our dreary, tiny town of Brighton Bay. I'd have to apply to another round of programs next fall. I'd spend another year at Seaside Middle, that is, if I was able to keep my job. Tom had promised me nothing beyond this school year. I thought I wouldn't need anything more after that. I thought I'd be gone.

By Thursday morning, I felt like I was crawling out of my skin. My parents had been acting oddly formal around me. My sister, Macie, and even Carter treated me as if I was a wounded bird. My life had been consumed by thoughts of my future for the entirety of the last year since the moment I boarded that plane in Heathrow. Before that, actually. The moment I sat down with the Dean of Admissions and the Disciplinary Committee at Oxford and was informed that my acceptance into the School of Archaeology Graduate Programme had been withdrawn. That I was being rejected, effective immediately, and that my Student Visa would be revoked. That was the moment I began to worry about my future. I've thought of little else since.

I sometimes allowed myself to fall into distractions. Thursday nights with Macie, or after-work binge watches with my sister. Carter had certainly been serving as a distraction, too. But it all still swirled in the back of my mind. Would I still be here in a year from now? What if my parents kicked me out? What if I never get to continue my education? I'd given up so much in pursuit of the career I always dreamed of. To think that I'd never get to see it through because of one mistake, that was the thought that haunted me most.

I moved through Thursday stuck in the haze I'd been in for most of the week. There, but not really there. I'd forgotten that Thursdays meant trivia. I'd forgotten to brush up on the tv shows that the bar would be covering. I'd forgotten entirely about the bet I made with Marshall until he started teasing me about it at lunch. I just shrugged. I agreed to drive with Macie, Jeremy, and Marshall to trivia, and Carter met us there. I watched Carter all week. More than anyone else. The way he breezed through a room, breezed through life. He was never worried about what would come next. Never scared for the future. He never failed because he never had to try for anything. He was effortless in everything he did. I watched him talk with students after class, the way they seemed to hang onto all his words. They were excited about his class, and not in the way anyone was excited about mine. In his classes, they were learning. In mine, they were blowing off steam. I couldn't understand how he did it. How he could be carefree, fearless, and breezy. I was none of those things.

I was still watching him when we made it to the bar Thursday evening. Watching the way he watched me. I felt completely out of the moment as Marshall asked me question after question and I never knew the answer. I didn't care to even listen to them. I didn't hear him when he told me to take a sip, but I still managed to finish my drinks. I could tell Carter was only half-listening to Jeremy as they sat at the bar and talked, because Carter was more focused on my movements. I'd been in a haze all week, and that haze only started to clear when I started on my second drink. The tightness I felt gripping my entire body only started to loosen with the alcohol. It made me feel free. I started to feel breezy. I didn't normally drink. I didn't like losing control. But watching Carter, knowing he was there, made it easier to let go. Halfway through that second drink, I wasn't thinking about the two college rejections I received that week, or the fact that I was a terrible teacher. I was no longer comparing myself to others, or worried about my parents hating me. I didn't care anymore. I felt free.

And Carter was there. Macie too.

They wouldn't let anything bad happen to me. So, it was okay if I let go.

I downed the last drop of my second Cosmo.

Marshall had a third one already in my hand.

Chapter Eight

"When someone can see the soul within, be grateful, for you've touched the stars."

-Amy Leigh Mercee

Carter

"I'm sorry. I'm so, so sorry," Penelope slurred, slouching between Macie and I as we half-carried her to the parking lot. As expected, she had gotten completely plastered. "I didn't think the questions would be so hard. I never would've made that stupid bet."

We arrived an hour before trivia began, and The Worm (The nickname for I made for Marshall that had now struck inside my head) immediately got her a mixed drink before the game even started. By the end of the first round, she was three drinks in. I'd been watching her. I'd seen her teetering on the edge of going too far. But I thought she was still in control. I thought maybe she did this often, that she knew what she was doing. I didn't want to overstep the boundaries I felt she and I had established. I should've realized that part of her hadn't changed. She wasn't a big drinker.

"I just wanted to say, 'fuck it.' I wanted to have some fun. I fucked it too hard you guys, too hard. I'm the worst at everything. I can't even fuck it good." I looked at Macie questioningly, she looked back with the same expression. She shook her head as if to say she had no idea what Penelope was talking about.

The first time I threw a party while my parents were out of town, Penelope tried a sip of beer and complained, a sip of wine and complained, and took one shot of tequila, where she then retched. I never saw her drink again, except for an occasional glass of champagne at a party or on New Year's Eve (her least favorite of holidays, although champagne seemed to be her most favorite of drinks). That is, apparently, until she discovered Cosmos, which now appears to be her drink of choice. Even so, she was stumbling after her second drink, and laughing at everything after her third. By her fifth, she hardly had coherent speech, and on her sixth and final Cosmo, she began standing on the table after every question was asked, accusing all the other bar patrons of having poor taste in entertainment.

We were winning, initially, but we only reached the halfway point in the game before we were asked to leave. Macie was clearly upset at losing her chance at winning a trivia night, which was how we reached the point of Penelope's hysterical apologies. We were headed in the direction of The Worm's car, since he had driven the four of them tonight, and I followed in my truck. I already didn't particularly like The Worm, but there was something about the glimmer in his eye every time Penelope took a sip of her drink that told me there was more upon his mind than the thought of winning a bet. Something that told me he had planned this out. I didn't trust him.

"Why don't I take her home? I'm staying with my parents right now, and they're across the street from her. It'll be easier than you guys going out of your way," I whispered to Macie. I tried to make my reasoning sound as innocent as possible, but I already knew there was no way I'd allow her to get into a car with The Worm. Though, I couldn't be sure if Macie could see what I was seeing, and it appeared she had had some sort of friendship with the guy. Macie glanced behind herself, as Marshall and Jeremy were a few paces behind us. Her eyes met mine quickly and she nodded.

I was parked next to The Worm, and once we reached his car, I unlocked my Bronco. Macie and I began moving Penelope around the passenger side as nonchalantly as possible, so as not to catch his attention. I was beginning to believe Macie and I were on the same page because she seemed to match my movements, as if she knew there was a protest coming. We stepped away from his car and around the front of my truck when he finally noticed us.

"Hey! What are you guys doing?" he asked, jogging up to close the gap between us.

"I'm going to be taking Penelope home." I said it with a conclusive tone, making it clear I would accept no other suggestions on the matter.

"Oh, you don't have to do that, man. I got her," he said as he weaseled his way between myself and Penelope, grabbing her arm. She was hardly conscious at that point, a fact he seemed all too aware of. I couldn't ignore the ill feeling that brewed in my gut. I'd always known to trust my instincts, and from the moment I met this guy, I knew he was bad news. He looked at Penelope with a hunger in his eye, and the slightest of a smirk on his face.

I decided I wasn't going to beat around the bush. I wasn't going to use reasoning around our locations or the convenience of her catching a ride with me. I realized that unless I spelled it out very clearly for him, he wasn't going to let it go. "No," I said plainly. "It's best if I take her home."

His face flashed with all the looks of shock and confusion before settling on annoyance. "No, dude, really. I drove her here, so I can take her home too. She'll be fine." He rolled his eyes at me as he yanked Penelope's arm. She let out a small yelp and Macie gasped.

I shoved him away, removing the grip he had on Penelope without offering a response.

"What the fuck?" he asked as he stumbled back a few paces. I took his place, and Macie let go of Penelope to hold Marshall back. As Macie stepped away, Penelope fell sideways and right into my chest. She landed against me with a thud, and instinctively I wrapped one arm around her hips and the other around her back, holding her up. Her head landed against my shoulder, her hair a mess across my face. I could smell her shampoo– coconut. Her nose nuzzled lightly against the skin of my neck, and I attempted to ignore the chills that radiated throughout my body. She let out a sigh that sounded almost like a moan.

"Are you okay?" I asked, wiping her hair out of her face and behind her ear.

"Where's Carter?" she responded, her hand sliding up against my chest and twisting into my shirt as she held onto me.

"I'm right here."

"Take me home," she groaned. The feeling of her soft voice vibrating into my skin caught me off guard, and I suddenly found it difficult to stay on my feet, let alone hold her up as well.

I glanced at The Worm, giving him a pointed look that confirmed it. He shook his head and stalked away. Still holding her against me, I swung open the door to my truck and lifted her into the passenger seat, buckling her in.

Macie handed me Penelope's purse. "Thank you," she whispered.

I nodded as I waved them off and came around the driver side of my truck. Penelope's light snoring stalled only briefly as I turned the ignition and the engine roared to life. Sometime in the ten minutes between leaving the bar and arriving home, Penelope woke up, though she never made a sound. When I pulled into my driveway and turned off my truck, I found her staring at me with her gemstone eyes.

"Hi," I chuckled. She blinked at me a few times before a grin appeared at her mouth. It wasn't the special smile reserved for me; it was a little different. It was dopey and sleepy and cute as hell. "We're home." She nodded and began to try unbuckling herself. I hopped out of the driver's seat and ran around to her side to assist.

When I opened the passenger door, she leaned back with her face held up and her hands covering her eyes. "Why is the world spinning?" she asked.

"Because you're hammered." I unbuckled her and rummaged through her purse for her keys, hoping I'd be able to sneak her upstairs to her bedroom without waking the rest of her house. As I sorted through her purse, I realized her keys were nowhere to be found. "Pep, do you keep your keys in some sort of secret pocket or something?"

"In my jacket," she mumbled almost inaudibly. I looked around her feet, and in the backseat. I noticed she was wearing a black sweater and tried to remember if she had a jacket earlier in the day. I think she had been wearing a coat because it had been cold in the morning. I think the coat was beige. I checked the truck once more before determining that she had definitely left her coat somewhere. Whether the school or the bar, I wasn't sure.

"Your jacket isn't in here, Pep. I don't have the keys to get into your house." I began searching for her phone so I could call Maddie and ask her to quietly come unlock the door. I checked time on my phone and it read ten-forty. Her parents would likely be sleeping but Maddie was probably still awake. "Do you have your phone? I'll call Maddie."

"In my jacket," she mumbled again, this time with an added groan as she doubled over.

Shit.

"Penelope, I don't have your keys or your phone, and I don't have Maddie's number. So, I'm going to have to knock on your front door, it'll probably wake your parents."

"No, no, no, no, no," she whined. "No, I'm already a failure." I opened my mouth to ask her what she meant when it happened.

She began to cry. *Shit, shit, shit.*

This couldn't be about her admissions, could it?I placed my hand on her back lightly. "Pep? Why are you crying?" She shook her head but offered no response. I let out a breath as I considered what my options were. Before I fully considered the possible repercussions of my next actions, I found my arm scooping underneath her knees, and my other arm coming behind the middle of her back.

"I can't go home, Carter," she whispered against my chest. It was almost heartbreaking, her tone. I can't imagine what could've happened that could cause her to feel so much like she was failing her family, like simply coming home after a night drinking could be so consequential. No, there had to be more to the situation than just her getting rejected from Stanford. Her parents had never been like that. They expected a lot from their children, but they never judged them. Not in the way Penelope seemed to be afraid of.

I glanced down at her. Her head was tilted inward toward my chest, almost like she was breathing me in. She grasped my shirt, the fabric knotting itself within her fingers. Almost like she was holding onto me for dear life. My stomach tightened at the sight of her. A lost, yet familiar instinct took over me. The instinct to protect her, to care for her, to have her need me. I remember feeling this way even as children. When she would fight with her brother, or when she would ride her bike without a helmet. The first time I watched a boy hurt her feelings. The way The Worm looked at her. Little things that burned me up inside.

"We're not going home, Pep. But you can't sleep in the truck," I said quietly. I shifted her weight onto one arm as I reached over the back fence to my parent's house and unlatched the gate. I tiptoed through the backyard to the pool house my father had converted into a studio apartment a few years ago– my current residence.

It was a small space, but had enough room for a queen-sized bed, a couch, a desk, and a kitchen. I flipped on the kitchen light since it stood separate from the remainder of the studio.

"Where are we?" she asked. I looked down and realized her eyes were still closed but tightened in reaction to the brightness when I had flipped the light on.

"The pool house behind my parents'. They turned it into an apartment. You can sleep here tonight." I left out the fact that it was my current living quarters, and that I too would be sleeping here tonight. I wasn't sure how she would feel about it, but I figured she was too drunk to care right now anyway. I could sneak over to my parent's house early in the morning before she woke up, so she would have privacy. There was no way I was leaving her alone in her current state, though. I laid her into the bed softly and took off her shoes before covering her with the blankets.

"You're such a good person," she whispered as she turned over the sheets. "Such a good person. Too good. Too good." I tried not to smile at her, but then allowed it since she wasn't looking at me anyway.

I shushed her and planted a quick kiss on her forehead before backing away from the bed. The motion took no thought at all, as if it was the most natural movement I'd ever made, but I instantly realized it may have been a bad idea when her eyes fluttered open.

"You know, nobody calls me Pep anymore," she said, chasing down some random train of thought. I walked around the corner into the bathroom and make-shift closet.

"I'll always call you Pep."

"Even when I'm eighty?" she asked, calling out from the main room as I changed into a pair of sweatpants.

"Even when you're eighty." I grabbed a change of clothes out of my closet for her in case she found herself uncomfortable in the middle of the night, and in a state of mind that would allow her to change herself.

Right as I stepped out of the bathroom she said, "When I used to kiss James, I would imagine it was you." I stopped abruptly, not yet in her line of sight. My heart dropped to the floor with a thud.

Who is James?

"I always imagined it was you," she added in a lighter tone. Almost sleepily. She hadn't seemed to notice that I wasn't in the room with her or that I hadn't responded.

I waited a few more minutes before reappearing, allowing her words to settle inside me. I wasn't sure how I should interpret them– if there was anything to interpret, even. She was drunk and saying things she didn't mean. Or maybe, things she *did* mean. Words she'd never utter in a solid state of mind, words she'd never intend for me to hear. As much as I wanted to ask her what she meant, probe her for further confessions, make confessions of my own, I didn't. I turned out the bathroom light and set a pair of pajamas on the nightstand next to her with a note and a glass of water.

I planted one more quick kiss on her forehead, afraid it'd be the last kiss I'd ever get. As I laid down on the couch, she whispered my name quietly in her sleep. I knew just then that she would ruin me, and I looked forward to it.

"Shit, shit, shit." Her stammered words echoed through the small space as I heard her stumble around. "Where is my–" She tripped over something. "How did I–" She tripped again. "Fuck!"

Clearly, my plan to sneak to my parents before she woke up had failed, and any attempt I made at sparing her embarrassment at this point would fail too as she stumbled around my apartment in the dark. I opened my eyes, noticing the black fade to blue as dawn approached outside the window above me. I sat up and yawned.

"Pep," I started, catching her glance as she jumped back startled. "Are you good?"

"Shit, Carter. I didn't know you were here." She stared after me with a pillow clenched against her chest, eyes wide.

"Sorry." I noticed she must've gotten up sometime in the night and changed because my high school gym t-shirt and sweatpants hung off her body. I swear she's never looked better than she does in my clothes. I couldn't help the grin that spread across my cheeks.

"I need to go home," she said, glaring at me through narrowed eyes. Even in the dark, her green eyes glimmered.

"You don't have your keys or your phone."

Her limbs dropped at her sides, and she tilted her head back. "Dammit. Is that why I'm here?"

"Didn't you see my note?"

"No?" she questioned. I pointed at the nightstand as her eyes followed my arm to the note beside her. She picked it up and read it before letting out a sigh.

A change of clothes in case those jeans get uncomfortable.

P.S. You left your keys and your phone in your jacket at the bar. I already called them and made sure they kept it safe until you could go pick them up.

P.S.S. You wouldn't let me wake up your parents to get you inside the house. This was my backup plan. Don't get mad.

– C

"You don't remember anything?" I asked.

She closed her eyes tightly as if she was concentrating. "Not since my third drink." She huffed, "I think."

"Do you want me to give you the briefing?" I chuckled.

"Do I want to hear it?"

"Probably not."

She closed her eyes and nodded. "Well, my dad is on the early shift this week, so he may be up by now. What time is it?"

I grabbed my phone off the desk and checked the time. "Five-thirty."

She let out a breath. "Yeah, he'll be up. I'll think of some excuse to tell him so I can get inside the house."

I wanted to ask her why she was so afraid to tell her parents she had been drinking, but I decided not to press. "Alright, what time do you want me to come by?" Her brows furrowed. "Your car is still at the school. I'll give you a ride to work." I could tell she was embarrassed, even with so much she couldn't remember. I tried to stay as casual as possible, as if it was no big deal, something that happened all the time.

She pinched the bridge of her nose and nodded. "Seven-thirty, I guess." I dipped my head and turned to set my phone back on the desk behind me as she opened the door to the studio. "Thank you," she murmured as she slipped out.

"Anytime, Pep. You know that," I whispered back.

Chapter Nine

"A bond between souls is ancient—older than the planet"

-Dianna Hardy

Penelope

Something about knocking on my own front door at five thirty in the morning felt so wrong. What was I supposed to say to my father when he opened the door?

Hi, Dad. It's me. The daughter who got expelled from the best university in the world. The daughter who got a renowned professor fired. The daughter who was deported. Oh, yes, the same daughter who's showing up on your doorstep this early in the morning because she got so drunk last night that she lost her keys. Oh, and she had to sleep in the backyard of the neighbor's because in her drunken state she thought she could somehow avoid you finding out about what a fuck up she is.

I turned away from the front door and took a seat on the steps, my head finding its place between my knees. Carter being back home made me feel bold. I think it was the way he ended up being exactly who he was meant to be without even trying that made me think I could do that too. He's a breeze, flowing wherever the wind takes him and never worrying about where he may end up. He has complete trust in the world around him, and that is a comfort I've never had myself. Yesterday, I allowed myself to ponder the idea that maybe if I was more like that, I would end up exactly where I needed to be. All that did was land me in Carter's bed.

The boldness that had set a fire to my stomach only a day before was now settling at the bottom of it, my former actions rising up my throat with the bile. I swallowed hard, unwilling to puke in my mother's hydrangeas. Once I knew Carter would be going out with us, I felt brave enough to make that bet. That stupid fucking bet.

I didn't even care about the bet. I really didn't. That night at the dance I was feeling hopeful and light for the first time in a while. I'd cleared the air with Carter, I was still living in the blissful ignorance that I may still be accepted to Stanford. Or Berkeley. Or anywhere for that matter. I knew when Macie looked at me with her puppy eyes, she would end up asking Carter to join us Thursday night. So, I made that bet because I knew he'd be there. That fact made me feel free. A feeling so rare for me. I had this unnerving urge to chase it. To remember what it felt like to be carefree, if that was a feeling I'd ever known in the first place. Then, as the week progressed, the shadows of my anxiety began to envelop me. They were choking me, suffocating me, slithering around my throat and pulling tight. It only loosened as the warmth of the alcohol settled in my belly.

The sky to the east was just beginning to brighten, the clouds emerging in shades of periwinkle. I could tell already that today would be an unseasonably warm and beautiful one. I used to love painting sunsets. There wasn't much else I could paint, since I wasn't particularly talented. Sunsets, though– sunsets I could do. It was really just a blend of every imaginable color streaked across the sky. I'd never tried to paint a sunrise, most likely because I was never up early enough to see them. I wonder if it felt the same way to paint a sunrise as it did a sunset.

My eyes were still fixated on the budding sky as I heard the gate I had just walked through a while ago become unlatched. A sound I wouldn't normally hear, but in the silence of the morning while the rest of the world slept, it echoed across the lawn. I watched him as he walked down the long driveway to his truck and threw his longboard in the back. Though I was visible to him if he had chosen to look, he didn't seem to notice me. That was, until the front door to my house creaked open behind me, his head snapping up to meet my gaze. It tilted to the side as he stared in confusion, likely wondering why I was still out here.

"Penny?" My dad's cool voice came from behind me, dripping with concern.

I hopped up from the steps casually and turned to face him, with only seconds to think of my excuse. It wasn't that my father would be angry if he knew I had been out all night obliterated, or that he'd even be upset, really. It was that he'd probably be disappointed to find me messing around with my coworkers, getting drunk, and sleeping in the bed of the guy who lived next door. I'm sure last night's actions were more like the activities he thought I had been doing during my time at Oxford, though that wasn't true either.

I glanced at Carter one more time, still watching us from his truck, and realized that he was my excuse. My knight in wetsuit armor. "Hi, Dad!" I said a little too brightly. Calming myself, I continued, "I'm glad you opened the door. I just realized I locked myself out."

My dad glanced down at his watch, noting the time. "Why are you outside at five-forty-four in the morning?" It was then that he noticed Carter and waved.

"I was about to go surfing with Carter, actually," I lied coolly. "I had just stepped outside to tell him I decided to join him when I locked myself out." I spoke loudly, hoping Carter would hear me in the otherwise silent morning.

My dad looked me up and down suspiciously. "Whose clothes are those?" I could hear the sharpness on his tongue that accused me of lying.

"Easton's." It wasn't a bad lie. Easton did have a dresser full of clothes he kept at home, and he was probably about the same size as Carter. "I was doing laundry and didn't have any pajamas." I spoke casually. My father huffed, a bit of disbelief in his eyes. His gaze landed on Carter and I thought I glimpsed a bit of accusation on his face, but he seemed to be letting it go for now. He held the front door open for me. "Thanks," I said with a smile. As I stepped inside, I yelled to Carter, "I'm going to go change! I'll be right back." He laughed and leaned against his truck, giving me a thumbs up.

I sprinted upstairs to my bedroom and watched from my window until my father had driven away before opening it. Carter was still standing next to his truck, staring at the front door as if he expected me to walk out of it any moment.

"Hey!" I shouted in a hushed tone.

He looked up at me and smiled. My heart faltered.

He held his arms out wide. "I'm waiting!"

I shook my head. "I was just saying that as an excuse to my dad. I don't really want to go surfing." He frowned as if it was the most ridiculous thing he'd ever heard.

"Don't tell me you're going back to bed," he dead-panned.

I shrugged as if to say, *not likely.*

"You better get a damn wetsuit on and get down here!" he demanded. There was a playfulness to his voice that removed any seriousness. An empty threat. "I don't want you to miss it! Come on, Pep. Live a little."

Live a little.

I wanted to snort at that, thinking of everything that seemed to happen to me whenever I 'lived a little.' Yet somehow, all the humiliation I felt earlier seemed to dissipate the longer he grinned at me. *That grin.* He knew he had me. He knew I wanted to live a little. He knew I trusted him to come to my rescue whenever my little bit of living bit me in the ass.

I sighed in defeat, holding up my hand and spreading my fingers. "Five minutes!" He tapped his wrist impatiently in the place an imaginary watch would be. My stomach fluttered and I struggled to suppress the giggle bubbling in my throat.

We turned off the 101 and headed down the narrow, empty road toward Rockaway Cove. I tugged at my brother's uncomfortable wetsuit, wondering why I'd bothered to put it on. There was no way I was getting in the water, let alone the board. My mind must still be hazy from the alcohol. I had never been into surfing, despite living in a coastal town. My brother used to surf when he was younger, a hobby he involuntarily dropped upon his move to Boise.

"Hey, Pep?" Carter asked, pulling me from my thoughts.

"Hmm?"

"Don't be alone with Marshall, okay?"

I looked at him apprehensively. "Why?"

I knew Marshall was into me. He was pretty open about it. What his intentions were, and what they weren't. He was kind of arrogant, brash, and could sometimes be a downright asshole. He wasn't someone I would typically choose to be friends with, but he knew Macie before I did, so I tolerated him. Even so, I'd never felt unsafe around him. Uncomfortable sometimes, at his advances. But never truly *unsafe*.

Carter's eyes flashed to me before landing back on the road ahead of us. "I know you don't want to talk about last night, but Marshall was acting weird around you. Almost predatory, I would say. He *really* wanted to see you get drunk. Then, he *really* wanted to be the one to take you home. He was ready to fight me about it." He shook his head. "I can't explain it, but something is off about him. I don't trust him. I don't think you should either."

He spoke slowly, with care. I could feel my nostrils flare as they worked to fight off the tears building behind my eyes. My stomach churned as I flashed through all the potential scenarios that last night could've turned into. Nothing happened. I *know* nothing happened. I only know that because I know Carter was there. I also know that if he hadn't been there, I wouldn't have allowed myself to go so far. I *know* that. Because I know, deep down, that I don't trust Marshall either. I never have.

"Okay," I said.

"Do you require additional explanation?"

I shook my head. "No. I trust you."

We pulled into the empty parking lot of the beach access point, and he killed the engine. He looked at me with a soft, sorry smile. "Well, okay then." He threw his door open and hopped out of the car. He must've sensed the notion that I didn't want to talk about the situation anymore. I'd ask Macie for more details later, but for now Carter's word was enough.

Carter had a wetsuit folded down to his waist, and a flannel on his upper body. The flannel was unbuttoned, revealing small glimpses of his perfect, muscled chest. I tried to ignore that, tried to ignore the way his dark curls poked out from the snapback of the hat he was wearing backwards. I failed to ignore how the way he looked—the way he was looking at me—made me feel.

He cocked his head as he caught me staring. "How much time do you need to get ready for work?"

"Twenty minutes if I don't shower, forty if I do."

He smiled mischievously, almost seductively. "Perfect."

He was jogging around to the bed of his truck and I noticed he'd swapped his surfboard for a stand-up paddle board. He must've made the switch while I had been getting dressed.

"I'm not getting in the water!" I shouted.

He was ahead of me, darting down the narrow path between the beachgrass on the top of the dune, and down onto the beach itself. I heard him mutter to himself, and I paused at the end of that path, looking down from the small hill. He took his hat off and stomped around the sand for a few minutes, picking things up and gathering them in his hat. If he wasn't doing it so angrily, I'd assume he was collecting agate rocks like we used to do as children. Agate was much more of a common find on the rocky Oregon coast than seashells were.

He jogged back toward me. "I hate people."

I was the one cocking my head at him now.

"Litterers. Are people not aware of the Great Pacific Garbage Patch? There are trash cans in all the parking lots and these assholes just leave their cigarette butts and gum wrappers in the sand for the fucking animals to eat. Have they never seen *Happy Feet*?"

I knew he was being serious, and I agreed with him wholeheartedly, but to see someone who is normally so calm, cool, and collected, lose his mind over plastic on the beaches... a laugh bubbled from my throat, and my entire chest cavity constricted.

"Unfortunately, I think there are a lot of people who don't know about the Great Pacific Garbage Patch, and many more who just don't care."

He frowned, and his eyes grew distant and thoughtful for a moment. "I'm going to do a project on it. For class."

"Inspire the next generation?"

He was smiling again as he nodded.

We both laughed quietly before he grabbed me by the hand and brought me to a cove just down the beach. A large piece of driftwood sat perfectly out of the morning breeze. He laid the paddle board onto the sand as I sat on the log and waited for him to join me. The sun was just beginning to rise in the east, turning the western horizon a soft purple hue. Behind us the sky would be painted with all shades of the rising sun, but out across the Pacific, it was a much softer display of color. Birds were beginning to wake all around us, and the waves crashed powerfully against the sand. In the distance, the nearly full moon was faintly visible. I was already feeling lighter than I had a few minutes ago.

"I think we're facing the wrong way," I protested.

He leaned back against the driftwood, his knees against his chest and his hands clasped between them. He was looking ahead, not turning to face me as he said, "That's what they want you to think." I chuckled lightly, perplexed by his words. I followed his gaze to the sky ahead of us, and the way it meshed with the horizon line. On the west coast, we never bothered to flock to the beach for the sunrise, since this was the place that it set. It's not something I'd ever thought to do before. "See, the sunrise to the east is so full of color. Beautiful, yes, but a little chaotic. Don't you think? Looking out this way, it's softer. I think it's more peaceful. A better representation of what early morning should feel like." The clouds turned from purple to magenta– almost matching, but a bit lighter than the fuchsia shade that surrounded the exploding sun. After another moment, the setting around me became shrouded in gold as the water reflected the rising sun behind me.

Whenever—if ever—I painted again, I wanted to paint this.

"It's pretty," I said softly.

"That's why I didn't want you to miss it," he whispered as if speaking too loudly would startle the slow waking of the sun.

"I'm not sure I've ever woken up to watch the sunrise at the beach. I've only stayed out to watch the sunset," I admitted.

"I guess it depends on where you live in the world. In Hawaii, we had the option to see the sun rise and set against the ocean. Sometimes I'd get to see both on the same day. I think the sunrise was always my favorite, though."

I sighed deeply, sinking down into the sand with my back against the driftwood. We sat for a while, watching the day come alive in silence. After the world no longer shimmered in a gold hue, he let out a breath and stood up.

"Alright, let's get out there." He pulled his board from the sand. "C'mon, kook." He stretched his neck towards the water as he smiled down at me.

"Absolutely fucking not," I stated, attempting, and failing, to stifle my laughter.

"Have you ever been on a surfboard, Pep?" I shook my head in response. His lips clustered in the corner of his mouth. "Alright. Well, there is nobody out here to see you make a fool of yourself but me."

"Exactly," I interjected. He held up his finger.

"Which means, it should be no different than anything else I've seen over the last twenty-four hours." He flashed me *that* grin. I clicked my tongue and glared at him. "Everyone should ride a wave at least once. Luckily for you, I'm an expert."

"Who says you're an expert?"

He stuck out his hip and scoffed, pointing inward at himself and wiggling his fingers up and down. "I'm Hawaiian?" he said, as if that automatically made him an authority on surfing. He stepped toward me and extended his hand.

With a defeated sigh, I took it.

"First, you're going to need boots and gloves. The water is cold as shit." From a bag I hadn't realized he was holding, he pulled out a pair of gloves and something that looked like socks. Both were the same fabric as the rest of my wetsuit. He put a set of his own on too.

"And put sunscreen on your face. It's in the bag."

I flicked a brow. "Carter, it's six-thirty in the morning. And it's March. In Oregon."

"I don't argue about SPF. Put. It. On."

I blew out a breath but obeyed.

We waded knee high into the water, and despite the fact that I was horridly aware of how cold I should feel, I wasn't cold at all. The morning breeze was soft and light. Inside the cove, the waves just barely rose to lap against our legs. Carter stepped in front of me and held the board steady as he beckoned me to climb onto it. I gave him an unsure look, but he returned it with an encouraging nod that was full of confidence. I braced both hands onto the top of the board and lifted my leg to swing it over. A wave came crashing just as I raised my leg, knocking me off my steady foot.

Absolutely sure that I would fall beneath it, I braced myself for the bitterly cold water to envelop my face. A strong pressure at my chest held me in place. "I've got you," he said against my ear. He gently pushed me back up until both my feet were on the sand. "Wait," he advised as he stared at the horizon. A few seconds passed before another wave crested over us. "Okay, go." I planted both arms on the board and hoisted my leg over, pulling myself up until I was straddling it.

The board tipped back slightly as another wave crashed over us. "Alright, lean to your left." I did as he said. From my right side, he swung himself over the board. Much swifter, more graceful, than I had. He brought both legs up behind him until he was sitting on his knees. "Put your feet out in front of you and lean back against my chest."

I caught my breath, taking a moment to prepare myself for the way it would feel to have my head against his broad, hard chest. Too afraid to fall, and too thrilled to change my mind, I leaned back. I could somehow feel the warmth of his body through both of our suits. He leaned forward, propping me into a sitting position. He began to paddle. I could feel the way the muscles in his torso, his arms, and his chest all moved in sync with each other. His breathing was labored as he panted against my ear. The air was warm against my neck.

We moved over the small waves as they rocked the board underneath us. Our bodies pressed together at the center of it, a balancing act. I held him steady, and he held me straight. It was exhilarating– moving against the wind and waves. At odds with the force of nature, moving in the opposite direction of where it was telling us to go. I couldn't imagine what it must feel like to move with the waves. To stand beneath them.

Carter paddled out just far enough that we were beyond the break, but not too far that the water was rough. He explained that the cove we sat inside blocked the wind, making the water calm enough to just wade above. Once he'd stopped paddling, the board stilled. Small ripples moved beneath us, but nothing in comparison to those that crashed against the shore.

I was too afraid to move, but I felt him straighten out and let both his legs dangle in the water. I stayed pressed against his chest, afraid that if I tried to turn around, I'd fall off. I could not believe I'd gotten onto a surfboard. I shook my head and let out a breathy laugh.

"What?" I couldn't see his face with my eyes closed, but I could feel him smiling.

"I just can't believe I actually agreed to this."

"It's amazing though, isn't it?"

"Yes," I breathed, "but I can't seem to open my eyes."

"If you feel safest in this position, then you don't have to move. But you should open your eyes, Pep. Look at the sky," he whispered against my ear. I could feel his chest vibrate against my back as he spoke.

I opened my eyes and looked up, but not at the sky. At him. He was watching the horizon as the day erupted from the clouds. I glanced down and ran my hand through the midnight blue, seemingly bottomless, water beneath me. It was becoming a deeper shade of indigo as the sun lifted into the sky.

"So, which beaches are your favorite? Hawaii, or the Pacific Northwest?" I asked. He looked back out at the vastness of the sea in front of us as he pondered the question.

"I feel like the easy answer—the expected answer—should be Hawaii. But it's not. Hawaii feels like home to me. The ocean is alive there. There is power within it that I think can only really be felt by the people who come from it. When I'm on the islands, I feel like I'm with *my* people. I've never had an entire culture to call my own before. It wasn't something I got to experience growing up with my dad. Living there allowed me to connect with something that was bigger than myself, and it just feels like a part of my identity now. It almost felt like a spiritual awakening. I think that's why for some time I was afraid to come back here. The mainland has always been my home, too. It felt like my soul was split in half on different sides of the ocean, and if I left the Hawaiian side, I'd lose it. That was why I got my tattoo."

I wanted to ask more about his tattoo and ask him to show it to me, but I could tell he wasn't finished speaking.

"But sometimes when I think about how the world was created, I think that if there is a God, they made the Pacific Northwest first. When I think of what heaven would look like, I imagine sprawling cliffs and pine trees. Snow-capped mountains and flowing rivers. The way that the green of the forest collides with the blue of the ocean. Painting the entire world around you the color of peace. It's the type of place I'd want to go when I die. It has its own kind of power. I remember hiking the cliffs along the coast for the first time as a kid and getting way too close to the edge. I stared straight down and watched the biggest wave I'd ever seen at the time come crashing against the rocks. The entire earth shook, and that was the first time I understood the power of the ocean."

I nodded because I understood. I remembered Lena always yelling at him to back up. I never dared to get as close to the edge as he did.

He sighed. "I don't know which I like more. I love both in different ways."

"Something tells me you'd feel at home as long as you were near the ocean. There are waves within your soul. I think it's just where you're meant to be." I shrugged. He broke his gaze from the water and looked down at me. I watched from upside down as his mouth curved upward slightly. I couldn't make out much of an expression, but something brewed behind his eyes.

They looked especially green in contrast to the blue floating all around him.

"I think you're right. Even though I'm here, and my mom—my people—are a whole ocean away, it's comforting to know that I can stick my feet in the water here and it's the same water that my mom feels when she dips her toes over there. Polynesians were voyagers, that's how they found Hawaii. They knew how to leave their families and venture out but stay connected through their spirit. I think it's ingrained in us to connect to each other through the ocean."

I smiled at him. It was silent for a moment. I didn't think there was anything I needed to say. I'd never spoken with him so deeply about something before, but it felt comfortable. I'd never realized that being alone with him could feel like this. It was easy, effortless, and natural. As if it was always supposed to be this way.

I glanced up at the sky, covering my eyes with my hand. "What time do you think it is?" I asked. He traced my gaze and lifted his head towards the sun.

"It's probably getting close to seven." He smirked. "Are you ready to ride one in?"

I shook my head no.

"That's the only way to make it back, Pep." He laughed. "Unless you'd like to swim?"

I squinted my eyes and looked towards the shoreline. We were at least fifty yards out. I realized for the first time that I had never been this far out at sea before without some kind of vessel keeping me afloat (I've now decided a paddle board doesn't count). In all the time we'd been out here, I hadn't accounted for sharks, riptides, or the Cascadia Subduction Zone finally faulting and causing the catastrophic tsunami we've always been warned about. For the first time in as long as I could remember, I was completely enticed by the moment I was in. Unafraid of the potential consequences. Carter made me feel that way. Bold and brave, fearless and carefree.

It would either be my salvation or my destruction.

Chapter Ten

"Two souls are sometimes created together and in love before theyre born."

-F. Scott Fitzgerald

Carter

I don't consider myself a violent person.

I'm pretty levelheaded, even when I don't like someone. Even in times I feel I've been wronged; I've never had an issue keeping cool. I don't really get angry, even. I've been in exactly one fight in my life (even if it could even be called a fight). I made a threat of violence one other time, something I never intended to act upon. Both instances were in protection of women I loved.

Once, picking up my sister from school when I was seventeen and she was about eleven, I noticed a group of boys following her to the parking lot of the middle school I now work at. She was trying to ignore them, but they were pushing her as she walked in front of them, sticking their feet out to try and trip her, pulling on the straps of her backpack to make her lose her balance. Her face was straight and stern, but I could see the tears building beneath her eyes. She kept her head down and walked in a straight line toward my truck. My sister would never expect me to step in, she wouldn't want me to. She was independent and stubborn. She was capable of handling herself, and if she wasn't, she didn't want anyone to know. Traits I think rubbed off on her from Penelope and Maddie's influence. I watched them intently but made no motion to step out of my truck. That was, until I caught one of those boys slap her backside as she stepped off the curb and into the parking lot. Their little parting gift.

My chest bloomed with fury at the sight of any child, especially my little sister, being touched in such a way. Against her will. I'd always held protective instincts by nature. I think it was a product of my father. He was a lawyer, a prosecutor. He dealt with the worst that society had to offer. He frequently heard stories so horrifying that I knew they kept him up at night. They haunted him. Many of those stories centered around the abuse of women. My father was many things: meticulous, strict, distant. Much of the time, more focused on work than family. I always understood why, though. His life's work is heavy, and hard. He takes on responsibility that probably shouldn't be his to bear, but he does it anyway and with pride. I may not have inherited his work ethic, but I think I inherited his sense of responsibility. One thing my father ensured to instill in me was respect for women. Watching the way he treated his wife, his daughter, even my own mother after they split, set the bar high for me. That was on purpose. Calculated. He'd never allow me to end up like the men on the bench opposite him in the courtroom.

The ones who harmed women.

In that moment, watching my sister as she jumped at the shock from that boy's hands on her body, the way she trembled and froze. It lasted only a second, but the look of utter horror was abundantly clear. I realized it was a look that my father must have seen dozens of times in a courtroom, when victims recounted their experiences and came face to face with their abusers once again. I wondered where it started, those cycles of abuse. I don't believe that people are born evil. It always has to start somewhere. Maybe it starts from touching a girl's behind in sixth grade and feeling a sense of power from it. Maybe it grows from there. It becomes more unwarranted touches, or unsolicited advances. Then, it becomes schemes to get a girl so drunk she doesn't know where she is and take her home. Or maybe it becomes impatience with a girlfriend and remembering the power that came from touching someone against their will. So, it turns into hitting her. Beating her. Worse.

I didn't know where it started, but I supposed it could start there. Start with the way he touched my sister. The next thing I knew, I was putting my truck in park and flying out of the driver's side, leaving the door wide open. My sister's cheeks blazed with embarrassment as she caught me walking towards them. I snapped at her to get in the truck and shut the door. All three of the boys in question stepped back several paces, shrinking beneath me with each one. I was still a kid then too, but I held at least a foot and fifty pounds on each of them. They stared at me with wide, terrified eyes that told me they had no idea Charlie had an older brother. I asked them if my sister gave them permission to touch her like that, they looked at me like I was insane before shaking their head no.

I straightened myself and smiled. I calmly informed them that if they ever touched my sister, or any girl like that again, I'd break every one of their fingers. I told them I knew their names (I didn't), and I knew where they lived (didn't know that, either), and that I had friends at the school who would tell me if they were messing with any other girls. They nodded slowly before sprinting in the opposite direction. Charlie and I drove home in silence. She was mad at first. I picked her up every day after school that year, and the year after. I never saw those kids again, never heard a peep from Charlie or anyone else about them. My threat worked, and though she never thanked me for it, I knew she was grateful.

My almost-fist fight happened when I was eight. Penelope spent her first year with the Mason's being homeschooled by Jenna. They thought she needed time to adjust to her new life in a private setting. After that first year, she started third grade with me. Easton was in fifth grade and the fifth-grade classrooms were on the opposite side of the school. They had separate lunches and recess times too. Our mothers worked to make sure Penelope and I were in the same class so she'd have a friendly face. I took it upon myself to be her friend and her tour guide, but most of all, her bodyguard. We didn't tell the kids she was adopted. Except that Easton went into fourth grade with only a two-year-old sister at home, and when he returned for fifth grade, he suddenly had a nine-year-old sister who looked nothing like him. It wasn't difficult—even for children—to put two and two together. It didn't help that we lived in a small town, and Penelope's family was well known. Parents would say things like: *that poor girl Dr. Mason adopted after her mother died in such a horrific way. Where is her* real *father? Her family? Why didn't anyone want her?* Failing to realize that their children would overhear them.

When Penelope started school with us, it was a nightmare. People asked her where she came from, who her real parents were. They made fun of her red hair and her freckles. They asked her if she was stupid. Asked her where her dad was and why he didn't want her. After that first day, I went home and told our parents. I told them all the horrible things that were said about her, desperate to get her out of the situation. She told me to stop, that she didn't want to be homeschooled anymore.

So, instead, I started telling people to shut up. I started defending her. Doing whatever I could to take the attention off her and put it on me. There was one particularly awful kid, Riley. He started taunting me as the first few weeks of school progressed. Asking me if I had a crush on Penelope, asking why I was defending her. I told him it was because she was like my sister, and even then, the words tasted weird in my mouth. I knew they weren't right. Riley then asked me if I had a crush on her because she was like my sister, or because she was– well, a slur I'd rather not even repeat inside my head.

I lost it. For the first, and really, the only time in my life– I lost it. I hated him. I thought he was the exception to the rule that people aren't born evil. I thought that he was pure evil. As the word left his mouth, I felt like I could see it float into her ears and down her throat, settling in her chest and her stomach. I expected her to cry or run away, but she just stared at him. As if nothing he said could penetrate her armor. I could see behind those walls. I knew that when she laid her head down on her pillow that night that she'd cry herself to sleep. That she would wonder if he was right. If all of them were right. If there was something wrong with her that made her unwanted. That someday the Mason's would discover whatever that thing was and leave her too.

I punched Riley in the face. Well, not really. I didn't close my fist. I drove my palm up into his nose. I held enough force to have him stumble back, to make his nose bleed. There wasn't the satisfying crack of contact, or crunch of his cartilage that a closed-fist punch would've granted. I didn't really know what I was doing. I think I meant to slap him at first, but then decided that wasn't enough. In the moment between my decision to hit him, and my contact with his face, I forgot to close my fist. Before his eyes even opened, a teacher's aide was on us, pulling us apart. I always wondered if she had been hovering close by the whole time but had only stepped in when it got physical. If she heard everything being said and made no motion to stop it.

Penelope and I were both sent to the principal's office. Like Charlie, Penelope never thanked me for defending her. But I saw her mouth twitch into a little bit of a smirk when I made contact with Riley's face. That was the first time I'd ever made her smile, the little smile that it was. That was enough reward for the consequences I'd face. I got an in-school suspension for hitting him. Riley had to write Penelope an apology letter, and he was transferred into a different classroom. He never bothered us again, even through high school.

The only discussion Penelope and I ever had about it was while we were waiting to see the principal. Penelope looked at me and said, "You're kind of bad at punching people." I didn't know why, but I laughed. Then, after a moment, she laughed too. I thought maybe Riley had been a little bit right about one thing. Maybe I did have a crush on her.

Pulling myself from my thoughts, I looked over at her as we made our drive back home from the beach. Her seat was leaned back, her feet propped up on my dashboard and her shoes kicked off. Her toes were painted green, wiggling to Børns as his voice flowed through my stereo. Her head was leaned against the window, her eyes were closed, and her lips were curved upward. The sun was hitting directly on her face, her hair glowing like embers in the morning light, and her freckles dancing across her nose.

I couldn't believe that she had agreed to come with me this morning. But she did.

I couldn't believe that she'd put on a wetsuit. But she did.

I certainly couldn't believe that she actually got into the water. That she got onto my board. That she'd leaned against my chest and trusted me to take her beyond the break. Or that she giggled when we rode a wave back to shore. But she did.

I couldn't believe that she let me talk about my family– my heritage, my culture. That she hung onto my words, that she cared.

But. She. Did.

"After school we can go back to the bar and get your stuff, okay?"

She nodded.

After a moment, I asked, "Do you remember Riley DeSantis?"

Her eyes snapped open, searching my face. *Emerald pools.* "Yes. Why?"

"Just wondering."

She was quiet for a beat. "You know, he messaged me on Instagram, like, a year ago."

I arched a brow at her. "Did he?"

"Yeah. He asked how I was doing like we were old school pals."

I scrunched up my nose. She caught my expression and laughed. "Did you respond?"

She shook her head. "No. I blocked him." She giggled. "Remember when you karate-chopped his nose?"

"I was eight," I argued.

"No, we were nine," she countered.

"Actually, *you* were nine. *I* was eight. It happened during that twenty-eight-day-span each year where we are not the same age." Penelope was born on September fourteenth; I was born on October twelfth. I don't remember which day the fight happened, but I know it was after her ninth birthday and before mine.

Her eyes narrowed at nothing in particular as she tried to remember. She shrugged. "Whatever. All I'm saying is you punch like a girl."

"Isn't that an insult to girls?"

She blinked at me. "You're right. You punch like Riley DeSantis."

I laughed, and she laughed. The sound of it filled the cab of my truck and it felt like the air was electrifying around us. Crackling with energy. A smile spread across her features. *My smile.*

I realized if I had ever crawled out of love with Penelope Mason, I'd just fallen back into it. Head first, right down the rabbit hole. I had no control over how fast or how far I fell, or if there would be anyway to stop myself.

Even though I was falling, it felt a little like flying.

Soaring. Swimming through clouds.

Maybe, I never even crawled out of it. I never stopped loving her. I don't think there was a time in my life I wasn't in love with her. I don't think there is a force on this earth or above that could've ever stopped me from falling in love with her.

I think I loved her the day I was born. Maybe even before.

I think I'll be falling in love with her until the day I die. Maybe even after.

Chapter Eleven

"But a true soulmate is a mirror, the person who shows you everything that is holding you back, the person who brings you to your own attention so you can change your life."

-Elizabeth Gilbert

Penelope

The sun dipped behind the rooftops, beginning its descent on this quiet Sunday.

For the first weekend in at least six months, I didn't volunteer at the museum, or frantically research graduate programs, or obsessively check my inbox for an acceptance. I watched my sister's softball game, the first one I've attended this year. I had dinner with my family for the first time in weeks. I went to the fucking Saturday market. It was glorious. I was fearful of my parent's reaction to seeing me take a break, to briefly halt the repentance of my sins. To my surprise, it seemed like they were genuinely happy to see me relaxing for the first time in a while. I almost believed they weren't pretending. My mother thanked me for going to my sister's game, and for carrying her bags to the car at the market. My father smiled at me when I helped him with dinner. For the first time in a very, very long time, I felt content with just being in my own skin.

I have spent the better part of the last year watching my life unravel at my feet as I frantically tried to hold it up. I was exhausted. So exhausted that I simply couldn't muster the strength to do anything but exist. What surprised me was that doing nothing but just existing over the last few days was a welcome relief. It was wonderful, actually.

I knew that eventually this carefree attitude would come back to bite me in the ass, and of course, it did. I leaned back against the exterior wall of my bedroom and closed my eyes. Trying to absorb the last of the sunshine as it warmed my face, ignoring the book in my lap. The rumble of the truck's engine chugging down our street broke me from my moment. I watched Carter's Bronco as it lurched to a stop in front of my house. He'd been gone most of the weekend. His truck wasn't in the driveway yesterday morning when I woke up (not that I had been paying *that* much attention), and it appeared he was just now returning. Wherever he'd been, he stayed overnight.

My heart stopped, dropped, and rolled right off the roof at the sight of the brunette in his passenger seat. Long, cascading, beautiful dark locks covered the face of the petite woman who was opening his passenger door. I tried to fight the urge to stare until I saw her face. I tried harder to ignore how sick it made me feel.

Especially once I realized it was *Charlie* stepping out of Carter's Bronco. I was about to become physically ill with jealousy, and it was his sister. *Get a grip, Penelope.* A moment later Carter himself stepped out. He handed Charlie a bag and hugged her, planting a soft kiss against her forehead before she hopped across the street and into their house.

I was afraid Carter would feel the singe of my heated gaze, but I couldn't will myself to look away. He stood next to his truck with nothing but a tank top and a pair of shorts, his bare arms staring right back at me as if it wasn't fifty degrees outside. A camera slung around his neck, just covering bits and pieces of the sprawling tattoo that covered his upper arm and broad shoulder. The design of it flowed across his body like rays of sunshine as they snaked out across his shoulder and his chest. Inside each ray held a detailed and intricate artwork of abstract flowers, waves, swirls, and triangles. I never cared for tattoos much. I wasn't against them, either. It just wasn't something I found particularly attractive.

Until now. His was different, that much I could already tell. Just as he mentioned in the water on Friday morning, I could see his soul within it. Exceedingly beautiful.

"Howdy, neighbor." His silky voice pulled me from the trance his body had me in. He was watching me with a knowing smile, silently acknowledging the fact that I had clearly been checking him out.

I cleared my throat. "I just haven't seen your tattoo before."

I sound like an idiot.

He chuckled deliciously, "Do you like it?" I gulped, hoping he couldn't see it from here and nodded. "What're you doing?"

I flashed the book in my hand. "I've got to present a lesson plan on this tomorrow and I haven't finished reading yet."

"Penelope Mason... *procrastinating*? I thought I'd never see the day." He laughed, wiping a fake tear away from his cheek. "I'm so proud of you." I flipped him off to hide the wince I felt inside my bones. He found it funny, but I found it an unwelcome reminder that I was no longer living up to my potential. "What's the book?"

"*The Alchemist* by Paulo Coelho," I called out.

He paused. "You've never read *The Alchemist*?"

I shook my head.

"I've got something for you, then!" he shouted as he jogged from his truck and toward his house.

I hit my head against the wall behind me and sighed. I couldn't believe how easy it was for me to fall back into the old patterns. Watching his every step, hanging onto his every word. Watching his parent's house from the spot on my roof, hoping he'd walk out. Knowing that I would make an absolute fool of myself just to hear him laugh. *Stop, Penelope. Stop, stop, stop.* I've got to stop looking at his body. Fixating on his eyes. Staring at his lips.

God, those lips.

I reminded myself that he isn't mine, he never was. I don't even know him anymore.

Except, I do. I know the parts of him I've always known, the parts that still remain. He still smiles the same. Still laughs the same. His eyes still light up when he makes a joke at my expense, and I not only take it, but throw it right back. His devil-may-care demeanor and go-with-the-flow style hasn't changed either. He still surfs. He still loves the ocean. He's always loved the ocean. All nature, really. I could see he still felt most at home when he was outdoors. It was also clear that his protective instincts hadn't diminished. Macie told me how defensive he got over me at the bar. The way Marshall had supposedly looked at me like I was *a snack, but not in the good way.*

Pushing all thoughts of Marshall far, far from my mind, I thought of the way Carter brought me home and let me sleep in his bed while he slept on the couch. So stereotypically gentlemanly of him. Exactly what I would've expected. He even left me a damn glass of water in case I got thirsty in the night. *And I'm not supposed to fall in love with that?*

Deep in thought, I must've missed him as he crossed the street because the next thing I heard was the sound of my bedroom window sliding open. I looked over to find him crawling out of it and sitting down beside me on the roof. He got comfortable, matching my position and leaning against the side of the house. I'd always been particular about my spot on the roof. I didn't allow my siblings up here, I didn't even really allow my friends. Carter never tried to come out here before though, he'd never tried invading this space until now. For the first time ever, I didn't feel like I was being invaded. I was happy to share my place with him.

He plopped something down at my feet. I glanced over to find a worn copy of *The Alchemist* with dozens of post-it tabs sticking out the sides. I picked it up and flipped it open. It was annotated all the way through. Some sentences highlighted, others underlined, notes written all throughout the margins. "I left your clothes on your bed too. I would've returned them sooner, but I was out of town yesterday."

Still focused on his notes, I replied in a forced casual tone, "Where did you go?"

"I took Charlie to Portland for the weekend. I haven't had any one-on-one time with her since I got back. Plus, do you know how much money photos of Multnomah Falls sell for?" He chuckled. "Thought I might as well get some shots of it while I'm out here."

"I haven't been to Multnomah Falls in years," I said, attempting to appear nonchalant. I held the book out to him. "Is this yours?"

His lips curled slightly. "Yeah. There might be some notes in there that'll help you with your lesson." He shrugged. "It's my favorite book."

I flipped through the pages again quickly. Almost all of them were filled with colored sentences and notes within the creases. Many of the pages were torn and the corners ripped. It looked like it had been read through a hundred times.

"Why?" I asked. I had started the book last week before the dance but had only gotten through a few pages before I became focused on other things. Even now, I'd only made it twenty-five pages in. But inside those twenty-five pages, I'm not sure I've found what would've made it Carter's favorite book.

"I've learned more about life between the pages of that book than I've learned anywhere else," he said casually. "I've read it every time I've felt lost, and every time I finish it, I feel like I've found myself again." He rubbed his hands down his thighs, almost nervously.

"How many times have you read it?" I whispered.

"More than I care to count." I looked at him, but he was staring out at the sky. His face was tense, serious. After a moment he met my eyes and softened. "What's yours?"

"My what?" I asked, only half-paying attention, still flipping through the pages.

"Your favorite book?"

"Oh. I don't really have one."

He dead-panned, "Everyone has a favorite book, Pep."

I shook my head. "I don't really read."

He craned his head to face me, a look of shock on his face. "Like, at all?"

"Not unless I have to for school." I set his copy of *The Alchemist* at my feet.

He scoffed. "Wow. I'm really surprised by this information. I would have pegged you as a reader." I rolled my eyes. "Why don't you like to read?"

I chewed on my lip for a moment unsure how to respond.

I wasn't sure I felt comfortable explaining to him that I don't read because it reminds me of my mother. She used to love reading. For a while, right before she died, we didn't have a television. I think she might have pawned it. So, she read to me all the time. She didn't read children's books, though. She read her favorite books. She used to say that she wanted to read all the happy endings until she chose which one she wanted for herself, and once she decided, she'd go make it happen. She would tell me to do the same.

"I guess I'm just so busy with work, and before I worked, I was busy with school. I never made the time for it. It just wasn't something I got into," I lied. "Plus, I kind of hate the way books romanticize the world." That wasn't a lie.

"Not all books are romance novels, Pep."

I slumped back. "I don't mean that, necessarily. I mean the way books always have a happy ending, because that's not real life. Some people—a lot of people—don't get happy endings." I paused. "But I do find the whole star-crossed lovers, forbidden love—soulmates—thing a little… repulsive."

I noticed him attempting to hide a smile. His lips forming a thin line, clustering beneath his teeth. "So, you don't believe in soulmates, then?" He let out a breathy laugh and added, "I guess I shouldn't be surprised, actually. You know what they say about redheads and their souls."

"Pretty sure that's exclusive to gingers." I shot him an overexaggerated eye roll. "I do believe in soulmates, but not in the way I see it represented in fiction. Or at least I think the kind of soulmates we read about are extremely rare, almost nonexistent."

I heard his head swivel just before I felt his eyes begin to study me. I kept my gaze toward the sky, refusing to meet his. "Well now you have to tell me more."

My stomach fluttered and my heartbeat as if it was outside my body. I begged it to calm down, afraid he'd hear the drum in my chest. I let a long moment pass before I spoke next. "A few months after I moved to England, I went out to a pub in London. There was all this writing on the bathroom door, and some of it caught my eye. In huge letters across the top the door was written: *Atoms are an endless, infinite existence.*" He nodded for me to continue. "Then, below it, someone had added in different handwriting: *The atoms that make up who you are right now are the same atoms that existed before the Big Bang.*" I chuckled. "And it was like people just kept adding onto this random train of thought that the first person had decided to write on a bathroom door. I mean these people could've lived all over the world, and they all collaborated to create this amazing theory on something unexplainable."

Carter glanced at me.

I blushed. "Anyway, in a third set of handwriting, it was written: *Someone told me once that all atoms lived in pairs. When the Big Bang happened, they were blasted across the universe and separated from each other. Ever since then, each pair of atoms has worked to find its way back to its other half...* and lastly, in a fourth set of handwriting someone added: *Sometimes those atoms find each other again in the form of human beings. We call them soulmates."* I looked at him then, and he was staring back at me, his eyes blazing with an unreadable expression. "I just never could get that theory out of my head again. I've always remembered it. I like to believe it's true."

He smiled softly. It wasn't a smirk or a challenge, but a real smile. "I like it."

"I don't think these are always romantic connections, though," I added. "I think that's even more rare. I think if we are lucky enough to find our soulmate in this life, the chance of it being our best friend, or dog, or anyone else is just as high as it being someone we fall in love with. I think it's just someone that we meet that we connect with on a level that is out of this world.

"I heard once that some scientist said that if romantic soulmates were real, only ten percent of people would find them in their lifetime. I actually feel like that might be in line with this theory, you know? A one-in-eight-hundred-million chance of finding *that* person."

"Alright," he drawled. "So, why does that make you hate romance novels, exactly?"

"Why would I want to read about something I am so unlikely to find?"

"Because it's just a theory, Pep. There are an infinite number of ways we can find our person, our *soulmate*, if you will. Your theory is solid, I'll give you that, but it's just one of a zillion. Another solid theory being that every person has a soulmate, someone that we're all destined to find. In that case, you've got nothing to worry about."

I huffed as I sat back up and crossed my legs.

He smiled triumphantly.

Except, when I said I hated happy endings, I didn't just mean the happy endings to love stories. There are much worse endings to much worse stories than love. Sometimes love isn't enough, sometimes it doesn't conquer all, sometimes it can't even keep us alive. I wasn't interested in reading books where everything works out in the end because for so many people that just isn't true. Sometimes... sometimes people just give up. They lose the fight. They crumble beneath the weight of their world. Sometimes people shut their own book before making it to the end because they've lost all hope that they'd get a happy one.

Carter didn't need to know that, though. Carter lived in a world where the glass was always half-full, where the sky was always blue, where both his parents—his birth parents—were alive and well and loved him. That last part will never be a reality for me. I hope maybe someday the rest of it can. I hope someday I can be a full glass, sunny days, flow-going type of person like he is.

"Plus, not all books have happy endings. Some books have tragic endings." He shrugged. I flicked my eyebrow at him. "I'm just saying, you should give reading a chance. At the very least, it's a great form of escape."

I nodded in consideration. I thought his words through before responding quietly, "I don't want a life I feel like I have to escape from."

He paused and leaned his head against the wall behind us, just as I had. He looked up at the sky, and I followed suit. The clouds were growing thicker, darker. "Then read to learn. Read to laugh. Books bring growth and knowledge; books bring peace. All things that make real life better. Don't read to escape, read to live." His eyes met mine again.

"What about *The Alchemist* made you feel like you found yourself?" I found myself asking.

"There is a passage toward the beginning of the book that stood out to me the first time I read it." He grabbed the book that sat between us. He opened it and pointed a finger at a highlighted group of text. "There."

I read it out loud: "*And, when you want something, all the universe conspires in helping you achieve it.*" I'd read that page already, but that hadn't stuck out to me. I looked at him, his eyes were matching the clouds above us: dark and storming. "And what is the universe conspiring to help you achieve, Edwards?" I asked, attempting at a lighter tone.

He only continued to stare at me with that same expression. I wasn't sure how long it lasted before he finally said, "That's for me to know and you to find out."

I blinked at him just as the first drop of rain hit the tip of my nose. He watched the water splash against my skin. I followed his eyes as they traced the raindrop that fell from my nose and onto my lips, cascading down my chin and onto my chest before disappearing underneath my shirt. I again felt compelled to ask him about all the thoughts in his head, but before I could, the sky opened on us and it began to pour.

We need to go inside. I know we need to go inside.

Except I felt warped as I watched the way his eyes are focused on my lips. The water was coming down faster, coating both of our faces in a sheen of moisture. I took note of the way his breathing became labored, the rapid and shallow movement of his chest. He inched forward, almost unnoticeably, like he was closing in on me. His gaze moved rapidly between my mouth and my eyes, his expression almost needy. Almost like he was asking me for permission.

I inhaled deeply, pulling my lower lip underneath my teeth. As if my faint movement broke him from a trance, his eyes snapped up to meet mine. He leaned back instantly and let out a breath he seemed to be holding in. "It's raining," he observed as if he hadn't noticed before.

"Yes," I said breathlessly.

Still facing me, but farther away now, he closed his eyes. "We should go inside."

"Yes," I repeated in a hushed tone.

As if my word was the answer to a question rather than an agreement to his statement, he nodded and quickly stood up. His face was unreadable, almost strained. Whatever it was giving off, it was far from the typical grin that charmed his features. I remained sitting, staring up at him through the falling rain. "Goodnight, Pep," he said, slipping through my window.

By the time I grabbed both copies of *The Alchemist* and crawled through the window myself, he was gone. I faintly heard him greet my parents downstairs before the front door shut. I watched him jog across the street and behind the gate of his parent's house without another glance back at me. Once he was out of sight, I slammed the window shut.

That was weird.

All of it was weird. Weird and wonderful and frustrating and enticing. If I hadn't known better, I would've thought he was about to kiss me.

But I do know better.

With a sigh of both relief and torment, I flopped down onto my bed. I pulled out Carter's copy of the book, flipping it open to that last passage we'd talked about, reading it once more.

Chapter Twelve

"We are attracted to another person at a soul level not because that person is our unique complement, but because by being with that individual we are somehow provided an impetus to become our whole selves."

-Edgar Cayce

Carter

I wasn't going to follow her. I really wasn't.

But I just so happened to pull out of my driveway the same moment she was pulling out of hers. We worked at the same place, so naturally, we had the same commute. I pulled into the parking lot directly behind her but parked a respectable distance away. Four spaces. I planned to hang around inside my truck and allow her time to get into the classroom without it appearing that I was following her. Except, when I watched her enter the school, I noticed her make a right turn towards the east wing, not a left toward our classroom. Instinctively, I found myself climbing out of my Bronco. I knew she was heading toward the teacher's lounge, and I had no reason to head towards the teacher's lounge, if the thermos in my left hand held any indication. I also knew there was a creepy guy with a wormy face who looked at her like she was his next meal, and he was roaming the school. So, despite my understanding that she could take care of herself, I followed her.

My intuition proved to be my ally when I saw Marshall conveniently leave the gym right as she passed the doors. I quickly dumped the contents of my thermos in a passing water fountain to make it appear that I had some reason to find myself in the teacher's lounge before school started. I tried not to think too much about the fact I would now be subjected to the shitty break room coffee rather than the good stuff I kept at home. I strolled into the lounge casually but couldn't help but glance at her as I entered. To my surprise, her eyes were glued to me, and if I didn't know better, I'd think I noticed a bit of a blush creep up her neck. She looked away quickly and appeared to hide a smile.

Despite attempting to be large enough to accommodate the entire faculty, very few people used the lounge. Some would filter in to grab coffee in the morning, or heat up their lunch, and then filter back into their respective classrooms. In the two weeks I'd been working here, I'd become accustomed to doing the same. I spent most of my day in the art studio, or the office adjoining it when Penelope's classes were in session. I noticed that though most teachers kept to their classrooms, Penelope and her friends didn't so much. They spent a lot of time in the break room. Macie seemed to be the tether that anchored them together. I was glad Penelope had found that in Macie. Penelope always seemed to need a person that kept her tied together. There were certain aspects of life that Penelope seemed unsure of, or maybe afraid of. Some things she couldn't do alone.

Walking into a crowded room.

Speaking to a large group of people.

Making new friends.

Kissing someone without first being pulled into a dark closet by them.

She lacked courage, I suppose, in certain situations. However, in others, she was fiercely independent. School work when we were younger, for example. She'd never welcome help or assistance with it, never asked questions. Each problem was hers to figure out alone. She excelled at that. I believe that could bleed over into all aspects of her life. Fiercely independent in her refusal to ask for help– even when she needed it. Even in scenarios where she lacked courage, even in the things she couldn't do alone, she would not ask for help with them. She avoided them. She'd never had a lot of friends, never willingly entered social situations, even turned down being Valedictorian for our high school to avoid giving the speech.

Sometimes I wonder how she was able to move across the world and attend college all on her own. How she moved to a place she'd never been, knowing not a single soul. That was how I knew her lack of courage was a choice, and not simply just who she was. Because she chose to have courage in order to chase her education. She was courageous and independent and impassioned in her quest for knowledge since we were children. Always curious, always wanting to know everything about the world around her. It made me wonder what might have changed, because the passionate person I used to know, the one who wanted—who needed—to know everything, seemed to have disappeared from the person I watched sitting with her friends and drinking coffee. As if she wanted to be the smartest person in the room, but she didn't want anyone to know she was the smartest person in the room. That made me sad because she should want people to know that. She should be known for that.

When we were kids, she went through a phase where she was obsessed with the Lost City of Atlantis. She would watch documentaries on it and fall down endless rabbit holes of YouTube conspiracies. I wasn't surprised to have learned that she graduated with a degree in archaeology. I knew when we were younger, she was most interested in Oxford because of its proximity to Stonehenge. She always had a thing for the Wonders of the World, especially the ancient ones. Maybe that's what she was doing on the other side of the world, still looking for Atlantis. Or maybe now she's given up.

I was pulled from my thoughts as I watched Marshall's arm come around her back, coiling its way around her shoulder, where his fingers brushed against her collarbone. Her body flexed at his touch–no, more like recoiled and tensed. The tightness around her shoulders made her collarbone become that much more pronounced, poking just above the neckline of her copper sweater.

Fuck. I love her collarbones.

I felt ill as I watched another man's hand brush along that part of her. The thought of any man touching any part of her made my stomach jump– but him, especially, made me sick. As if I'd actually expressed that thought out loud, her head snapped up to mine. I only knew I hadn't said it because nobody else looked at me. She shook off The Worm's arm and stood, grabbing her coffee mug that was still half full, and walked over to me. His eyes followed her before landing on me and narrowing in a glare. I was standing with my back against the counter, facing the room. When she reached the sink, she poured her coffee down the drain.

Without turning around, she said, "Macie told me everything." I assumed she meant about The Worm, about that night at the bar. I hoped it meant that Macie had the same feeling I had about him. That whatever she had told Penelope had been a warning. "When I first started, he was nice. He was charming, actually," she scoffed in disbelief. "It was a fucking performance. One he gave to women often. But Macie knows him well, and as she and I grew closer, he made his... *intentions* clear." She shivered. "But I didn't think he was dangerous. I knew he was into me, but I thought he was always just messing around." Her voice broke with fear. "I guess a few weeks ago Jeremy asked him why he hadn't given up on me yet. Marshall claimed that it was just a matter of time. That the easiest way to get to me would be to get me drunk. Jeremy never told Macie that. I guess he thought it was a joke."

"Fucking pig."

"How did you know?" she asked. "I mean, I've been working with him for six months and it took me that long to see it. Jeremy and Macie have known him for *years*, but you figured it out right away."

I sighed, knowing the truth was because I was always watching her myself. Always protective even when she didn't need it. "He was acting possessive over you from the moment he met me. Like he thought I was a threat." I looked at her. "The only reason he'd find me a threat was if he thought he had some sort of claim on you already, and I could tell you didn't return his interests. So, that was the first red flag." I shrugged. "Plus, he looks like a fucking worm."

Penelope laughed, loudly. So loud that the rest of the room stood stared at the two of us. Her face brightened as she threw her head back. For someone who hated the spotlight, she sure knew how to pull a room to attention. I thought I noticed a small smile creep from the corner of Macie's mouth. She said something loudly, pulling the attention back to her. It almost felt like she was trying to give Penelope and I privacy.

"Why are they still talking to him, then?"

"Marshall and Jeremy are roommates," she sighed. "But Macie hates him. She's only tolerating him because we're at work. She's refusing to go to their house anymore and demanding Jeremy find a way out of their lease." I nodded. She turned fully to her side, looking at the thermos in my hands. "Did you actually need coffee, or did you just come in here because you saw him follow me?" I felt my cheeks grow red and I stared down at my feet. When I didn't respond, she looked at me. "Thanks."

"Anytime–"

"Pep. You know that," she finished for me, a soft smile on her lips.

We both chuckled before The Worm broke the laughter. "Penelope?"

She grumbled, "Yeah?"

"I was just asking about trivia this week. You're still going, right?"

Just then, the first bell rang, signaling that school was starting in ten minutes. "I can't," Penelope muttered, setting her mug in the sink.

"We can't either," Macie said. "Dinner with my parents, remember?" she asked Jeremy, nudging his ribs lightly. He nodded quickly as both stood up and gathered their things before heading off in the direction of their respective classrooms.

Penelope turned to follow them out, but before stepping away she whispered in my ear, "We're definitely still going. You should come too."

I filed out the door behind her, failing to hide the stupid grin that accented my features. The Worm sat in the same spot he'd been in since I walked in, staring at the doorway his friends left out of with an annoyed, if not concerned, look on his face.

I was fifteen minutes early to the bar. I don't know why. I sat in a booth towards the back because I thought Penelope would like that best. Close enough that we could easily participate in the game, but far enough away that the M.C. would never single her out.

I sat awkwardly, flexing my fingers together and attempting to look anywhere but the door when Macie and Jeremy walked in. Macie stopped and glanced around before her eyes settled on me and she smiled. She grabbed Jeremy by the hand and dragged him over to the table I was sitting at. "You know her better than I thought." She laughed as she slid in across from me, Jeremy next to her.

"Does she always ask to sit in the back?" I asked.

Macie nodded with a smile. Jeremy drummed his fingers on the table awkwardly before waving a waiter over and ordering drinks. "So, Carter, are you coming back to Seaside Middle next year to teach?" Jeremy asked after the waiter walked away.

"No, Mrs. Carlson should be back from maternity leave by the fall. After the school year ends in June, I'm a free bird."

"And what do you plan on doing after that?" Macie raised a brow.

I cleared my throat. "I'm not sure. I'm hoping to save up enough money from this contract and some freelance work I'm doing on the weekends to travel for a while. I'd like to check out California, maybe." I shrugged. The truth was, that had been my plan before I moved back in with my parents. I was tired of taking the same old photos for the same old brochures and hotel websites in Hawaii. I wanted to grow my skills and doing that meant trying something new. More challenging. When my dad offered me the substitute position here in Brighton Bay, I thought it would be an easy way to make some extra cash and then I could go off to California for a while.

"Interesting," Macie said slyly. Her head tilted slightly as she studied me. I wondered how much Penelope had told her of me. I could almost see the thoughts that clouded Macie's mind, telling me she knew more than she let on. "So, was Penny your first kiss?"

I let a chuckle escape my mouth, unsurprised by her questions. Jeremy seemed the same, except he wasn't laughing. He was rolling his eyes. "You really have no filter, do you?" I asked.

Macie shrugged. "Just curious."

I snorted, "My first kiss was with a girl named Becca during a game of seven minutes in heaven at Penelope's brother's birthday party. I was twelve. But it *was* in Penelope's bedroom." Macie's face then twisted into something disturbed. I held up my hands. "I didn't choose the location. Easton did."

Macie laughed then. "That's rough."

I smirked. "Well, Penelope's first kiss was in my swimming pool," Macie's face lit up until I continued, "with *my* best friend, Dominic."

Macie gasped dramatically while Jeremy was looking down on his phone uninterested.

In looking at the two of them, I hadn't noticed the door to the bar open until I heard, "Yeah, well you dared us to do it." Penelope smiled as she sat down. "Hi."

I smiled back at her. "Hi, Pep."

Macie's eyes darted back and forth between us, sparkling with amusement—or maybe mischief—I couldn't tell. "Penny, two drinks maximum tonight, okay?" Macie warned.

Penelope threw her hands up in surrender. "Trust me, I'm never drinking more than two ever again."

"I think you're fun when you're drunk." I propped my elbows on the table and leaned my head into one as I looked at her.

"And I'm not fun when I'm sober?" she mused.

"Not nearly as much fun as you are when you're drunk."

She shoved me with a playful giggle. "You ass."

The trivia game started, and by halfway through, we were losing miserably. I wasn't even sure what the theme of the night was supposed to be. Some television show none of us had ever heard of. We'd all but given up, not even bothering to provide answers anymore.

"Penny, have you heard back from UCLA yet?" Macie asked, her eyes darting to me briefly.

Penelope huddled her hands in her lap and brought her shoulders in on herself, as if she was embarrassed. "No, not yet." She looked away from the rest of us as if she was a little pained. "But I did get accepted into Pepperdine!" she exclaimed quickly. Almost like she was trying to make up for the fact that she hadn't heard back otherwise. Or as if to make up for the other rejections she'd received.

I tried to ignore the warmth that bloomed inside my gut at the thought of her moving to California too. We'd always orbited each other in different directions, and it suddenly felt as if we may change course. As if we'd start moving toward each other rather than away from. We all granted her our congratulations at her acceptance.

"I was invited to an academic conference there. Typically, only current graduate students are permitted to attend but I received a special invitation in my acceptance. An opportunity to meet with the program leaders and professors, as well as other students." She shrugged. "It's not my first choice, though."

"What's your first choice?" I asked.

She cleared her throat awkwardly. "Oxford, obviously. But I was...expelled." She let her hair fall across her cheek, once again hiding her face. "UCLA was my second choice, and they are the only school I still haven't heard from."

She clasped her hands on the table in front of her, staring down at them. I met Macie's eyes across the table and craned my head toward the bar. She nodded and grabbed Jeremy's arm. "I'm hungry. Let's go order food," she said.

"What happened?" I asked Penelope quietly. "With the schools."

She chewed on the inside of her lip. "I knew you'd ask eventually. It's just... it's embarrassing to admit." I opened my mouth to tell her she didn't need to say anything, but she spoke before I could. "Technically, I forged a recommendation letter in my graduate application at Oxford. They accepted me initially, but after it was discovered that my application was.... fraudulent... they withdrew it. I lost my student visa. I had to move home. It tainted my academic reputation. When I apply to other schools, many of them are informed or find out about my... *situation* at Oxford. It makes them reconsider accepting me."

I was the one now chewing on my lip, unsure of how to respond. I was surprised, but somehow, not shocked. I knew Penelope valued her education, and I knew that in a moment of sheer desperation, she may have made a mistake in hopes of securing her future. It wasn't the right choice, clearly. She was eaten up over it, I could tell. But I wasn't sure I could blame her for it, either. "Do you think you wouldn't have been accepted if you hadn't given them that letter?"

She shrugged. "I don't know. I had someone tell me my chances of getting in were low. That I may not have been cut out for the field at all. I got desperate."

"That someone sounds like an asshole," I muttered.

"It was one of my *professor*s..." She said the word with disdain. "So, I took him seriously. Took his words to heart. I know I shouldn't have done it." Her voice was hollow.

I turned toward her. She was staring down at the table. "Pep." She glanced at me. "I know how seriously you take your education, and if someone like a professor was beating you down, well, I can't blame you for getting desperate. Do you beat yourself up about it because you know it was wrong and you feel guilty, or because it hurts your chances of getting into other programs?"

"Both," she admitted. "But the former, mostly." She said as if it was something she thought about often.

I nodded. Hesitantly, I grabbed her hand underneath the table and squeezed it. "You made a mistake, Pep. You deserve to forgive yourself for it. God knows you're facing the consequences." She only shrugged once more. "I know you, Penelope. You're not the sum of your mistakes. You're caring, thoughtful, empathetic. You're good, all the way down to your bones. Don't let this one thing eat you alive."

She smiled, but it didn't reach her eyes. As if the words I spoke went into her heart, but not her head. As if she appreciated them but didn't believe them. I sighed in defeat before giving her hand a final squeeze and pulling mine away.

Macie and Jeremy settled back into their seats.

"Are you going to the conference at Pepperdine?" I asked.

She shook her head. "I don't think so. It's next week."

"Next week is spring break," Macie cut in.

"Yeah?" Penelope said.

"So, we must go. We can go down there together. You can go to your conference while I lay on the beach in Malibu for three days." Macie smiled as if she'd hatched a grand plan inside her head.

Penelope began to shake her head. "I don't think that's a good idea. The cost of the flights and the hotel... it's too expensive."

"We'll split the cost of the hotel. It won't be too bad," Macie countered.

"I can probably use my mom's discount for plane tickets," I found myself saying. My mom has been a flight attendant for years and gets significant discounts with her airline.

Penelope looked at me, her lips clustered at the side of her mouth in a sly smile. "Are you inviting yourself?"

"No," I said too quickly, "I just meant for you."

"Wait, that's perfect," Macie said, grinning like her plan was back in action. "If Jeremy and I come, we can help split the cost of lodging, and Carter's discount can help pay for your flight–"

"If we go, you know Marshall is going to expect to come too," Jeremy cut in.

Penelope went rigid and began to shake her head.

"Marshall can go *fuck* himself," Macie spit.

Jeremy rolled his eyes. "Calm down, Mace. I'm just saying, he'll expect to. Why don't you two just go, make it a girl's trip?"

"No, I want you to go," Macie said. She was looking at me when she said it, and it almost felt like she wouldn't be opposed to a girl's trip, but for some reason she wanted me to be there more than she cared if Jeremy was. She narrowed her eyes, staring at nothing.

We all remained silent as we watched the gears turn in her head. "Marshall thinks there is something between the two of you now," she said, nodding between Penelope and me. "His fragile ego can't handle being rejected by a woman, especially when he thinks it's because of another guy. He's still burned by what happened last week at the bar–"

Penelope snorted. "*He's* upset?"

"Let me finish," Macie held up her hand. "What I'm saying is, if Carter comes, Marshall won't butt in. Not that I'd allow him anywhere near you, anyway. But because he's a misogynistic piece of shit, he'll be a lot more threatened by Carter than by me."

"So, basically, you want Carter to come on the trip so that we can use him as a ploy to keep Marshall away?" Jeremy asked. His face was a hard line. He seemed almost uncomfortable, which rubbed me the wrong way. Friend or not, roommate or not, I wouldn't stand to associate myself with someone who had done what Marshall did.

I looked at Penelope, and she looked at me. Both of us were attempting to read the other, looking for permission. "Think of it as a work trip," Macie said to me.

"I wouldn't mind going down to visit Dom," I said to Penelope.

"You and Dom still talk?" she asked.

I nodded. "I don't see him as often as I'd like, though."

She chewed on her lip as she considered things. "Okay, I guess we'll go."

Macie cheered, and I smiled. Jeremy took a sip of his beer as if he didn't feel any particular way about the plans.

"I'll find us a rental," Macie said.

"What day does the conference start?" I asked.

"It's just one day. It's next Thursday," Penelope said.

"How about we fly out Wednesday morning, then? Come back on Friday?" I asked. Macie frowned. "We're going for Pep. The less time we're there, the more money we save."

Macie nodded and pulled out her phone as she began searching for a place to stay.

Chapter Thirteen

"Tis hard to discover that you have found in the mate of another; he who travels with a part of your very soul."

–Renee A. Lee

Penelope

I technically had the aisle seat, but I asked Carter if we could switch because I like looking out the window.

He obliged without hesitation. I settled in my seat and laid my head against the window. We somehow both got upgraded to first-class, and our seats were next to each other, while Macie and Jeremy were back in coach. He slipped into the seat next to me and I realized for the first time our proximity. Even in the larger sized first-class seats it was difficult to be comfortable without our knees and shoulders colliding. It was slightly painful, the way the chills shot through my body as his arms grazed my thigh. He wasn't even touching me on purpose, and yet I shivered.

Just being in Carter's presence set a fire deep inside my gut–below it. I could smell the fresh scent of rain on him and the warm mahogany undertones of whatever body wash he used. I glanced at his arms, the way they sat hesitantly at his sides. His forearms flexed and I realized how smooth his skin was. I studied his hands and wondered what it would feel like to be touched by them. How they'd feel dragging along my skin. He seemed bigger now than he did at eighteen, and I wondered if his hands would feel different, if he grabbed me now, than they did back then.

He cleared his throat and my eyes shot up to his face. He was grinning at me. I realized I'd been checking him out. *Again.* The morning sunlight shone through the window of the plane, making his eyes appear particularly green. "Pep?"

"Yeah?"

"Who's James?"

I blinked at him a few times. "How do you know about James?"

He chewed the inside of his cheek and looked as if he wished he hadn't asked. "You said something about him a few weeks ago. The night you got wasted." I threw my head back against the seat of the plane and sighed. "I'm sorry, I shouldn't have brought it up."

"No, it's fine," I ground out. "He's my ex, I guess. We dated for a while back in England, but things ended before I moved back here."

His brows furrowed. "So, James isn't still in the picture, at all?"

"No," I said. "Not at all."

He was quiet for a minute before he asked, "Were you in love with him?"

"No," I said too quickly.

He nodded, as if that was enough of an answer. We sat quietly as the rest of the plane boarded and the flight attendants gave the safety presentation and took drink orders for us. The only thing I was able to focus on was him, though. I kept my eyes glued to the window, afraid that if I looked at him, I'd again ask him to tell me all the thoughts running through his mind.

Allowing myself one quick glance, I turned my head toward him. I was pinned by his hazel eyes. They were blazing, and it wasn't just because of the sunlight. He had thoughts brewing behind them, and I needed to know what they were. I opened my mouth to ask him what he was thinking about when he asked me instead, "Have you ever been in love with anyone?"

My breath caught in my throat as I considered his question. *Just you,* I wanted to say. I tried to untangle his words, read his face, and understand what he was truly wanting to ask me. "I've only... *been* with James, if that's what you're asking."

Might as well rip off that Band-Aid.

He blinked at me as if he was surprised at my revelation. I opened my mouth, about to get defensive, when he stopped me with a chuckle. "It's not. That doesn't mean anything. I've *been* with a lot of girls but I wasn't in love with any of them."

I arched my brow. "Define *a lot of girls.*"

He bit down on his lip, the corner of his mouth tilting into a smirk. "Are you jealous, Pep?"

"No," I muttered. I shook my head and looked away, feeling my cheeks begin to blaze.

He roared with laughter. "You have nothing to be jealous of. None of them would hold a candle to you." I leaned my head against the seat window, watching the airport creep by us as the plane slowly began to move away from the gate.

I turned slightly towards him. "You can't say that. You've never had sex with me."

Oh my God, did I just say that?

I looked down at my lap to hide my face.

"Penelope, look at me." I kept my head down but glanced up through my lashes. He was studying my lips as he leaned in slightly and said just above a whisper, "If having sex with you is anything at all like kissing you, then I am certain that nothing else could ever compare."

It seemed as if the pilot themself was hanging on those words because once they left his mouth, a force pulled me back against my seat as the plane began to pick up speed. My heart was hammering in my chest and my stomach was fluttering. His eyes were still focused on my lips, but the way his chest moved told me that he might be feeling exactly what I am.

"Have *you* ever been in love?" I found myself asking.

He broke his gaze and his brows furrowed softly before he let out an exasperated sigh. "Not with anyone I've fucked."

My breath caught as the plane began to accelerate down the runway. His response was a non-answer. I was too afraid to ask more, to even consider what he could've meant by it. I was afraid to think too deeply about all the other girls he didn't love. I'd never much minded cursing, but the word *fucked* hung in the air around us, causing a bubble of jealousy to bloom inside my gut. I might hate that word forever now.

After a moment, he cleared his throat, and I realized I hadn't responded. I looked up at him. "Right. Well, to answer your question, no I don't speak to James anymore."

Carter only nodded, gripping the armrest we lifted off the earth. I looked at his hands again and reminded myself of how ill I felt at the thought of those hands touching someone else's body. I looked at his face and wondered if that's how he felt about James. If he was thinking of James touching me. Kissing me. Being inside me. Something in his expression tells me that's exactly what he's thinking about, and I want to tell him that it's all true. James did all those things to me.

And all of them reminded me of Carter.

I wasn't sure exactly what kind of friendship Carter and I were falling into. It was different than when we were kids. We spent time together, time that wasn't forced upon us. I felt like I was finally getting the chance to really know him. I was finding that I really enjoyed the person I was meeting. There were zips of electricity that blazed through my body every time I was near him, and there may be a part of me that thinks he feels it too. I know those zips can't be ignored forever, and that means that eventually I'll have to tell him the real reason why I moved home.

I felt guilty, lying to him. I'd told him I was tossed out of Oxford due to a fraudulent letter of recommendation. While that hadn't been *entirely* untrue, it hadn't been the whole truth, either. When I told him, he was kind. He understood. He accepted it– accepted me. If I'd told him the whole truth, I couldn't be sure the reaction would've been the same. In fact, I was almost positive it would've been the opposite. There was no motivation that warranted what

I'd done. The actions I took. I know that now, but I needed the time to show Carter that I knew that. That I'd made the worst mistake I'd ever made, and that it wasn't something I'd ever do again. I couldn't have explained that to him in a crowded bar, though. But I would tell him. I had to.

Except, I knew there was a good chance that once he learns that about me, he'll want nothing to do with me. I want to prepare for that to happen, and I'm not there yet. A part of me knows that getting close to Carter—in any way—could just cause me more pain down the road. Another part of me doesn't care. A third part of me knows the inevitability of it all crashing down and wants to hatch an escape plan for when it does. That escape plan being school. In the meantime, though, I'm going to hang onto him as tight as I can and hope it doesn't hurt too much when everything falls apart.

"Don't freak out," Macie pleaded from the front steps of the villa she'd rented. She raced inside the house the moment Jeremy put the rental car in park, only to return a moment later with the horrified expression she was giving me now. "There is only one bedroom... I– I swear the listing said it was two rooms."

I stared at her blankly, all too aware of Carter's gaze on me as he grabbed my bag from the trunk. I walked up the steps and into the house with him on my heels. I glanced around the room and made note of the surroundings. It was very small. A short hallway past the kitchen held two closed doors. One door must've led to the bathroom, meaning the other was the only bedroom in the house. "Two rooms? Or two *bedrooms*?" I asked. "Because this is a room." I waved my hands in the air referencing the living room we were in, glancing at the couch that clearly held a hide-away bed. "A living room. That," I pointed at the closed door in front of me, "is a bedroom."

She crossed her arms over her chest. "Well, it said it slept four people!"

Carter looked at me with concern as he gently set my things down onto the floor. I could demand the bedroom, but that would make no sense. It would leave the three of them left to fight over the couch. Plus, Macie already called dibs on the king bed, and we took dibs very seriously. That meant Carter and I were left to sleep out here. Much to my surprise, I laughed. "Two people per bed." I soon found myself unable to stop.

My friends looked at me like I had gone completely insane.

Maybe I had, because this was starting to sound like the beginning of those cheesy rom-coms– the ones where there is only one bed. I was laughing so much because, despite that, I had no problem sharing a bed with Carter. I would love to share a bed with Carter. In fact, I'd spent our entire plane ride thinking about all the things I'd love to do in bed with him.

I shook those thoughts away, along with the irony. "You're sleeping on the floor," I said to Carter. He held his hands up and nodded, as if to tell me there would be no argument on his end. "And if any of you fucks with me while I'm sleeping, I'll…" I tried to think of an idle threat. "I'll throw you off one of these cliffs."

They all laughed at my expense as I grabbed my bag off the floor and found a corner of the room to make my own. We all took turns freshening up. It felt strangely reminiscent of the family trips we used to take as kids. I expected to feel a little uneasy traveling with Carter, but I wasn't. I realized we'd done this a dozen times before, at least. Our dads used to be joint owners on a cabin up in Northern Washington, at the base of Mt. Rainier. We spent weekends every summer in the cabin by the lake. The cabin only had four bedrooms, so me, Maddie, and Carter's sister, Charlie, shared a room. Easton and Carter shared one too. Our rooms had adjoining doors and sometimes, on the rare occasions where we weren't fighting each other, we'd open the doors and have one big sleepover. They decided to sell the cabin when we were teenagers because we'd all become so busy that we never made it up there anyway. We couldn't have been older than ten the last time we had a sleepover.

When I finished showering, I stepped outside the back of the house to admire the view. The veranda had a few chairs, a bar-b-que, sweeping views of the ocean below, and a hammock. While the rest of the crew meandered around the house getting settled in, I hopped into the hammock, popped in my ear buds and decided I'd try to nap.

I was up late last night preparing for the conference I'd be attending tomorrow. We had to leave for the airport this morning at seven, and I hadn't fallen asleep until after two. While the rest of them were on vacation, I had a reason to be here. Sure, Pepperdine wasn't my first choice of school, but I still needed to make a good impression in case my other options fell through. Plus, I didn't think I'd mind living here all that much.

When I woke up, the first thing I noticed was that I was cozy. While hammocks are relaxing, and the weather is wonderful, an outdoor nap shouldn't be cozy. I opened my eyes and realized I was covered in a knitted blanket. *I don't remember bringing this out here with me.* I pulled my phone out of my pocket to check the time. It was just before six. I rubbed my heavy eyes and tumbled out of the hammock, wrapping that blanket around my shoulders before walking over to the edge of the veranda, peering down at the beach below it.

I didn't bother looking back to see who else was outside when I heard a door shut and heavy footsteps made their way toward me. A moment later, Carter was standing next to me. I took out one of my ear buds when he asked, "Sleep well?"

"Mhmm." I smiled sleepily.
He chuckled. "Good."

Chapter Fourteen

"When you exchange energy with some places (soul-places) or people (soulmates), you feel that youre not just flesh, blood and thoughts; youre something beyond"

-Shunya

Carter

I don't know why I kept stepping out onto the patio to check on her.

The first time I brought her a blanket when I realized she was sleeping. Later, I walked outside again to make sure she was still okay. Maybe I just liked watching her sleep. She looks unchanged from the child who used to nap anywhere at any time. I'd watch her sleep in the car on family trips or in her dad's lap after dinner. I shouldn't have been surprised to find her sleeping outside now. I still find myself walking the fine line between the Penelope I used to know and figuring out the person she is now, but when she's asleep, she looks exactly like her younger self.

I was there the very first day she came to live with the Masons, before she was their daughter. I remember the horrified look in her eyes. The way she seemed far too tired for any seven year old to be. Far too drained of life for any child. She was so fragile. She was broken.

I didn't fully know why she was broken for several years. Not until my own father felt that I was old enough to comprehend her story. Something she actually had to live through at seven, my father felt I wasn't mature enough to even hear about until I was twelve. Even now, I don't think I know all of it. I'm not sure anyone does except for her. I was too afraid to ever ask her about it, too afraid to bring up the hauntings of her past.

I've always felt protective of her. From the moment I first looked into her grief-stricken eyes. Though, when I finally understood the true reason for her fragility, it was the only thing I could see about her for a long time. Protecting her became my primary instinct. I never wanted her to hurt again. Even in the way of a fight with her brother or kids being mean to her at school. I couldn't stand it. I was so caught up in protecting her that I forgot how to do anything else.

I forgot how to be her friend.

Now, I think I realize that everyone who loves her feels the same way I do. I think that her brother was so focused on repairing her that he forgot to accept her for who she is. Her parents were so focused on making her feel loved that they forgot to teach her how to love herself. Her friends were so focused on making her feel accepted that they forgot how to have fun with her. I think everyone around her treated her with kid gloves. I think she grew so tired of it that she literally ran away the first chance she got.

Now that she's back, she's grown. Whatever she did on the other side of the world has clearly taught her how to protect herself. Though, I'm not sure she ever learned how to accept herself, how to love herself, how to have fun. Maybe I could be those things for her. I could be the person to teach her all of that. I still feel there is a line to walk between what I think she needs and what she wants.

Now, I see the way she looks at my body with fervor, and I know what she's thinking. I try—without words—to make it clear that I want her too. When I kissed her all those years ago, I thought it was selfish. It was what I needed, not what she needed. That's why I stayed away for so long before it. Why I never tried. I never thought I was what she needed. At least, not in the way that she was what I needed.

But now, I think I may be exactly what she needs.

She yawned again, and I noticed the ear bud that she was holding in her hand. Its pair was still in her ear, and I realized she must've been listening to music while she was napping. My curiosity peaked and I plucked it from her hand, putting it in my ear. "What're you listening to?"

She shrugged. "It's just a random playlist of songs that remind me of my mom." By the way she said it, I inferred that she wasn't talking about Jenna, the mother I knew. She was talking about her birth mom.

"You never talk about her."

"I don't remember much about her." She sounded so sad when she said those words. I felt my chest quiver. My instinct was to comfort her, to change the subject to something lighter.

I reminded myself that wasn't what she needed from me anymore. She knew where to draw her lines. Maybe what she needed more was to talk about her mother. Maybe speaking about her would breathe life back into those memories.

"You've never told me the story about your adoption," I said apprehensively.

"I figured someone would've told you," she murmured.

I shook my head. "It's nobody's story to tell but yours, Pep. I wouldn't allow anyone to tell me something *you* didn't want me to know. The only thing I knew was that your mom died." She crossed her arms over her chest, and I wondered if she was about to stop the conversation short and tell me she didn't want to talk about it. Instead, she looked at me with that same admiration in her green eyes.

"The hard thing is that it's not really my story, either. I don't remember a lot from before I was adopted. I just have glimpses of things I think I remember. They feel like dreams. I remember my mom singing when she did laundry. I remember her reading to me all the time. I remember her telling me she loved me. I remember she had red hair like mine. She told me never to change it because I'd never be able to get the right color back. I remember her being sick a lot. I remember the day she died. Sometimes, though, I wonder if I make up the good memories to replace the bad ones. I wonder if I'm imagining things."

I looked at her and her face was stern, like she was having an argument inside her mind. Arguing whether to tell me about the day her mom died. I looked up at the sky above us.

I won't push her on this.

"Do you look up songs because you remembered your mom singing them, or do you just happen to come across them one day and they remind you of her?"

"Depends. There was one song that I could remember the lyrics to but not the song. One day the lyrics were floating in my head, so I googled them. When I heard it, it felt like I was hearing my mom's voice again."

"Then the memory is real. The lyrics already existed in your brain, you just had to find the melody," I said.

She rubbed her palms against her knees, and for a moment, I thought she was bracing herself to stand up and go inside. Instead, she let out an extended breath and closed her eyes while she tilted her head toward the sun.

"I was in bed. We shared a one-bedroom apartment. It was the evening. I had just gotten out of the bathtub and crawled into bed when I heard her body hit the floor. I knew it was her body. There is a certain sound a body makes when it falls and the person falling doesn't even try to catch themselves. Nothing else makes that sound. I waited for a second, waiting for her to say something, but she never did. I opened the door and I could see her feet sticking out into the hallway from inside the bathroom. At first, I shut the bedroom door again. I ran into the bed and hid under the covers. I don't even know how long I stayed in bed. Sometimes I wonder if she was still alive at that moment, if she heard me shut the door and run away, if her last thought was that her daughter was abandoning her." She almost shivered along with that sentence.

Taking a deep breath, she continued, "Eventually, I creeped back out and went into the bathroom. She was laying back with her head craned against the bathtub, her body sprawled out between the tub and the sink." I winced at the thought of finding my own mother in such a position. "There was so much blood. I didn't know the human body held so much blood and how it could flow so freely from our veins. The blood was everywhere, there was no way to tell where she was bleeding from. I knelt and tried to shake her awake, but nothing happened. The only thing I could think was that I was too small, and I couldn't shake her hard enough. I needed someone bigger to shake her awake for me."

Her fear of blood. She's always feared blood. Whether a scraped knee or a bloody nose. Her blood or others, it didn't matter. It all terrified her. I'd always thought it was some kind of irrational fear that some people are just born with. Like heights or clowns. She had a reason, though. A reason that ran so deep she couldn't even look at red paint without seeing it.

She looked at me and all I could see was numbness. As if she was talking about nothing but the weather. That broke my heart. Yet, she continued, "I ran outside and downstairs to our neighbor who lived below us. I didn't even know her name, I had never spoken to her before. She was older, probably in her sixties. She had three grandchildren that lived with her. I knocked on her door and when she opened it, she screamed. I couldn't figure out why she was screaming, until I looked down at myself. My pajamas were sticking to my body with blood. I told her my mom wouldn't wake up. I remember seeing the color drain from her face. She knew before I did that my mother was dead. She called nine-one-one and waited with me outside for the ambulance. She gave me a pair of her granddaughter's pajamas to change into.

"When the ambulance took my mom, I rode in the back of a police car to the hospital. There was already a social worker waiting there for me. She sat with me in the lobby for probably six or seven hours, but in my little-kid brain it felt like days. My dad– well, Dan. Not my birth dad. I don't even know who he is." She sighed. "My dad was the one to come out and tell us she had died. He said it to me, not the social worker. He bent down on his knees to meet my eyes and placed his hand on my shoulder. He said what all doctors say, 'We did everything we could, but her injuries were too severe. I'm sorry, but your mother has died.' He was the first person who didn't tell me it would be okay. He just told me the truth. I hugged him. Much to his confusion, and the confusion of my social worker. I don't even know why I did it. I just already felt safe, like his guy would never lie to me. My social worker left to make some calls, trying to find me a placement for a foster home. She asked my dad to wait with me, and he did. We played go fish, and he told me he liked my name. I obviously wasn't present for any of these conversations, but it turned out that my dad and Jenna had already become certified to foster. They had been interested in it for a while, but Jenna was always afraid she'd become too attached to a child and then lose them. They'd always wanted a third child but had a hard time getting pregnant. I don't think my dad even called Jenna to ask if he could take me home at the end of that shift. He just did it. Regardless, she accepted me immediately. They all did."

"Kids at school used to say your mom died of an overdose?" I asked, immediately regretting the words as they came from my mouth. Living in a small town, there were a lot of people who were privy to her mom's death and her adoption. Rumors flew around, and she was used to hearing them, but I hadn't meant to ask so bluntly.

"She did." Penelope cleared her throat. "I didn't know that for a while. My parents told me a few years after it happened. Her official cause of death was cardiac arrest. The number of opiates in her system determined that she overdosed first and fell back against the bathtub and hit her head. That's where the blood came from.

She was addicted to just about any kind of prescription med she could get her hands on, apparently. I don't remember that about her, though. I don't remember anything ever being wrong with her. Other than the fact that we were poor, I guess. I remember her being sick a lot. It kind of always seemed like the cold, though. I never thought much about it," she said as she shrugged.

"After a few weeks, my social worker came for a visit. She asked me how I liked it there, and of course, I said only the best things. They are the best parents. But my dad– he really felt like my dad. He felt like my dad from the minute he told me I didn't have a mom anymore. I was afraid that if I said something wrong, the social worker would take me away. I was always walking on eggshells when she was around. Even after I was adopted, I sometimes still felt like I was walking on eggshells. Like if I said or did something wrong, they'd un-adopt me."

"You can't un-adopt someone," I scoffed. I was still trying to process all the things she said prior to that sentence.

"I know. I didn't even really know what it meant to be adopted, though. My parents have never, ever, done anything to make me feel this way. This is all me, but I sometimes feel like their love is conditional. They took me in and gave me everything, so I owe them something back."

I leaned forward, my head falling between my knees. Anger burned the back of my throat. The way she spoke about her experience was so casual, and that almost made it worse. It felt as if nobody had ever told her they were sorry for what she went through, as if she felt like she didn't have a right to hurt from it. "I'm so sorry, Penelope. I'm sorry."

She rubbed my back. "I know." *She was comforting me.* As if she had expected this reaction. As if this was how she had to handle the situation every time she told someone this story. No wonder she never brought it up. It was more strenuous for her to tell the story than it was to keep it hidden. In one movement, I sat up straight and hardly noticed the confusion on her face as I grabbed her and pulled her to my chest. I ran my fingers through her hair as my arm held her head against me.

"*You* are the one who should be held, Pep," I whispered. "I'm so sorry."

She deflated in my arms and one hand lightly landed on my chest. "I feel like I don't have the right to be sad. I feel like I should feel lucky to have been adopted by my parents. I could've spent my entire childhood in foster care or group homes."

"You are lucky in that regard. But you can still be sad about losing your mom," I said. I took a moment to absorb her words as I rubbed her head. She feels like she has to earn the love she's given. I wonder if she has ever told her parents that. Surely, if she had, they would've done something to make sure she knew. "'*One is loved because one is loved. No reason is needed for loving*,'" I whispered to her, quoting *The Alchemist*.

She moved her head away from my chest and looked up at me. "What?"

I chuckled. "You didn't finish the book?"

Her eyes fluttered. "I skimmed. I mostly focused on what I needed to know for the class's lesson plan."

"Well, you should read it again. Not for work, or because I told you to. For yourself. I think there are some messages in there that you should hear."

She smiled softly with a slight nod.

"You can always talk to me, Pep," I said.

"I know that." I knew she was ready to change the subject. As if on cue, she cleared her throat, "Speaking of the book, my class will be finished with the project after spring break, and I'll return it to you then."

"Keep it as long as you want," I said. "Keep it forever."

"What happens when you get lost again? And you need it to find yourself?"

"Then I guess I'll just have to come find you."

A flush ran to her cheeks.

"I have one more question," I said. She looked at me inquisitively. "You said your mother liked to read to you. Is that why you don't read? It reminds you of her?"

She nodded once. "She never got her happy ending."

I suddenly understood. I stood up abruptly. "I'll be right back."

I sprinted inside the villa and sorted through my bag until I found what I was looking for. A part of me was hesitant about my next move, but a bigger part of me felt like it was an involuntary reaction. I walked back outside holding a copy of a mystery novel about an Archaeologist. An Indiana Jones type of story. I found it years ago, and it had always reminded me of Penelope. She used to love Indiana Jones when we were young.

I couldn't stop thinking about all the things she said when she told me she doesn't like to read a couple of weeks ago (I found myself stuck on her soulmate theory, too). I wanted to try and see if I could get her into it. She was always so high strung. So stressed. I planned to give it to her on the plane, but the moment hadn't been right.

"I'll preface this by saying I had not expected the conversation to go the direction it did today." I huffed. "But I did bring this for you. It's not a romance, and it doesn't really have a happy ending either. It's about a treasure hunter searching for a lost city. It's like Indiana Jones meets Atlantis. It reminded me of you. There is a whole series." I smiled softly. "I understand if you're not there yet. I didn't realize the reason you don't read is because of your mom, but–"

She snatched it from my hands, her eyes glimmering with gratitude. She sighed in mock defeat. "Alright, I guess I'll give it a try."

She was just opening the first page when Macie's voice rang out.

"Maybe in life you get all kinds of soulmates. Multiple people who vibrate at the same level you do."

-Samantha Irby

Penelope

"I want to go real housewife hunting!" Macie yelled from the doorway of the patio. She then gasped, as if startled. "Oh, sorry. I thought Carter was inside."

We both glanced back at her. "What the hell is Real Housewife hunting?" Carter asked.

"Don't encourage her," I muttered under my breath.

"First of all, I heard that, Penny. Secondly, I just made it up. But I want to go to West Hollywood and see if I can find any of the Real Housewives of Beverly Hills."

I snickered and shook my head.

"I'm in. Sounds fun," Carter said. I shot him a horrified expression. "Not the Housewife hunting part, but I've never been to Hollywood."

Before I could argue with either of them, Macie was squealing and grabbing me by the arm, hoisting me onto my feet and inside the house.

Macie didn't do anything half-assed. If we were going out, we could bet that she was finding the top tier restaurants and clubs in L.A. She was definitely going to dress me in something with sequins. I'd probably have to wear fake eyelashes and insensible shoes as well. It wasn't that I didn't like dressing up. I just had a *very* different style from Macie's, and tonight I knew she'd want her way. She already had her hair done, her eyes fully smoldering with dark eyeshadow, making the brown within them appear more of a honeyed shade.

"I only brought one dress," I warned her. "It's that black one with the cinching at the front and the short sleeves," I said, jogging her memory back to the dress I'd worn multiple times.

She tsked and shook her head. "No, that won't do."

I already knew she'd say that.

Forty-five minutes later, I was thrown into a lace bralette (which was too small because I was at least a cup size bigger than Macie); with a sheer, long sleeve, black mesh top, paired with a tight, black, faux leather mini skirt. She finished the look off with hot pink strappy heels to add *a pop of color to the all-black ensemble.* I had to admit that I actually didn't hate it. I looked good. I wasn't wearing sequins, either. It wasn't my taste whatsoever. I'd rarely ever be caught dead in something tight and see through, or bright pink heels. But I didn't have the energy to argue with her about it. I stared at myself in the mirror, turning side to side to examine the finished product.

"Wow." Carter's voice pulled me from my reflection just in time to catch him staring at me from the hallway. I noticed the slow roll of his throat as he swallowed. His tongue snaked out across his lips as he checked me out. He started at my feet as his eyes roamed across my body, lingering on my hips and my skin underneath the top that left nearly nothing to the imagination. He wasn't even trying to hide the way he looked at me. It both empowered and excited something deep inside me. I took a moment to look at him too. He had on another one of his sheer button-ups. This one appeared particularly white in contrast to the color of his skin. The top two buttons were undone, giving the slightest glimpse of his tattoo. He had on dark jeans and a watch that looked like it would cost what I make in a year. I assumed it was a gift from his father.

He looked good. Really good.

Feeling bold, I sauntered past him, pausing briefly at his side. "Stop drooling or Macie's going to make me dress like this all the time."

"That threat gives me zero incentive to stop drooling," he rasped.

Macie's housewife hunting was a flop, but running around West Hollywood while we observed her scavenger hunt certainly was not. She had us going to a nightclub she had been told was frequented by several her favorite reality-TV stars. Carter called Dom at dinner and asked him if he wanted to meet up with us at said club. Macie was promising it was just another two blocks, even though she said that seven blocks ago and we'd been walking for what felt like hours. My pinky toe kept falling out of the strap on my shoe. I stopped against a telephone pole to stick it back in. Macie and Jeremy trudged on ahead, but Carter only made it a few paces before he realized I was no longer next to him and he stopped too.

I finished fixing my shoe and stepped up to reach him as we fell back in line. I was walking next to the street, whereas Carter was to my right. After a few paces, he lightly grabbed my waist and pulled me in front of him as he stepped sideways and took a place to my left. "What're you doing?" I asked.

"Walking next to the street," he said offhandedly.

"Why?"

"It's safer for you." I could tell he was slowing his pace to keep back with me. He had at least six inches in height on me, so of course his strides were larger. The heels didn't help me much. I knew I was walking slow. "What? Did *James* not do that?"

I raised my brow accusingly. "Why do you keep asking about James?"

He rubbed the back of his neck as he refused to meet my gaze. "I guess I'm trying to figure out what I'm competing with."

He's flirting with me.

"There isn't much to compete with," I muttered, trying to remain cool. "He never walked next to the street. Or held doors open for me. Or pulled out my seat at dinner." Not like Carter had earlier tonight. "It just wasn't that kind of relationship, I guess."

Carter's face contorted. "The kind where a man treats you the way you deserve to be treated?"

I snorted. "Yeah, apparently."

My stomach knotted when I looked at Carter's reaction. He thinks I'm the victim, but really, I'm the villain here. James may have taken advantage of the fact that I was an awestruck, naive, barely-legal college freshman. I was astonished by his accomplishments, his intelligence, and the life he'd made for himself. But I took what I wanted too, and his consequences for our actions were much more severe than mine were.

I smiled softly. "It's fine."

I skipped ahead to meet Macie and Jeremy at the corner they were waiting at. We crossed the street and finally arrived at the club Macie had insisted on. Once we made it inside, we found a couch in the quietest corner, though it was still far too loud to hear ourselves think. Macie offered to get us all another round of drinks from the bar. The club had two stories. We were on the second where most of the sitting areas were located. The bottom story held the large dance floor, bar, and main entrance. It was particularly crowded tonight.

I had two drinks at dinner but wasn't fully feeling the effects of alcohol yet. I decided I'd make a temporary amendment to my two-drink-rule and asked Macie to get me something from the bar as well. She returned ten minutes later with a round of shots.

Dammit. I shook my head in protest, but she pouted about how much they cost so I took one anyway. Then one more.

It was tequila. I hate tequila.

"Alright, alright. That's it for me!" I shouted over the music. She patted my head like I was a dog. I was already feeling the warmth settle in my stomach. She was mouthing something at me, but I had no idea what she was saying through the pounding of the music. She started pointing downwards at the level below us. She looked at Jeremy, but he shook his head and settled onto the couch across from Carter and me. She pouted and looked at me pleadingly. "I'm going to have to go dance with her," I groaned at Carter.

"Might as well go get it out of the way so she stops hounding you." He playfully elbowed my ribs. "I'm going to stay here and wait for Dom."

I slapped my knees and moved to stand up. I knew that if I truly refused, Macie wouldn't force me into anything I didn't want to do. As the alcohol flowed through me and flushed my cheeks, a small part of me *did* want to go dance. A part so small that if I wasn't with the people I was with, I wouldn't do it. Macie could read me in a way very few people have ever been able to. She's able to read the line between the things I want but am too scared to take. She pushes me into being the person I want to be. Almost as if some of her boldness, her adventurousness, and maybe a little recklessness, rubs off on me. Whereas I'm normally reserved, she makes me daring. It wasn't something I ever noticed until Carter came back.

Because Carter makes me feel safe. Safe enough to be bold, and adventurous, and daring, without fear of falling because if I do, he'll catch me.

I stood up but found myself to be a little more buzzed than I had initially realized. Losing my balance, I began to wobble when something steadied me. I glanced down to find Carter's hands on each side of my waist, holding me in place. I became hyper-aware of the fact that my ass was in his face, so I jumped to turn around and face him. Only, it was now my boobs that were in his face. His hands didn't move away as I turned. They stayed exactly where they were, and my body spun within them. He was still holding me by the waist as his line of sight narrowed directly at my chest. Slowly—so slowly—his gaze moved up to meet my eyes. He looked almost as if he was panting, a blush coming to his cheeks.

"Sorry, I lost my balance."

"Don't be," he said gruffly.

I was steady now, there was no reason for his hands to remain on my body. Regardless, I didn't move. Neither did he. I wanted his hands on me. I didn't want to walk away. "Do you want to come dance with us?" I asked. *With me. Just dance with me.*

He took a long time to answer. After a moment, he shook his head as if he was trying to clear his mind of something. "I told Dom I'd wait for him here."

I frowned, covering it quickly with a non-convincing smile. Maybe that moment wasn't for him what it was for me. Maybe none of these moments mean to him what they mean to me. Maybe it's all in my head. I nodded and stepped over him, his hands falling from my waist. I ascended the staircase and waded through the pool of bodies in search of Macie.

Once I found her, I was surprised to see the dance floor hadn't been cleared for her. She looked like something out of a movie. Her tight blonde curls whipped back and forth, moving in unison with her hips. Her red dress sparkled in the light as she threw her head back and moved in the exact rhythm of the music. She didn't even care that she was by herself. Didn't care who was or wasn't watching. Perfectly content in her moment.

I grabbed Macie by the hands and started to dance with her. I was sure that in comparison to her, I resembled a wounded giraffe. As the music flowed, I let all my insecurities go and focused on moving along with it and with Macie. I twirled with her and wrapped my hands around her neck as we danced. I made a few noticeable glances at the second floor where Carter stood over the railing with a beer in his hand. His gaze pierced through me. He wasn't even trying to hide it. I ran my hands up my own body and through my hair. I knew I was attempting to tease him. I didn't know why. I guess I wanted him to see what he was missing.

The longer we danced, the more his face began to harden. After a while, I caught sight of Dom. They were dressed similarly, except where Carter's shirt was white, Dom's was black, complimenting his skin tone, which was slightly darker than Carter's. It appeared Dom now kept his hair cut short, but when we were younger he'd grow it out like Carter still does now. Dom's curls had always been tighter and more coiled, while Carter's fell onto his forehead. Dom's teeth flashed at me and he waved, but I pretended not to notice. The two of them were almost annoying, looking like twin Adonis' staring down at us.

I turned away and continued dancing. Not long after, I felt a pressure on my lower back. I whipped around to find a pair of blue eyes looking down at me. The man was tall, couldn't be older than thirty. He was decent looking. His hair was buzzed, his beard was long, and he had a tattoo of a cross splayed across his forearm. He smiled at me. "Hi, I'm Hunter."

"Penelope!" I shouted over the music.

"Penelope, do you want to dance with me?" His smile seemed sincere. I wasn't sure how these things worked. Is this how you met people at clubs? You just asked utter strangers to dance with you? That seemed weird to me. I looked up at the second floor again, and Carter wasn't even there. He wasn't even watching me anymore.

With that, I shrugged and nodded at Hunter. He brought his hand back to my hip when his shoulder was pulled back suddenly by an invisible force.

No, not invisible. It was a hand. A dark hand, with a way-too-fancy watch on its wrist. Hazel eyes blazed at us, fixated on Hunter's arm that splayed across my waist. "She's not available," Carter said. To Hunter, it sounded like a stern statement accompanied by a stoic face. For me, it was a growling assertion in comparison to his usual demeanor.

I tried to determine if I was embarrassed or turned on. Or if I should be embarrassed that I'm turned on. I couldn't believe he was doing this. At the same time, this was exactly the reaction I wanted from him earlier. Hunter's hand left me and he gave me a look that asked: *who the fuck is this guy?* I looked at Carter and saw pure fury in his eyes. The only color winning the war tonight was red. Or maybe green. I wanted to hate that I loved it. Really, I love that I love it. Looking back at Hunter I mouthed: *my brother.* Hunter only shrugged before sauntering away.

Carter was staring after me. "I'm not available?" I asked.

"Your brother?" His eyes were still glinting with something I couldn't recognize.

"I didn't need you to protect me." I didn't *need* him to step in. I had just *wanted* him to.

Carter slid his hand up my arm and yanked me into him. He leaned his head down until his mouth met my ear and whispered, "I'm not protecting *you.* I'm protecting myself."

I leaned back. "Protecting yourself?"

He resumed his previous position, his arm holding me by the elbow. His lips weren't touching me, but they might as well have. I could feel the air blow across my ear as he spoke, sending chills up my spine. "Seeing another man's hands on you is fucking infuriating, Penelope."

My knees went weak and my stomach dropped between my legs. *Yes, please say more things like that.*

I straightened myself and tried not to appear affected by his words. I was far too into the game we were playing."Well, I'm not done dancing."

"What does that mean?"

I inhaled and craned my head so that my mouth was at the base of his neck. "It means, if you don't want anyone else touching me, you better do something about that. I'm not leaving." I turned around again, walking back to the center of the dance floor.

I found Macie at the corner of the dance floor, talking to Dom. He caught my eye and waved at me again, more exaggerated than before. I waved back. I noticed him looking Macie up and down, eyes lingering on the hem of her sparkly dress. He craned his neck toward the dance floor. She laughed, and I thought I may have seen her blush before she shook her head. She pointed above them, toward the second floor where I knew Jeremy was sitting. Dom nodded, then held his hands up in front of him as if surrendering. Macie shrugged before they both ended up dancing again. They didn't touch. Macie took over the space as she had before, almost as if she was a force of nature. Dom watched her as if he'd never seen anything like it.

Only a moment later, a pressure came to my lower back, mixed with the scent of fresh rain. I didn't need to turn around to know who it was. Both hands slid slowly from my back and onto my hips. I put my hands over his to let him know it was okay. I pushed my body lightly against him to show him I approved of what he was doing.

He took my hands and guided them up to wrap around the back of his neck. I felt his hands then melt down my body as his arms coiled around my waist. I felt electric as our bodies moved in sync to the rhythm of the music. It felt almost artistic as we painted the dance floor, him the hand and me the brush. He spun me around to face him as my hands interlaced behind his head. He explored my body and a sense of familiarity washed over me. It was the same way he moved against me during that kiss all those years ago. I let my head drop back, focused solely on his touch. The club, the people, and even the music, seemed to melt away as we danced. I closed my eyes and felt his presence all around me. The heat of his body, the way his nose glided up my neck and against my cheek, coming to rest against my forehead. One song could've passed, or twelve, I had no way of knowing.

I opened my eyes to find him looking down at me. Forehead to forehead, nose to nose, mouth to mouth– almost. I could feel his breath against my lips, hot and wanting. That hunger was back in his eyes and I was sure mine were giving off the same thing. The past and the future made no difference to me now. Everything around me ceased to exist except for him.

"Kiss me," I begged.

A tortured sound rose from the back of his throat. He closed his eyes and leaned in until his lips feathered against mine. He exhaled against my mouth. "Not here, Pep."

"Take me home, then."

He smiled against my lips, but it still wasn't enough. He shook his head softly. "Not when we're drunk." I admired his resolve because I had none. If he offered it up, I'd fuck him in the bathroom right now.

He must've read my expression, my disappointment. Because he leaned into my ear, close enough that I'd be able to hear him clearly. That there'd be no mistaking his words. "Penelope, when I kiss you, I need you entirely sober. The only thing I want intoxicating you is me."

He pulled back and studied me. All I could do was blink. And blaze. And melt.

"Take me home anyway. Let's go home and go to bed." If he would give me nothing else tonight, I just didn't want the touching to stop. I wanted to fall asleep in his arms.

"Anything for you."

I felt a little empty as his hands pulled away from me, but he grabbed my wrist and maneuvered us through the crowd. We spent less than a minute grabbing my purse and saying goodbye to our friends. Dom seemed to be getting along well with Macie, and as usual, Jeremy was glued to his phone. I almost felt bad leaving them there, but not bad enough to ignore how good it felt to leave with Carter.

Carter ordered us an Uber, and after arriving back at the villa, I was already sobering up. We readied for bed in silence, and I was thankful I had remembered to set up the hide-away bed before we left. I looked over at Carter as I pulled the covers back and crawled into it. He leaned against the wall that separated the front door from the kitchen. "I won't hold what you said in the club against you. Do you want me to sleep on the floor?"

"Get in the bed," I demanded as I turned over and flipped out the light. In the second it took the room to fade from light to dark, the bed dipped and two strong arms came around me. One across my pillow and underneath my cheek, the other across my stomach. His knee tucked between my legs and his chin at the base of my neck. His fingers stroked a circle around my thigh, soothing me to sleep.

Somewhere in the darkness between dreaming and consciousness, I thought I heard him whisper, "You're all I ever wanted, Pep."

"A soulmate is not a person you find, but one who helps you find your soul."

-Jeffrey Fry

Carter

A sharp, radiating pain in my kneecap woke me from my sleep.

After taking several seconds to adjust to my surroundings and remember where I was, my arm instinctively spread across the mattress searching for her. My hand met her arm and I opened my eyes. I shivered a little as I realized she'd stolen all the blankets, and that pain in my kneecap was her foot. I slid my arm behind my head to prop myself up and looked at her, realizing that she was laid out, stomach down, across the bed, every blanket piled on top of her.

She turned her head my way and her eyes popped open. Her eyelashes fluttered as she registered her surroundings. I smiled at her as she began to take me in and her eyes went wide. My heart stilled in realization that maybe she didn't remember last night. She wasn't that intoxicated. But maybe she didn't remember asking me to come to bed with her. Maybe she wasn't okay with this. Maybe she thought–

"You don't have any covers," she stated groggily.

My heart began to beat again.

"You stole them," I chuckled.

She lifted her head and looked down at herself, just realizing the cocoon she was wrapped in. "Oh, shit. Sorry." She began to fuss underneath the blankets. Kicking around and moving her arms to get out of them, but she was so tightly wound that she was only making herself more stuck. "Dammit," she muttered.

I leaned over her and pulled the blankets away from her. She lifted her hips so I could grab them from underneath her. Then, I pulled the sheet over both our heads and laid next to her. I just needed one moment with her– cut off from the rest of the world. Morning light shone through the window behind her head, and even through the sheet it illuminated the space around her. Like a halo.

I couldn't kiss her last night. I couldn't kiss her because I didn't know what she meant when she asked me to. She was intoxicated from tequila, but I was intoxicated from her. I think that kiss would've meant two very different things for us. I didn't know what she wanted in the long run. I could only remember the last time I kissed her, and the words she'd said after.

I can't do this.

My soul couldn't handle hearing them again. Not from her. My soul was tormented by her. My body was tortured, and I was terrified of the potential fallout of it. So, if all she wanted was a drunken release– I couldn't handle that.

Yet, finding myself beneath the covers with her felt like the rest of it didn't matter quite so much. It felt like nothing existed outside of this little bubble we'd created, that no decision we made here would have consequences outside of it. I knew how stupid that sounded, but I propped myself onto my elbow and let my fingers dance across her collar bone anyway. Her breath hitched as I made contact with her skin. Her eyes sparkled, even in the muted tones underneath the sheet covering us.

I ran my hand up her neck and across her jaw, savoring every inch she allowed me to touch. I ran my thumb across her bottom lip, considering whether I had the courage to close the gap this time. Her chest moved faster as my thumb met her mouth. She stared at me in anticipation and I decided that maybe I wasn't concerned about falling out of orbit with her. Maybe I was ready for our planets to collide.

If kissing her now, or if one night with her was all I'd ever get–it'd be enough.

A door opened somewhere in the distance, but it didn't register in my ears as I fixated on her lips. Her eyes, her flushed cheeks, and her dancing freckles. The curve of her hips and the way one leg bent over the other. How her legs looked a million miles long when they're not hidden underneath clothing. I noticed—for the first time—the freckles that dotted her chest, matching those across her nose.

"Shit. Sorry. I thought I'd be in the clear by now," Macie's shocked voice quipped from the hall. Penelope and I froze, looking at each other. Footsteps began to retreat, and I sighed in relief at the thought of getting the moment back. "I just...Penny, do you know what time it is?"

Penelope's eyebrows clustered at her forehead. She threw the sheet off us and sat up. I turned over just in time to watch Macie shield her eyes. "We're not naked." I laughed. She hesitantly lowered her hand and opened one eye as if she didn't fully believe me.

"What time is it?" Penelope asked.

"A little after nine," Macie confirmed.

"Fuck!" Penelope hissed as she jumped from the bed and began to storm around the room in a flurry, almost like a cartoon character. After a moment of her running in circles, the bathroom door slammed shut. I leaned back against the top of the couch and crossed my arms. Macie mimicked my pose as she leaned against the doorway that led from the hallway to the kitchen, giving me a smirk.

"Nothing happened," I said.

"Sure it didn't. It's fine, you can lie to me now. She's just going to tell me everything later."

I chuckled, "I know that. That's why I'm not lying. Nothing happened."

She frowned. "You were in bed together. Penny didn't have any pants on."

I rolled my eyes at her lack of boundaries. "Other than sharing the bed, nothing happened."

"So, you guys pretty much skipped all the steamy shit and went straight to the old married couple shit?" Her response had me cackling. "You've got it bad, Mr. Carter." I shrugged because I couldn't argue with her. "You know she does too, right?"

I shrugged again, but this time because I wasn't sure I believed it.

Macie opened her mouth to say something, but the bathroom door swung back open and Penelope walked out. She'd pulled her hair back into a tight bun at the base of her neck. She had on a solid black dress, tight down the middle, accentuating her curves. It had frilly sleeves and stopped at the knees. It was nothing like what she wore last night. I think I liked it more, though. It was her.

She paid no mind to Macie and I as she flew back through the room and frantically finished readying herself for the conference. "I need to take the rental car, I don't have enough time to Uber," she said breathlessly as she squatted down and sifted through her bag.

"That's fine. Jeremy and I planned on laying out on the beach anyway," Macie said. "Oh, and we're going to dinner later tonight–just the two of us. We'll probably be back late." She winked at me.

Penelope nodded as if Macie's comment didn't fully register. She then looked at me expectantly. "I'm just meeting up with Dom today, but I can have him pick me up," I said. She nodded. "I might go catch a wave when I get back. I found a couple of boards in a shed against the side of the house. You want me to wait for you?" I grinned.

She shook her head without looking at me. "No, that's okay." She said it without a hint of the playful tone I was trying to pull out of her. She stood up and straightened out her dress before grabbing her purse and making her way to the front door. I hopped out of bed and reached her in two strides. She looked at me impatiently.

I grabbed her forearms. "Hey, you're going to do great today. You know that, right?" She dropped her eyes and looked down at the floor. She was nervous. She was frustrated that she overslept, that she forgot to set her alarm. She's regretting last night. Regretting the drinking, the staying out late, the distractions.

I don't want her to regret me.

I moved one arm to her chin and tilted it up so her face would meet my eyes. "You are the smartest person in every room you walk into, including that conference. Just be yourself. By the end of the day, they'll love you so much they'll be begging you to attend Pepperdine."

She smiled softly and nodded once. Her eyelashes batted and her lips pouted, and I wanted to kiss her. *God, I want to kiss her.* But she was in a hurry, and she was nervous and already overthinking things. Macie was still standing in the hallway staring at us. The moment wasn't right. Instead, I moved my hands from her arms and slid them around her waist, pulling her into me. She sighed against my chest and one arm found my lower back. I kissed the top of her head and wished her luck. She smiled again and slipped through the front door without another word.

I turned back to Macie who was still staring from the door to her bedroom. I waited for her to make a comment, but she didn't. Her face looked strained, almost sad. I watched her for a long moment before she blinked a few times and shook her head. It seemed as if she didn't realize she had been watching us. Or that I was now watching her. She smiled once and retreated into her room.

"Sorry you had to drive all the way out here to get me," I said to Dom as I climbed into his car. I took mental note of the fact that he was driving an Audi. Brand new, by the looks of it. "Pep had to take the rental car."

He smiled at me and mouthed, *Pep*, before turning back to the road. "It's all good. I've got something I wanted to show you in Venice anyway. Plus, I'm never going to complain about a drive along the PCH."

"I wouldn't complain about any drive in this car."

He smiled at me again, his perfectly straight teeth gleaming. "Isn't she pretty?"

I rolled my eyes but nodded. It had been over a year since the last time I saw Dom. We made a point of seeing each other at least that much. It was easier right after high school. He didn't move right away, even after he did, we always made sure to go visit our parents at the same time. Until a couple of years ago when his parents moved to Arizona to be closer to family. Maybe even more than everything else, I moved back to the mainland for him. To make it easier to see him. As much as it hurt to admit, he was more a constant in my life than either of my parents. He was a lot of the reason I considered California as the place to come next.

We flew down the highway with the windows down. The aquamarine of the sea and the periwinkle of the sky clashed together, making the entire world a piercing azure. He looked at me again with a question in his expression, though his face was difficult to read with his eyes hidden behind his sunglasses. "So, Pep."

I shook my head. "Can it wait until we get to the restaurant, please?"

"I've got somewhere I wanted to show you first."

We spent the rest of the ride to wherever it was he was taking me, talking about his life here. His work as a realtor and his friends. All the things he's seen and done. I know it's a coveted way of convincing me to move down here. He's been hung up on the idea ever since I mentioned it a few months ago. But damn if he wasn't a good salesman. It was easy for Dom and I to fall back into our friendship. Bicker and joke as if no time had passed. There were no boundaries between the two of us. He may be the person who knows me better than anyone, which meant he already knew there was a larger conversation to be had about Penelope. He was the only person who knew the extent in which she'd haunted my dreams.

"So, Penelope's friend, Macie," he said after a few moments of silent driving. He didn't look at me when he said it.

"She's unavailable," I stated.

"Yeah, well, her boyfriend's a douchebag."

I snorted. "He didn't leave you with a great first impression?"

He shook his head. "What kind of idiot has a woman who looks like *that* and leaves herto dance alone? He hardly even noticed her. If she'd been on my arm, I wouldn't have been able to keep my hands off her. I would've been looking like *you* out there."

I laughed. I shouldn't have been surprised that Macie caught his eye. He always liked girls who glittered like she did. Girls who were loud, who demanded attention, and knew what they wanted out of life.

"For once, I agree with you on something. Jeremy doesn't let her... sparkle?" I shook my head. That was the only way I could describe it.

Dom grunted.

He pulled into the carport behind what appeared to be a three-story apartment building off the highway. It was a white-washed building with blue shutters on every window. I could see the upper floors had two balconies on each side. Taking a closer look, it appeared the bottom part of the building may be some kind of retail space. Dom turned the car off and stepped out of it before throwing his arms out wide as if he was presenting it.

"Do you live here or something?" I asked.

"I wish I could afford to live on Venice Beach."

I arched a brow and nodded toward the car. "You drive an Audi, dude."

He chuckled. "I drive an Audi *because* I live in a dump." He pulled out his keys and waved toward the backdoor of the building, beckoning me to follow. "Anyway, Tom and I have been talking. He wanted me to show you this."

My father?

"What the hell are you talking about?"

He didn't respond as he opened the door and stepped inside. I followed him in and took immediate notice of the way the bottom floor was one huge room. How there were panels of wall constructed throughout the large space strategically. I took note of the two smaller rooms on either side of the studio space. They had no doors, they weren't meant to be cut off, just separate. Ahead of me there was a long wall of paneled windows that stared straight out at the ocean across the street. A front door that matched the shade of the shutters outside stood next to the panel windows. I knew exactly what this was supposed to be. "It's a gallery," I said.

I noticed that he was chewing on the inside of his cheek. He was nervous, gauging my reaction. "That's what the owner wanted. Until she went bankrupt. She's selling now. Before she owned it, this was a clothing store." I shot a look that told him to continue. "My point being that it could be whatever you want."

"I'm not following," I said.

"I've been talking to your dad for a while. He's interested in buying some investment property, and I convinced him that this is a good area for it."

"How come neither of you told me?" I asked.

"At first, he was just asking some general questions about real estate. I didn't think it was anything worth mentioning to you. I just...You mentioned moving here after your contract with the school is up. The seller contacted my office a couple of weeks ago, and I haven't been able to get this property out of my head since. Then, you told me you'd be coming down here *with* Penelope. I couldn't *not* show it to you."

My laugh echoed through the empty room as I ran a hand through my hair. "I was so drunk that night, Dom. You know that was just some... some drunken thought I decided to share out loud."

"You meant it," he said quietly.

"It doesn't matter," I rubbed the tension out of my jaw.

"I saw you guys' last night."

I shook my head. "It's not like that. We didn't– nothing happened."

"It's *always* been like that, Carter." He sighed. "How long did it take you?" I looked at him, eyes narrowed in confusion. "To fall back in love with her."

I cupped my neck and paced the floor in front of me. I thought back to what I'd told him after my first photos were published in *This Week Hawaii*. The issue happened to get published while I was visiting my parents for Thanksgiving, only about a month after my twenty-first birthday. Dom took me out to celebrate, and several shots later we found ourselves huddled around my parent's firepit in their backyard. I was crying, admitting that I still thought about Penelope all the time. Wishing I could share the news with her about my publication. Wondering out loud whether she still drew, or if she ever got into painting. I told Dom about the dream I had of opening an art gallery, filled partly with my photos and partly with her paintings. In a different lifetime, perhaps.

"You really think it's a coincidence?" he asked. My head snapped up in question. "That you guys just so happened to work at the same school? That you both moved back in with your parents at the same time?"

"Yes. My dad set up the job for both of us. He's on the school board. It's not that spectacular of a circumstance," I argued.

He shook his head in defeat. "There are eight two-bedroom apartments above the studio. Four on the second floor and four more on the third. I showed it to your dad last week. He likes it. You could live in one of the units, manage the other seven to offset the cost of your rent. You could still travel, build your portfolio, sell your work. Do whatever you want with the bottom floor, or nothing at all. If you filled all seven units, your dad would make a profit." He walked to the back door and held it open for me. As I passed him, he said, "You didn't answer my question."

"I never stopped," I murmured, exiting the building and climbing into the car.

"I will look for you in every lifetime
and love you there."

-Kamand Kojouri

Penelope

I began the descent down the steep steps behind the villa that led to the beach. I tried not to think too much about having to climb back up them later. The villa was empty when I got back from the conference. Carter mentioned something about going surfing after seeing Dom, and I knew Macie and Jeremy were going to get dinner. It was after seven, so I wasn't surprised they were gone already.

I told myself that I wasn't going down there to look for Carter, specifically. I wanted to watch the sunset, even if I was doing it alone. I was still reeling from waking up next to him this morning. Waking up next to him and missing my alarm.

I wasn't the kind of person who missed alarms. Who was late to things. I normally wasn't the type of person who went out the night before an academic conference. Or, better yet, I normally wasn't the type of person who got drunk and begged people to kiss me. Take me to bed. Except, maybe I was. Maybe I am, now. I couldn't decide if it was Carter's influence on me or Macie's that had me behaving this way. I couldn't decide whether it was good or bad.

I always struggled with that– balance. I had very specific goals in life, and it had been my experience thus far that those goals didn't go hand in hand with a fun, carefree nature. When I got to Oxford, I met James and he rationalized every belief I'd ever had that balance wouldn't exist for the exceptionally ambitious. He'd reinforced all the ideas I had that if I wanted to excel in my industry; get my PhD, travel the world, discover lost cities– I'd have to give up everything else. There'd be no family, no children, few friends. For a long, long, time I believed him. I accepted it.

Sometimes I'm not even entirely sure why I want to be an archaeologist. All I know is that it's the only thing about myself that I feel isn't in constant limbo, ever changing and impossible for me to grasp onto. When I was about five, I fell in love with that Disney movie, *Atlantis*. I became obsessed with the legends of Atlantis. I wanted to find it. I was convinced it was real. My mom told me I should become an archaeologist, and I've never wanted to be anything else since.

I'd always struggled with finding balance, but never ambition. James used that to his advantage. He found me alone, on the opposite end of the world from everything I'd ever known. Lost and forgetting who I was. Forgetting who I wanted to become. He fed on those weaknesses like a vulture, until only scraps of me were left. When things went sideways, he left me for dead.

Sometimes I still feel like I'm just in scraps. I don't know which scraps are really me and which scraps are the me that he created. Carter makes me feel like I can still feel myself, somewhere deep inside. I want so badly to pull her out. But sometimes, I don't know if Carter's making me see the real me, or if he too is creating a version of me for himself. Not intentionally, not on purpose. But maybe I'm such a broken shell that I can't help but mold into what others want.

Because, somehow, I don't think I'm the type of person who forgets to set my alarm.

I want to be fun. I want to be carefree. I want love, and life, and friends. But I also want success. I want to travel the world. Discover lost cities. Find Atlantis. That part is the only part I know is me. Before James, before Carter, before I was adopted, before my mom died.

I wanted to find Atlantis.

I stumbled down the last of the steps feeling faintly nauseated, as thinking about James often made me. I sat down on the bottom step and peered out into the horizon as I let the setting sun warm my face. My eyes caught sight of the broad shoulder silhouette who was now staring at me. Backlit by the sun, it was difficult to make out his features, but I knew he was smiling at me. His arms moved to the center of his chest, and then lifted to his face. He was holding something, but it took me a second to realize it was a camera.

I heard one shutter, then two. Then, I flipped him off.

I could hear the thunder erupting from his mouth as he stumbled back a step and held his chest, as if I'd wounded him. I looked away to hide my smile, and no sooner did he begin to yell my name. Incessantly. I reluctantly got up and made my way towards him, if for no other reason than to shut him up. And maybe because I missed him too.

"I thought you were going surfing?"

"Waves are mush." He shrugged. I nodded, pretending to know what that meant. He smiled because he knew that I didn't. "Decided I'd try to get some pictures of the sunset."

"Well, don't stop on account of me. Get back to work." I shooed him toward the landscape behind him. The gold was fading into orange as it dipped below the horizon. He gave me *that* grin and stepped back a couple of paces before turning around. I watched him for a couple of minutes. He would tilt his head as if he was seeing something nobody else could see. Take a few steps in one direction or another, squat down, angle his camera, and move again. He seemed fluid, natural. In his element.

I watched the world change color across his face. His expression was determined, calculated. He studied the space around him, and I wanted to know so badly what he was seeing. He jogged backward a few paces and cut across the sand in front of me. He shuffled sideways, snapping pictures as he went, until he was knee deep in the tide. He seemed to be moving with urgency, as the sun was seemingly setting faster behind the earth. He moved deeper until the water reached his waist. He began splashing water in the area right before he took the photos. When a large enough wave came through, he'd bend at the crest of it, seeming to attempt catching the sun within it.

It was mesmerizing; the way he created art with nothing but the world around him.

Once the orb of the sun had finally peaked, he waded out of the water and placed the lens cap on his camera, letting it hang around his neck. He ran a wet hand through his hair, damping his curls. Without saying a word, he grabbed my hand and walked with me back to the steps that would lead up to the rental house.

"How was the conference? Did you blow them away?" he asked before adding, "You don't need to answer that, actually. You blow everyone away."

I hid my blush. "It went really well. I forgot how much I missed it."

"Missed what?"

"The academic environment. Being a student."

He glanced at me with a smile. "How do you feel about Pepperdine now?"

I thought for a moment before answering. We made it back to the stairs and he began to climb. I hesitated. The world wasn't quite dark yet, the cotton candy clouds still accenting the fading sky. He must've understood me because he instead sat down on the bottom step, and I sat next to him. "I think UCLA is still my first choice, but Pepperdine doesn't feel so much like a back-up school anymore. I think I'd be happy there."

He squeezed my hand and we watched the world move from day into night in silence.

We heard cheers from a handful of people in the distance. Only their silhouettes were visible, but a way down the beach, someone was on one knee, while another stood in front of them squealing with joy.

We both sighed, and then pretended we didn't hear each other.

"Did you ever think you'd marry him?"

"No." I cackled as if it was the most ridiculous sentiment I'd ever heard. "I don't really ever think about that at all, actually." Marriage rarely ever crossed my mind. I mostly thought about it in moments it was right in front of me, like the proposal we just watched. I never thought about it with James. He didn't want me to believe in marriage. He guided me away from any belief that something like that could work for someone like me.

His face twisted into something unreadable. "What? You don't have a dream wedding? Something you've imagined since you were a kid?"

I chuckled. "Oh, of course I do." I used to love looking through my parent's wedding album when I was little. I used to imagine what kind of dress I'd wear or what color theme I'd go with. As I got older, I realized that my parents were the exception, not the rule. I wasn't sure if I had what it took to be another exception, so I just stopped thinking about it entirely. Now, the thought of being paraded down an aisle and having to profess my love in front of people– it freaked me out. If it were to ever happen for me, I think I'd find myself as more of a civil ceremony type of person. "A wedding and a marriage are two very different things."

"Why does marriage scare you?"

I snorted. "I didn't say it scares me. I said I don't think about it."

He tilted his head as if he didn't entirely believe me. "Okay, then. Why don't you think about it?"

I chewed on the inside of my cheek. "I want to be a doctor. I want to travel. I want to study the Wonders of the World and find ancient civilizations that we don't even know about yet. That's my priority, and I don't know if I have the focus for much else. I'm afraid I wouldn't be able to put another person before my career goals... and, well, who would want to deal with that?"

He glanced down at his clasped hands thoughtfully. "So, you're saying there are no archaeologists out there that are married? That have families? No way to do both?"

That stung. He couldn't have known that it would and wouldn't understand why. I did, in fact, know a married archaeologist that has a family. *Had* a family. Until he ruined it. Until *I* ruined it. "I'm not saying that. But I've seen the way this kind of career can destroy a relationship."

"Sounds like it's just about finding the right person. Someone who accepts everything you are. Everything you want to be. Who wants to see you succeed just as much as you want to yourself. Your *soulmate*, or whatever." He grinned.

"Exactly. Shouldn't that be the prerequisite for marriage?"

"Ah, so that's why you're afraid of marriage, then. Because you don't believe in soulmates."

I shoved him playfully, rolling my eyes. "I didn't say I don't believe. I said it's rare. Much rarer than marriage is."

"You're afraid of marrying someone who isn't actually your soulmate."

"I guess." I shrugged. He kind of hit the nail on the head, but I didn't realize that was the way I felt until he said it. That was the thing I was actually afraid of.

"Why?"

"Imagine you die, and you show up wherever it is we go after that. What if you get there and you're given your soulmate, and they end up being someone different than the person you spent your whole life loving?"

He spent a moment considering what I'd said. "Maybe that's why they say, 'til death do us part.' It's the only promise we can make. We don't know what will happen after that."

"I don't think I could do that," I said, shaking my head. "I don't think I could agree to just life. If I loved someone enough to marry them, if I found the person I thought was my one-in-eight-hundred-million, then just this lifetime wouldn't be enough for me."

His face was relaxed but deep in his thoughts. He stared at the darkening water, but I knew he wasn't seeing it. I was staring at him, but I realized I wasn't seeing him either. Not really. I felt like I was seeing through him. Through his skin, his muscles, his bones. All the way down into his soul. I wondered if just a lifetime with him would be enough. Not as a friend, or neighbor, or even a lover, but as a person. Would I get to know him beyond this life? Beyond the bodies that we're in right now? Not knowing the answer to that question terrified me.

Because I wanted to know him in every lifetime.

I hoarded that thought inside my gut, unwilling to consider what it may mean. "How can you promise more than just this life? That's what a vow is. That's the vow you make when you get married because you can't promise anything beyond that."

"Isn't that the point, though? Shouldn't we be able to promise, 'I'll love you beyond this life. No matter what, my soul will find yours, every time.' Isn't that the goal? To love someone so much that we believe even death couldn't keep us apart. That we'd continue to find each other again and again?" The words flew through my throat on their own accord. I had no control over them as they spilled from my body.

Breaking his focus on the water, his head snapped to mine. His face twisted into so many emotions, and yet I was unable to decipher a single one. I could see the pools of light reflecting in his eyes as the sun fell, changing the color of them with it. I didn't break the contact either as he looked into mine. For a long while, we just looked at each other. He smirked as he broke the silence. "You've got a lot of soulmate theories for someone who doesn't believe in love."

I stifled a laugh. "I didn't say I don't believe in love, you ass."

"Right. Just that it's repulsive," he shot back. "Doesn't that kind of contradict your main theory, though? The one about the atoms traveling across a millennium to find their O.G. companions?"

I blushed at his remembrance of my soulmate theory. "Yeah, I guess it does. Except, maybe it's not across a millennium, just a lifetime. Maybe when we die, our atoms get blasted across the universe. Like our own personal Big Bang. Then, as we begin our next lifetime, the atoms work to find their way back to each other again, the form of two new beings."

He shook his head with a soft laugh, this one rainfall where it's normally thunder. "Oh, so we believe in reincarnation too now?"

I nodded. "Definitely."

"Maybe that explains why people meet their soulmate at different points in life. Maybe if one person dies first in the previous lifetime, they have to spend time in the new one waiting for their soulmate to catch up. Or maybe that's why some people don't find their soulmate at all. They're living in different lifetimes and haven't met yet."

I flicked my brow at him. "Look who's stuck on soulmate theories now."

"You got me hooked, Pep. Next thing you know I'll be spouting off Atlantis conspiracies."

"I look forward to that," I said, my voice dripping with a tone I didn't intend to produce. I cleared my throat. "Maybe people who meet their soulmates as children died at the same time in their past lives. Now, they get this whole new life together."

He smiled, bringing his mouth to my hand and letting his lips feather against my knuckles. We watched the rest of the sunset in silence. Once it dropped completely below the horizon, and the sky had that flash that suddenly moved the world around us from day to night, Carter stood and tugged at my arm. I allowed him to lead me back to the house. We took the climb slowly. Mostly, because I'm out of shape. Carter matched my pace anyway.

When we finally got up that last step and into the house, I headed straight for the kitchen. He followed me in and sat at one of the bar stools as I stumbled through the fridge for wine that I knew Macie opened the night before. "Did you eat?" I asked.

"I did. Dom and I had a late lunch, early dinner. Linner, if you will."

I lost control of my laugh, which came up faster than my mouth could open. The sound of an out of tune trumpet—or maybe a dying elephant—tore from my nose. Once I caught my breath, I peeked up at him behind the fridge. It wasn't even that the word itself was funny, but the way he said it so casually. As if it was a part of his everyday vocabulary. "Linner?"

His mouth was gaping, his eyes huge. "What the fuck kind of sound did you just make?" I laughed a second time, but again, it came out as a rumbling snort. "Did you just snort?"

"Stop," I pleaded between fits of laughter.

He quieted suddenly. I couldn't see him as I bent into the fridge. "You know I think you're the most beautiful girl in the world, right?" I snapped up and looked at him, opening and closing my mouth several times, unsure of what to say. A wicked grin tugged at his lips. "But that might have been the ugliest noise I've ever heard come out of that pretty mouth."

I knew my face had dropped into a look of pure vexation. *Ass.*

Roaring laughter flew from his throat. He threw his head back, pure delight dancing on his face. I peeked back into the fridge, ignoring him. I grabbed the bottle of wine and slammed the door shut. Without facing him, I opened a cabinet and pulled out two glasses. Before I turned, I straightened my face into an expression that I hoped looked sultry and spun on my heel. "You think my mouth is pretty?" I asked, my voice dripping with seductive curiosity.

His laughing ceased. His eyes glimmered with pleasant surprise, and his mouth parted slightly. I watched his tongue glisten his lips as he watched me walk towards him. "Devastating," he said, his voice rough.

The chemistry between us was a tangible thing. The tension alone was enough to send me over the edge most nights. When I'd allow myself to picture him. His hands– where'd they explore, where they'd touch. His lips– where'd they kiss, his tongue. I'd think about his mouth, his voice. What it would sound like when he moaned my name. I shivered.

Just the thought of him brought me to my peak more often than not, and I knew that the moment I'd gain the real thing, I'd be ruined. I didn't need to test the theory. I knew that nobody else would ever compare to him. That awareness used to scare me. Scare me to the point of retreat from him. I'd given up on that a while ago. No matter how brief, how fleeting, I wouldn't deny myself this anymore. Deny both of us this feeling regardless of the fallout.

I pulled my eyes back to him. He was still glimmering at me. *He was taking the bait.*

"Wine?" I asked. He only nodded. He had moved from the barstool on the other side of the counter and was now standing next to me. Once I'd poured both glasses, I turned to him, my chest so close it'd brush against him if I only arched enough. So, I did. He saw it coming, and he began to smile. I could almost see the scenes that began to play out in his head. The ones that started on this counter and ended on the couch. Clothes strewn across the room. He'd seen the look in my eye as I thought about his hands, his mouth, his tongue. He thought he knew where I was headed.

I felt playful. It was a rare feeling for me. Something I was unwilling to let go of just yet. As I arched my back, I *accidentally* tipped his glass of wine and watched it spill through down his shirt. Soaking the fabric right into his perfect skin. "Oops. Me and my ugly snorts are a bit clumsy. Sorry." I set his now empty glass of wine down on the counter next to us and leaned back, sipping on my own full glass smugly.

After staring down at his shirt for several moments, his eyes found my face. He read my expression as if that was the telling factor that it had all been on purpose, as if he hadn't even heard my words. Then, he smiled. It was *that* smile. That grin. He lifted his shirt from the back of the neck and pulled it over his shoulders in one fluid motion. He tossed it across the room and I suddenly found myself face to face with his chiseled chest. His muscles were hard, his skin soft. Broad in all the right places and tapered in others. Then, there were the sprawling rays of sun that swirled along his body, filled inside with different symbols. The clash of the ink against his golden skin. The rough and smooth, the hard and soft, it was enough to make me pant. Late at night I thought about his hands, I thought about all the things he could do with that body. All those nights—all those thoughts—had done nothing to prepare me for what stood in front of me now.

He's beautiful. I knew he'd heard my breath hitch as I took him in. He re-poured his glass of wine and looked at me, his gaze piercing me until I finally moved my eyes from his body to his face. He raised a brow and smirked, as if to say *checkmate*. I leaned back against the counter. It wasn't far enough, not enough distance to cool the heat that pooled between my thighs. This game felt a little like foreplay– who'd last the longest before giving in. I launched myself up onto the counter, allowing my legs to dangle off the edge. A little space from him, to keep me from losing the game already.

I cleared my throat in an obvious manner and attempted to change the subject to something more casual. "What do all the symbols inside your tattoo mean?"

His eyes flickered with uncertainty, but swiftly relaxed into his classic breezy expression. He pointed to a place on his bicep, a set of symbols that looked like waves. "Those are waves." He laughed.

His hand drew up to his shoulder, resting on rows of triangles. "Those represent shark teeth."

"Do you like sharks?"

Stupid fucking question. I couldn't think straight.

He smiled knowingly. "It's not personally my favorite animal, but they are highly respected in Hawaiian culture. They're believed to represent strength. A lot of my tattoo is made up of waves because I surf. I made a career photographing the beaches– the water. I must respect the ocean and all it's given me. Sharks are a big part of that, and I think that incorporating them into this gives me strength when I'm far away."

"I love that," I whispered.

He laughed. He pointed at a design on the top of his shoulder that kind of looked like a flower. "That means wisdom." And his hand dragged to his chest, to something that looked like a hook. "Courage."

I leaned into the cupboards above my head, as if to admire the tattoo from a grander distance. "You know, the whole thing kind of looks like a big sun. The symbol for wisdom on your shoulder looks like the center, and all the other rays that snake out from there down your arm and across your chest."

"Yeah, that was my own little touch. I told the artist what I wanted incorporated, but she handled most of the design itself. I told her I wanted to have the sun involved in some way. A tribute to my mom. She always called me her *ray of sunshine.*"

I noticed that he'd taken a step closer to me, inching into me little by little as the conversation had bloomed. He was almost in between my legs, but we hadn't touched quite yet. He was still playing the game. He'd been closing in on me, hoping the focus on his bare skin would break me. Instead, it entranced me. Instinctively, I reached out and traced my hand across his chest before realizing my actions and snapping it back quickly. "I'm sorry, I don't know why I did that."

I'd expected the night to lean toward touching, hoped it would. But sometime between the moment I asked what his tattoo meant, and the time I glided my hand across it, things had become intimate. Intimate in a way that wasn't sexual. Or physical. He'd told me about his tattoo, something that was deeply important to him. And although I was sure he didn't mind my touch, I wasn't sure if it had been right for me to touch him there. To snake my fingers across something that quite literally bared the depths of his soul.

He grabbed my hand and put it back on his body, right over the center of his sun. The heat of his skin felt nearly electric. He nudged my knees with his thighs and stepped between them, peering down at me intently. "You can touch me, Penelope."

I pulled my gaze from his chest, from the place he held my hand against, and looked up at him. His eyes sparkled with cocoa undertones.

Brown was winning the war today.

I think I loved his eyes the most when they looked brown. Or maybe it was just because that's how they looked right now. They were hungry, yes. There was something more that shimmered behind them, though. Something that felt like yearning, understanding– love. I allowed my instincts to continue their driving force as I traced the line of one of the rays of sunshine up his peck and across his sternum, until I reached his throat. My fingers continued their journey to his jawline– to his lips. I studied them. The way they parted, seemingly with permission. How his breath escaped through them in short, shallow bursts. I ran my thumb across his silky lower lip, savoring the way it felt against my skin.

A sound rumbled from deep in his chest, almost impatient. "Penelope," he rasped, my thumb still on his mouth. The sound of my name rolling out of his throat in a tone deeper than I'd ever heard– it was my undoing. A whimper escaped me as he replaced my thumb with my lips. We both seemed to have forgotten about the game we'd been playing. There was no way to know who caved first, but we both won.

Where his first kiss was timid, this kiss was brazen. He braced himself on either side of the counter as his mouth smashed against my lips. I opened mine in invitation, clasping my hands behind his neck and pressing myself into him. It wasn't enough. I couldn't get close enough. I needed to feel more of him. All of him. My legs wrapped around his waist and something hard nuzzled against my inner thigh. A moan of approval escaped my throat.

I felt his smile against my mouth, and I slid my tongue across his teeth. He hissed as they parted to allow my tongue though. I entangled it with his, eager to explore, to memorize every part of his mouth. Yearning, searching, begging for the closeness I needed. He pressed farther into me, the hardness between his legs rubbing against the molten between mine. Painfully aware of the fact that all that separated us now were our clothes. His tongue stroked mine, his teeth nipped my bottom lip before sucking it beneath them.

He tasted like wine and the ocean.

He tasted like the sun, the stars.

He tasted like home.

He groaned into my mouth, and I swallowed it like he was water and I was parched. I arched my back, pressing my chest into his and his lips found my neck. He bit down, and then licked the spot where his teeth had been. Nipping and tasting his way down my neck until his lips reached the collar of my cardigan. He pulled at the scoping neckline until it was down past my shoulder. His mouth returned to my body at my collar bone.

He took his time there. He dragged his bottom lip across it, then followed back with his tongue. His fingers crawled up my bare thigh, underneath the hem of my cotton shorts. His mouth caressed my skin as it moved back up my neck, along my jaw, against my ear. I could feel the heat between us, the fire that we'd started with our lips– I could see it spread throughout the space around us. I could hear his heart pounding in rhythm with my own. His mouth found mine once more, and I could again taste the salt water that lingered on his skin. I could smell it in his hair, mixed with the smell of rain and the scent of his shampoo.

All of my senses were enveloped in him. Only he existed.

My hands descended down his chest, until I met the waistband of his shorts. His breath hitched against my mouth as my fingers met the buttons. I could feel him right beneath my fingertips, pressed against his lower abdomen. In a desperate hurry to remove what was between us, I fumbled with his zipper. His own hands moved quicker now, away from their place on my thigh and underneath my sweater. He began to lift it slowly– as if he was savoring each inch of exposed skin he was about to see. Our mouths did not leave each other as we worked to strip away the layers that separated us.

A door slammed in the distance. Too close to be the neighbors. We paused, the defeat in both of our eyes apparent as we pulled away from each other. The gravel outside crunched under two pairs of feet, hushed voices whispered back and forth. His face was slack in disappointment, and I was sure mine read annoyance. We didn't move, but I noticed him lean away, taking a slight step back. He was still in between my legs, but I could no longer feel the hardness against my thigh. He tugged the neck of my sweater back over my shoulder, his hands moved from my hips and to my face.

He leaned in once more and kissed me. This time it was tender, soft. He took his time with it, not even flinching as the front door opened. The fire between us, moments ago roaring and ready, had simmered into embers. A moment ago had been a promise of what was to come. The kiss he was giving me now was a gift. He pulled away just as the door clicked shut.

Macie and Jeremy appeared in the hall on the other side of the counter. Their expressions held no surprise as they stared after

Carter and I. Macie's expression felt faraway, almost as if she was unaware of her surroundings. Her eyes seemed red and puffy, like she had been crying. I glanced at Carter and noticed his forehead crinkled in worry. He saw it too. Jeremy waved and apologized quietly, making his way toward their bedroom. Macie smiled apologetically. "Sorry," she whispered.

Carter smiled at me softly, tucking a strand of my hair behind my ear before stepping away and leaning back against the counter. "Mace?" I asked. "Are you okay?"

She laughed unconvincingly. "Yeah, my allergies just really act up around here." She waved us off. "I'm going to sleep. We have an early flight tomorrow." Before I could get out another word, she slipped behind the bedroom door.

I huffed, unconvinced by her explanation. She'd never complained to me about allergies before. I looked at Carter, who was still leaning back against the counter, arms crossed, watching me. I chewed on my lip in concern. Carter scooted himself over to me and turned around until he was boxing me in. His body covered mine as I leaned back against the counter. I noticed his eyes roam my face, his expression unreadable. He stopped at my lips, his eyes focused. He paused like he was considering something before dipping his head and pressing his lips to mine. It was soft, hesitant, like it was straining him. It was almost painful– the way his mouth tensed just before he pulled away.

I moved to follow him until I found myself leaning far forward, my eyes popping open to find him leaning back. He tried to smile, but it didn't quite reach his eyes. I knew he could see that I was still leaning toward him, that I was trying to re-close the gap between us. He shook his head. "Pep," he whispered, seeming almost frustrated. I wasn't ready for it to be over. I needed more of him. "We shouldn't continue."

I recoiled back against the counter, feeling as if I had been punched. My forehead crinkled with concern. My stomach sank.

Earlier in the evening, for one small second, I believed that he may be my person. *That* person. I thought he felt it too. I was sure he did. Now, the way he looked at me with an apology plastered on his face told me that I was wrong. I was so, so wrong. Maybe everything I saw before wasn't real. Angry tears built behind my eyes.

The fire in my blood turned to ashes as my heart erupted, magma pouring out of it– soaking me in his rejection.

"And he would give her everything he had, every part of his soul, even the broken pieces."

-Lisa Kleypas

Carter

I winced as the bathroom door slammed shut, shaking the entire house with it.

I let out all of the air trapped in my lungs, blowing out the unspoken words that somehow got lodged inside me. All the things I should've said. I watched her face fall. I knew what it looked like—what it felt like—to face rejection upfront. I knew that was what she was feeling.

I had opened my mouth to try and explain myself, but I found that the words wouldn't come. My voice refused to follow my thoughts. I was too distracted by the devastation I found on her face, too afraid to make it worse. I just stared at her until her cheeks reddened to the point of crimson, and she dropped her head, shoving past me as she muttered something like *I get it,* and slammed the bathroom door behind her. I heard the pounding of the shower head from inside the bathroom and figured I'd have about ten minutes before facing her again.

Ten minutes to get my shit together and explain to her that my body often betrays me, and I absolutely did not mean that I didn't wish to continue kissing her. I'd kiss her forever if she'd let me. But I needed to know what it meant. I needed to know if this was just a release or something more. I needed to at least try and protect my tormented soul, my agonized body.

Plus, I couldn't continue *here*. Because her friends were in the other room. Because I didn't want to fuck her on a shitty sofa bed.

Because by the way she was touching me, I couldn't be sure I'd even make it to the couch before losing myself completely. I just have trouble speaking when she looks at me a certain way. In those moments when she's zoned in on me, focusing on my mouth as if she's trying to guess what I'm going to say before I say it. Her eyes deepen and stretch, her lips part slightly, her brows raise, and her cheeks flush. When she is hanging onto my words as if anything I could say could make or break her world.

In those moments, I lose the ability to speak.

Knowing me, as soon as I would try explaining that I'd lose my words again, or I'd say something equally as stupid. I sighed and ran a hand through my hair, untangling the curls that had wound together when whipped through the beach breeze. The room felt colder than it had a minute ago, quieter too. The absence of her was palpable and I couldn't stand here helplessly while I waited for her. I stepped outside onto the veranda. The ocean wasn't visible in the darkness, but the sound of the crashing waves reminded me of its presence. It soothed me as I caught my breath and waited for Penelope.

I wasn't sure how much time had passed, but it felt like more than ten minutes. I leaned back in my chair and glanced through the window. The bathroom door was ajar, and the light was no longer on. She must've been done in there, though the living room looked dark too. As quietly as I could, I snuck back inside the house. She was nowhere to be found. The bed-slash-couch was empty, the bathroom and kitchen dark and barren. I darted towards the front door to check if she was outside– if she had left.

Where would she have gone in the middle of the night? Could I have upset her that much?

A door creaked and footsteps padded in the hall behind me. Somehow, by the sound of them alone, I knew they weren't Penelope's. She tended to stomp everywhere she went, even when she thought she was being stealthy. I turned around to find Jeremy standing in the hall. His lips clustered to the side of his mouth as he gave me an evident shrug. "She's in there," he said, craning his head towards the bedroom door.

I blew out my nose and hid a smile. "She kicked you out of bed, then?"

"I was already on the floor." I tilted my head in confusion. "Mace and I got into it earlier."

"I'm sorry," I said.

He waved his hand. "She'll get over it. You know how dramatic she is." Rolling his eyes, he added, "Looks like you're not faring much better."

I tried to ignore what he said about Macie. "I'm just an idiot."

"Everyone who's in love is an idiot," he chuckled as he strode into the kitchen and got a glass of water.

I gripped the back of my neck. "Yeah, I guess so."

"Good luck," he chimed as he returned to the bedroom.

"I booked two first-class seats. One under Edwards and the other under Mason." I said to the airline agent as I slid my driver's license across the counter. "I'm Carter Edwards. Penelope Mason will follow me in a moment to check-in herself." The agent nodded absently as he checked my identification and typed something into the computer in front of him. "I'm going to need you to tell her we got a first-class upgrade. She thinks I booked us in the main cabin."

The young man paused and looked me over. "You want me to lie to your girlfriend for you?"

"Well, she's not exactly my girlfriend. *Yet*. And she's actually kind of mad at me right now. If she knew I upgraded her flight and paid for it without telling her, it would just make things worse."

I spoke quickly as I heard Macie's voice from somewhere behind me.

He smirked. "She would be *upset* that you paid to have her flight upgraded?"

"She's independent." I shrugged, hiding a prideful smile. "She's the one with the red hair. Please, please, lie for me," I pleaded one last time as I stepped back from the podium.

Penelope skirted past me to the counter but didn't look at me. She greeted the agent in a kindness that was in stark contrast to the coldness she showed me. He looked at me with an eyes-wide expression, and a smirk. "Well, Miss Mason, it appears that you have received a first-class upgrade. Congratulations." He smiled as he handed her the boarding pass. She whipped around to scowl at me. Her eyes narrowed in accusation. The agent cleared his throat. "Um. Mr. Edwards booked your tickets using a friends and family discount through the airline. We always put these bookings on first-class standby in case the main cabin is overbooked. It looks like you guys got lucky," he lied.

Her face relaxed slightly, but she didn't smile. She accepted the boarding pass and thanked the agent before she took off towards the line for security. *Thank you,* I mouthed to the agent.

"Only because she seems like a keeper."

We made it through the security in awkward silence. Only Penelope and Macie were in conversation. It seemed as if Jeremy hadn't had a chance to sort things out with Macie either. Both girls ignored our presence as we sat at the gate. Jeremy and I shot each other side-long glances every so often. I understood why Penelope was ignoring me– why she was upset. I also understood that the moment we stepped onto that plane, she'd have nowhere to go, and I'd make things better then. I'd let her sulk for now if that's what made her feel in control at this moment.

She didn't speak to me as we waited to board. Not as we crossed the jet bridge and entered the plane. Not even when she sat down and I filed in next to her. She was trying to be angry, but the only emotion I saw on her face was hurt. It destroyed me to know I'd caused it. I took one final deep breath as I threw my backpack down at my feet and sat next to her, knowing she'd have nowhere to run. Knowing she had no choice but to hear me out. I wasn't going to sit here in silence for the next three hours and then allow her to run away again once we got home. I didn't want to do this on a plane, but I had no other choice because I knew if I didn't do it now, she wouldn't give me the chance to once we returned.

"Are we going to talk about last night, or are you going to run away again?" I asked as she fastened her buckle.

"I don't really have anywhere to go." She waved her hand about, in reference to the fact we were on the airplane and I was in the aisle seat, blocking her exit.

Exactly.

I rolled my eyes. "Is that the only reason you're not running?"

I waited for her to respond, and a long minute passed in silence before I had the nerve to look at her. Her head was leaning against the window. I think she was afraid to look at me too. "I can't be casual about this, Carter. I can't just kiss you like it means nothing."

"Believe me. There was nothing casual about the way I kissed you last night."

She turned her head to meet my gaze. Her eyes bore into me with enough intensity I felt like I may dissolve right there. "I can't fall in love with you," she said, barely above a whisper.

I let my head fall back against the seat behind me. *Yes, you can.* I wanted to scream.

Fall in love with me. Fall in love with me. Fall in-fucking-love with me.

Her words sounded like daggers and felt like a stab into my stomach. "And why is that?"

"Because..." She paused, looking defeated. "You've rejected me twice already. First at the club, and again last night. I– if you're not interested in me that way, we need to put a stop to things right now." She looked away from me again. In a tone much more timid than before she said, "Every time I'm with you it feels like I'm flying. But when you push away it feels like falling. When you reject me, it feels like my heart is imploding and... I just can't." She shook her head, and for the first time I realized that she might be struggling to find the words too.

Every time I'm with you it feels like I'm flying.

Flying. Soaring. Swimming through clouds.

I inhaled deeply, my chest constricting almost to the point of pain. Like my body had forgotten how to breathe. Like I hadn't been breathing for years, and air was just now entering my lungs again for the first time. It's happened before– this feeling. A couple of times when I'd fall off my board while surfing and gotten sucked underneath a wave. Being flipped and kicked and whirled within the water, not knowing which way is up or down. Forgetting how to swim. Going so long without oxygen I was sure I'd die but somehow just kept moving. Both times it happened to me, my feet hit the ground and everything else righted itself. I was able to push off the bottom, straight up towards the surface. When my head broke the water, it felt like I had to teach myself to breathe again. I would suck in gulp after gulp of air, to the point I was almost choking on it. That is what Penelope's revelation felt like. Like I had been stuck beneath a wave all this time. Unsure of where to go, of what I was doing, or how I'd escape. Her imploding heart is the earth beneath my feet, and I am just now pushing up towards the surface, breaking it and breathing again.

I haven't breathed in five years.

I interlaced my hands and flexed them side to side. I had to find a way to explain to her exactly how I feel about her. To convince her that she *can* fall in love with me. To tell her that I fell in love with her years ago, and I've been waiting for her all this time. I steadied my breathing before I spoke again. "Do you know the first thing I loved about you?"

She didn't respond.

"Your hair. I loved your hair. I'd never seen a color quite like it." I grabbed a strand from her shoulder and twisted it through my fingers. "The same hair you have now."

Again, she said nothing.

"Then, your eyes. Huge– always wide as you interpret the world around you. By looking at your eyes alone, I could see the gears cranking in your mind. Always observing. And the color. Do you know how rare your eyes are? In general, green eyes are rare, yes. But your eyes are deep emerald, not a hint of any other color. An endless pool of green. Do you know how easy it is to get lost inside those eyes?"

She blinked at me as if it was the first time she was realizing the color of her own eyes.

"Then, I got to know you. I got to see who you are as a person. I got to understand your *soul*, Penelope. Your compassionate, kind, artistic soul. Your humor, your wit, and your unrelenting curiosity. That smart-ass mouth," my lips twitched upward, "and even smarter brain. And I couldn't understand how someone with such a beautiful soul—a beautiful mind—could also look like you." I sighed and shook my head. I knew my words were sounding almost angry.

"But I was lost completely the first time I heard you laugh." I was frustrated that she couldn't see the things about herself that I see. That she could believe for one second that I wouldn't want her. That I hadn't done a good enough job of showing her how much I did. "Do you know when I fell in love with you, Penelope?"

"When?" she peeped. Her first response since I decided to rip my chest open for her on a crowded plane. I assumed her silence was in shock, not indifference. She was looking at me with those widened eyes, the parted mouth, flushed cheeks. She was breathing hard, her hands shaking a little. I could see in her eyes that she wanted to smile, but her mouth wouldn't move yet. She was still too afraid. As if she was hanging on my words for dear life.

"The first time you gave me *my* smile." Her expression changed, only in that her brows furrowed slightly in confusion. "Do you not realize that you smile at each person you love in a different way?"

She shook her head.

"You do. Some people get teeth, some people don't. Sometimes you grin, other times you smirk. Your mouth leans to the left or to the right. Your eyebrows raise or fall. Your nostrils flare. They're all a little different depending on who you're smiling at. But, once you create a smile for someone, it's always the same. It never changes.

"The first time you smiled at me that way, we were nine. I noticed that it was a little different than how you normally smiled. Your normal smile is a little sarcastic, a little reserved. A slight tilt of your lips and a little breath blown out your nose." Her eyes flickered again, like she was trying to remember her own features. I continued, "When you smile at me, your brows furrow a little, and you tilt the left side of your mouth a little higher than the right." She started to shake her head in disbelief. I chuckled, feeling lighter. "I'm telling you, it's true. You don't smile at your parents like that, or Macie, or Christine, or Maddie. That one is just for me. It's mine." She bit down on her lip and looked away briefly, seeming to blink back tears. "The first time you smiled at me like that we were nine. I fell in love with you at nine years old and not a goddamn thing has changed since then, Pep. None of it. I loved you then, and I love you now."

For so long she stared at me. I stared back. Her eyes were misting. She would breathe in, and I braced myself for her to speak, but words wouldn't come. Her brows were raised like they were trying to get her mouth to lift too. She wanted to smile, but she couldn't.

"Then, why didn't you want me last night? The night before?" she finally asked.

I laughed. "The first time you were drunk, and I was afraid it wouldn't mean anything to you. That you might not have remembered it. That you might have regretted it. Last night..." I sighed. "God, Penelope. Last night was just a game to you. This isn't a game to me."

"It's not a game to me either," she whispered.

"Do you have any clue how much restraint it took for me to say no in that club, with your hands all over me? *My* hands all over *you*?" I closed my eyes and let out a breath through my nose. Willing myself not to get hard at the thought alone. "To tell you no last night after kissing you?" I let out a low laugh. "Do you know how hard it is to just sit next to you and not fuck you on this plane right here and now?"

I let my eyes fall closed as I looked away from her. I'd found myself losing control the longer this conversation lasted. Even with my eyes closed, I could feel hers on me. I could smell her shampoo. I could almost taste her lips. I breathed through my nose, hoping I hadn't gone too far.

I think she stopped breathing entirely. I finally opened my eyes and glanced at her. Her cheeks were flaming, but her eyes were dancing with fervor. She licked her bottom lip, and I realized the plane was now moving. It was accelerating, and I hadn't even noticed the doors close. Missed the safety presentation too. My stomach lifted into my chest cavity. I wasn't sure if it was because of the plane's suspension into the air, or if it was because of the way she was staring at me.

"I wasn't rejecting you, Penelope," I continued. "I was halting things before they went too far because I *want* you to fall in love with me. I want you to know that I think you're worth more than dancing in a club or having sex on a pull-out sofa." I leaned into her, my mouth against her ear. "When I do fuck you, I want to be able to show you exactly what you're worth." I pulled away and studied her. I watched her flood with heat, watched the panting of her breath, the rapid rise and fall of her chest. I tried not to stare too closely at the way her thighs clenched together, the way her breasts peaked through her t-shirt. I saw the roll of her throat as she swallowed audibly.

The plane leveled out, the pilot's voice came above us, but I couldn't hear a goddamn thing as I leaned into her. As her lips feathered mine, as her hand came to grip my neck, and mine rested on her thighs. I deepened the kiss. A promise to her of what would come. A confirmation of everything I'd said before.

The man across the aisle from me cleared his throat and I growled into her mouth. She giggled as she pulled away. She looped her arm through mine and laid her head on my shoulder. I didn't move my hand from her thigh. Moments passed in silence.

"Did we really get a free upgrade both times?" she asked, her voice sleepy.

I smiled, staring down at the top of her head. "No."

"I knew it."

"I did get a discount though, so I didn't pay anymore for these seats than Macie and Jeremy paid for theirs. But I knew you wouldn't accept it. So, I convinced the ticket agents both times to tell you that you got upgraded." She swatted my arm and pouted sarcastically. "You're going to have to let me spoil you sometimes, Pep."

"Only sometimes." She yawned, snuggling back into her previous position. Her head fell in between my shoulder and my neck, mine rested atop hers. "So, where do we go from here?"

"I think we're en route to PDX."

She snorted. "You're an idiot."

"I've been told," I laughed. "I just want to keep flying with you, Pep."

"Then you've got to catch me when I fall," she whispered.

"Deal," I promised.
"Deal," she agreed.

Chapter Nineteen

"Our souls are dyed in the same colour."

-Krishna Chhertri

Penelope

The day had been painfully long.

It was hard to believe that it was only this morning I'd woken up in bed with Macie. It was only a few hours ago that Carter professed he loved me, and I didn't say it back. That had been chewing away at me for much of the day. He didn't seem upset about it. It almost seemed as if he didn't even realize he had said it. That was part of the reason I couldn't return it. Not because I didn't feel it. I did. I always had. But also because I knew once I let the words leave my mouth, there would be no going back. It would all become real.

It was an emotionally draining day, but I felt that in a good type of way. I had no doubts anymore about Carter. I knew the way he felt about me. I was ready to fly with him. Prepared to fall into him. I knew eventually there would be harder conversations to be had between us, but for now, I felt at peace with all of it. I felt like I could trust him.

Getting to this point had been tiresome. I hardly slept at all last night. I tried speaking with Macie about what had happened between her and Jeremy, but she wouldn't tell me, especially since he was in the room with us. I asked again at the airport, and she just promised we'd talk later.

By the time we arrived home, I was so ready for a nap that I hardly noticed the awkward tension between us as we said goodbye.

I wasn't ready for anyone to know about us yet, and he must've understood that look in my face because he didn't even so much as hug me. He grabbed my bag out of the trunk after Maddie had driven us back home, setting it on the doorstep. He thanked Maddie for picking us up and disappeared through the back fence of his parents' house. I bound straight for my bedroom, texting him that we'd talk soon before I fell asleep.

I woke to the golden light of the evening sun shining through my shades, and the clinking of pots and pans in the kitchen as my parents made dinner. I stretched, yawned, and wondered if I should call Carter. It had been precisely two hours since I'd texted him. He responded with a thumbs up emoji. I wasn't sure how these things worked. Relationships– the start of them. I'd only ever known secrets. I wasn't ready for our families to know because I wasn't sure what we were myself. I wanted the space for us to figure it out for ourselves. But I also wanted it to be as easy as calling him and asking him to come have dinner with me. As easy as holding his hand and falling asleep next to him at night.

Except now, I felt like a teenage girl who just got home from her first date and doesn't know what the next move is supposed to be. I felt naive. Unprepared.

I looked at my phone just as a text popped up on the screen.

Carter: I'm coming up.

Only a moment later, there was a knock. Not on my door, though. I flew to my window, pulling up the blinds and throwing it open. Carter squatted on his knees, his entire body fitting into the panel of my bedroom window. *That* grin plastered on his face.

"Are you absolutely fucking insane?"

He didn't answer, and before I could yell more, his hand came around the nape of my neck, pulling me halfway out the window until my lips met his. This kiss was soft, tender, yet playful. As if he was expecting me to flip out on him, and he found his lips to be the antidote for shutting me up. He pulled away, laughing. I almost pulled him inside, but the sun sprawled across my cheeks, making the night unseasonably warm. Purples, pinks, oranges, and golds began to splotch the sky. So, I crawled outside with him. We leaned back against the window, arm to arm.

"How in the hell did you even get up here?" I asked.

"Your parents have a trellis against the side of the house. It's so overgrown with ivy it almost can't be seen, but I was still able to climb it."

"You are actually insane," I gasped. "You could've just walked right through the front door. They wouldn't have cared."

He smiled. "I thought the climbing would be more romantic. You know, *Romeo and Juliet* kind of thing."

"As you pointed out, *Romeo and Juliet* is a tragedy. They both die by the end."

"Well, even better, then. Since Penelope Mason hates romance." He winked.

I shoved him. "Ass."

He only chuckled as his arm slipped behind my back. He pulled me between his legs so that my back fell against his chest, his chin resting atop my head. Both of his arms moved down my shoulders, down my own arms, until they reached my hands. His fingers interlocked with mine as he brushed his lips along my temple.

I settled in against him. It was only a few weeks prior that we'd been sitting in this same spot. That I felt he may have wanted to kiss me but was so sure he never would. "Anyone could walk outside and see us out here."

"Would it bother you if they did?"

"I don't know," I breathed. The honest answer. "You know how our families can be. I– I don't know. I want us to be able to explore this—whatever this is—for ourselves first before needing to explain it to everyone else too." I tilted my head up to look at him, trying to read his eyes.

"We don't have to explain this to anyone, Pep. We don't owe anyone anything, except ourselves." He inhaled. "But I understand. I don't want you to feel like there is any pressure on this. On us. I want this to grow naturally. If you think that keeping things between us for right now is the best way to do that, then I agree with you."

I nodded into his chest. I lifted my arm, and his came with it. Opening my hand, I ran my fingers along the length of his. I studied the veins that ran up the backside of his hand, the calluses beneath his knuckles. I rubbed my thumb across his palm as I said, "I need you to be patient with me."

"What do you mean?"

I sighed, still playing with his fingers. "I have a tendency to overinflate. Overthink. Overstress. Over worry. Then, I find myself floating up into space, trapped within the chaos of my own mind. I might do that, with us."

He was quiet for a second. He brought his mouth against my ear, moving his hand away from mine so he could brush my hair away from my face. His lips tickled my temple again as he whispered, "And I have a tendency to drown beneath the pressure of mine. So let us be the tether that ties each other back to earth."

I scrambled out of his embrace so I could turn and face him. Sitting up on my knees between his legs, I leveled my face with his. I could feel tears brimming behind my eyes. That tether he spoke of swirled within my stomach, my chest, my heart. He watched me intently, seeming content with the amount of time I was taking to respond.

I placed a hand on the side of his face, studying his eyes. He was beautiful. Not just in his skin, his face, or his body. Not just in the way he made me feel. He was beautiful into the very depths of his soul. He was all that was good and kind. Pure and free. More than

I ever thought he'd become. More than I could've ever imagined for myself. More than I deserved.

I placed my other hand against his chest, right over his heart. I leaned into him, sealing my mouth over his. The moment the contact was made, I had let go. Let go of my heart, giving it to him entirely. Every wall broke down within me. I could almost feel the tether solidifying between us. His hands held my waist, mine held his face. I was grounded. I was understood. Anchored.

And despite what we had just agreed upon, I didn't care who saw us. I was ready to shout it from the literal rooftop in which we were sitting. I was his. He was mine.

My mother shouted that dinner was ready through my closed bedroom door, forcing us apart. His knuckles brushed against my cheek bone, and he smiled at me. One of those smiles that could knock the wind out of the woman receiving them, but even more so. An expression so reserved, I wondered if he'd ever given it to anyone else. It was adoring, raw, *love*.

He nodded toward the window behind him. "Go spend time with your family." I shook my head. I could miss dinner. I could sneak away with him. Spend the night with him, even. I wanted to. *Needed* to. I opened my mouth to protest but he cut me off, "Go spend time with your family, because tomorrow I'm stealing you away."

My mouth shut and I flicked my brow. "Are you?"

He smashed his mouth against mine once more. Brisk and effortless. Unworried. As if he'd done it a thousand times before, and he'd do it at least a million more. He lifted me off him and stood up, trudging over to the ledge of the roof. "Yep. Meet me outside at six o'clock tomorrow morning."

I groaned and he laughed. "It's kind of a work thing. I've got to get out there when the lighting is right, before the sun gets too high. Plus, it's supposed to rain tomorrow afternoon."

I huffed but nodded. "Can you at least not scale the house again? Just go inside and down the stairs. Please."

He squatted down at the edge of the roof before turning back at me. "And explain to your parents how I got into your bedroom in the first place?"

He flipped around and swung the lower half of his body over the edge of the house, holding himself up by his arms. "I'll be fine." He smiled arrogantly. "Watch." Then, dipping below the roof, he disappeared from sight. I walked to the edge and peered down. He was scaling down the trellis as if it was a ladder. Within a moment, his feet were back on the ground and he was staring up at me, smirking.

"Night, Pep." He winked.

My alarm sounded at exactly five-forty-five in the morning. I'd texted Carter the night before, asking for hints as to what we'd be doing so I could be prepared. He told me we were going somewhere called Opal Creek but demanded that I not research it. It *had* to be a surprise.

I quickly readied myself, unsure of what I was supposed to wear. I had a feeling hiking would be involved. I threw on a pair of leggings, a tank top with a knit sweater over it, and boots. I thought the boots may not be necessary, but I made the mistake of wearing sneakers during a family hike a few years ago where I slipped and severely bruised my tailbone. Even in early April, without knowing where we were going, I couldn't rule out the possibility of snow or ice in the Cascades. I also grabbed the copy of the book Carter had loaned me so I could return it. I left a note for my parents, informing them I was going hiking with Carter. *And Macie.* I had added as to not sound suspicious.

As I quietly slipped out my front door, I couldn't help but spend a moment taking him in. He was standing against his truck, looking down at his phone. He was wearing a flannel, rolled up to the elbows. I allowed my eyes to roam his legs underneath the faded jeans. He too had on hiking boots, and a large camera bag wrapped around his chest. He ran a hand through his curls, allowing them to hang off his forehead limply. I took a breath in and bounced across the street. He smiled as I climbed into the passenger seat of his Bronco.

We headed south down the Oregon Coast Highway from Brighton Bay, other than our current direction, I had no clue where we were headed. We turned east down Highway 26 toward Portland. The small beach towns slowly turned into scattered residences as we descended into the Coastal Range. Soon, the residences disappeared too, and the highway became narrow, winding through the canyons. Tunnels of trees towered over us on both sides of the road, their silhouettes faintly visible in the rising sun and still dripping with last night's rain. "I like the woods," I said. "I know there are woods—forests—everywhere. But something about it is different here. Like, this is what the forest is supposed to feel and look like. So mossy and wet. It's pretty."

"Because these forests are your home, Pep."

"It never really felt like home growing up. It was just where I lived. It's not like I could go anywhere else. I didn't choose Brighton Bay. It's just where I was. I didn't even think I'd miss it when I went to college."

He frowned.

I found myself continuing, "After I'd been in England for about a month, I got so homesick. Like, physically sick. My anxiety was at an all-time high and couldn't keep any food down. I didn't realize it rained so much over there. Maybe even as much as it rains here.

At first that annoyed me, because I wanted out of it. I've never liked rain. Then, after I started getting really homesick, I thought it would be comforting. But it wasn't. The rain was different. I hated the rain more there than I ever did here. There was even one point, my first Thanksgiving over there, that I actually took the train from Oxford to Heathrow. I called my dad and I told him I was getting on a plane and coming home."

"I don't remember you coming home that first year."

I shook my head. "I didn't. My parents knew I'd been homesick those first few months. They kept telling me to stay, promising it'd get better. When I called my dad, I think he heard the desperation in my voice because for once he didn't argue with me. He just said, 'Okay, Penny.' Then, he added, 'Carter is here too.' And I don't know why he said it. I know he didn't know anything had happened between us. I didn't know if he thought I'd find that to be good news or bad, but he just said it." He took his eyes off the road, only for a moment, to glance at me. "I stepped off the train and got immediately on another one back to Oxford."

"You didn't want to see me?"

"The issue was that I *did* want to see you. I wanted to see you more than anyone else. I couldn't see you. If I'd gone home then, if I had seen you—been with you—I wouldn't have been able to come back. Leaving you after the graduation party broke my heart. I wasn't strong enough to do it again."

He didn't say anything. He didn't take his eyes off the road. His right hand leaned over the center console and found mine resting on my thigh. He folded his hand over mine and squeezed it. After a moment, he asked, "Does it still feel that way? Like it's not home?"

It did. When I first moved back, I was hollow– empty, sad. The rain was suffocating. I hardly went outside at all. I didn't go hiking or visit the mountains. I didn't go into the forest. I didn't appreciate the trees or the smell of the rain on them. I didn't notice the green. The air didn't feel light and fresh. I never noticed the saltwater in the breeze– the way it feels now. The world still felt dreary and small, the way it felt in England. I didn't go to the ocean, not one single time. Not until that morning with Carter a few weeks ago. "At first it still felt like that. But I don't know, over the last few months I've been growing to appreciate it."

He nodded, as if agreeing with me.

I leaned my head against the window and propped my feet up, watching the shade of the pines and the evergreens become deeper as the day brightened.

Carter squeezed my hand again, and I'd never felt more at home.

The only sound that seemed to echo for miles was the sound of the gravel underneath our feet. Still early in the morning, the path was deserted. Underneath a thick canopy of cedar, we trudged along the seemingly never-ending trail. Even though the morning was chilly, the sun beat down overhead. The trail wasn't particularly steep, but after what felt like hours (it had been one) of hiking, I was panting.

We'd only stopped a few times. All our breaks had been because Carter found trash on the trail and wanted to stop and pick it up. He even brought an empty reusable grocery bag to fill with any litter he found today, so he could recycle it once we got back home.

"How far is the hike in?"

"Three miles in, three miles out, baby," he chimed from several paces ahead of me.

"Shit," I panted.

"We're almost there, Pep." He was right, because only a hundred or so yards down the trail, we veered off down an embankment that led to a rocky waterfall.

"Oh my God," I gasped as the landscape came into full view. The morning sun sparkled, just as Carter promised it would, over crystal clear green water. The only sounds in the space around us were the chirping birds and the creek as it plummeted over the rock face and into the pool below.

I found myself struggling out of my boots as I stumbled, desperate for my toes to touch the calm, crystalline water as it lapped at the shore of the pool. The entire world existed in shades of green and gold in this silent space. The vivid shade of the moss meshed with the evergreen of the trees and the brightly colored wildflowers that sprouted throughout the banks. The water was so transparent that it reflected all the colors around it, including the bright blue sky and the sunlight, making it truly appear translucent opal. "It's so beautiful," I whispered as I sat down on the flattest rock I could find along the shore.

Realizing for the first time that he hadn't said anything, I pulled my gaze from the setting in front of me and looked at Carter. He'd been watching me. His hands were on his hips as he stood above me at the top of the bank. His backpack was still on, his camera hanging around his neck. "Breathtaking."

An effortless grin broke out from my cheeks.

I nodded towards the waterfall. "Get to work."

He saluted me. "Yes, ma'am."

I watched him for a long while. He brought all kinds of camera contraptions that I couldn't even begin to understand. He'd move all around the area, taking photos of different things. Sometimes he explained to me what he was doing, as if I had any clue what long exposure meant, or why he needed a tripod. Regardless, I'd listen to him forever. I'd watch him forever.

"Pep?" His voice was soft, breaking me from my trance. I realized he was standing ankle deep in the pool of water behind his tripod as his camera sat on top of it facing the waterfall.

"Yes?"

"I asked if you'd put your feet in yet."

I shook my head. I stood up and stepped forward, into the water. It was exceedingly frigid, but nearly welcoming as the sun beat down on us. I bent down and ran my hand through the water. Despite the waterfall plummeting into the far end of the pool, the water lapping at my feet moved so slowly, it almost appeared still. I watched the ripples my hand created as they cascaded beyond my reach. "Penelope?"

I snapped my head up at him and blinked, wondering if I'd been lost in my own thoughts once again, unable to hear him.

"Will you...will you get in the water?"

I scowled, thinking he was making a joke. "Absolutely fucking not." The water couldn't be warmer than fifty degrees.

"Pep." His voice was an unwavering plea. Almost desperate. "I have never, not once, been interested in photographing another person. Not until now."

My scowl deepened into something puzzled. "Me? You want to photograph *me*?"

He nodded.

"Why?"

He swallowed. "I've never thought anyone was more beautiful than the landscape around them. I've always been more drawn to nature than people. Until now. You are more compelling to me than anything else here. You are pulling all of my focus. Let me photograph you. Please."

I studied his face. The sincerity in it. I'd known what he was feeling because I'd felt it too. Ever since I was a child, I loved to draw. I used to draw everything I'd see. Trees, buildings, cars. As I got older, that narrowed down into something more niche. I liked to draw history. I would imagine what ancient ruins looked like in their prime, inspired by other artist's renderings. I loved it because there was no true way for anyone living to know what these places looked like before. We could only interpret based on what we had now. So the idea that I could take something old and weathered, making it brand new and beautiful inside my head, was inspiring. It made me feel full inside. I imagined that's what Carter felt like when he studied nature through the lens of his camera.

Like him, I'd never been interested in sketching people. Even when I drifted into painting for some time, like my mother, I only focused on landscapes. Things that were open to interpretation. Then, I lost all interest in any of it. Sketching, painting, admiring the work of others. I didn't even imagine ruins anymore. I only studied what I could see upfront. Only studied it for school. Only focused on what was absolutely required of me. I'd lost the passion I once felt. Passion for everything. I never wanted Carter to feel like that.

I'd never wanted to draw or paint people, but as I stared into his sunlit eyes, I thought that maybe I'd want to paint them someday. Maybe I'd be interested in sketching the look on his face when his jaw tightened in concentration, or the way he smiled at me. *That* grin. And I understood why he was suddenly asking me to get in that freezing water for him. And I knew that if I had asked him myself, he would've.

"Okay," I said. His eyes widened, his face taking on a look of complete astonishment. I stepped out of the ankle-deep water and began peeling off my leggings so that I'd have dry clothing to put on after coming out of the water.

He beamed at me as he shrugged out of his own flannel, tossing it onto the shore next to me. He began to unbuckle his jeans as he stepped out of the water to slip them off.

"What're you doing?"

"I'm taking my clothes off?" He said it like a question.

"Why?"

He scoffed, "I wouldn't ask you to get in cold-ass water if I wasn't getting in with you."

"Oh." I blinked as I lifted the hem of my sweater.

"Leave the sweater on," he said. I looked up at him, frowning. "If you can."

"I won't have anything dry to put on if I get this wet."

"I have a shirt you can wear."

I nodded, adjusting my sweater so that it fell off my hips once again. It was a loose-fitting, cream-colored, knitted sweater that hung off one shoulder. I wasn't sure why he'd asked me to keep it on, but I realized that the neon pink sports bra I had on underneath it probably wouldn't fit the aesthetic of the environment as well. By the time my feet were back in the water, he was knee-deep. He held his hand out to me as I inched in. "You know, I don't think I'm a particularly talented model."

He clasped my hand and waded me through the water until I reached him. The water lapped at the back of my knees, inching up my thighs. It was so cold it almost burned. My toes going numb, I began to shiver. "You're absolutely perfect."

I couldn't reply through my chattering teeth. Or my pounding heart.

His arm coiled around my back, scooping beneath my ass as he lifted me around his hips and slightly out of the water. I crossed my legs behind him and threw my arms around his neck. He stepped in deeper. "Fuck," he hissed as it splashed over his hips. He exhaled deeply. "Okay, I think this is deep enough. We'll do it quickly, Pep. I'm going to let you go so I can step back and get enough space between us. I'll tell you what to do. It shouldn't take more than a minute."

I nodded. I braced myself, closing my eyes and waiting for him to let go of my legs and let my body drop into the icy water. Instead, I found his mouth against mine, warm and inviting.

I kissed him as I felt myself begin to fall backwards. As startling as his kiss was, his next movement was staggering. He held me tightly as we both tumbled into the water below us.

That numbness bit more than just my toes. The icy water nipped and tore at my face, my arms, my torso. Frigid streams wafted through my nose as I went under completely. Carter's arm moved away from me, and I could no longer feel his presence at all. My body stung with ice, until the shock began to settle. My feet still touched the bottom of the creek bed, and I planted them down, pushing off and propelling upward. I broke the surface, inhaling sharply.

"To the right, Pep," I heard.

My ears still ringing, my body still in shock, I couldn't process what was being said. I began to move my hands toward my face to rub my eyes and open them.

"Penelope, stop!" I froze. "Shift to your right, about a foot. Don't open your eyes yet, don't touch your face." As I realized what he'd done, realized that he was still standing near me, I realized I was furious. He'd dunked me, then let go and stepped away.

For some reason, I listened to him.

Dropping my hands back beneath the surface, I shuffled to my right. "Good girl." I grumbled in disapproval. A burst of light shone through my closed eyelids, the warmth of the direct sun hit my face. "Now move your hands above your head, like you're pushing your hair out of your face. Move slowly and tilt your head up toward the sky." I heard shutters of the camera, the water sloshing around him as he moved within it. By the sounds, it seemed as if he was standing a few feet in front of and to the right of me. "Perfect. Relax your face. Now move your right arm down, around your ear and against your neck. Slowly. Open your eyes once your arm meets your collar bone. Keep your face relaxed."

I did as he asked. More shutters sounded around me. I realized he was getting closer. I let my eyes flutter open as softly as I could manage. I blinked rapidly as the sunlight hit my face, allowing a moment for my surroundings to come into focus.

I'd hardly noticed the sound of the waterfall in front of us, but with my eyes open once again, the roaring of it seemed to become more apparent. Carter was standing not two feet in front of me, camera at his face. Three more shutters sounded before he moved the camera back to his chest. His eyes glistened in the sun as he smiled at me.

"Y...you... a... ass," I shivered.

"I'm sorry, I'm sorry, I'm sorry," he rambled as he waded to me. "I thought it would be easier if I just dunked you, instead of having you try and inch into it." As he reached me, he dipped his head down to meet mine, planting a kiss on my mouth. His lips were hot where mine were ice. He pulled away, that pleading look from earlier back in his eyes. "One more?"

I frowned.

He began to back up toward the shore, bringing the camera up to his face. "Just come out of the water slowly. Lean forward so that your face hits the surface, gently though so you don't cause ripples. Cross your arms in front of you and lay your cheek against them. Turn towards me and look up." He moved so that he was standing at my side. I bent forward, the bitter cold constricting my chest as it dropped beneath the surface. I struggled to keep my lips from chattering as I crossed my arms and laid my face across them, looking up towards him. "I know it's cold, baby, I know. Try to relax your face."

Warmth bloomed, starting in my chest and stretching all the way through my toes until every molecule in my body was buzzing with it. He'd never called me that before. I liked it. No, I loved it. I settled into my position, looking up at him. Looking through the lens of his camera that covered his eyes and seeing him through it.

I didn't move my mouth. I left it relaxed, but I was smiling. I knew he could see it underneath.

"Stunning," he breathed. After that, I couldn't keep my face straight anymore. A smile spread throughout my cheeks, and a giggle burst from my throat. The camera dropped at his chest and he matched my smile. "Come here."

I stood up, feeling even colder as the air pricked my skin. I stepped toward him, but he was quicker. As soon as I was standing upright, he was scooping me into his arms. His chest was warm against my soaked skin. He carried me past the trail we'd come down from, and up a smaller, more secluded one that led around the backside of the waterfall.

He set me down on a large rock, which was almost sizzling from the heat of the sun. It instantly relieved me of the shivering. I splayed across it, trying to soak up as much of the warmth as I could. Leaning over me, he grabbed the bottom of my sweater and began to pull it off me. His hands were steady as his fingers brushed along my stomach, over my ribs, and around my breasts. I was propped up against the rock on my elbows, watching him. He was only watching his arms as they moved my clothing, exposing inch after inch of my skin. I sat up as he peeled it up my arms and over my head.

He laid my sweater out on the rock next to us, along with his shirt and jeans. I realized, for the first time, that I was laying out in front of him in almost nothing at all. He was wearing nothing but wet underwear. He must've realized it too as he said, "This is not what I had in mind when I was hoping to get you naked on our first date." He slung a backpack off his shoulders and onto the ground.

"Is this a date?"

He laughed, tossing a dry sweatshirt at me. "I do realize that risking hypothermia may not have been the most ideal way to go about it, but yes. That's what I had intended originally."

"Did you plan on taking pictures from the beginning?"

"Of the scenery, yes. I've had Opal Creek on my list for a while. It's a hidden gem. The pictures of you, however, were not planned. Not until I watched you step into the water. Until I realized how much you were distracting me anyway. The only thing that was capturing me—captivating me—was you."

He leaned back on his hands in the grass below me, his eyes closed as his head tilted toward the sun. "Are you going to try and sell any of the photos of me?"

He shook his head. "No, those are mine."

A chill raced through me, but I knew it wasn't because I was cold.

"I'm going to go grab the rest of my clothes." He stood up and brushed his hands on his knees. "Your leggings are in the backpack. You should put them on. Lay your wet clothes in the sun to dry. I packed a picnic. Oh, and there is some sunscreen in there, too," he added as he trudged back down the trail.

I rolled my eyes.

"I can hear your eye roll, Pep. Put the damn sunscreen on!"

My laughter echoed throughout the trees.

Chapter Twenty

"...everything under the sun has been written by one hand only. It is the hand that evokes love, and creates a twin soul for every person in the world. Without such love, one's dreams would have no meaning."

-Paulo Coelho

Carter

Her feet started to drag about a mile into the hike back to the truck. Two miles in, she was beginning to yawn. With only a half-mile to go, she started to complain. Now, less than a quarter of a mile from where I parked my Bronco, she was getting testy–irritable.

I was several paces ahead of her when I stopped. "What is it, Penelope? Are you tired, or are your feet sore?"

"Both," she muttered, catching up to me.

I turned around, slipping the backpack off my shoulders and holding it out to her. She looked me up and down with a scowl. "You take the backpack."

"Why?"

"I can't carry you both."

She rolled her eyes and crossed her arms across her chest, sticking out a hip in defiance. She had such a typical posture when she was readying to throw a fit. She'd done it ever since she was a kid. She didn't do it often, but when she did, she always stood the same. As if her crossed arms were protecting her from the words of others–or maybe others from her. Her extended leg was giving her extra foundation to hold her ground. "You do not need to carry me."

"I'm not letting you ruin our date because you're cranky."

She pouted. "I am not cranky."

I snorted, dropping the backpack at her feet and turning around. I dropped my hands at my sides, then held them out slightly. I beckoned her with a wave of my fingers, telling her to jump onto my back. She sighed, but I could almost hear the smile that accompanied it. The gravel crunched from behind me, hard and swift. A second later, I felt her leap onto my back. My arms scooped underneath her knees as I hoisted her up behind me piggy-back style. She wrapped her legs around my waist as her arms clasped lazily around my neck.

She planted a soft kiss on my temple. "You are insufferable."

"*Me*?" She snickered, biting on my ear. I groaned. "Save that for later."

She whimpered in agreement.

I groaned at that too.

She fell asleep within twenty minutes of reaching the truck. I think I was beginning to admire that trait about her. She could sleep anywhere, and she did. Whether the plane or the car, or her near daily after-work naps. She was a frequent napper and became rather cranky when she didn't get one. She slept the entirety of the drive home.

The evening was turning into night as the colors of the trees faded into nothing but shades of black and blue and gray. As we closed in on the Coastal Range, dense fog settled in around us. Once we passed the Brighton Bay city limit, I placed my hand on her thigh and shook her lightly. "Pep, we're almost home," I whispered.

She began to stir, opening her eyes and blinking a few times before nodding. She shifted in her seat and was silent for a few minutes. As we grew closer to our houses, she reached between her legs and pulled something out of her bag, setting it on the dash in front of her. "Just returning this," she said.

I noticed it was the book I gave her last week. I attempted to hide my disappointment as I asked, "How much did you read?"

"I finished it."

The disappointment was wiped from my features. "You finished it?"

"Yes." She smiled. "It was really good. You were right, I– I think I did enjoy living there for a little while."

Something like pride exploded inside my chest. I craned my neck behind me. "Look beneath the back driver's seat."

She raised a brow but turned around and looked down. She pulled the bookstore bag from the floorboard behind my seat. She opened it, finding the full series set, brand new. "Carter."

"I wasn't sure if you'd ever finish the first book, and I wasn't sure if you'd be ready for that. But I wanted to be prepared in case you did. In case you loved it."

I moved my eyes from the road only for a second to see her expression. Her eyes were glassy. Her face stunned. Breathless. "Thank you."

I smiled. "I kept that book for a while. I thought you'd like it, so I held onto it just in case." I glanced at her again, her eyes were glued to me, hanging onto my words. "In case we ever found our way back to each other."

My next words flowed from my mouth effortlessly, as if my body knew there was nothing it needed to hold back from her any longer. "When I moved to Hawaii, I was still reeling over our kiss, still reeling over you. I felt lost. Half of me wanted to board a plane to London instead of Honolulu. I wanted to come after you. I got to the airport hours before my flight. I begged the Universe for a sign on what I should do. I wanted you– I'd always wanted you, Pep. But more than that, I wanted what was best for you. I wasn't sure if that was me. While I was trying to make a decision, I found

The Alchemist in the airport bookstore. I read it right there in one sitting and decided to follow through with moving to Hawaii.

"About two years later I stumbled upon that book," I nodded toward the one in her lap, "and it made me think of you. At first, I thought it was a sign that I should go after you. But then I realized it was a sign I should do the opposite. That I was already on the right track because if I had never gone to Hawaii, I may have never stumbled upon that random book in the random garage sale I was at with my mom that day. I thought maybe it was a sign I should hold onto it– wait. I knew that the Universe would bring you back someday if that's how it was supposed to work out. I knew that you were where you needed to be. And for whatever reason, Hawaii was where I needed to be at the time too. So, I kept waiting."

Only silence followed my admission. Long, agonizing silence. I threw a few glances her way as we drove through the darkening town. Each time, her head was dropped, staring down at her hands clasped between her legs.

"You waited five years for me," she said in a whisper that sounded almost heart broken.

"Yes," I answered, even though it wasn't a question. "I knew I wasn't capable of falling in love unless you walked back into my life." I exhaled deeply. "And I'd wait five years again. Ten. Hell, I'd wait this whole lifetime for you if it meant I could have you in the next one." I looked at her again. "You are what I've been conspiring to achieve, Penelope. You. Always you."

She shook her head. "I'm sorry."

Her head still cast down, her hands between her legs. I looked back at the road then looked at her again as it registered that her shoulders were shaking lightly. *She's crying.* I turned down our residential street just as the realization set in. I didn't respond until I'd pulled into my parent's driveway and killed the engine.

"Pep." I faced her. "Why are you crying?"

"I don't think I deserve you."

I unbuckled myself and threw up the center armrest. I tried to scooch closer to her, but she shrugged away, leaning against the window. Her tears were quiet. I almost couldn't see the streams that fell down her face in the darkness, but I knew they were there.

"Penelope, why are you saying this?"

She faced away from me, staring out the window. "I have nothing to offer you."

"I'm not asking for anything from you. It's not about deserving, Penelope. You do not need to earn my love, or anyone else's. I need you to understand that." I sighed. "Can you look at me?"

She shook her head. I settled into my seat, refusing to get out of the truck until she spoke to me. Long moments passed, only the sound of her tears filling the space around us.

Finally, she turned towards me, but refused to meet my eyes. "Carter, you are not a ray of sunshine, you are the entire sun. You bring joy, brightness, and warmth to everyone you come across. You deserve the sun, too." She looked at me, finally. "But, if you're the sun, then I'm the moon. Dark and dull."

I grabbed her face with both hands and tilted her head up to meet mine. The moment the words left her mouth, I knew exactly what to say. For once, I knew exactly what would make her understand. "Penelope, do you remember what you said to me the first time I took you surfing?"

Her eyes were wide, unyielding as they bore into mine. She shook her head.

"You told me that there were waves inside my soul." Her brows clustered at the center of her forehead as confusion floated across her face. I shook my head as I tried to hide the smile forming in my mouth. She had no clue.

"Maybe I'm the sun and the tides, and you're the moon and the stars; but all that means to me is that you are light in the dark. You're every wish in my night sky, and I'll follow you wherever you go."

And this time I didn't wait for her to close the gap, I leaned my head down until my lips met hers. I showed her what it felt like to be the tides in the sea– drawn to the moon.

As I pulled away, her eyes popped open. I saw the understanding settle in her features as my words poured into her ears and flowed throughout the rest of her body. Her eyes were wide, almost glowing in the dark as they sparkled behind her tears.

She unbuckled herself quickly as she crawled across the seat and into my lap. She straddled me, her knees coming to rest on either side of my hips. Her back was pressed against the steering wheel, as her chest leaned into mine. My arms had been pressed against my sides, but I brought them up to wrap around the back of her thighs, holding her flush against me. I looked up at her expectantly. I could tell she had something more to say. She cupped my face between both hands.

"I love you," she whispered.

My hands froze in their place and I felt my mouth drop open as we stared into each other. I'd told her as much on the plane, but at the time I wasn't sure she'd registered it. I hadn't expected her to say it back, even when I knew she felt. I thought it would be a while yet before I heard those words come from her.

My heart began to beat quicker as those three words poured into my own ears and flowed into my body. Right down to the depths of it. Right into my soul. The silent moment seemed to defy time and physics as we studied each other's faces. Only a few moments could have passed, but as if the Universe itself was interfering, we felt as if we were given all the time we needed. Her emerald eyes glowed like they were on fire. My hand found its way to her face as I cupped her cheek and rubbed my thumb across her perfect bottom lip.

Our mutual breathing grew heavier as her hands slowly made their way away from my face and down my neck. One moved behind my head as she pulled me into her. Because she was the moon and I the tides. When her lips touched mine, I felt the heat of the sun and the force of the stars.

"Say it again," I begged into her mouth.

"I love you," she whispered between my lips.

Chapter Twenty One

"I loved the way I could feel him deep in my soul."

-Jacqueline Simon Gunn

Penelope

"I love you," I said as he opened the door.

I whispered those words again against his lips as he stepped out of the truck, hands gripping my ass, my legs coiled around his hips. Another time as I nipped against his ear and he unlatched the gate that led to his parents' backyard, and again into his neck as he reached the pool house, adjusting me in his arms to open that door.

"I love you," I whispered a final time as I kissed his jaw.

I couldn't stop. I'd bottled those words up inside my body my entire life, waiting for the time I'd finally let myself speak them to him. I never wanted to stop saying it.

He slammed the door shut with his foot. The closest piece of furniture to us was his desk, set next to the door. He sat me atop it. My mouth crawled along his jaw as his hands reached the hem of his sweatshirt I was wearing– entirely bare beneath it. Mimicking his movements from earlier in the day, he slowly slid the sweatshirt up my body. His fingers trailing along my stomach– my ribs. Caressing my skin, sending shivers down my spine.

He pulled away to slip the sweatshirt over my head, tossing it on the floor below him. His eyes simmered as he beheld me. His breathing seemed to grow more labored the longer he stared. My breasts peaked beneath his gaze, growing needy. He ran his hand down the center of my chest, beginning at my throat. It swooped underneath my breast, cupping it as his calloused thumb flicked across my nipple. I whimpered at the feeling of it hardening beneath his finger.

"You are so beautiful."

A moan was my only response. I let my head fall back and I arched toward him, hungry for more of his touch. He groaned as his mouth closed around my breast. His teeth grazed it, his tongue flicking back and forth across my nipple. Molten heat rushed between my legs. I clawed at his back, desperate for more of his skin. He pulled away just to take his shirt off before returning to my other breast.

His hands traced along my spine until he reached the waistband of my leggings. I lifted my hips, a whimper of permission escaping my lips for him to slip them off. He pulled them down to my knees as his mouth left my breasts and peppered kisses down my stomach as he crouched and removed my leggings completely.

Squatting down, Carter looked up at me. "I've wanted this for so long."

He pressed his mouth against my calf. "Me too," I whispered.

He spread my legs slightly, his hand moving between them, pressing at my core through my panties. He sucked in a swift gulp of air and I knew why. I was embarrassingly wet, my arousal humiliatingly apparent. His thumb navigated to that spot between my legs that would make me shudder, and he began to rotate it in lazy circles.

"You're so fucking wet, Penelope," he rasped. "Is this all for me?" The low level of his voice, the way he moved his finger, even through my underwear, I was clawing into the desk below me. I couldn't focus on what he was saying. I couldn't remember words. "Answer me, baby," he demanded.

A high pitched, "Mm," was all I could get out.

He pressed his mouth against the place his thumb just was as his fingers looped through the waistband of my underwear. Tugging them off in a pleading, desperate, pull. He tugged them down my legs and over my knees, until my panties were hanging around just one of my ankles. I kicked them across the room.

He fell to his knees in front of me. Tilting his face to mine, he stared at me with an expression I'd never seen in him before. Soft and hard at the same time. His brows rose together, and his eyes were wide, seeming like a plea. His mouth parted slightly. "Penelope," he whispered my name like a prayer.

His lips feathered against my knee, moving up my thigh as he parted my legs with one arm and moved his head between them. His mouth was searing, sending flames straight into my core, leaving embers in their wake. That molten heat had pooled between my thighs, my body clenching tightly the closer he got. My hands found themselves inside his curls. "Carter," I whispered, pulling him away. He looked up at me, that same pleading expression mixed with confusion on his face. "I've never..."

I had never done this before. James wasn't a particularly generous, or adventurous lover. He never offered, and I had been too afraid to ask. It wasn't something I ever felt I had been missing, though. Not with him, at least. Having a man's mouth between my legs felt almost more intimate than sex itself, and I wasn't sure that was something I'd ever have been comfortable doing with James anyway.

My body was screaming at me to let Carter continue, screaming at me in a way that it never had before. I'd never wanted something more. Despite it, I wanted him to know that this was new to me. Wanted him to know that it wasn't something he *had* to do. Wasn't something I expected of him.

He took a moment to consider what I was attempting to say. Then, the most seductive smile rose from his mouth. Planting another kiss against my thigh he said, "Let me be your first."

I rested on my elbows, bringing my head up to look at him. He was frozen, his arms wrapped around my thighs, holding me open.

He was meeting my eyes, but his gaze kept dropping between my legs. His breathing was heavy. He licked his lips. His expression looked something like a starved man staring at a feast. I knew what his face was giving off, and yet I found myself saying, "Are you sure? I mean, you don't have–"

"Penelope, I am on my knees for you. Seeing you like this, spread in front of me..." He shook his head as if words were lost on him too. "*Fuck*. You have no clue how long I've waited for this." Echoing the words he'd said on the plane, "Let me show you what you're worth. Let me fucking worship you."

Something inside me snapped at that. The sheer desperation in his voice. "Please," I whimpered. I shouldn't feel dumbfounded by his words anymore, not after his revelations yesterday. Not after the things he said on the plane. The way he explained to me how he felt. How he *always* felt. Since day one. It had knocked me the hell off my high horse. I had been disarmed. I had melted. A puddle at his feet. I'd never believed that another person could feel so fiercely about me.

All further thoughts eddied from my mind as he ran one finger up my center, splitting me open. He watched me with delicious concentration as his mouth inched closer. His grip on my thighs tightened, spreading them wider.

His tongue followed the path his finger had just forged, setting my entire body aflame.

Nothing—*nothing*—had ever felt like this before. I bucked and moaned beneath him. He groaned with approval as he pinned my hips down to the desk. He draped one of my legs over his shoulder, the angle allowing him even deeper. He tasted in me in long, sweeping strokes, until his tongue reached the center of my thighs. He slipped that bundle into his mouth, sucking on it and nipping gently. His tongue pressed flat, then rotated in circles the way his fingers were moving before. Sounds– foreign, inhuman sounds bubbled out of my throat.

I had no control over them.

No control over the buckling of my hips or the trembling of my legs.

His tongue was unrelenting as he slipped a finger inside me. He pumped into me. Once. Twice. Then, added a second finger. I bowed off the table, his mouth pressing into me harder. He curled his fingers, just so slightly, that they hit a wall deep inside me.

His tongue and his fingers moved in swift rhythm. A warmth bloomed and spread throughout my core, building and building as he worked on me relentlessly. Groans of his own would vibrate against that spot, causing me to thrash against him further.

He continued that humming of approval, almost as if he knew the way it felt against that place between my legs. Almost as if he was taunting me with it. He took it between his teeth, snaking his tongue through them to flick rapidly. I could feel the building reaching its breaking point, I could feel the walls cracking within me.

"Carter–" My voice was scratchy, strained from the cries of pleasure.

"Yes, baby. Let me taste you."

I shattered.

An orgasm tore through me, more intense than anything I'd ever known before. My body fractured, splitting open as that heat spilled out of me. Spilling onto his fingers, his tongue. He continued the pumps of his fingers, until I was sobbing, limp with pleasure. His tongue continued to lap at me until I was spent. Until there was nothing left of me at all.

When I finally had the strength to lift my head, I found him still between my legs, his eyes on mine. Looking past his face, I noticed him adjust himself in his pants. That near sent me into another spiral. He pulled away, wiping his face with his hand to reveal a devilishly feral grin.

He stood, towering over me. He grabbed my hips and pulled me to the edge of the desk so that my hips and his were flush together. Even through his jeans, I felt the hardness of him straining against them. Against me.

"Oh," I gasped.

His mouth found mine in a clash of tongues, lips, and teeth. He palmed my ass again, scooping me up and turning me around, laying me on his bed. I scrambled back onto the pillows as he unbuttoned his jeans. Even in the darkened room, the contours of his muscles were highlighted in the moonlight peeking through the window. I traced his tattoo with my eyes, the way it meshed into the hardness of his abs. The way his stomach went into a v, disappearing underneath his pants.

Until the pants were removed. My eyes were already there, watching, as he sprang free. I swallowed hard as I took in the size of him. I knew he'd be big. I could feel as much that night in Malibu as I had palmed him through his pants. But feeling and seeing were different.

He was huge. All of him was huge. And beautiful. And *mine*.

That last thought must've garnered a sound from me because he grunted in agreement. The bed dipped underneath his knee as he crawled onto it, bringing his body over mine. He reached over his nightstand, pulling the drawer open and fishing out a condom. I took the moment to grasp him. I wanted to feel him. The satin skin over the hard as steel shaft. I pumped him a few times, admiring the length. Admiring the way he felt in my hand. The way his body tensed on top of me.

"Mm, Penelope," he groaned.

He replaced my hand with his as he rolled the condom over him. Knocking my knees wide with his own, he cradled between my legs. He nudged at my entrance, but didn't push in. I knew he was waiting for my permission. I grabbed the back of his neck, pulling his head down until his mouth hovered over mine. "Fuck me."

He moaned into my mouth, his tongue parting it open. "Keep talking like that and I'm going to come before I even get the chance." He inched in slowly. Pleasure and pain morphed together as I adjusted to his size, stretching open for him. "You're so tight," he said, his teeth gritting.

The first two thrusts were punishingly slow. Tender and timid. Filling me until I could fit all of him inside. On the third thrust, he slammed into the hilt, hitting my innermost walls. That warmth bloomed inside my core once more.

"You feel so good," he whispered. "So perfectly tight. So wet. *Fuck.*" He growled into my mouth, "It's like you were made just for me."

An accompanying moan was the only response I could produce. His tongue plunged into the depths of my throat, kissing me deeper than he ever had before. He unleashed himself on me completely as his thrusts became rapid. Those inhuman sounds tore from his throat too, mixing with mine as our mouths danced together.

I believed that some things were always meant to happen. That certain points in time had always existed– since the beginning of it. That no decision, no force, no power, could stop those moments from existing.

This was one of those moments.

He and I. Since the start. Since those atoms went soaring across the Universe. He and I were there. This moment has always been. Will always be.

I watched his eyes, every imaginable color swirling within them, as he slid into me again in a powerful thrust, pausing as he buried himself inside me.

My body, my mind, my own name became foreign to me. There was only him. He pulled out, almost all the way, before thrusting in again. Harder. Deeper. With purpose. Nothing existed except for that. The feeling of him within me. The heat. That building pressure, pounding like a drum between us.

Forehead to forehead, nose to nose. Mouth to mouth. We didn't kiss. We only breathed. Breathing life into each other. Into this moment.

"I love you, Penelope." Those words came right out of his chest and up his throat, into mine. I swallowed them as if I'd die without them.

That pressure continued rising as he gripped my hips and slammed into me. His arms moved up the backside of my thighs until they reached my knees. He pushed both legs forward, knees met my shoulders, spreading me wider as his strokes went deeper. Deeper than I thought possible, deeper than I could comprehend. Reaching a place I hadn't known was even there, my toes curled and my body tightened. My nails dug into his back, feeling his muscles tense as he worked inside of me.

Something heavy felt like it was buzzing at the center of my thighs. Like it was stuck inside a box and needed to be released. A type of release I wasn't sure I'd ever experienced before.

Carter held my legs up, somehow navigating deeper still. His strokes became unrelenting as he drove into me, unyielding as he pulled out and crashed into me once again. Over and over.

He spoke with every powerful thrust, "Every second,"

"Every minute,"

"Every breath I take."

He pulled out near completely, bringing his face back lightly so he could look at me. "I love you." He drove into me. "I *fucking* love you."

That heavy buzz burst like a dam. Flying through my chest, expelling between my legs and out of my mouth as I cried his name. Every muscle tensed around him. My face found his neck, my legs found his hips as climax ripped through me, tearing me apart.

Stars exploded in my mind.

Planets collided.

The entire Universe ruptured.

He lifted my hips at an angle, and plummeted with one final, all-consuming thrust. My head fell backwards, baring my neck to him as I tried to remember where I was, who I was. Remember anything at all. I couldn't see, or hear, or think. I could only feel.

Until his mouth found the hollow of my throat and he moaned, "Fuck, Penelope. Fuck. *Fuck.*" The rasp in his voice undid me.

Maybe fuck is my favorite word after all.

I unraveled around him, melting into him entirely. Never-ending waves of pleasure cascaded over me. Those exploding stars pouring down like infinite rainfall.

I could never have enough of this.

Nothing else would ever compare.

He shuddered as he came. He whispered my name into my neck again and again. Until he had stopped spilling himself. Until we both came down from the stars. He didn't pull out. I didn't release the hold my legs had around his hips, my arms around his neck. His mouth stayed on my throat. For an eternity we stayed there, only breathing. It was a comfortable silence. The kind I could live in forever.

Through heavy breaths he said, "That was... that was." He paused. "Otherworldly."

I nodded. "Yes." I couldn't think of any other response, any other way to describe it myself. Only, "Yes."

He reared back, and I felt painfully empty as he pulled out of me. Shivering as his body became absent from mine. He sat up, peeling the condom off and disposing of it in the trash next to his bed, before he laid down next to me, tucking his arm underneath my neck. I rolled sideways, draping my leg over his thigh. "Stay with me tonight."

He said it like a statement, not a question. But I answered, "Yes."

He looked at me, hazel eyes gleaming in the night. "You are perfect, Penelope." He brought his lips to my temple, kissing it softly. One arm splayed across my stomach, drawing circles around it. “So perfect. Ko’u mahina.”

“What does that mean?”

He smiled against my skin. “My moon.”

My heart leaped.

“Your mom calls you her ray of sunshine,” I responded.

“Kukuna o ka lā.” The words dripped like honey from his mouth. “But you, Pep. You are the moon. The stars.”

“How do you say stars in Hawaiian?”

He snorted. “I can’t remember.”

I chuckled as I flipped over more so that I was laying on top of him. His leg in between both of mine, my arms across his chest. I kissed his nose. “I love you,” I said. “How do you say that in Hawaiian?”

“Aloha au iā 'oe,” he whispered into the darkness.

Chapter Twenty Two

"Suddenly, two shooting stars collided. Our souls merged."

-Melody Lee

Carter

Madness. Utter madness.

The only word capable of describing how it felt to have her. Hold her. Openly love her.

It was an all-consuming, all-encompassing, breath-stealing type of feeling. It was as if I dissolved into her, forged my body and my heart with hers until only our souls were left. She destroyed me. Salvaged me. Ruptured me, and then healed me again.

There would be no recovery from her. She'd infect me for the rest of my life.

For the rest of time.

I'd told her as much Saturday night, long after I'd taken her for the first time. We'd talked deep into the night about everything. About the world. The stars. The moon and sun. How we fit into all of it. Then, that talking turned into so much more. Only when we were spent entirely and on the cusp of sleep did I tell her some ideation of the words I wasn't even ready to echo inside my own mind, let alone say out loud. That our connection was out of this world.

A connection outside of time and space, created by eternity itself.

She only sighed a simple, *yes*, before drifting into unconsciousness. I woke Sunday morning with her hand on my cock, followed soon after by her mouth. We didn't leave the pool house all day, fucking each other on nearly every durable surface. We'd only made it to her house in the afternoon to get enough items to last her through the night again.

By Sunday night, the roaring in our blood finally simmered enough that we were capable of lying next to each other without having me inside her. We talked about nothing and everything. She'd trace the lines of my tattoo and I'd play with her hair. Or we'd hold our hands together and she'd rub her fingers across my knuckles. Or her thumb against my lip. Or her hands in my hair. Never not touching each other, we talked until we both drifted to sleep.

I woke up much earlier than I should have, more interested in watching her than sleeping myself, only realizing how early it was when my alarm began to sound. She groaned and stuck her head beneath her pillow, draping her arms over top of it.

I chuckled, inching the sheets down her bare back and drawing circles down it. She shivered beneath my touch, her groans becoming whimpers. I was tempted to place my mouth there, to move it lower. But with less than an hour before we had to leave for work, I scrambled for any semblance of self-control. I knew if I started kissing her back, if my hands moved below her waist, we surely wouldn't make it on time.

She must've felt the same because she arched her back and grabbed the blankets, yanking them back over her before pulling her head out from the pillow. She turned to look at me, her expression sleepy and irritated. "You can't touch me right now or I won't make it to work today," she said, parroting the thoughts in my mind.

"Ditto."

She smirked at me as she slowly sat up in bed, stretching and yawning. As her arms came over her head, the sheet fell down her chest, pooling at her hips. That self-control I'd been building was quickly dissolving, along with my sanity. I hopped out of bed and grabbed a t-shirt off the ground, throwing it at her. "Please put this on before I lose my goddamn mind."

We got ready for work together, moving around each other effortlessly, even in my studio space. We'd decided to carpool this morning, since Penelope had told her parents she was staying the night at Macie's and it wouldn't make sense for her to go home to get her car anyway. I thought she was overthinking things– keeping us a secret. But I wasn't about to argue with her about it either.

After we were both dressed and ready, I peeked my head out and scanned the windows of my parents' house to ensure all the blinds and curtains were still closed. I stepped out and motioned her to follow me. Our dads already left for work, and our sisters wouldn't leave for school for another hour. So long as we weren't spotted by Marlena or Jenna, we'd be in the clear.

We made it to my truck without being seen. Though, the moment we pulled into the school parking lot, we both sighed as we caught sight of the petite blonde tapping her foot impatiently by the back entrance. Once she'd spotted us, her eyes lit up. Penelope and I hopped out of the truck and made our way towards the school.

"So, how much detail are you going to be disclosing to her?" I asked, nodding at Macie.

"You know she's going to want all of it."

I grunted. "At least try to talk me up, okay?"

She snickered. "I was just going to tell the truth."

"And what's the truth?"

"Oh, y'know, that it was at least thirty seconds. Solidly four inc–"

I cut her off, "You wound me."

She laughed just as Macie reached us and grabbed Penelope by the arm, pulling her a few paces in front of me without even so much as a greeting. I hung back and let them enter the school ahead of me, whispering in giggles.

We continued the dance we'd been doing for the previous month while our classes took place. Though our orbits were now accompanied by heated glances and electric stares. By lunch, I was ready to get away from our students and just have a few moments to be myself around her. To stop pretending that she wasn't affecting me. We had the same lunch period, and my free period took place right before it so I left campus to get us food and met her in the teacher's lounge. I'd begun to allow a few of my yearbook students to use the art room during lunch to work on it since the school year would soon be coming to a close, which meant our classroom was rarely ever empty.

Penelope smiled at me as she entered the break room, but she was looking much less relaxed than she had been all weekend. She rolled her shoulders as she sat down at the table across from me, and I could tell she was attempting to shake off any tension in hopes I wouldn't notice. But I did.

I slid the sushi roll I got her across the table. She thanked me for it, but made no motion to dig in. I nudged a set of chopsticks at her. She smiled as she grabbed them, but then only picked at her food. She tried to make small talk, asking me about my classes and my day thus far. But not once did she put a morsel of food into her mouth.

That was how I knew something was up. She couldn't eat when she was stressed out, when she was anxious. She'd always been that way, but I noticed it again when I first moved back. Over the last couple of weeks, she didn't seem to struggle with eating, at least not in front of me. So, I knew something must've been wrong at this moment for refusing her lunch.

"What's wrong, Pep?"

She sighed, as if she knew I'd realize it and didn't feel like bothering to hide it. "I'm supposed to hear from UCLA this week."

"You're nervous?"

She nodded. "You've been a good distraction." She blushed. "But now it's eating at me. By Wednesday I'll know whether or not I was accepted."

I grabbed her hand from across the table. "I have a good feeling about it. You'll get in. I have faith." She gave me a strained smile, then her face promptly dropped as I heard the door click open behind me. I didn't turn around, but I could've guessed who it was. Ignoring him entirely, I squeezed her hand. "You have to eat, though. I'll go get you something else if you don't want sushi, but I need you to eat something."

She opened her mouth before being cut off by a snide laugh. "She's a big girl, Carter. I'm sure if she wants to eat, she will." Marshall stalked into the break room, the three of us being the only ones inside. Penelope just shook her head at me, as if telling me not to engage. Marshall paused, as if waiting for us to respond. When we didn't, he asked, "How was your *trip*?"

She rolled her eyes but finally popped a piece of sushi in her mouth. He laughed again. "Or maybe she just needed a little convincing from me instead." As he walked past us, he winked at Penelope. "Good girl."

My jaw tightened as I bit back a response.

He stopped at the back counter and began preparing a new pot of coffee. I was now the one facing him. Penelope swallowed. "Fuck off," she muttered more to herself than to him.

His mouth curved into an expression I'd only describe as vile. "Oh come on, Penelope. You know I'm just joking."

"Except jokes are funny, and you're not," she murmured.

My mouth was the one curving upward now, and she smiled back at me. My eyes peeked at Marshall as he watched us, his vile smile becoming a scowl. "I see Carter hasn't managed to pull that stick out of your ass. I thought getting laid would make you less of a bitch." Her jaw dropped, her face reddened, and I thought I might have seen tears just beginning to brew behind her eyes. Marshall murmured, "Maybe he's not doing a good enough job." Penelope blinked hard, and those tears were gone. Her walls had risen. The Worm smiled as he poured coffee into his cup and began walking toward the door, brushing Penelope's shoulder as he passed her. "Let me know if I should step in."

Penelope physically recoiled.

I stood from my chair. My movements were far more calm and calculated than the rage that swirled inside me. "What the fuck did you just say to her?" I asked, though nothing about my tone made it sound like a question. Marshall's face straightened as he opened his mouth. I cut him off, "No, you know what? I think you've actually said enough. I think opening your mouth again would probably be something you'd regret." I inched toward him and he took a flustered step back.

I could see the hesitation, the kernel of fear in his eyes as he took that step. Penelope had recoiled from him, but I'd make him run from me. His eyes flashed before an easy smirk took over his face. "Are you threatening me in the workplace?"

I snorted, "Only if you continue to sexually harass women in the workplace."

"Whoa. *Sexually harass*? That's a loaded statement. I take that type of accusation very seriously." He crossed his arms over his chest. "I wouldn't want to have to get my lawyer involved."

"Like what? Defamation?" Penelope scoffed. "As if anyone gives a shit about your character."

He picked at his fingernails nonchalantly. "Well, maybe I'll need to speak with my lawyer about it, just to be sure. You know, he's a member of the school board. I'm sure he'd hate to learn about faculty members making threats and causing scenes in the breakroom." He looked up at me. "Or how about coworkers fucking each other? What's the policy on that?"

I shook my head with a breathy chuckle.

All this because he's jealous.

Pathetic.

Penelope's eyes bugged at me as the realization dawned on her. I knew I was giving away the most feral of grins. I turned toward Marshall. "Your lawyer is on the school board? For the Seaside District?"

He nodded with a vicious smirk.

I cackled, "And that wouldn't happen to be Thomas *Edwards*, would it?"

The Worm froze. His eyes widened as they darted between Penelope and I rapidly.

I nodded. "Right. Well, before you go seeking personal defense council from the County Prosecutor, *you fucking idiot*, you should know that Penelope is like a second daughter to *my* dad." I paused, crossing my own arms and leaned against the table casually. "I'm sure he'd hate to hear about the guy who publicly pants over her like a goddamn dog, harasses her at work, and purposely tries to get her drunk to take advantage of her." He began inching toward the door. I pushed off the table and took a step forward. "And I promise you, if it's your word against hers, she will win. Every time."

He threw his hands up and shook his head. Looking only at Penelope, he stuttered, "No, I wasn't. I mean, I was interested, of course. But I never meant to make you uncomfortable. I just– I'm sorry. I–"

Penelope stood up abruptly, cutting off his speech. Leaving her lunch uneaten on the table in front of her, she threw her bag over the shoulder and walked between us. "Just leave me alone, Marshall."

He looked back at me, no longer trying to hide that fear in his eyes. "I don't want you ever looking in her direction again. And if I hear a single peep about the way you treat another woman, I will go to my father. I'll ensure that you don't just lose your job, but that you never step foot inside a school again. I'll ruin your entire fucking career."

I exited the room after Penelope.

I made a mental note to report Marshall's behavior to my dad anyway. I wouldn't use her name if she didn't want me to, but assholes like him didn't deserve warnings.

She was stalking down the hall toward our classroom. She only moved faster as I jogged to catch up to her. Our room was fortunately void of students now that much of the lunch period was over. Penelope stepped inside our classroom and shut the door behind her as she stood back against the door and crossed her arms.

She held her face in a dead-pan expression, arching her brow at me. "I didn't need you defending me like that." She was in her *I'm-about-to-throw-a-fit* stance.

I mimicked her position. "And how would you have preferred I acted?"

She rolled her eyes and huffed. "I didn't need you to save me."

I ran a hand down my face. "I know, Pep. I'm sorry. I couldn't–" I thought back to the look on Marshall's face when he called Penelope a bitch. His smug expression, as if he'd just won a game only he was playing. "He does not deserve to even speak to you, Penelope. He does not deserve to breathe the same air as you." I shook my head. "I should have fucking killed him for what he said." I stepped toward her until she leaned back against the door to our office. "I'm sorry you didn't like it, but I'm not sorry about how I reacted. I will not sit around and allow anyone to ever speak to you like that. *Ever.*"

Her features took on an expression I couldn't quite place when she nodded. I sighed and leaned back from her. "Except, the only part he'll remember about that interaction is that I didn't say anything. That I had to be protected by you. That I wasn't capable of standing up for myself."

I nodded. The sound of running footsteps padded down the hall right outside our door. Kids were laughing, and I knew if we could hear them, they could hear us too. I nodded towards our office and Penelope opened the door to it. We both stepped just inside the doorway and away from the main door that led to the hall.

"I'm sorry. I understand what you're saying, but I think you're wrong, Pep. I think he'll remember that interaction as the last time he ever fucks with you, or any other woman, ever again."

"Only because you were there," she muttered. "What happens next time if you're not there? What happens if I don't get into UCLA and I have to keep working here? And you move on to go do your photography stuff and I'm alone?" She looked down at her feet.

There it is.

The truth. The real source of her distress. She had a brilliant way of beating around the bush. I'd never encountered anyone else with such a talent for it. I almost laughed. "Whoa, whoa, Pep. First of all, you already got accepted at Pepperdine, so you will not be working here next year. Second, even if you were, I'm not going anywhere." I grabbed her chin, tilting her face up to meet mine. "I let you go once. You're fucking crazy if you think I'm doing that again. I go where you go, baby. I'm right where you are."

She deflated against the doorway, and her eyelashes fluttered a thousand miles an hour. "That scares me too," she murmured. Before I could even process her statement, offer a response, and have a dreaded feeling about what she was saying, she continued, "The last time I tried to balance my love life and my academic life, everything around me fell apart horribly." I opened my mouth to ask what she meant by that, but she shook her head. "I told you I don't know how to do this. I don't know how to have that balance. I only know how to make my entire life about my education, and my career, and my future. Right now, I feel like my entire life is you. And I *love* it. But I don't know how to do both. I don't know if going back to school is going to make me lose you."

"Penelope, I don't need to be your entire life, I just want to be a part of it." I laughed. "Trust me when I tell you I know exactly what I am agreeing to here. I've seen you shut people out and live off granola bars for an entire week while you studied for your A.P. finals. I watched you chew your nails to the point of bleeding when you were waiting for your college acceptance letters." I rubbed my thumb across her lips. "I saw the look on your face the first time we kissed, and I knew exactly how you felt about me. Then, I watched you leave anyway because you were determined to chase your dreams. I know what to expect being with you, and I accept all of it.

"Let me show you that you can have both. You can prioritize your education, and your career, and I will still be here. I'll help you see that all of it has a place in your future, including me. You don't have to choose. Never again. You will always, *always* have me."

The faintest of smirks clustered at the corner of her mouth. I matched it with my own as it morphed into *my* smile. "I don't know how you think I'm ever going to be focused on my studies when you're saying things like that to me."

I pressed against her, backing her up until she was completely inside our office, shutting the door behind me. She leaned back against our desk. I braced my hands against it on either side of her as she arched into my chest. I pressed my lips to her throat, "I know you may be tempted to skip out on class, or homework, or whatever prestigious ass internship you'll inevitably find yourself in, so you can stay home and jump my bones all day." Her chest was heaving, her heart pounding in sync with mine. "But if I have to physically pry you off of me in order for you to stay on top of your shit, I will."

She snorted, "I don't imagine I'll struggle with that as much as you think I would."

I smiled against her jaw, dragging my mouth up to her lips. "I suppose I'll have to prove you otherwise, then." I sucked her bottom lip under my teeth and bit down on it.

She gasped. "That..." She moaned. "That would be very unprofessional," her hand found its place around my neck, pressing me into her tighter, "in the workplace."

I released my hold on her lips so they could move freely on top of mine. She flicked her tongue across my bottom lip, releasing a groan of my own. "Then I'll just have to wait until after work to show you just how addicting I can be."

"Bold of you to assume I'm addicted to you."

I chuckled, removing my mouth from hers and bringing it to her ear. "Tell me that again the next time you're coming on my tongue." I nipped on her earlobe. "On my cock."

I felt her body tighten against me, I felt her legs squeeze together and imagined the wetness pooling there. "The bell is going to ring soon," she whimpered.

I nodded, knowing I'd need a moment to come down from this. Remembering how insanely inappropriate we were being in the workplace. Remembering I had a class to teach in ten goddamn minutes.

She planted her hand on my chest as I pulled back from her. She straightened out her sweater and brushed her fingers through her hair. As if any of it would hide the fact that she was entirely flushed. "I've got to get to class." She stepped toward the door. I kissed her once more before opening it for her. "Oh, and Christine asked me to stay a little late with her and help her grade some of the projects the students had been working on over spring break." She chewed on her lip. "I can have Maddie come pick me up later?"

I shook my head. "That actually works fine, Pep. I was thinking about going surfing after work, anyway. So maybe I can drop by and grab you on my way back home. Around six?"

She gripped the handle to the main classroom door when a smile bloomed on her cheeks. She leaned in and kissed me once more. It was quick and effortless. Casual in a way that felt permanent. It stirred up something in my stomach that felt like flight. "Sounds good," she chimed before she slipped out the door.

I leaned against the door frame, watching her as she disappeared down the hall knowing the smile that shadowed my face. Stepping back into the classroom, I pulled out my phone.

Dom picked up on the third ring.

"I need you to call my dad. Tell him he and I can talk more about it tonight, but I need you to handle whatever needs to be done to get an offer put in that apartment complex in Venice. Tell my dad I'll manage it for him. Tell him I've got ideas for the studio, too."

I could hear him smiling on the other side of the phone.

Chapter Twenty Three

"A soulmate doesn't have to be a romantic relationship. Sometimes in life, you meet people when you need them..."

-Alison G. Bailey

Penelope

We made it all of one night in separate beds before I found myself crawling back into his late last night. I told him on Monday that I thought it would be best for me to stay at home during the week. It wasn't realistic that I'd be spending so much time with Macie. I loved her, but I wasn't a fan of sleepovers with my friends as a child, let alone as an adult. It'd be unconvincing to my parents that I'd be sleeping there so often.

Despite that, I found myself somehow being talked into another surf lesson yesterday after work. Carter claimed it was to get my mind off of the pending admissions decision from UCLA. I was adamant there were more effective ways of distracting me, but once I found myself pressed against his chest in the water again, UCLA was not at the forefront of my mind. Afterwards, I told my parents I was going out with Macie and Jeremy, but I really went back to Carter's. It was ten-thirty before we realized we'd spent over three hours grading assignments together in his bed. He'd suggested we deserved a break, and I agreed. After our break left us spent and breathless, I was too exhausted—too enticed—to leave.

Waking up next to someone was not something I'd ever felt I had been missing. I never felt lonely when I was asleep. The last time I slept next to another person on a consistent basis was my mother when I was young. We couldn't afford a place with more than one bedroom, so we shared it. Shared the bed too. When I was adopted and was given a room of my own, it was something almost incomprehensible to me. But there was something about sleeping alone that I knew should have scared me. I'd never slept by myself before. Instead, though, it became something that I had only ever shared with my mother. A piece of me that wouldn't belong to anyone else.

It felt different with Carter, though. Four nights in the last week I've spent sleeping next to him. I was beginning to hover dangerously in the area of having this as a routine. And yet, that didn't scare me at all. I'd spent so much of my life hoarding this feeling to myself, that I never allowed myself to savor the way it felt to share someone's body heat. To slip just out of consciousness in the middle of the night and be unaware of almost everything around you except for the breathing of that other person.

To feel safe, protected, by that person's breathing. By their presence.

I never had that with James. We rarely spent full nights together, and even when we did, it didn't feel like this. It didn't feel like waking up next to someone and knowing that the immediate start of your day will consist of your mouth on theirs. Of their smile being the very first thing you see, accented by the morning light. That the first thing you touch will be them. The first sound being their shallow breaths, their beating heart, their voice. To wake up knowing that you're offering them the same experience. That they're savoring it in all the ways you are too.

This feeling was something I hadn't known I was missing.

Something I never wanted to sleep without again.

His face was somehow even more relaxed when he slept than when he was awake. I wasn't sure that could even be possible. If his consciousness was a breeze, I imagined his subconscious as a flowing river stream. No trace or hint of struggle, fear, or uncertainty reflected in his features. I wondered what my features gave away on the mornings he woke before me. I wondered if he watched me sleep too, and if he did, were the hauntings of my mind apparent on my face, or did I appear as peaceful as he does now?

Sleeping next to him brought me comfort I hadn't known existed before. I knew within that I was sleeping better—more deeply, more soundly—than I had in months. Years, probably. Though certain moments flashed behind my eyes from time to time that held enough weight to crush my chest. Sometimes I could still feel those tendrils of anxiety coiling around my throat and threatening to cut off my air supply. Those tendrils could creep up on me in my dreams. I wondered, if he'd been watching me during one of those moments, would he have been able to see them too?

It killed me that I was still lying to Carter. Well, not lying, per se. More like omitting the truth. I admitted to him that I cheated in order to get into the grad program at Oxford. It went onto my transcripts and severely impacted the way other schools see me. I told him I had a fraudulent letter of recommendation for the program. Which wasn't *technically* true. At least, I think James meant what he'd written in the letter.

Even so, it'd been eating away at me for weeks. Now that he'd vowed to move to California, to follow me, I knew I needed to tell Carter the entire story. He deserves to know before he commits to me.

I know that, and yet, I can't seem to get the words to come every time I think I've gained the courage to do it. Carter has accepted every part of me. Even the parts I don't like, even the things that drive him nuts. He accepts them, I think he may even love them. To imagine the disappointment in his face, to imagine him losing his trust in me, his belief in who I am; I don't think I could bear it. He's the only person I've felt may love me truly, deeply, unconditionally. My past may be a condition he can't overcome. I'm not sure how I'd overcome not only losing him, but knowing without a doubt that I'd done something that even unconditional love can't conquer.

He'd been wrong all those times when he accused me of not believing in love. I did. I always, always had believed in love. What I wasn't sure I could believe in was whether or not love was something that was in the cards for me. If it was something I deserved anymore. Because for a time, my morals changed. I was selfish, greedy, and reckless. I created a path of destruction and ran away from it when it blew up in my face. I wasn't worthy of someone like him. I wasn't deserving of the love he could give me. To know that while I had been turning into the worst version of myself, he had been waiting for me– that had almost broken me.

So I now stood at a crossroads of having him and hating myself. Or giving myself over to him, every ugly part of who I am, and facing the chance that he may not accept it.

A ray of morning sun shone through the crack in the blinds, illuminating just over his lips, as sparkles of light floated down to accent his skin. I traced the outline of his tattoo around his bicep, moving my fingers up along his shoulder. Thoughts emptied from my mind entirely as I found contentment in this moment. Watching him sleep, running my fingers along his skin, savoring the warmth his body provided. The quiet of the early morning, the belief that the rest of the world slept along with him.

He was the tether that tied me back to earth.

He was still heavy with sleep when my phone chimed. I started at the sound because I was sure I had silenced it last night before I fell asleep. My phone chimed again and Carter's eyes fluttered open. He blinked at me as a lazy smile spread across his face. "Good morning," he said.

I ran my fingers through the curls that nested on top of his head. "Sorry my phone woke you. I thought I silenced it last night."

He sat up out of bed quickly, eyes lingering on me only for a moment before he lunged for my phone. He scrambled toward the other end of his bed and held it against his chest. "Don't get mad at me."

"What?" I asked. I'd been awake longer than he had, but it had been that peaceful, lazy, early morning consciousness. His sudden movements made me painfully confused.

"I turned on notifications for your email after you fell asleep last night so you'd be notified when you received the decision from UCLA."

"Carter," I growled.

He held his hand up. "I know, I know. You can be as mad at me as you want to later. I've already thought through the ways I'll make it up to you." He bit down on his lip. I shivered. "But let's rip the Band-Aid off, Pep. Just check your email, and then you'll know for sure. I am not going to watch you anxiously wither away all day long lost inside your own head. Anxious to the point you can't eat. Can't hardly speak." He pulled my phone away from his chest and glanced down at the screen before looking up at me. "I can't stand it. So let's just find out, and then we'll figure out where to go from there."

I huffed. "Is the email even from UCLA?"

He nodded.

My gut twisted into knots. I nodded back.

He entered the passcode on my phone (my birthday, which he had correctly guessed on the first try) and opened the email. I watched in panic as his eyes dragged across the screen, reading the school's response line by line. His eyebrows rose up and his eyes widened. His mouth gaped slightly. I couldn't tell if the expression was shock, disappointment, dismay, or excitement. It would have been any of them– could have been all of them. It couldn't have been more than a few seconds, but I swore it felt like years as I waited for him to look at me. To speak.

Instead, he smiled. A smile so wide, so bright, it felt like I was being licked by a ray of sunlight. It was more than excitement, surprise, or shock. "Miss Penelope Mason," he drew out my name knowing it'd build my suspense, "welcome to the Graduate of Archaeology Program at the University of California Los Angeles."

The sob was already bubbling up my throat before he'd finished speaking. It erupted from my mouth as his words ceased. I could feel my eyes swelling as the emotion settled around me. Tears overflowed as the realization set in. All I could do was drop my face into my hands as I heaved and cried. I'd been so scared for so long. Afraid I'd thrown my entire life away over one bad judgment call. I'd been stuck in this purgatory for over a year. A door only appeared when Carter entered my life, and now that door had finally opened.

UCLA had been a top choice school for me since the beginning. I wanted to stay in Oxford if I could, but when I had thought about moving home in my first few years of college, UCLA was the school I saw myself attending. It wasn't just the fact that it was a top-rated school. Or that their program was renowned. Or the career opportunities that would come with connections there. It was the environment too.

After a lifetime of rain, I wanted sunshine.

When everything came crashing down and I had to leave Oxford, I was set on UCLA. Until I'd been rejected from nearly every other program I'd applied to. When I had been rejected from programs less extensive, less demanding, less prestigious. I'd all but given up hope on this dream.

It didn't feel real.

The bed dipped and shuffled as I was being pulled by two strong arms into a hard body. I pressed my cheek against his chest. "It's real, Pep," he said. I realized I must've said it out loud. "It's real. You did it. You did it."

He rocked me for a long while as I let out all of the feelings I'd held back for so long. I let out everything that had dragged me down. That had drained me. All the fear and guilt, all the pain. Until the only feelings left were hope and love.

He wrapped both arms around my hips and sat up, whirling me back so that I fell against the bed. He pressed his lips to mine once more before he pushed off the bed and stood up. I braced myself on my elbows and looked at him. He smiled as he threw a t-shirt at me. “No sex until you go tell your parents the good news.”

I pouted.

He walked into the bathroom. I slipped on my bra and threw the t-shirt over my head. I began sorting through the pile of my clothes that had accumulated on his bedroom floor throughout the week, looking for a pair of sweats that would resemble something I may have worn at Macie’s. I walked up to his door and slipped on my shoes while simultaneously pulling my hair into a bun when he stepped out of the bathroom.

I turned to face him and stepped forward to press against his chest. I pressed up on my toes to level my mouth with his nose and planted a kiss there. “I love you,” he whispered.

“I love you,” I returned as I stepped out his door and into the chilled April air.

I wasn’t worried about running into any of our family members at this time of morning. Tom was likely already at work, and my father had Wednesdays off. Our sisters were probably still in bed since school had a late start. I still snuck across the Edwards’ yard on the far side of the shrubs. Another routine I found myself falling into.

Sneaking across the street felt dangerously close to a walk of shame, though I wasn’t sure why. It likely had something to do with the way my hair sprouted from my head, flailing in all different directions. Or the fact that I hadn’t washed the shirt I was wearing in a week. Or maybe that I’d put on Carter’s shoes instead of my own, which I’d failed to notice until I was standing at my front door. We had similar pairs of slip-on sandals, except his were about three sizes bigger than mine.

Hoping I'd be able to sneak up stairs before anyone noticed me, I unlocked the door and slipped inside. My hopes were stopped short when my mother's face peeked past the wall that separated the kitchen from the entryway. She tilted her head. "Penelope?"

"Hi," I whispered.

"I thought you were at Macie's?"

My sister then stepped out of the kitchen, past my mother, and looked me up and down. Her eyebrow flicked in accusation. It was clear she had assumptions about what I had actually been doing last night. What concerned me was her assumptions of who I may have been doing those things with– and if she'd voice them.

I pointed at the door behind me with my thumb. "Yeah, she just dropped me off. I have some news. Is dad up yet?"

I walked into the kitchen, just realizing how suspicious it was that I didn't have a bag with me. I'd left everything at Carter's as if I was casually strolling over to my parent's and would be right back. I also realized, subconsciously at least, that's what my intention had been. Even though it made no sense. My mom glided down the hall to my parents' bedroom to get my dad. My sister stared at me as if she was searching me for evidence.

"Whose shoes are those?" she asked.

My toes curled under her stare. "Macie's boyfriend. I spilled wine on mine last night and so he lent me these." I almost winced at how bad the excuse was.

She nodded, unconvinced. "You've been staying at Macie's a lot lately."

"Congratulations on your observation," I muttered.

Our parents' door opened as they both breezed through it. My father still looked groggy, his dark hair uncombed and messy. My mother had always been an early bird. She was in loungewear, but it was clear she had already showered this morning. She handed an already made cup of coffee to my father as they gathered around the kitchen. "Do we need to call Easton?" my dad asked.

I shrugged. "Not right now. It's not worth waking him."

I dove into the news with them, relaying the information that Carter and I had discovered this morning. I told them I hadn't ironed out the details, but that I had gotten in. That was all that mattered. My father gushed with pride, and my mother teared. I willed myself not to cry again as well. I felt the relief flood and settle through all of us. As if this wound in our relationship may just begin to heal.

Maddie leaned in for a congratulatory hug. "I knew the news must've been good, given that you were braving a walk of shame to share it," she whispered. Flustered, I pulled away from her but she held me in place. "But for real, Pep. You deserve it. All of it. I'm really happy for you."

She just called me Pep.

It'd been years since anyone had called me that except Carter. Her words felt weighted as she let me go. I could only smile at my sister, who somehow was looking like a woman. She was devious and playful and meddlesome. Carter told me once that Macie reminded him of her, and I could see it too. Also, like Macie, Maddie was fierce and loyal. She'd always supported me, believed me. From that very first night I came back from England, she'd been my rock in the most discreet of ways. As I looked at her, I felt a wave of gratitude wash over me. It felt foreign and overwhelming, as if it was something that didn't wholly belong to me.

I shook it off, those threatening tears pounding behind my eyes. I cleared my throat. "Thank you." Blinking rapidly, I turned toward the hallway. "I'm going to go get ready for work. I'm meeting Macie for coffee before school so I can tell her the good news." I smiled.

Until Maddie's palm hit against her forehead.

My father's forehead creased. "But weren't you just with Macie? You haven't told her?"

Fuck.

"Right. Yeah, well, I wanted to tell you guys first."

My mother snorted, as if she didn't believe me either. I realized it was obvious at this point that I had not been with Macie last night, or likely any of the other nights this week. It was painfully obvious that I had been with a guy. Maybe it was even obvious I had been with Carter, but I wasn't ready to dive into that with them. My father shrugged, his way of letting it go. I followed suit as I bounded up the stairs. My sister's stifled laugh was trailing behind me.

A massive cinnamon roll and a steaming mug of coffee sat on the table in front of the empty seat next to Macie as I walked into the coffee shop. "A cinnamon roll?" I asked.

She beamed. "I hear congratulations are in order."

I frowned. "Who told you?"

She nodded toward the front counter of the coffee shop. I found myself surprised that I was able to make it inside and to our table without noticing him. Carter leaned against the counter and watched me with a smile. "You ruined the surprise!" I shouted across the room at him.

The barista handed him his coffee and he walked toward Macie and I. He set his drink down at our table and stood behind my chair. Leaning in against my face he said, "I know how you hate surprises." He kissed my cheek. "And Macie is annoyingly persistent."

I shrugged because I couldn't argue with him. Macie watched the both of us with a fascination that was almost childlike. He grabbed his drink and backed away toward the door. He pushed it open with his hip, mouthing, *love you*, at me before leaving.

My heart fluttered and I wondered if I'd ever get used to it.

Somehow, I didn't think so.

"Well, that was disgustingly adorable," Macie muttered.

I leveled her with a stare. "That sounded pretty bitter coming from someone who is supposed to be in love herself." She rolled her eyes at me. "You want to finally tell me what the hell is going on with you and Jeremy?"

She'd been dancing around the topic every time I'd tried to bring it up. She'd tell me that they had a fight, they were working things out, and everything was fine. But I hadn't seen them together once since we came back from Malibu. Macie arrived at school each day alone and left each day the same way. They weren't having lunch together either. She'd been glued to her classroom, ignoring me too.

She sighed. "It was just a lot of little things that built up over time. He never wanted me to be myself. He was always telling me I'm too loud or too obnoxious. That I cause a scene. I get too excited about things. That I'm too stubborn, too high maintenance."

"Mace–" I started, but realized I didn't know what to say.

She nodded. "And that's fine. I'm fine with that. I *am* like that. And I had twenty-six years to accept that about myself. I *like* who I am—my personality—no matter how big it may seem to some people. That's what I told myself. That I had twenty-six years to accept who I am, and Jeremy has only known me for three. So, I gave him time." I nodded. "But it all kind of came to a head in Malibu, and I tried telling him how I felt, but he wouldn't even acknowledge it. He wouldn't entertain for one second that what I was saying could be true. I just realized he's never going to change." She shrugged. "I also realized that maybe I want someone who is a little more like me anyway. But I love Jeremy enough to not ask him to change who he is for me. He wasn't willing to do the same. So, I ended things."

"I'm so sorry, Macie," I said. She gave me a closed mouth smile that wasn't quite genuine but was at least grateful. "What was your breaking point?" I found myself asking.

She scratched her neck, her face looking more solemn than I'd ever seen it. "Carter." I tilted my head, willing her to say more. "The way he looks at you. He said something to you before you went to the conference. He saw that you were anxious, and it was making you irritable. But he didn't try to make you different. He adjusted what he was saying, how he was handling things, to accommodate what you needed at that moment. He told you how smart you were. He knew exactly how to speak to you, how to touch you, how to comfort you to make you feel better." She smiled a little. "Jeremy never did that with me. He's never looked at me the way Carter looks at you."

I stared at my hands and noticed them tremble. She was correct. Maybe it was the way he studied me for so many years that made him accustomed to who I was. I don't know. But she was exactly right. I knew she was right about the way Carter looked at me too. Another beating reminder in the back of my mind that I didn't deserve him. I never would.

I also knew she was right about Jeremy. I'd noticed it before, the way he'd cringe at things she said or the way she acted. He never shared her excitement for anything. I'd never said anything because I figured Macie saw it too, and I always knew if she wanted to do something about it, she would. Macie was the last person on earth who needed someone else to step in and save her, but I wondered if I should've said something sooner. I wondered how much weight I may have held.

I now wondered if she'd stay here in Brighton without him. She didn't have family here. She had friends, but none she liked as much as she liked me. She had her job, but teachers were in short supply. She could work anywhere. I wondered if she'd consider moving to Los Angeles with me. I wanted her to live somewhere she could glitter. I feel like she couldn't do that with Jeremy, and she couldn't do that here alone either.

"He dulled your brightness," I said. "He didn't want you to shine brighter than he does."

She nodded. "I know. That's why I know I'll be fine." She shook her head and it radiated down through her shoulders as if she was removing the weight of the conversation from her body. I could tell she was ready to change the subject. I knew she'd turn the focus back on me now.

"Do you think it's wrong of me not to tell Carter the truth about James?" I found myself changing the subject for her.

Her face scrunched. "That's hard for me to say, Penny. You've never told me the truth about James. Not really."

I glanced at my phone. We had just over an hour until school started. I glanced around the coffee shop though I wasn't sure why. Nobody here knew me, nobody cared about my past. Yet, I looked around as if someone may be eavesdropping. I'd told Macie some of the truth. The same way I did with my parents, and Carter, and the disciplinary committee at Oxford. Everyone got bits and pieces.

I wasn't sure myself if I was really ready to share the story in its entirety. It wasn't something I'd ever told anyone before. But for the first time, the truth wasn't something that just affected me. It would affect Carter too. The burden of whether or not to tell him when to tell him was something I was struggling to come to terms with on my own. Macie was the only person in the world I trusted to help me make the decision.

With a heavy sigh, I dumped it all out on her. I told her everything. Every gross detail.

How I had been a nineteen-year-old virgin (not that the virgin part mattered *that* much) when I arrived at Oxford. That my only identity was my major. What I wanted to do in life. How I thought, before I left, that new identity would give me some kind of power.

I'd no longer be the adopted girl, or the girl whose mom overdosed, or Dr. Mason's daughter, or Easton's sister, or the weird girl who turned down being Valedictorian. I was just Penelope, just me. And somehow, that didn't make people more drawn to me or less drawn to me. I wasn't sure how to feel about that. I spent the first six months at Oxford floating around in my own head. Homesick. Heartbroken.

The only connection I made during that time was the professor for my ancient technology course that first semester. Dr. James Martin. He was a renowned archaeologist, credited with multiple discoveries. There were several Oxford professors I wanted to learn from that had inspired me to attend there, including him. His was the only class I was able to enroll in that first semester, though. I ate up every word he said and I attended every lecture. I began going to his open office hours to try and learn more. I was mostly looking for a mentor, but at that point I'd met nobody. I made no friends. I hardly spoke to my roommate. I think I was really, maybe, just looking for a connection– a companion.

James was interesting and intriguing. He had so much knowledge and advice. More than that, he seemed to believe in me. Believed I had what it took to succeed in the industry. He began to offer me tutoring sessions and extra credit opportunities. I believed he was taking an interest in me because he saw my potential. I started to see the signs that maybe his interest in me extended farther than just the academic level, but I ignored those advances. Too afraid that I was either misreading them, or that if I backed away from them, I'd lose my mentor– my friend, too.

Then, one day I decided to take the train to London at the insistence of my parents. I hadn't been since I moved there. I traveled across the world by myself, and I think that had wiped all of the courage out of me because I wasn't able to explore London on my own. The culture shock was more intense than I had prepared myself for, and I became overwhelmed. I somehow ended up in a small pub outside the Liverpool Station. After sitting there for over two hours, and twice as many cocktails, I stumbled out of the bar, ready to go back to Oxford. In my state of mind at the time, I ended up getting off at the wrong station. Somewhere between London and Oxford, though I didn't know where. I realized then that the only phone number I'd managed to get in my first six months there was James'. So, I called him, just to get directions on how to get back to Oxford. I was horribly embarrassed, drunk, and crying. I was homesick and struggling more with classes than I had expected to be. I wanted to move home, but I also didn't.

And I missed Carter. I remember missing Carter that night.

The night I found that soulmate theory written on the bathroom wall.

James figured out where I was and drove to pick me up. He said he couldn't take me back to my dorm and risk being seen by another student and having someone *get the wrong idea*. So, he took me back to his apartment near campus. He was kind, supportive, and even a little funny. He didn't make me feel stupid, or young, or naive. Or out of place. When he brought me back to his apartment that night, I let one thing lead to another. I never told him I was a virgin, and if he figured it out afterwards, he never said anything.

After that, for almost two years, that's what our relationship consisted of. He gave me guidance, advice, proof-read my essays and helped me with homework, and got me into special conferences that under-grads normally couldn't attend. He promised to help me make connections, he promised to help me get into grad school, to support me through my PhD. In return, I had sex with him. And it wasn't the worst thing in the world. We both gave each other the only thing we wanted, the only thing we could handle. I had no desire to fall in love, and he wouldn't want that from me anyway. So it was fine. It worked.

Until I learned he was married. That he had two kids– twin boys. I found out after he snuck me into the grand opening of a new exhibition at Ashmolean. He introduced me as his intern to everyone we met. Until a colleague of his asked where his wife was. He mentioned she was at home, and then that colleague asked how his boys were.

I'd been devastated. Not because I loved him or because I saw a future with him. Not even because I was jealous. But just because he was a cheater, and he'd conned me into being a homewrecker. He first told me their relationship was open, and I said he was a liar. Then he told me how unhappy he was with his life, and for some reason, I sympathized. But not enough to continue the affair.

That was two months before my graduate application was due. He was on the evaluation committee. He would be directly responsible for whether or not I may be accepted. He'd written a stunning letter of recommendation for me as well. Though, he hadn't given it to me yet. He merely told me that ending things with him wouldn't be in my best interest. That he had on good authority that I was unlikely to be accepted into the program without his *help*.

I'd become so reliant on him, I so surely believed that I couldn't be successful without it.

That no class I'd passed, no exhibition I attended, no connection I had made had been done without him. That *he* had chosen *me* and had deemed me worthy of him. Of his guidance, his mentorship, his presence. I believed him when he said those things. I was desperate.

I wanted to be just like him.

I continued that affair for another three months, until I got accepted to the Graduate Programme at Oxford. Not long after, his wife found some emails between us on their home computer. They were incriminating. Incriminating for me. There was one email where I, in a little game we'd play, offered various sexual favors in return for answering questions I needed for different class assignments. The email was old, from before I knew he had a wife. He hadn't responded to it because he'd just called me and explained to me what he wanted in person.

She'd found condoms in his car. Apparently, she found my underwear in one of his bags too. So she knew he was having the affair, even though the only concrete proof she had was the email I sent. She reported the email to the school. When James was called in for questioning, he claimed that it had all been me. That I was desperate for acceptance into the Graduate Programme, that he'd taken me on as a mentee, and so I offered him something more in exchange for his letter of recommendation. Even when everything in both our lives had blown up, even when there was no more hiding things, no way out; he still shredded me apart to uphold any ounce of his reputation.

He held no regard for how it would affect me.

I was so numb by that, by what he did, that when the committee held my hearing, I did nothing to defend myself. I didn't even speak. I only nodded or shook my head at their questions. They asked me if I had an affair with my professor. If I offered sexual favors in exchange for his letter of recommendation. I had to say yes, because he hadn't been lying. He'd just downplayed the role he played in it too.

In the end he lost his job. He lost his credibility. He lost his family. I lost Oxford. I lost my reputation. I lost my dignity and my identity. I moved home after that. I've been crawling through the last year of my life, through the shattered pieces of myself, trying to find a way to glue her back together. I had thought I'd at least begun to recover, but speaking all of it out loud to Macie, the first time I'd ever done so, made me feel like I was shattering all over again.

I didn't realize I was even crying until I felt the tear drop off my chin. I looked up at Macie and realized she was crying too. Crying for me, or because of me, I wasn't sure. I couldn't tell if she was shocked that I wasn't the person she thought I was or angry that I could do something so awful.

"Penelope, are you serious?"

It felt strange to hear my full name come from Macie's lips. She started calling me Penny the day she met me. I wasn't sure she'd ever used my full name before. I buried my face in my hands. "I know, I know. It's the worst thing I've ever done."

She leaned across the table and pulled me hands away from my face. "The worst thing *you've* ever done? Penelope, I– I think you have Stockholm Syndrome or something."

Stockholm Syndrome?

"What the fuck are you–"

"Do your parents know about this?"

"Of course they know, Macie. I had to call them when I was kicked out of school over it. My visa was revoked. I had to move back home."

"*No*, Penelope. Do they know what James did to you? Did Oxford? Have you ever told anyone the full story?"

I opened my mouth and shut it again several times. I just shook my head. My parents had been informed that I'd offered a professor sex in exchange for help getting into grad school. That was the extent of what they knew. I think they believed I had sex with him one time. Carter knew there was a man named James and that I was a fraud. He didn't know the two were related. Maddie and Easton knew as much as my parents did, or maybe less. We didn't talk about it.

"Penelope, you have to tell someone. He...he *groomed* you. He *made* you do those things. Do you understand that? Do you understand what happened to you? Penelope, you need to tell your dad right now. You need to tell Oxford. Is he still teaching there?"

I shook my head profusely. "No, Mace. You're not understanding. I did–" I stuttered. I wasn't sure what to say. I couldn't comprehend what she was talking about. I'd heard that word before, *groomed*, but it wasn't what this was. I was an adult. Stupid, naive, but an adult. A consenting adult. I made those choices as much as he did. I blew through my nose. "No, he's no longer teaching. He was punished just as much as I was. There is no point in re-opening all of it. That's not why I was telling you."

She sighed, wiping her face. I'd never seen her look so serious. "*You* shouldn't have been punished for this, Penelope. You are the victim."

"You're not understanding. I'm not. I– I am not a victim. I fucked up, big time. And I am asking you if you think I need to tell Carter. If you think it'll make him rethink being with me." I looked down at my lap, murmuring that last sentence. It had been the hardest one of all to get out.

She glanced at her phone and stood up, throwing her purse over her shoulder. We only had fifteen minutes before we both needed to be back at school. My cinnamon roll sat untouched in front of me. "I think you should tell him, but not for the reasons you think. I think you need to come to terms with this situation for yourself first before you involve him. You need to understand what happened to you." I stood up with her, caught by surprise as she embraced me. She said into my shoulder, "And you need to talk to someone about this, Penelope. If not your parents, if not me, then a therapist. I don't think you've even begun to process this, and you need to. Before you can move forward, with Carter or otherwise, you need to talk to someone about what happened to you. *Please*."

I was too stunned to respond, so I nodded. I followed her to the parking lot, then into the school. She hugged me again before she went to her classroom. I went straight to Christine's because I was late. My chest, my stomach, and my head felt hollow. But I could only come to the conclusion that Macie was horribly confused. She had misunderstood everything I said. Which was fine, I guess.

Because I somehow felt relieved that she agreed I wasn't ready to tell Carter about it. That made me feel less guilty.

I agreed to think about seeing a therapist, but I wasn't sure I'd follow through on her request. I vehemently avoided therapy since I was about twelve. My parents made me go for years after my adoption, my mom's death. But at some point, it became more tedious than helpful. I asked if I could stop going, and they didn't push it. But maybe I could try again. Maybe, at the least, it'd help me find a way to tell Carter. I wasn't convinced it would fix me. It wouldn't fix the actions I'd already taken, the things I've already done. But maybe it could help me get him to understand.

My head throbbed with all the conflicting thoughts that floated through my mind.

I navigated throughout my day in a blur. I told Carter I had to stay after work again to help Christine. Our parents had already made dinner plans on our behalf to celebrate my acceptance and we agreed to meet directly at the restaurant. We agreed to act platonic while we were at it. We agreed not to tell anyone about us yet.

After work, when I knew Carter had left for the day, I snuck back into the art room. Christine hadn't needed my help, just like she didn't need it any other day this week. I sorted through the closet I knew Carter never used until I found everything I needed. I locked the classroom door to be safe.

Throwing on my smock, I stood in front of the easel and stared for a long while, determining my next move. The process of painting was feeling a little like my life. Maybe that's why I kept coming here day after day. Where life felt stagnant before, it was flowing again. Just like my inspiration. I began mixing blue and white together, then orange and white, then pink and purple. Creating three different shades of the soft, peaceful sunrise that I was remembering in my head. I swept my brush across the canvas.

Chapter Twenty Four

"Our souls speak a language that is beyond human understanding. A connection so rare the universe won't let us part."

-Nikki Rowe

Carter

She laid back in the chair opposite mine, the fire roaring between us as she took another bite of her pizza. "I just don't understand."

I pinched the bridge of my nose. "*I* don't understand, Pep. It is disgusting."

"But you're Hawaiian! *This* is in your blood, Carter." She held up the pizza above her head, tilting it at me so I'd have to look at it. I watched a piece of pineapple fall off the tip of the slice and splatter on the ground in front of her.

My face twisted into something that spelt disgust. I shook my head as she inhaled another mouthful. Penelope now was absolutely glowing in comparison to the person I'd come home to a few months ago. Gone is the woman who hid herself from the world. Who punished herself for every mistake she ever made. Who believed she wasn't lovable. She was lighter, and brighter. She was excited about her future, but content in her present. She was painting, she was drawing, she was reading. She was loving herself, loving others. Loving *me*.

I fucking love her.

I'd caught her painting a couple of weeks ago when I found her in the art room after work one afternoon. She wouldn't show me the canvas she was working on, but she had green paint smeared across her face and hands. Sometimes she did show me her sketches, though. I wasn't surprised by that. Drawing was her natural talent, but painting was a skill she had to build. She was still the same in that she liked to be the best at something, or she didn't want to do it at all. So painting for her, I believe, was a much bigger deal than she even realized. I wouldn't push her to show me her work until she was ready to. She liked to sit on the couch in the pool house and draw while I sat at my desk and edited photos. Or sometimes she'd come with me on trips to shoot locations, and she'd bring her sketch book. Content to draw while I took pictures of the world around us. And of her, too. She was incredibly distracting.

The girl staring at me now, picking the grilled pineapple off her pizza and eating it by itself, was a stark contrast to the hollow shell I'd found when I moved home. She'd done all the hard work of putting herself back together. She was the one who worked her ass off to get into UCLA, she was the one who chose to start seeing a therapist several weeks ago, she was the one who continued to get back up every single time the Universe knocked her down. Yet, she liked to try and give me the credit. I think that maybe I helped. Maybe I helped teach her how to accept herself, how to love herself, how to have a little more fun in life.

But at the end of the day, it was her. It was all her.

She dropped the half-eaten piece of pizza onto the box next to us and clapped her hands together before rubbing the grease down her leggings. Walking around the firepit to the bench I was sitting on, she picked up my arm and ducked underneath it, snuggling into my side.

We sat in silence for a while, watching the flames pop and blaze in front of us. My parents were out of town for the night, staying in Portland, and my sister was staying with Penelope's parents. Early June provided pleasant enough weather that I thought we could light a fire and have take-out in the backyard rather than huddling in my bed and hiding like we normally do. Do something that was more out in the open, for once.

It was glaringly obvious to her parents she was seeing someone. Whether or not it was obvious that she was seeing *me* remained unknown. They had never asked her about who the man in question was, so she was convinced that they must not assume we were together. I thought the opposite. They assumed it was me, but since she hadn't said anything, they wouldn't either. But we kept it a secret regardless. Penelope decided we'd tell our families once we moved.

It was harder to hide from her parents than mine since I lived in a separate building. Though the hardest challenge of all was to hide it from our sisters. I first disagreed with keeping things secret until I caught our sisters trying to install a doorbell camera outside the pool house last week. They were trying to catch whomever it was *I* had coming in and out of the pool house.

Whether because they thought it was Penelope or someone else, I didn't ask.

After that, I thought it may not be a bad idea after all to lay low until we move. With the way our families operated, it may be news best served over a phone call than a family dinner.

Luckily, within the next three weeks, both of us would become residents of Southern California. We were technically moving down separately. Penelope was getting an apartment near the UCLA campus, which was, thankfully, only ten minutes from Dom's apartment in Culver City, where I'd be staying. My dad bought the building in Venice, and I was waiting until he closed on it to move down there. Penelope would be moving a week before I did. We had months of work to get done on the apartments before they were ready to rent, so I'd live with Dom in the meantime. Once we finished them, Dom and I would move into one (and Penelope, if I can convince her by then).

"You sure you still want to move for me?" she asked.

I sighed. She still appeared unsure at times of how much I actually wanted to be with her. Like she wasn't entirely convinced

I'd chosen her yet. "I told you, Pep. I go where you go." I had told her that after what felt like a thousand times since the first time I said it to her a couple months ago. She brought it up again and again. At one point, I finally told her about my own opportunities there. I told her I had thought about moving to California long before I even knew she'd walk back into my life. Before I knew she would end up there too. I reminded her of Dom. Of all the reasons I had for moving outside of just her. Though none of them mattered as much as she did, and if I was honest with both of us, I knew I'd move to goddamn Nebraska to be with her (not that there was anything inherently wrong with Nebraska, but I couldn't think of a place farther away from the ocean, and that made me claustrophobic).

She shook her head against my shoulder. Without looking at me, she asked, "What about your family? Didn't you move back to be closer to them?"

I chuckled. "I think they're more than fine without me." The one reason I hadn't entirely disclosed to her, though I wasn't sure why, was that I just felt like I wasn't needed here. I had never felt like I was needed here. Or in Hawaii either. I always felt a little like a house guest. Like my father had a complete family with Marlena and Charlie, and I was kind of just... there. Living with my mother felt the same sometimes.

If our soulmate theories prove correct, I think my mom is one of those people who lives in a different lifetime than her soulmate. She appears perfectly content with that, though. My mom has been alone for so long, and she's so used to it that living with her almost felt like being in her way. She'd spent my entire childhood on the other side of the ocean, traveling around the world for work, and though I understood why she had to, it sometimes felt like my moving in with her was more of a favor to me. I think that feeling was more a reflection on me than her, but it didn't make it difficult for me to leave again. Feeling a similar way around my father wasn't giving me a ton of motivation to stay here in Oregon either.

She pulled away and looked up at me. "What do you mean?"

I shrugged. "My mom lived without me for fifteen years and was just fine. Then, I went to go live with her and my dad, Charlie, and Lena fared just fine too. They have no problem living without me. Sometimes I'm not even sure they miss me when I'm gone."

Those words sounded ridiculous as they came from my mouth.

"Carter."

I shook my head. "It's nothing." I was quiet for a beat. "Plus, you know I have opportunities down there too, Pep. I'll be plenty busy." Penelope knows about the apartments my father bought and how I'll be managing them, but she doesn't know about the studio space on the bottom floor. Mostly because I haven't entirely decided what I wanted to do with it. Though, seeing her interest in painting grow over the last six weeks has certainly given me hope.

"You think your family didn't miss you when you moved away?"

I shrugged again.

"Carter." She wiggled out of my arms and sat up on her knees, making her face level with mine. I looked down to find her hands brace on my forearms. "Your spontaneity and care-free spirit are the best qualities about you. Your ability to just go wherever life takes you is something that everyone loves about you. Nobody would want to hold you back from that. If you told me tomorrow that you had to go spend six months in the Himalayas to photograph mountain goats, or whatever it is you do, the last thing I could ever ask of you was to not go.

"You weren't meant to live a sentient life. You were forged to move freely about the world, to make it your own. Your parents know that, your sister knows that, *I* know that. We would not ask you to be anything other than yourself." Her hands traveled up my arms until they grasped my face. She leaned in to kiss me, slowly. "It does not mean they don't miss you. That they don't wish you were here. It means that they love you enough to let you go." I closed my eyes and sighed, pressing my cheek into her hand. "Do you feel that often? Feel like you're not needed? Not loved?"

Giving myself time to respond, I grabbed her hand and pressed my lips against her palm. "I used to, sometimes." She kissed me. It was soft, tender. When she pulled away, I said, "But I don't feel like that anymore. Not when I'm with you. *You* make me feel loved, Pep."

"You are," she whispered.

She settled back into my arms, her head resting against my shoulder. I twirled a piece of her hair between my fingers. "You said I wasn't meant to live a sentient life."

"Yeah, like you were always meant to travel. Not live in the same place forever."

I nodded. "Do you think you were meant to live a sentient life?"

I could feel her giggle against my chest. "Not until I've swam in every ocean, stepped foot in every country, and seen every Wonder of the World."

Flying. Soaring. Swimming through clouds.

"Penelope Elizabeth Mason," I pressed my lips against the top of her head. She turned to look up at me, the fire reflecting in her eyes, making them glow. "I think you're my perfect match."

A smile exploded from her lips. She shook her head and looked down into her lap. "Ditto."

I grabbed her hand and wrapped her fingers in mine, hoisting her up. She swung her leg across my lap so that she was straddling me. I ran my hand down her spine until I reached her backside. She giggled, settling into my lap. I moved one hand to her face, tucking her hair behind her ear. "You know, someday your initials are going to be P.E.E."

She blew a raspberry with her mouth. "Well, that settles it, then." Leaning back from me, humor highlighting her face, she tried to scramble out of my arms. "There is just no way I could ever marry you. I mean, it's clearly a sign from the Universe."

I tightened my grip on her, pulling her back to me. "You know, I like to think that the Universe is a little mischievous. If anything, I think it's a sign that you should absolutely marry me." I leaned into her lips. "I think it's a sign that you definitely will."

"You seem very confident in that statement," she breathed into my mouth.

"Oh, I am. I've known since I was old enough to understand what marriage meant. It was going to be you or nobody at all."

She let out a small moan as she kissed me. Pulling away, she chortled. "I used to scribble *Mrs. Penelope Edwards* in my diaries. Until I was like, eleven. Maddie found one once."

"Manifestation," I hummed. "It works."

Her head fell back, her hair tickling my hands where they grabbed her waist. She laughed. I knew she was probably still afraid of marriage. I knew it was something in such a far-off future for us. Especially since we'd only been dating two months. I knew it was probably crazy that I was even thinking about it. Yet, it somehow felt longer between us. Like I'd already seen, and known, and experienced everything I needed to with her. Everything I needed to know that she was it for me. The fact that I could talk about it openly, and she didn't cower away, or change the subject, only solidified that understanding that much more.

She gripped the back of my neck and sighed. "But just so you know, I want my PhD to have my name on it. My dad's name. I want to do that for him."

I think she was more so trying to tell me that she wouldn't be ready to marry me until she finished school. Which I had been fully prepared for. I believed what she said about her name, too. But I think it was a different way of her telling me she wasn't ready and wouldn't be for a while. I think she knew that I wouldn't give a shit if she actually changed her name. Hell, I'd take her name. I didn't care, as long as I got to marry her.

I nodded. "Okay. So, no proposing until you finish school. But the day you graduate, the day you hold in your hand a degree that reads your name as it is now, I'm going to be dropping down to one knee. I'm going to make you P.E.E."

Her face straightened for a second as she stared at me. Her features then contorted into something both amused and horrified. She fell into my neck as she wheezed. "That is the worst pre-proposal I've ever heard."

"How many pre-proposals *have* you heard?"

She snorted. "Well, none. But you're not setting the bar high."

Laughter filled the air between use, buzzing with its own kind of electricity. She sat up and stared down at me again, but her eyes kept darting toward my parent's house behind me. She tilted her head to the side as if she was considering something.

"What?"

"I was just wondering if your parents have stuff to make s'mores."

I stood up with her wrapped around my hips. Her legs dropped to the ground, and she stepped away from me but I kept her hand in mine. I craned my neck toward the backdoor of my parent's house. "Let's go check."

Iopened the door to my parent's kitchen pantry and stepped inside. There was a box on the bottom shelf that Lena labeled: *campfire kit*. There was chocolate and graham crackers– but no marshmallows. I turned and began sorting through the baking section of her highly organized pantry.

"I haven't been in here since... you know." I glanced at Penelope and found her standing just against the doorway, not fully inside.

I smiled to myself. I'd always associate this space with our first kiss, but I'd of course been inside it a countless number of times since then. In the years she lived on the other side of the world, the years I tried to force myself to give up on her, I also had to force myself to associate this closet with something other than her. So, I hadn't even thought about it when I walked inside.

I stood up and straightened myself, forgetting entirely about the missing marshmallows. I grabbed Penelope's hand and pulled her all the way inside, shutting the door behind her. She leaned back against it as I pressed into her, interlacing our fingers and pulling her arms above her head. "Should we recreate it?" I asked, bringing my face closer to hers.

She hummed, her warm breath coating my lips. "Tempting." She sighed. "But I'm not sure I like the taste of you quite as much as I like the taste of s'mores."

"Well, unfortunately for you, I can't find marshmallows. You may have to settle for my mouth instead." She flicked her tongue across my lips. I suppressed a moan. "You know what I used to think about all that time after our first kiss?"

"Hmm?"

"If your mom had never come looking for you, I would wonder how far you would've let me go."

She snorted. "I can't imagine very far. I don't think I would've been able to lose my virginity against a door in a kitchen pantry." Her face twisted. "With all of our friends and family just outside."

"Me either. But if I knew it was the last of you I'd get for five years, I sure as hell would've tried."

Her grip on my hands loosened and I let hers drop. They fell to her side as her brow furrowed. "You were not a virgin."

"Yeah I was?"

She shook her head. "No way."

"Penelope, please tell me who you think I would've been fucking in high school? I never even had a girlfriend." I laughed.

Her eyes dropped to the floor and a moment passed before they reached my face again. "I don't know, I just always assumed... I don't know."

I braced my forearm on the door above her head, allowing me to lean into her even more. "I never had sex with anyone on this side of the Pacific until I had sex with you. I was a virgin until I was twenty. My first time was with my friend Alaina, and I'm pretty sure it's because she felt bad for me. It was quite embarrassing, and I'd rather never speak of it again."

Her nose scrunched up before her features morphed into something like amusement. "Why'd you wait so long?"

I shrugged. "Waiting for the right person, I guess. After I realized she was too far out of reach and I'd blown all of my chances, I just wanted to get rid of the pressure."

She sighed. "Me too." Her face was almost sad. I realized she was thinking about *him*. I'd be damned if I'd allow thoughts of any other man drift through her mind while I was the one pressed against her.

I leaned off the door, but kept my arms against it on either side of her head, boxing her in. She was staring after me as if she was expecting a response, but I didn't have one to provide. Instead, I dipped my head and brushed my lips against the skin underneath her ear, knowing it'd make her shiver. I'd learned that somewhere within the last two months. I learned every inch of her skin. Some places I touched brought her comfort, others brought her chills, and a few made her cry my name. "As I was saying, I used to wonder how far you'd let me go. If we'd had privacy, no interruptions, nothing but time." I met her eyes. "Kind of like we have right now."

Her face flushed with heat and her eyes burned with lust. She tilted her head just slightly upwards, as if she was attempting to resist. Though, I knew she wasn't. She didn't want to.

She liked our games too much. She liked it when we both won.

I kept one arm against the wall but slid the other down slowly until it met her shoulder. I let my fingers trace the bit of skin that peeked out above the neckline of her sweater. Sliding past, my hand followed the curve of her waist, brushing against her breast, until it reached her hips. I let one finger inch above the hem of her top, warming the skin beneath it. "Would you have let me do this?"

"Yes," she breathed. Her eyes were fixed on where my hand was as two more fingers found

themselves beneath her clothes.

I slipped my entire hand beneath her sweater and inched it up her stomach, to her breast. I feathered a touch right underneath it, savoring the fact that she wasn't wearing a bra. I let my finger tickle dangerously close to her nipple. "What about this? Would you have allowed me to go this far?"

Her eyes closed as her head fell back against the door. She nodded. "I think so."

I cupped her breast, feeling her nipple harden beneath my palm. I then took it between my finger and my thumb, twisting it lightly. Just close to, but not quite reaching, pain because I knew she liked it that way. I dragged my other arm from the wall and down her body, until it reached the bottom of her sweater.

Rather than slipping beneath it, I grabbed hold of it and pulled it up. Removing her breast from my grasp I lifted her top over her head with both arms, letting it fall to the floor. Before it even reached the ground, my mouth was back on her. I wasn't kissing her, because our first kiss in this closet was earth-shatteringly perfect and for some reason I felt this space should remain untouched from that.

Not that any kiss from her wasn't earth-shatteringly perfect, but that first kiss was innocent, pure. Nothing about what I was doing to her right now was innocent, or pure, or juvenile. So, my mouth landed around her breast, her nipple now finding itself beneath my teeth while the other fell between my fingers.

She let out a moan.

I sucked hard and pulled away. "What about that, Penelope?" She didn't answer. I hadn't expected her to. I loved the way she lost the ability to speak when I touched her like this. I loved that she was at my mercy. That in these moments she belonged wholly to me.

My free hand found itself at the waistband of her leggings, one finger teasing through the fabric. I paused, waiting for her permission to continue. She grunted impatiently, bucking her hips towards me as if to force my hand inside her bottoms. I grinned.

I dipped my hand beneath the fabric, but outside of her underwear, feeling the sheer lace of it hardly separating us at all. My hand dove between her legs as I found the edge of her panties and slid them aside. I could already feel the wetness and the warmth blooming there. "You're so wet," I breathed into the skin of her chest. Attempting to pull any piece of myself together, attempting to keep up the game we were playing, I added, "Do you think you would've been this wet for me back then?"

My thumb moved in circles as she panted and writhed, a silent beg for more. She still didn't answer me, though. I slid my hand down, her legs spread wider on instinct to give me more access. I dipped one finger into her. "Penelope. Pay attention, baby."

Her teeth grit as she let out a sound that was somewhere between a moan and a growl. I taunted her by adding a second finger. I moved them in slowly, wanting her to feel every second. I savored the way I became coated in her. The grip she had as her legs clenched around me. I found myself gripping the waistband of her leggings with my free hand as my other hand pumped into her furiously. I squatted down to the ground, tugging her leggings off with me as I lowered. I exited her so I could get them all the way off. She didn't hesitate when she stepped out of them and kicked them aside. "Would you have liked me on my knees for you back then? I know you like that now." I pressed my lips against her navel. "Do you like me down here, Penelope? Do you like seeing me beg?" I bit her thigh, and then dragged my tongue across the same spot. The moan that roared from her throat could only be described as carnal.

She made me fucking crazy.

Absolutely insane.

How did we get here? How could she entrance me to the point that I was about to fuck her right in my parent's kitchen? Right next to the canned goods. She rendered me incapable of even walking the hundred yards to the pool house where I could fuck her in my own bed. I wouldn't make it. I needed her right now. I needed her against this door.

I found her pulling on my shirt, a request for me to stand. As I did, her mouth crashed into mine. Her tongue was already swirling in my mouth, desperate and hot. She was nipping at my lips as her hands were clawing at my back, grabbing my shirt and yanking it up over my shoulders. I pulled away to take it off, then her mouth was back on me.

So much for leaving this place untainted.

I gripped her hips and dove into her mouth. She tasted like wine and pineapple and the answer to all of my fucking prayers. She tasted like heaven. She was intoxicating and blinding and *fuck*. I'm going to fuck her against this door. I have to, because if I don't get inside her soon, I think I might die.

I pulled away and spun her around so that her chest pressed against the door. I licked, and nipped, and kissed my way down her spine until I reached her phenomenal ass. Looping my finger through her panties, I tugged them down her legs. Once they reached her ankles, I paused just so I could stare at her. Her legs were spread just slightly, but enough that even in the dark I could see her– all of her. She was plump, swollen, and wet. I was so hard it hurt and she looked ready for me and– "*Fuck.*" My head fell against the back of her thigh. "I don't have any condoms."

Logically, we could easily dress and make the short walk across the back lawn to the pool house where I had a drawer full of condoms, but I couldn't strain the disappointment from my voice. I stood up, dragging my hands up the back of her legs. She was still pressed against the door, her face turned just slightly, her chin resting on her shoulder. "Actually, I got on birth control a couple of weeks ago. The pill. I heard you had to wait awhile for it to become effective, but we should be in the clear now if you wanted to..." she trailed off.

Oh God. My cock was straining against the fabric of my pants. Throbbing at the thought of taking her bare. Taking her raw. I pressed my face against her back and let out an animalistic sound of my own. "I've never had sex without a condom before."

"Me either," she whimpered.

That undid me.

Another first.

In one swift movement, my shorts found themselves on the floor. I placed my hand at the center of her back. "Bend forward." She did so immediately. I tapped her ankle with my foot. "Spread your legs." She did that too. "Good girl," I growled.

She whimpered. Her hands were planted against the wall, and one of mine came to grip over hers while my other guided myself into her entrance. I nudged her legs a little wider with my knee as I slid home.

Holy fucking hell.

I felt everything. She was mind-bendingly tight, and wet, and warm. Every time I plunged into her felt like her body was made for me. Fitting into her like puzzle pieces. But this was different. Maybe it was the position we were in. Maybe it was because of the setting, and the desperation, and desire that had us doing this in this place. Or maybe it was because we were entirely bare to each other, and it felt as if I was melting into her for the very first time. As if our bodies were truly forging together.

She let out a small gasp, the same noise she always made when I first entered her. As if she'd forgotten what it felt like to have me inside, forgotten what it felt like to stretch around me, to feel me plunging into those inner walls. Every time she let out that gasp, I felt myself unraveling. I wanted to remind her exactly what it felt like.

I wanted to remind her every single day for the rest of her goddamn life.

One of my hands squeezed hers while the other found itself twisted in her long, thick, perfect auburn hair. I grabbed a fist full of it and pulled her head back just enough to make her moan. I pulled out, almost all the way, and then thrust back into her. My movements were slow, precise, purposeful. I wanted her to feel every single inch. I wanted to move slow enough that I wouldn't blow this too quickly.

The gasps and whimpers escaping her throat with each movement of our bodies were driving me wild, and once those whimpers became whispers of my name, I knew I was about to lose it. Her breathing was quickening, her moans growing, and I knew she was getting close too. But it wasn't enough, I wanted to see her face.

"I want to watch you come," I whispered into her ear as I pulled out of her.

I felt her body shudder against me as she moaned, "Yes."

She turned around so that her back was pressed against the door. I lifted her so that her legs wrapped around my waist. Her hands were tangled in my hair as I looped both arms beneath her knees, her ankles crossing behind my back.

"So big," she breathed as we both watched me plunge back into her.

"And look how good you take it, baby."

Nothing about it was slow this time. It was hard, and fast, and still purposeful. Our mouths fused together but we weren't kissing, we were just swallowing each other's noises, each other's names.

Her legs began to tremble, and I could almost see her release gathering around her like a haze. Mine zipped down my back like electricity, gathering in my spine. I pulled back slightly so I could see her face better. Her eyes were watching mine, and she didn't shy away as she ran one hand around my neck and down my chest until it reached that place our bodies were joined. I dropped my gaze from her eyes to her legs and watched her fingers as they moved in slow circles just over that spot.

Fuck.

I found her face again. She was almost smirking, as if she realized just how hot I found the way she was touching herself. Her eyes were glazed over, clouded with passion and pleasure. I felt her hand moving faster between us, her legs tightened and she began to move her hips, matching me stroke for stroke. She was clenching around me and I swore I was about to lose my mind. My fingers were digging into her legs as I slammed her onto me. My thrusts were losing rhythm, becoming chaotic and unchecked.

I was so close, but she hadn't come yet and I couldn't go without her. I moved faster, wilder, burying myself so deep inside her I thought I may never come out. "Penelope can I..." Her head fell back against the door, her eyes clamping shut as her body jerked and shook against me.

"Yes," she whimpered. "Please."

I exploded.

She cried my name as her hand moved from between her legs and began to claw at my back. Her grip around me tightened as she pulsated around my cock, coaxing my release from me. I stilled, spilling myself inside her as I pushed us both against the wall, hardly able to stand. She was holding onto me, face buried in my shoulder, teeth scraping against my neck as I filled her.

We held each other, gasping for breath, trying to find our way back to earth.

I kissed her hard as I let her legs fall. She wobbled when she hit the ground as if she couldn't stand straight. I stepped back and found her underwear next to my feet. I squat down to grab them and hold them open. She glanced back as I grabbed her ankle and slipped it through. She lifted her other leg as I slipped her panties over that foot and pulled them up her legs. Once they were snug around her hips, I let my fingers drag up her back as I stood. I pulled her hair back from her shoulder and planted a kiss there. "You're incredible," I whispered.

"You too," she breathed. She turned around and lazily clasped her hands around my neck. Her eyes fluttered as if they were still swimming with passion, though she blinked as if just remembering where she was. Her eyes roamed around the pantry we were in before she met my face again and her mouth gaped open. She clamped a hand over it and laughed. "Oh my God. Did we actually just have sex in here?"

I grabbed my clothes off the ground, then stood against the door as I watched her dress. "You render me incapable of logical thought, Pep. What can I say?"

She slipped her sweater back over her head just as I heard the house alarm beep, indicating that the front door had been opened. Penelope's head popped through the neck of her sweater, her eyes wide with terror as she looked at me.

I held my finger to my lips, letting her know to stay quiet. I placed my hand on the doorknob to the pantry so that I could try and keep it closed in case someone came to open it.

Giggles echoed throughout the silent house. Giggles that could only be the product of teenage girls. "That's weird, the alarm is off."

Penelope's mouth was clamped shut, as if she was afraid to even breathe. Her eyes grew wider as the sound of my sister's voice registered.

"Is your brother here?" That voice belonged to Maddie.

"I don't see why he would be."

Their voices grew as they neared the kitchen. Penelope now held a hand over her mouth. Footsteps passed us, but thankfully, did not stop at the door we stood behind. I mapped out their movements in my mind, and by the sound of their steps, I thought they may be heading into the dining room.

I heard a clattering of cabinets, and a clinking of bottles. I gave Penelope a side-long glance. It sounded like they were getting into my dad's liquor cabinet.

"No," Maddie hissed. "Not whiskey. Are you crazy? Get vodka."

"I can't. He'll notice if that's missing. He doesn't drink whiskey as often."

"What about rum?"

"All that's here is Malibu."

"Oh, hell yes. That's the best kind."

I was clenching my jaw to keep from laughing. I wouldn't dare look at Pep because I knew her expression would have me cracking up, blowing our cover.

"The firepit is on outside." It sounded like Maddie was the one making that observation. "Oh my God, there are two wineglasses out there. Do you think–"

"Shh!" Charlie hushed her. "Carter?" She called out. "Carter!"

I noticed Penelope move out of the corner of my eye. I glanced at her, and she was doubled over, both hands covering her mouth to keep from laughing.

"Okay, he must be in the pool house. We should be good but let's get out of here before he catches us."

There was more bottle clinking, before the footsteps passed the pantry door once again and faded down the hall that led to the front of the house.

"I highly doubt he'd catch us, Charles. He's probably in bed right now with–" the front door clicked shut behind them, cutting off the rest of Maddie's sentence.

Penelope and I looked to each other then, both gaping, before we erupted in laughter.

I ran my fingers down her spine, noticing the way her hair splayed across her back in a messy tapestry. She had the sheets pulled down to her waist as she laid on her stomach next to me. She must've woken up a while before I did, but she was significantly farther into the fourth book of the mystery series I'd bought her than she was last night.

She liked to read early in the morning, though it wasn't often that she woke before I did. She didn't say anything when I began to stir, and that was at least fifteen minutes ago. She had the book propped against my shoulder, her arms crossed and her chin resting on her hands as she read. She must know I'm awake now since I've been rubbing her back, but she still hasn't said anything.

Which is fine. I'm content to watch her read.

Sometimes I wished I was the painter out of the two of us, because this moment could be a painting. I wish I could transition it to canvas and keep it forever. Her perfect skin, and her hair reflecting in the morning light. Her brow furrowed in concentration on the book in front of her. Mesmerizing, intriguing, beautiful.

I never think about anyone else when I'm with Penelope. She is the being at the forefront of my mind. But as I run my hands up and down her spine, I allow myself to think about every other woman I've done this to. Every other pair of lips that have been pressed against mine, every mouth I've tasted. I think about the skin I've touched and the laughs I've heard.

The all-consuming thought raging through my brain is that none of them are remotely comparable to this. To the simple feeling of my hands against her skin. Not even the way it feels to kiss her, or be inside her, or bare myself to her– mind, body, and soul.

No, just to touch her. Just to be in her presence, to know her name. That alone outshines every other experience I have ever had. My chest, my stomach, and my heart swell at the mere thought of spending my life with her. I realize that I have nothing to compare this feeling to. I've never seen it reflected in a book, or a movie, or heard it spoken about by another person.

"How would you describe what it feels like to touch me?" I asked.

She let the book fall closed, thudding against my shoulder before it rolled onto the bed next to me. Propping herself on her elbows she looked at me, brushing my hair off my forehead. "To touch you?"

"Or, just– I don't know. I can't describe it. Yeah, to touch me. To lay here, like this. How would you describe the way *this* makes you feel?"

She considered it for a moment, as her pointer finger ran down the side of my face and into my neck, until her palm laid against my bare chest. "This loving you feels like flying and falling at the exact same time. Drowning but also floating. Being in outer space but feeling my toes dig into the ground. Like, so much adrenaline that my heart is leaping out of my body, but so much comfort and calm that I could also fall asleep." Her lips clustered to the side of her face. "That doesn't make sense, but... yeah." She shook her head and laughed.

I think she feels the same way.

She perked up a little. "Like I would find you in every lifetime. That's how it feels. It feels like nothing has ever been a coincidence, and you know I strongly believe in coincidences. I refuse to believe that there was ever any good reason for my mother dying.

"But, being with you makes me feel like maybe if she *had* to die, if she's out there somewhere able to see me, maybe she played a role in all of it. She pulled some strings with whoever it is that calls the shots. There is a reason our dads are best friends. A reason your dad met your mom, a reason my parents adopted me. A reason we grew up as neighbors. There are a million reasons, and a million more benefits for all of those coincidences, but I don't care about any of them as much as I care that I met you.

"That's how it feels to be next to you. To touch you. To love you. There is a reason for everything, even the bad things. And that I have to appreciate you so much that it almost hurts because for all the bad in the Universe, there is a lot of good too, and you are proof of that. And just this lifetime with you isn't enough to appreciate all of it, so I have to make sure I find you in all of them– that I know you in all of them. And if I'm really, really lucky, I'll get to love you in all of them too."

I knew exactly what she was saying. What she was trying to express indirectly. How she was able to put it into words, I didn't know. I was beyond words, beyond coherent thoughts. I could only feel her. As if what I felt for her extended beyond language, beyond bodies, beyond minds.

I didn't have words for it, but I tried to find them anyway.

"I love you, Mahina."

She smiled. "Aloha, ko'u lā."

She remembered how to say *my sun* in Hawaiian– well the closest thing to it, the direct translation being closer to 'day'. She remembered that aloha did not just mean hello or goodbye. That it was a spirit in and of itself. That it could also mean, *I love you*. I felt that swelling in my heart puncture completely. I was painfully aware of how truly insignificant the two of us are in the grand scheme of things but knowing that she's my moon and I'm her sun made it feel like the entire Universe orbited the two of us alone.

I dipped my head between her arms and kissed her. I bound from the bed and pulled on a pair of sweatpants. It was Sunday, and Sunday was the one day a week that she and I had decided to set aside for each other alone. We didn't make plans, we didn't run errands, and we didn't worry about anything outside these walls.

She turned sideways and watched me quizzically as I dressed and sat down at my desk. “Keep reading, Pep. I’ve just got a project I’m working on here.”

I’d taken one mixed media class at a community college back in Hawaii a few years ago, but it had never been something I’d dabbled in extensively. Though, imagining Penelope in a painting was something my mind wouldn’t let go of. I knew I couldn’t ask her to paint a portrait of herself, and even if I did, I don’t think she’d capture herself the way I see her.

I logged into my computer and began sorting through the photos I took of her that day at Opal Creek. I was going to try my hand at something new. She’d inspired me.

She was my muse.

My Aloha.

"Whatever happened, I'd met my person, the one my soul connected to."

-Kiera Cass

Penelope

"Mace, have you even started packing yet?"

Macie bit her lip and glanced at me guiltily as she bent over a box.

I'd asked her a month ago to move in with me. I began thinking about it the day she told me she'd broken up with Jeremy. She told me she'd been thinking about it too but was waiting for me to ask. Even though I hadn't asked yet, she'd already started looking for jobs. She'd already quit at Seaside Middle too. I told her she was crazy. She told me she had a hunch.

"You know me, I'll probably wait until the day before."

I snorted. I finished packing up the contents of my desk and slid the box onto the floor.

We only had a couple of weeks before we moved, and I, being the most responsible of us all, had already done most of my packing. I think Carter was closer to Macie in that he hadn't started either.

I'd been seeing a therapist for a while, one that I got in contact with through UCLA itself. I'd only held virtual sessions thus far but planned to start seeing her in person once I arrived. I was still feeling guilty about keeping the entirety of my past from Carter, but through therapy I started to realize that it was more important for me to come to terms with it for myself before I could be fully honest with him. I hated lying to him, and I was still afraid of how he'd react when he found out. I was afraid he'd change his mind about me. But I also knew that healing from my past was something I had to handle on my own first. I had to forgive myself before I could ask it from any other person.

"My mom thinks my decision to move was too impulsive," Macie said, pulling me from my thoughts.

I shrugged. "You're an impulsive person. It's one of your many charms."

She sighed, placing a hand on her stomach as she stared up at my bedroom ceiling. "My mom thinks I'm having a quarter-life crisis, but I think I've been having a quarter life crisis since I was twenty-three. That's why I started dating Jeremy in the first place."

"That seems to make sense." I laid next to her. "God, Mace. He was such a dud."

"The sex was awful. I don't know how I survived."

Laughter bubbled out my throat as I turned to look at her. Her eyes met mine, serious at first. I could actually see within her gaze how terrible her sex life must've been, and for some awful reason that made me laugh harder. Our laughter was still filling the room as I heard a commotion at the bottom of the stairs, then heavy footsteps bounding up them.

I sat up. "Shit, he's here early," I muttered. The drive from Boise was around eight hours. He must've left before it was even light out this morning.

Macie looked at me puzzled just as my bedroom door swung open. "Baby sister!" Easton shouted as he strolled into my room. He bound straight for where I was sitting on the ground and dove across my lap, wrapping his arms around my head. "Missed you."

I patted his arm. "Missed you too."

He pulled back and gave me a crooked smile. His hair was longer than the last time I saw him, pulled up into a half bun and shagging down to his shoulders. His facial hair was scruffy and uneven– he'd always had trouble growing a beard.

"You look... rough." I couldn't think of another word for dirty.

His brows furrowed, his ice blue eyes growing sharp. "Thanks. I was going to say you look beautiful, but you know what?" He pressed his finger into my chin before I could jerk away. "You have a zit right there."

I swatted at him, and as he dodged my arm he turned, noticing Macie for the first time. She patiently sat against my bed, arms resting in her lap as she watched us. "Oh, shit. Hi." He smiled, eyes roaming her body as he decided whether or not she'd be his next conquest. "I'm Easton Mason."

I scoffed and rolled my eyes.

Macie's face lit up with amusement, not in a way that showed interest but a way that said she'd like to make a fool of him. "That's a name straight outta Nashville."

He cocked his head. "I don't think that's the proper way to introduce yourself, Macie." She shrugged. "Fortunately, since Penelope only has one friend, I already know who you are."

They began to argue back and forth about whether Easton's name was inherently Southern and better suited for a country music singer. Reading both their expressions, I could already tell Easton was under the impression he'd have a chance. Macie's eyes glistened because she knew that he didn't.

I love my brother, but he's the definition of pretentious. He just finished his second year of law school. He took a gap year after finishing his undergrad to backpack through Mexico and Central America, posting his adventures on YouTube to show others how they too could live the nomad life (only if their parents were paying their way, of course).

Now that he finished school for the summer, he'd come home for a few weeks before returning to Boise. Sometimes I think that's why he's attending law school to begin with. He's just not ready to be done with the college experience yet.

"So, Macie, will I be seeing you again at dinner tonight?" he asked.

She shook her head. "No, I've got to go start packing up my apartment. You know how Penny is, a real hard-ass. Apparently, I'm slacking." She slapped her knees as she stood up. Easton was still on the floor next to me. His eyes ate her up as they dragged up her body at a disgustingly slow pace. She blew me a kiss as she walked out my door, and Easton reached his arm out and pretended to grab it before turning to me and grinning.

"You're disgusting," I muttered.

He smirked as he stood up, turning in a circle with his hands on his hips as he studied my room. "You need help bringing some boxes down to the garage?"

I nodded as I grabbed the box off my desk and pointed toward my closet for him to grab another box of clothes. I heard him stumble through my closet door before he paused.

"Damn, Penelope. Did you do this?"

I froze. I couldn't see him from where I was bent over, but I knew exactly what he was looking at. I'd been hiding it in the art room at school for weeks and brought it home when the school year ended. I wasn't ready to share that piece with anyone yet. I'd given my other paintings to my mom, but that one I stuffed into the back of my closet.

"Just grab a box, Easton. Don't snoop through my stuff."

His head popped out from behind the door, two boxes in his arms. "I wasn't snooping. You told me to go in there and grab a box," he scoffed. "It's really good, though. It almost kind of looks like–" He shook his head, as if whatever thought he had was crazy.

I didn't let him finish his sentence as I left my bedroom and started down the stairs.

Family dinner was at the Edwards' again. To celebrate Easton's visit, my move, and the girl's last summer before their senior year of high school. Also to celebrate that Carter and I survived the end of the school year as teachers.

It actually ended up not being as bad as I had imagined. Maybe someday, once I've seen all the Wonders of the World and discovered ancient artifacts and lost cities, written a book, and appeared on an episode of *Ancient Aliens*– maybe then I could become a middle school art teacher again. Just for fun.

The families were aware that Tom had purchased a rental property in Southern California, but it wasn't known yet that Carter was going to be moving down there too. I don't know how Carter convinced him to keep that part a secret, and I wondered if he'd told Tom the truth about us. Tom never seemed to be aware of anything, though.

I snuck over to the pool house an hour before dinner, under the guise that I had items from our classroom that I had to return to Carter. In reality, I had to hide all of my things that had started to accumulate there over the course of the last two months since I was staying the night so much. I wasn't sure if anyone would be using the pool house during dinner since Carter was living there, but typically that bathroom got used when everyone was in the backyard.

Carter hadn't been inside when I walked in, so I assumed he was helping his parents with dinner. Once I'd properly hidden everything I could, I wanted to check the time. Everyone was supposed to meet in the backyard at six. I didn't want to be uncomfortably early, but I also didn't want it to seem like I was hiding in the pool house. Realizing I left my phone at home, I turned on Carter's desktop to see the time. The screen lit up, and I was startled by my own face.

A photo of me from that hike to Opal Creek was staring back from the locked screen of his computer. My heart leaped and I could feel myself blushing, though I wasn't sure why since I was the only one here. I glanced at the time in the bottom right corner. Five-forty-seven.

I was smiling to myself as I exited the pool house. It was such a small gesture; it shouldn't warrant such a reaction. But I liked the idea that he wanted to see my face every time he logged into his computer. I liked the idea that he'd taken photos of so many beautiful places, and above them all, it was me he chose to stare at.

"Hey, you." That silky voice radiated my skin as I shut the door behind me. Carter was on the other side of the pool, setting a bowl on the outdoor dining table.

"Hi." I smiled. "You need some help?"

"I'd love nothing more."

I followed him into the house and grabbed plates and silverware as he finished setting food out on the table. The scent of the grill lingered in the air as Tom appeared downstairs with an apron on.

Our sisters showed up first, then my parents, and Easton not long after. Everyone grabbed drinks and greeted each other as we settled in around the table. Easton asked to use the pool house bathroom, and I was thankful I'd thought to move my things.

Tom was setting steaks and chicken on each person's plate as Lena passed around a salad bowl. My father held a platter of corn and the girls were giggling into their phones, showing each other something. Finally, our fathers took each end of the table. I sat next to my dad, across from my mom. Carter was between Lena and I, with our sisters on the other side of Tom. My mom squeezed a chair between herself and my dad to make room for Easton.

Everyone had begun eating, making small talk to each other as Easton returned from the bathroom and settled in next to my mom. She asked him if he'd made sure to wash his hands. I snorted at the fact that he was twenty-five and still had to be reminded.

He glanced at me, his jaw tight and eyes swimming with mischief. An evil, wicked smirk rose from the corner of his mouth, and I knew he was about to make fun of me. Likely to get back for my reaction to my mother's comment. I glanced down at my dress, patted my hair, looking for whatever piece of me was out of place and would become his target.

Instead, he turned his gaze to the person next to me. "So, Carter, how long have you been fucking my sister?"

Eight forks clinked against eight plates as they were all dropped at the same time. I heard Tom choke on whatever he'd been chewing on. I heard Carter swallow. I heard Easton settle back in his chair, no doubt looking triumphant. I saw nothing, because my eyes were glued to my lap, afraid to make contact with any of them.

Way too many seconds passed.

Carter coughed, "Um."

I should've been mortified. I should've been humiliated. I should've been angry at my brother, but the only thing I could think of was how the hell Easton found out. Unless he'd gone digging through Carter's closet, he shouldn't have found a single thing.

"Easton." My mother sighed.

I glanced up to meet my mom's eyes across the table. I realized she, and everyone else, was staring directly at me. This is my nightmare. Everything I was trying to avoid.

My brother glanced around. He scoffed, "Oh, please. Don't tell me that I've been here for six hours and already figured it out, and the rest of you haven't known."

I felt Carter's gaze but I couldn't meet it. I didn't know what to say. My mouth wouldn't move. He cleared his throat. "No, nobody knew. We decided it wasn't anyone's business but ours. So, thanks for that." I felt his hand land on my knee beneath the table and squeeze it. I realized I was shaking.

With anger or embarrassment, I wasn't sure.

After another beat of terribly, horrendously, painfully long silence, my sister snorted.

Both Carter and I snapped our heads up at her.

"What? It's not like you guys were very good at hiding it."

I glanced at Carter. He shrugged.

"You came home wearing his shoes, Penelope," Maddie added.

My dad stifled a laugh.

"It was a little obvious, you know, when Dan called me to tell me about Penelope's acceptance to UCLA, and then Dom called me not thirty minutes later and told me Carter wanted to move forward with the rental property." I looked at Tom, he was smiling. "I looked up how far the property is from the UCLA campus. Thirteen minutes."

I hadn't even thought about that.

Carter gave me a wide-eyed expression that told me Tom had known the whole time.

My forehead fell into the palm of my hand as chaos erupted.

"You guys are moving in together?" My father's eyes bugged.

"It's that serious?" My mother gasped.

"No," I said too quickly. Carter's gaze landed on me, his face twisted. "I– I mean," I was stuttering. I hated being put on the spot. I hated this attention. This embarrassment. I hated my brother most of all, I think.

Carter sighed, his hand squeezing my knee again before coming up to the table and grabbing mine. I watched seven pairs of eyes fall to the place our hands were held. "We're not moving in together yet." I heard the emphasis in the word *yet*. Carter continued, "But it's serious."

Seven mouths were gaping open at us.

"Well, I really opened a can of worms, didn't I?" Easton said as his fingers drummed against the table awkwardly.

"We all thought you were just hooking up," Maddie said. Her confirmation that my family had been talking about me *my sex life* behind my back. My family knows I don't like to talk about myself. They know that I've always been that way, but even more so after what happened with James. Especially with my personal life. I was a private person by nature, and even being adopted into a family that was open about everything, it wasn't something I ever completely adjusted to.

I'd always thought there was at least some level of unspoken respect about that. I thought it was why they weren't questioning things when it became clear I was seeing someone. They knew me. They knew I would only share information I wanted shared. Now, they're airing my dirty laundry at the dinner table without regard to how that would make me feel.

My stomach twisted as my chair screeched across the cement beneath me and I stood. I was well aware of the eyes on me, but I couldn't handle this dinner for another second.

"Oh come on, Penelope. Why are you leaving?" Easton asked.

"Because you're all fucking crazy."

I turned to leave, in absolute need of escape from this humiliation when I felt my arm being gently pulled. A force on my hip spun me around until I was facing Carter. One of his arms wrapped around my waist, holding me in place, while his hand grasped mine.

I was seeing red. He was chuckling. *Chuckling.*

"Why are you *laughing*? It's not funny."

He shook his head. "It's not funny. But I'm going to keep laughing at you until you come back down to earth."

I softened immediately. His hazel eyes bore into mine, looking golden beneath evening light. I felt myself begin to settle as he smiled at me. That golden thread tugging at my heartstrings as I floated back to earth, back to him.

His hand ran up my arm until it reached my face and he tucked a piece of hair behind my ear. His eyes were studying my lips, but in a flash, they met my own again. His arm cupped the back of my neck as he pulled me in, letting his lips brush my temple. "It's okay, Pep. They all knew you and I were inevitable. They always knew this was meant to happen," he whispered quietly enough that only I heard.

Inevitable.

Meant to happen.

He and I. Suddenly, my feet were planted back on the ground. The whipping wind inside my mind had settled into a sea breeze.

I found his eyes with mine, conveying a look that spoke all the words I couldn't. I nodded.

We both sat back down, Carter casually draped his arm over the back of my chair, I think in an attempt to relieve the heavy tension that came from the way our families were looking at us. My parents knew that when I boiled over, it took hours for me to simmer. But for Carter, it took two sentences and *laughing at me*. It was clear that I was putty in his hands. I'd do anything he asked.

I cleared my throat and lifted my chin towards my sister. "If you ever talk about my sex life again, I'll smother you in your sleep."

Maddie frowned as she glanced between Carter and me.

Carter shrugged, brushing his fingers across my collar bone. "Oh, I'm now officially required to help her bury bodies. Don't look to me to save you."

My eyes were watching my brother and my dad as their eyes focused on his movements.

Tom chuckled, breaking the tension, "Great, so it's settled. None of us talk about our children having sex, or we die."

For the first time since dinner started, everyone laughed.

Despite it, my father kept looking between Carter and I uncomfortably. Carter seemed to catch his stare because his arm removed itself from the back of my chair as he straightened. "Okay, let's talk about literally anything else."

My mom cleared her throat. "So, Carter, you were telling me about that project you're working on?"

He smiled at her with gratitude and nodded. "Yeah. It's called digital painting, or mixed media, and it's using software to edit digital photos into something that looks more like a painting and then putting it on canvas..." Their conversation trailed off as I studied my brother.

I leaned toward him, attempting to cut off the rest of the family. "How did you know?"

Carter continued talking with my mother and Lena as the girls began to clear the table. Easton leaned back in his chair and smiled at me, "Oh, Carter had a picture of you on his computer." He held his hands up. "Wasn't snooping, I swear. It was on when I walked in." He leaned forward. "And the way you're looking at the camera tells me you've definitely seen him naked."

My father squeezed his forehead. "Good Lord," he muttered.

I knew by the way Carter's words stalled and stuttered that he'd been listening too. He didn't turn towards us, though. "I hadn't seen him naked at the time that photo was taken," I murmured.

Easton arched his brow. "Well, you were in a pond or some shit, so he was at least half-naked."

I shrugged because that was true.

My dad flexed his neck, and I noticed a vein popping out of it. "Penelope, in these pictures, were you–"

"She was clothed," Carter chimed in without turning to face us.

Easton busted up with laughter, and my father's mouth twitched into something that could've almost been a smile as he raised his beer to his lips. "Well, thank God for that."

The space was feeling a little tight around me now. I knew that even though the girls had excused themselves to clean up, my mom was talking to Carter, and his parents were speaking among themselves, there was a tension in the air that wouldn't dissolve for quite some time. It felt like that tension was choking me and I needed to step away from it.

I stood from the table and grabbed my plate. "You done?" I asked Carter.

He smiled at me and nodded. "Thanks, Pep." I grabbed his plate too and carried them into the house. I noticed him get up from his chair and slide into mine. He had his arms resting on the table as he seemed to be speaking with my dad, my brother listening in too. I stepped back outside to grab the rest of the silverware off the table when I heard them laughing.

That's a good sign, at least.

"I don't know about you, E, but I'd say Penelope could definitely do worse," my dad said.

My heart swelled. I couldn't be sure what Carter had been saying, but whatever it was seemed to be working. I'm sure he was trying, in his own way, to clear the tension. I picked up my pace as I walked toward them, searching my brain for an excuse to pull Carter away and rescue him. Give him his own kind of respite from the shit show that was this family dinner.

"Ha, yeah," Easton chortled. "At least she's not hooking up with her college professor anymore, right?" He started laughing, as if he expected everyone else to also.

I froze.

"What?" Carter asked in a tone that was pure ice where he was normally sunshine.

Time suspended itself and everything moved in slow motion as I watched Carter's body turn in his chair. A hundred years passed, and at the same time, it was instant. I had all the time in the world to consider every expression that could mirror his face: Shock, confusion, anger, disgust, hatred.

Yet, there'd never be enough time to prepare for how he would actually look at me.

"But how could you love another soul the right way, if youve your whole life loving yourself in all the wrong ways..."

-Samiha Totanji

Carter

Penelope rose from her chair. "You done?"

I smiled at her, trying to convey all the words I couldn't say here.

I know this was a shit show. It's almost over. Stay on earth. I love you.

I nodded. "Thanks, Pep."

She grabbed my plate and walked into the house. Once she was through the doors, I removed myself from the chat between our moms and slipped into Penelope's chair next to her dad. I cleared my throat. Dan clasped his hands between his elbows on the table and raised an eyebrow at me as if anticipating what I was about to say.

"We obviously didn't expect any of this to happen today. In hindsight, considering the family dynamics, maybe we shouldn't have been so secretive." I flexed my fingers together. *Fuck.* I'm so nervous. I don't know why I feel this way. I've never felt like this around Dan before. "I guess what I'm trying to say is that I wasn't not telling anyone because I see things casually, or…" I shook my head. *Why can't I talk right now?* "I respect her, and I respect you– all of you. I just want you to know that I had no intentions or expectations with Penelope when I moved back. Things progressed quickly because I've been– I've felt very strongly about her for a long time. Before either of us moved. And when we began working together, I realized those feelings hadn't really gone away." I tried squeezing the tension out of my jaw. I sighed. "She became my best friend before she became anything else. She's still my best friend, and our friendship will always come first."

Dan seemed to take a moment to consider what I'd been saying. I was trying to make it clear that I was in no way asking for his permission. Penelope wouldn't tolerate something so traditional–nor would she listen if he refused to give his blessing. I think Dan knew that, though. I suppose I was having this conversation more for myself than anything.

I could see how secretly hooking up with the daughter of my father's best friend, a man who himself has felt like a father to me, could become a gray area. It may paint the idea that I was only using Penelope for sex and wanted to avoid other people knowing about it so I could easily walk away. I wanted to make sure Dan knew that wasn't the case. More for myself than for anyone. I always felt like Dan and I had our own kind of relationship, and when I was younger, I imagined I would be someone he'd approve of. I wanted to make sure that hadn't changed.

Dan opened his mouth to respond, but more words had gathered at the tip of my tongue and I cut him off, "I know Penelope has had a really tough year. I know she's been through a lot with all of the college stuff, so I want you to know that I'll make sure she keeps working through it. That I've been helping her through it and I'll keep doing that. I'll make sure she always knows how capable and brilliant she is. And I won't be a distraction. I know how demanding her schedule will be and I won't pull her away from that. I want her to succeed in all of her goals as much as you do, and above all else, I'll be her best friend and her biggest cheerleader."

My word vomit seemed to have spilled across the table in front of us and was laying out for all the world to see. I don't think I'd ever been more vulnerable with anyone outside of Penelope before. I was almost embarrassed of all that I said, but not enough to take it back. I needed to say those things, and I needed him to hear them.

I looked at Easton who was watching the two of us like it was his favorite soap opera. Dan's eyes were dancing with amusement as he watched me spill my guts. Dan paused for a moment, seeming to ensure I was finally done talking. He cleared his throat. "Carter, are you asking for my blessing to date my daughter?"

I immediately shook my head. "Nope." I laughed. "You know Penelope better than that, and so do I. If she wants to be with me, she will. If she doesn't, she won't. If she even thought I would dare to ask your permission, she'd kick my ass."

All three of us erupted in laughter.

Dan nodded. "I don't know about you, E, but I'd say Penelope could definitely do worse."

I breathed a sigh of relief. I didn't do it for Penelope, or Dan, or Easton, or anyone but myself. I'd never ask for permission on anyone's behalf. Penelope would always make her own choices regardless of the opinions of any other person. But Dan was someone I respected, cared about. I held him in high regard, and I needed to know he thought the same of me. Especially now.

"Ha, yeah," Easton snickered. "At least she's not hooking up with her college professor anymore, right?"

"What–" I began to ask. Dan's face looked stunned, and then dropped as his eyes focused on something behind me.

What the fuck *is he talking about?*

Penelope told me the only person she'd ever been with before was James, someone she met at Oxford. My mind raced backward, thinking through every conversation I'd had with her about him. I had assumed he was a student, but I couldn't remember a time she'd actually specified it.

I couldn't fathom why she wouldn't just tell me that. I supposed it was taboo, but I'd heard about it enough times to know it wasn't illegal. I thought most policies were that students just couldn't date one of their direct professors.

Unless James was one of her professors?

My temples ached as my brain worked a million miles a minute to connect the details that Penelope had apparently failed to tell me herself. She said she was rejected from Oxford because she submitted a fraudulent letter of recommendation. Unless...the letter itself wasn't fraudulent, but a conflict of interest. If she was dating her professor, a professor in her department, and he wrote her a letter of recommendation because they were seeing each other, then surely that could be grounds for rejection if her relationship ever came to light, right?

I turned around to find Penelope frozen halfway between the door to the house and the place I was sitting. I noticed Jenna and my father had been standing by the backdoor. The girls and Lena were nowhere to be seen.

"James? James was your *professor*?" I asked her.

I could see her eyes misting over, her bottom lip trembling as if she was already on the point of tears. Her face looked defeated. She shook her head. "I..."

"Shit," Easton hissed quietly.

I just couldn't understand why she wouldn't tell me. Why would she blatantly lie, for months. I'd told her everything about myself. All of my fears, all of my shortcomings. I'd worked to show her she could trust me. The level of trust between us had been the foundation everything else was built on. That level of trust that existed our entire lives felt as if it was falling out beneath our feet. That world-leveling earthquake Penelope always talked about had just begun to tremble, but only I could feel it.

She told me about her mother. She told me about all her insecurities, her fears.

She told me all of her soulmate theories, the reasons she didn't believe them, and I thought I had shown her all of the reasons she should. I even thought that maybe she had...had started to believe.

So why wouldn't she tell me she dated a professor? A detail inconsequential to so many others she'd disclosed to me. Why wouldn't she trust me with something as simple as this? I tried to think through what about her dating a professor would make her so secretive. Oxford was one of the top universities in the world, so he had to have been highly qualified, experienced. Was he old? Was that why? It still didn't seem like a large enough reason to hide for so long.

To lie for so long.

"Why lie?" I found myself asking.

She stepped closer to me, shaking her head. Her mouth was gaping with no response.

"How old was he, Penelope?"

She stopped again, her head hanging in defeat. "Thirty-seven...when it started."

A gasp echoed my own, and I realized Dan was still here too.

"How old was he when it ended?" Dan asked.

"Thirty-nine." Her hair was a curtain across her face.

"It happened for two years? *Two years*, Penelope? You were nineteen!" Dan sounded more shocked than I even felt, and I began to wonder how much she'd been keeping from her family too.

"Was he married?" I asked. I hated that I even had to tolerate the question. It was the only thing that made sense to me. Hooking up with a professor who was eighteen years her senior was embarrassing, being rejected from the University because of it was humiliating and disappointing, but none of that was enough to hide it from everyone she knew.

Not enough to make her hate herself.

She brought her hands to her face, covering it.

My heart dropped into my gut and was dissolved by my stomach acids.

She lifted her head, and as her eyes met mine. They told me everything I needed to know. They answered the question her mouth couldn't bear. I may vomit my acidic heart out onto the table. Right on top of all the words I just told her father.

I felt my throat tighten, and I stood on instinct, my body begging to get away from the environment. My name was a whisper on her lips as I turned my back to her and walked toward the pool house. The conversation continued behind me, her brother's voice raising above the rest, but I couldn't hear them. I'd heard enough. I slammed the door behind me and stared blankly at the wall.

I wasn't sure how much time had passed while I stood there. There was a numbness between my ears that didn't allow me to think, or move, or even react. All I could do was stand. It dulled as I felt the pressure of the front door against my back. Someone was trying to open it. My instinct was to shut it again, but Penelope's soft, broken voice made me pause. "Carter, please."

I stepped out of the way and she stepped inside, shutting the door behind her. Penelope took a few steps into my room and turned to face me. I couldn't read her expression entirely. I saw despair, regret, and fear. Maybe even, defiance?

I was sure the only expression my face was producing was devastation. Maybe pain.

"You've been lying to me for months."

"I know," she whispered. She closed her eyes and took a calculated deep breath. "I just... I was trying to process it. I am still trying to process it. I wasn't ready to share everything yet."

I scoffed. "Right, so you conveniently picked and chose what details you wanted to disclose. I got one story, your parents got another, and the truth is something else entirely."

Her hands came to her hips as she craned her neck toward the ceiling and blinked. "Carter, this is *my* trauma. Something that

I went through. Alone. I am the one who gets to choose who knows, how much they know, and when I tell them. Easton was wrong to say that. He—you—nobody knows what the hell I went through."

"Because you didn't tell me shit, Penelope!"

"I planned on it. Once we moved. I planned to tell you everything. I just needed to get out of this environment. I needed time to process things."

I leaned onto my desk, bracing my forearms. My head dropped between my shoulder blades. "That's fine, Penelope. But you lied. Do you understand that? You just made up some version of events that did not even happen. For what? For my sympathy? My attention? Why did you fucking lie to me?" I straightened up and turned back at her. "For months!"

"Because I was afraid of this!" She waved her hands in between us. "Afraid that you'd think I was just a horrible, selfish, homewrecker fucking her professor to get ahead."

I didn't think that. I never would. I was disappointed in her decision, but it was clear that the guilt had been eating her alive. She wasn't a selfish person. She wasn't a horrible person. She made mistakes. What was killing me was her lies. That she had spent months fabricating a version of events that wasn't true, all so she could hide that truth from me.

Because she didn't believe that I could forgive it. That I could accept the darkest parts of her. I'd spent my entire life trying to convince her of exactly that. Trying to support her quietly. Protect her firmly. Love her in silence. In the last few months I thought I'd proven that love out loud. I just told her father I'd been supporting her in her quest to overcome her past, only for it to be shown that I knew nothing at all. How was I supposed to prove anything to her, to him, to anyone when I was being lied to? I thought I had shown her how deep those feelings ran for me. For us. I thought

I had shown her that there was no force on earth—nothing she could do—that could stop me from loving her.

Yet, it wasn't enough.

It made me wonder if it would ever be enough. If *I* would ever be enough.

I shook my head, pressing off my desk and turning to face her.

She couldn't meet my eyes, her own dropped to the floor as she whispered, "That's what I used to think about myself. I *hated* myself. That's why I couldn't tell you. I'm still trying *not* to hate myself. Still trying to understand and accept what really happened. What happened *to* me."

It broke me apart to hear that, but a deeper, darker part of my soul wondered whether or not it was another lie. That whisper of doubt destroyed me. "I don't know what to believe right now."

I saw her jaw tighten, and then her face crumpled entirely. Head falling into her hands, her chest began to heave with heavy sobs. The sound of it sent my stomach cascading into a bit of black. My instincts took over as I stepped to her. She had her arms crossed around her chest, her head dropped toward the floor as her hair covered her face. Her entire body vibrated with her cries as I lifted a hand to her chin and tilted her head to meet mine.

Watching the tears stream down her face pulled my own from me. I stretched my thumb up to her cheek, and wiped away the moisture beneath her eyes. She only breathed, her chest heaving as she slowly lifted her own hand and did the same with my tears. She moved that hand to the back of my neck, pulling me toward her.

Like the sea to the moon, I followed. No matter my anger, no matter my hurt, I was within her orbit. Drawn to her. She may compare me to the sun, but it was my world that revolved around her.

Her lips brushed against mine. She was trembling, and I was too. I deepened the kiss, noting the taste of salt on her mouth as our tears mixed together. I wanted to lay her down on my bed, I wanted to take away both of our pain. I wanted to wipe away the lies, wipe away her regret. I wanted to imprint myself into her body and her soul until she could understand how deep my love for her ran, but I still feared that even that wouldn't be enough.

A strangled whimper clawed its way out of my throat as I pulled away from her. I couldn't do it right now. I couldn't kiss her. I couldn't fuck her. I couldn't breathe. I felt helpless. Helpless in my efforts to convince her I love her. To convince her she deserves it. I felt overwhelmed. I felt betrayed. Not by her actions, but by her lies. I felt like I was slipping beneath that wave, being flipped upside down and inside out.

I needed to find the surface again. I needed to find it on my own.

I dropped my forehead to hers, our breath still mingling though our lips no longer touched. "Penelope, you don't fucking trust me. You couldn't trust me enough to tell me the truth. You didn't have enough faith in me—in us—to believe that I'd love you through this. Because I would." I blinked back the emotion I felt building in my eyes once more. "I know that's not you, Penelope. I've known you your whole life, sometimes I think I know you better than you know yourself. So, I *know* that what you did was a mistake and not who you are. And I can love you through that, but it breaks my heart that you didn't trust me enough to even let me try." I swallowed, my throat suddenly constricting. "Even after everything. Everything we've talked about, everything we've been through our entire fucking lives, have I still not done enough to prove myself to you?" I let my hand drop from her cheek. "I don't know what more I can do. I don't know how this," I pointed my finger between us, "could ever work if you don't trust me." I closed my eyes, my forehead still pressed against hers. "I just can't do this right now, Pep. I need a second to process things."

A shallow sob bubbled from her mouth, but I felt her nod against my skin as she stepped back from me. As if she was swallowing all the words she had left to say, I saw a lump move down her throat. She refused to meet my eyes as she brushed past me without another word.

I felt her presence disappear before I heard the door shut behind her. I braced myself against my desk again, feeling it all rise up my throat. I found the lamp I kept next to my computer flying across the room and shattering against the wall.

I think I threw it, but I'm not sure.

That numbness roared throughout my entire body, and I couldn't be sure how long I stood there, staring at the broken lamp on the other side of the room before I heard a knock sound at my door again. I turned around and noticed the darkness behind the window shade, which meant I'd been standing there for a while.

The knock came again, and I could already tell it wasn't her. The door opened just a fraction and I saw my father's eyes peeking in at me. "Can I come in?" he asked.

I answered by slumping into my desk chair and turning it to face him. "I just don't understand how she could've hidden this for so long. How she could've lied to *everyone*."

My dad's face creased with confusion. He sighed, taking a seat on the couch next to me. "Carter, do you understand how common it is for victims of grooming to misinterpret their own experience? When someone is manipulated, especially for extended periods of time, it can be difficult for them to unravel the truth and the manipulation and–"

"What?" I asked. "What the hell are you talking about?"

He looked up at me, the same expression he held before. "I know that some people don't consider it 'grooming' if the victim is over the age of eighteen, but that doesn't change the fact that she was naive, inexperienced, and alone. She was the perfect target for a man like that. Being stuck in that environment for so many years..." He shook his head.

I pressed my hands to my eyelids as my pulse sped up. My skin felt tight over my bones, like I needed to get out of it. My breath was no longer in a normal rhythm. "What do you mean she was a target for a man like that? What does that mean? What are you talking about?"

"Were you not listening?"

I blinked at him as I thought back to everything that had been said in the last couple of hours. How Penelope referred to her trauma and the need to process it. Something she went through alone. I'd been so angry at her that none of those sentences had settled in me. The underlying message she was trying to convey.

But my father hadn't been present for that conversation.

I gasped, my hand flying to my mouth as I remembered. I remembered it.

Just as I had been opening the door to the pool house, Easton said something.

His voice had been sharp, more serious than I'd ever heard him before. *"So, in other words, he was controlling you by dangling your academic future over your head? Essentially forcing you to fuck him by threatening to have you rejected from the school?"*

I could still hear it, could feel those words stabbing me in the heart.

I felt my face get hot, and wet. I felt the saltwater drip off my cheeks and into my neck.

My dad, who'd been watching me, only looked down at his hands. "I had a client once who was a victim of a similar situation. She explained that she felt like her entire life was covered in a fog. That fog being the reality that her abuser gave her, and how it separated her from the reality of the true world.

"Penelope probably told a different piece of the truth to all of you because she was struggling to understand the truth herself. Her parents only knew a small fraction of what happened to her, and based on their response to that bit of information, she interpreted things in a very specific way. She spent months believing the worst of herself because that is what she had been manipulated into believing. And deep down, she probably knew she was being abused. But maybe it was harder for her to face the truth than it was for her to believe that she had done something wrong. I don't know."

My chest cracked open. I hid my face in my hands as my body wracked with emotion.

I always wondered how she had the courage to move across the world on her own. Now I realize that maybe she didn't. Maybe once she got there, she absorbed back into her shell. She got lost. She was vulnerable. She was alone.

He preyed on that. On how young she was, how naive she was. He took advantage of that, and through the course of *years*, he convinced her she was nothing and nobody without him. That she not only needed to be saved, but he was the one to save her. Fix her. Help her. That she wouldn't survive without him.

He used her, he manipulated her. Abused her.

It broke me that she'd endured that.

It broke me that instead of trying to understand, I pushed her away. When she was forced to confront those demons against her wishes, in front of an audience, I blamed her for it. I told her to leave. I focused on my own hurt and didn't for one second consider the hurt that she'd been suffering from for so, so long. I spent my entire life trying to protect her from men like him. Yet, she found herself wrapped up in a cycle of abuse despite it.

I spent my entire life protecting her, and now I feel like I'm the one hurting her most of all.

I had justified every reason she had for keeping this from me. Played into every one of her fears.

I jumped up from my couch, running an anxious, frustrated hand through my hair. "Fuck." Pacing across my floor, I ran that hand down my face. "Fuck. *Fuck*." I actually felt as if I could vomit. I could see her face in my head. Could see those tears streaming down her cheeks. Her gemstone eyes strained and red.

Every time she said she wasn't good enough for me.

Every time she asked me if I was sure about her.

Every time she felt less than. Felt unlovable. Felt unworthy.

This was why. *He* was why. He'd actually manipulated her into believing that she was to blame for all of it. That *she* had done something wrong. That *she* was a villain. Penelope carried that guilt, that pain, that denial around by herself for over a year. She'd been suffering in silence, allowing everyone around her to think the worst of her, because even after it was all said and done, she was so brainwashed that she still wanted to protect him.

And the way I reacted to it made her think that she had been right all along.

I looked at my dad. "She called herself a horrible, selfish, home-wrecker and I... I didn't..." I shook my head. I hadn't responded to her. I hadn't told her that wasn't true. I let her continue thinking that of herself. Think I agreed.

I had to go talk to her. I had to apologize. I had to make sure she understood that my reaction was in no way a reflection on what had happened to her, or what she thinks she did, but everything to do with myself. I could be hurt that she lied to me. I could be upset that she didn't trust me. But I had no right to make her doubt herself and all the growth she's attained over the last few months.

I brushed past my dad and opened the front door before his hand gripped my shoulder, halting me. "Carter, everything you heard out there– that was the first time Jenna and Dan heard it too." I turned to face him. "They have a lot to discuss as a family. Give them time to talk to her first."

"How long should I give them?"

He scrunched his nose as if he was thinking about it. "Give them the night. Go over there tomorrow morning." My face dropped. I couldn't wait all night to speak to her. I couldn't allow her to think I'd given up on her—on us—for that long. "For what it's worth, I think she was still stuck inside that fog before you came back. I could see it, when it began to clear, and she was ready to try and wade through it. I think you helped her *want* to wade through it."

"She told me she was going to therapy. She started going a couple of months ago." I hadn't thought much of it. Nobody needed a specific reason to see a therapist. "Why didn't she fucking tell me?"

"Only she can answer that. And Carter, if this is too much for you. I– I understand. I expect all of us to support her in this, but if it's too much for you to continue your relationship with her, I understand. And *I* will support you through that. If we need to postpone renovations on the apartments, or if you decide you no longer want to move down there, I'll sell it."

I immediately shook my head. I would not even entertain the idea. "Dad," I rarely ever addressed him that way, "it'll never be too much."

He nodded. "I know."

"I've loved her my entire life."

He smiled at me, maybe the most genuine he'd ever given me. "I know." He stepped past me but his hand remained on my shoulder. "Come on, why don't you stay in the house tonight? We need some genuine family time before you move, anyway."

I reluctantly stood up and followed him out of the pool house, realizing the reason he'd been standing out there in the first place was to stop me from going to the Mason's. Probably at the request of Dan. I'd give them space for now, but I wasn't waiting until tomorrow. I'd sneak up to her window later tonight if I had to.

As we walked across the yard, my father said, "And come and visit more this time around. You didn't visit enough when you were living in Hawaii. The family doesn't feel complete without you here."

I smiled but didn't disclose to him how much I truly needed to hear that.

Chapter Twenty Seven

"He was a catalyst for my soul. I didn't need him in order to exist. I needed him in order to be a better me."

-Angela N. Blount

Penelope

I didn't remember opening my front door or shutting it behind me. I didn't remember any step I took until I was standing in the entryway of my parents' house, my entire family staring after me from the hall, apparently waiting for me.

The same devastation in Carter's eyes now shined in all of theirs.

Along with pity.

My throat began to tighten. Tendrils of invisible black smoke gripped around my neck, clenching it shut. My stomach was a funnel swirling with despair, my chest was concaving inside me and– I couldn't breathe. I couldn't breathe. I couldn't breathe.

My limbs were going numb, and my brain felt mushy, the room spinning around me. I needed to get away. Get out. I couldn't face them. I couldn't face any of this anymore.

My father stepped toward me but I shook my head and made an immediate right, bounding up the stairs and racing to my room, slamming the door behind me and hoping it would speak the words I couldn't.

I grabbed a duffle bag from underneath my bed and filled it with the clothes I had kept unpacked to get through the next ten days before my move. I threw in my toothbrush and maybe some other things, unable to even comprehend what I was packing. All I knew was that I needed out. I needed to leave. I was going to start driving tonight. That's what L.A. had always truly been, my escape hatch. My plan when this all blew up in my face.

Because I'd always known it would.

Except, I hoped it wouldn't. I *really* hoped it wouldn't.

When I began unraveling my past, my therapist convinced me I could not only heal from it, but that I move forward from it too. With Carter. With my family. With myself. That I wasn't a villain, but a victim. I began to believe her. I let myself believe her. I thought I could take all the pain and turn it into something more. Something better.

I was so fucking wrong.

I should've never even tried.

Because it hurts less to hate yourself than to believe you deserve love and realize you don't.

I couldn't hear through the raging in my head, I couldn't see through the watery veil that coated my eyes. The only thing that existed in this darkness were the words that echoed through my ears over, and over, and over again: *You deserve this.*

It was screaming, pounding as my skin was being ripped apart from the inside out.

I wasn't the type of person who could be loved and accepted unconditionally, I never had been and had always known it. Deep inside the depths of my body, the pit of my stomach, that awareness was there. I pressed it away, pushed it down, ignored it. But I'd always known I was a burden. A burden on my birth father, so much so that he left before he'd ever even seen my face. A burden on my mother, so much so that she turned to drugs and died. I was adopted into a new family out of pity for the orphan my dad found in that hospital waiting room. I tried to give it back. Give back all that I had taken from others. I tried to be the best at everything I did. A daughter worth having. I couldn't– I failed. I became a burden to them too.

A burden and a disappointment. A person incapable of being truly loved, that look on Carter's face being all the confirmation I'd ever need that those deepest fears held true. He'd never forgive me. If even he couldn't love me, I wasn't sure I'd ever find someone who could. And I didn't want to. I'd only ever wanted him.

If even he couldn't love me, then I wanted to be alone.

I wanted to leave– run.

A knock sounded at my door.

"No," was all I could croak through the streams of tears.

I stilled my trembling hands as I realized that in order to leave, I'd have to get past my family. They wouldn't let me go. My throat began to constrict again, my lungs collapsing in on themselves. I tried gulping back mouthfuls of air but nothing was going in. I felt like I was gagging on my own tongue as I slipped to the ground, pulling my knees to my chest.

The haze only started to clear when the rocking began. I wasn't moving my own body, something else was. Vibrations bounced inside my ears, but I couldn't understand them. My eyes were closed. I couldn't remember where I was. Splashes of light dotted the inside of my lids as I realized I'd been squeezing them tightly. My entire body had been clenched and tense. Even though I couldn't breathe, I became aware of my chest moving up and down, the air going in and out of my nostrils. Those vibrations in my ear came through sharper, clearer. Someone was whispering to me.

"It's okay." The voice was calm, nurturing. I became aware of the hand against my forehead, the chest my nose was pressed against. Slender and soft, smelling like my mom. "It's okay, Honey. It's okay, you'll be okay."

Her fingers rubbed across my forehead as she swayed side to side with me in her arms. I let my eyes open, realizing where I was. Kneeling down at the foot of my bed, my mother leaned against it as I spilled into her. My father sat cross legged on the floor across from us. His chocolate eyes were soft and kind. Fearful, too.

"I'm sorry," I whispered to him.

"You had a panic attack," my mom breathed into my ear. "But you're okay. We're here, and you'll be okay. Just breathe."

I clenched my eyes shut but listened to her.

After a moment, my gasping breaths began to subside and I let my eyes fall open again. My father's hand rested lightly on my knee, and I could tell he was faintly trembling. "Dad, I'm sorry," I said again. I wasn't even sure what exactly I was apologizing for. There were so many things.

He shook his head. "No, Penny. I am sorry. I'm so sorry." His voice was hoarse and hollow, like speaking into an empty shell. Whether I was the empty shell or he was, I wasn't sure. "We don't have to talk about it right now."

We did, though.

Because I was still leaving. I'd figure out a way to leave. I wouldn't sleep here tonight. I never wanted to sleep in this bed again. It'd only serve as a reminder that I wasn't sleeping in Carter's.

Whether they let me go or not, I was leaving tonight. I'd sneak away in the dark if I had to. And if that's the route I'd be forced to take, I needed my parents to know that they were not the reason. I am the reason. I am the only reason I run away time and time again. I would not let them feel the guilt that I can never seem to escape from. I would not leave them with the look on their face that they're giving me now.

I curled into my mom's side, dragging a blanket off the top of my bed and covering the both of us. "I just wanted an identity other than being the girl with the dead mom. Or the girl that was adopted by Dr. Mason. I wanted an identity that was about who I am, not what happened to me. I thought moving somewhere where nobody knew who I was would allow me to have any identity I wanted, but once I got there, I realized that I didn't have any identity at all."

My dad let out a defeated sigh, and I hoped he didn't take my words too personally. He saved me from a childhood that I didn't even want to imagine. I was grateful for him, I owed him everything. All of them.

Returning his sigh with my own, I launched into the same tale I gave Macie several weeks ago. The only other person I'd shared it all with. Including myself. For many, many months I allowed myself to block it out. Carter was right in that I had fabricated a version of events that didn't happen. What he didn't know—what he hadn't allowed me to explain—was that I fabricated those events to myself, just as much as I did to him. I was in denial even when I spoke with Macie about it. It wasn't until I saw the gutted look on her face, until she begged me to seek counseling, that I had considered there may be more to the story than what I'd always thought I believed.

It wasn't until I actually began speaking with a counselor that I was able to unravel the truth and the lies.

Even in all the change that's happened since the first time I spoke the words out loud to Macie, I still found them spilling from my mouth the second time with the same numb coolness they had with her. I couldn't find it in me to shed tears over him anymore. I had far more important things to shed tears over now. Despite my dry cheeks, both my parents had moisture coating theirs. I couldn't look at either of them.

They were quiet for a long time, even after they realized I was done talking. My mom pulled up her sleeve over her fingers and dabbed her eyes. My dad wiped away his tears with his bare hands. "Why didn't you tell this to the disciplinary committee? They never would've expelled you if they knew the truth."

"I..." I couldn't explain it. I didn't defend myself because I believed everything James had told them was true. I believed that I had cornered him, that I had taken advantage of his mentorship and coerced him into becoming something more because I was lonely. That I had pressured him into helping me academically in return for what I offered him. He convinced the school that I had nothing to offer the relationship other than my body, but he had everything to offer me. I believed it too. But more than that, I think a small part of me wanted to come home, so I didn't argue and I didn't defend myself. I let them kick me out.

I only regretted the decision when it affected my ability to get accepted into other programs. Even then, I didn't have the courage to face the truth of what happened or come forward or do anything but believe the things I'd been told to believe. And hate myself for them.

"I believed every accusation they made. There was nothing to argue with them about."

My mother's fingers brushed through my hair. "Well, we know the truth now. I'm so sorry we ever let you believe anything different. We should have pushed more." She looked at my dad. "We knew something was wrong– off. We thought you needed time to... sort through things. But I never imagined..." She trailed off, sniffling.

Picking up for her, my dad said, "We always wanted you to have the freedom to handle your trauma the way you saw fit, because it wasn't something we could relate to. When you stopped going to therapy, stopped talking about her..." He sighed. "We thought you were okay. When you came back from England, we wanted to let you handle that on your own too. We had no idea..." They both seemed to be at a loss for words. "Penny, if you still want to move to California, if you want to go to UCLA, you can. You should. But you've got to start talking to someone. You've got to promise me that, or I can't let you go."

I said quickly, "I already am. I have been. For a couple of months."

"Good." He nodded. "Good. And if you don't want to go, if you want to take another year off, or never want to go back to school again, that's okay too." I began to shake my head. "Then you have to tell the school. If you're going to go to UCLA, you need to tell someone there the truth. I won't allow this to continue affecting your academic reputation."

I opened my mouth to tell him that the therapist I found was through the school itself. That I had been having virtual sessions with her and had my first in-person one scheduled for the week I moved down there, but my mom cut in, "You know, we should contact Oxford. There might be more that can be done there. If we can explain, maybe you can even go back. If you wanted–"

"You can't be serious?" My sister gasped from the hallway. My door had been left cracked, but it opened widely as her body appeared. "No." Her eyes were red, telling me she'd heard every detail I gave my parents. "That happened to her because she was *alone*. She can't be alone again." She then turned to me. "You just moved back. I can tolerate you living one state away, but not a world away. No. Pep–"

My chest sank as those letters left her lips. My eyes grew heavy again at the reminder of the person sitting just two hundred and ninety paces from me at this very moment, wanting nothing to do with me. My chest sank– not my heart. Because my heart was there, with him, and I wasn't sure he wanted it anymore. "Don't call me that," I whispered. I buried my face in my hands, unable to control the emotions but refusing to show them.

"Oh, well that's just bullshit. I'm sorry, I don't care what's going on with you and Carter. That is *my* nickname. I made that nickname and he stole it from me. So he can fuck off for all I care. You don't get to associate that name with only him."

A broken whimper escaped my mouth, muffled by my hands. My mother drew my back. "What happened?"

I shook my head, pulling my knees up to my chest. I didn't want to talk about it with them. I remained silent as I let the wave pass over me. Lifting my head once I could control myself. "I still want to go to UCLA. I already have a counselor setup there. I've already spoken to them about everything." Surprised by my sudden calmness, I lifted my chin, looking to my dad. "And I'd like to leave tonight. I need to leave tonight."

I needed to leave because I could still hear the beating of my heart where I left it.

My hollow chest couldn't bear the sound.

He almost laughed in disbelief, before his eyes settled on me and realized the seriousness of my own. "No, Penny. You can't just drive down there in the middle of the night on your own. That's almost an entire day of driving. Your adrenaline is spiking right now, but soon you're going to become emotionally exhausted and you'll never make it all the way down there. Plus, you're not supposed to move in for another week and a half. And what about C–"

I cut him off before he could say his name. I couldn't hear it. "I signed my lease as of the fifteenth, actually. I already have the keycode to get into the building. My apartment key is in a safe in my mailbox, and I have the code for that too. I could've moved in already but I was waiting..." I didn't explain that I was waiting for him. Waiting for him because I hated the thought of having to spend three weeks apart from him. I had also hated the thought of paying a month's worth of rent without actually being there, so we settled on a week apart. And I knew even that was going to hurt.

I almost laughed at that now because he'd probably never want to speak to me again. I might have laughed at the irony, if I wasn't so close to crying.

"I'll go with her." It was Easton who appeared in the doorway now. Except, unlike my sister, he barreled straight into the room. Straight to me, crouching down to meet my face. "I'm so sorry.

He said something about you having a tough year, about your 'college stuff'" he brought his hands up, making quotations with his fingers, "and I assumed he knew. I was already upset that I had embarrassed you earlier, and I was just trying to make light of a heavy situation and I obviously made things worse. Please tell me he's not still upset with you."

My bottom lip trembled as I said, "I told him I cheated on my grad school application and that's why I was expelled. I didn't just withhold information. I made up something completely inaccurate." I bit my lip, fighting back tears. "I was afraid he wouldn't want to be with me once he found out I'd..." I couldn't finish the sentence, *had an affair with a married man*. I couldn't look at any of them as I spoke that truth. That grain of fear that had dissolved so deep into my gut I almost forgot it was there. "I was right. He doesn't." I blew out a shaky breath as emotion built behind my eyes once more. "He worked really hard to build trust between us, and I was lying the whole time. He has reason to hate me for it. All of it."

Easton's jaw went tight. His blue eyes crisp with glacial rage. "Seriously?" He turned to my father. "Were we having two separate conversations?" He shook his head, and through gritted teeth he muttered, "That's bullshit."

"He'd never hate you, Penelope. Trust me when I tell you that Carter would never, never, hate you," my mom said.

Both of my siblings nodded in agreement.

"He asked me if he could marry you when you guys were about nine. I don't think he fully understood what he was asking. I think he'd picked up somewhere the whole thing about asking a father's blessing before proposing. I think he thought proposing meant asking someone to be your friend." My dad laughed. "I don't know. I told him to ask me again in twenty years."

We all laughed at that. Then I felt the tears on my cheeks again as my soul broke right open in front of everyone.

That could have been us. That could've been real. He could've asked my dad to marry me at nine, and asked again at twenty-nine, and it would've been a moment straight out of one of those cheesy romance novels I hate so much. The ones about star crossed lovers, soulmates, and everything else repulsive. Except, I would've read that romance novel.

"You two will work things out, I am sure of it," my mom whispered.

I shook my head. I wanted to agree. But in an attempt at preserving any part of my soul that could remain intact, my despair prevented me from finding hope.

"I should kick his ass," Easton growled. "None of this is your fault. Do you understand that? *None.*"

"He'll come around, Penny. I am sure of that. He just needs time. I am positive he'll be over here tomorrow morning looking for you, if not sooner. Another reason you need to stay home."

"Fuck that. We should go. Give him a little scare. He can crawl on his knees down to Los Angeles himself for all I care," Easton muttered.

We all looked at Easton, astonished. Easton had been a stereotypically protective older brother when we were younger. In a way that he thought made him look more interesting to his friends. A way that inflated his ego when boys my age would cower from him. I'd never thought any of it stemmed from true care, though. Something in the tide had changed, whether because he felt responsible or because, for the first time ever, he noticed that I had actually allowed someone close enough to crush me, I wasn't sure.

"Look, I really think you need to sleep on it. Give Carter a little time. It's reckless to start a drive like that in the middle of the night, regardless of if Easton goes with you. Stay home tonight, and if by tomorrow you still want to leave, then I'll let you go." My dad threw Easton a pleading look as if to stop encouraging me.

Easton nodded, and reluctantly, so did I.

I had no interest in sitting here and waiting for Carter to come around, mostly because a large part of me believed he wouldn't. Or if he did, it would be to lay confirmation to all of the fear swirling in my gut right now. I didn't want to be here to see any of it.

"You wanna sleep in my room tonight?" Maddie asked, as if she'd read my thoughts.

I shrugged as I stood up from my bedroom floor. Maddie disappeared into her room, as did Easton. Both of my parents pulled me into them. "We love you, Penny," my father said.

I squeezed them both.

✷ ✷ ✷

"Penelope...Penelope!" My eyes flashed open. Darkness. Cool darkness.

My sister stirred next to me, but her heavy breath told me she wasn't the one whisper-shouting my name. My foot shook. I raised my head to find my brother standing at the foot of Maddie's bed, arm outreached and gripping my toes. I could just make out his features in the approaching gray of dawn. "What?"

"Do you still want to go?"

I sat up, wiping my groggy eyes. Hazed with sleep and heartbreak. "Go?"

"L.A. Right now. If you still want to go, I'll go with you," he said. Maddie groaned as she turned over, now facing me but still appearing to be asleep. I ran a hand through my hair. "You shouldn't have to sit around and wait for him to come to you."

"I–" I suddenly couldn't decide. Last night I was so sure, but now...

"We'll leave mom and dad a note. They'll be mad but they'll get over it." He sighed. "I'm just saying, I understand what it feels like to have these four walls suffocating you. If you need to breathe fresh air, I'm with you."

"Me too," Maddie said, half-awake.

I glanced between my two siblings. I'd never felt such support from them before.

I knew I was being cowardly. I already knew this was one of those moments where I should stand my ground. I started to think that Carter was the person who'd run with me. Or maybe even the person who'd hold my hand as I faced fears head on. The person who'd make me not want to run so much.

Yes, running right now was just a way of me delaying the inevitable. The inevitable conversation that would ultimately lead to the total destruction of my heart. But my heart wasn't here with me anyway. It was there with him. He could keep it because I didn't want it anymore.

What I wanted was fresh air.

And the two people sitting in front of me were holding out their hands and telling me it was okay to run, because they were right there next to me.

"Okay," I whispered. "Let's go."

We silently loaded my car with all the boxes that would fit. I'd ask Macie to bring the rest down with her next week. As Maddie and Easton grabbed enough items to get them through three days, I snuck into my closet and retrieved the painting. Thankfully, in the dark, I couldn't see it clearly. I didn't have to examine it closely. I wrapped it in a blanket and placed it in the trunk, away from anyone else's prying eyes. I'd sneak it into my apartment once we got to L.A., and I'd hide it in that closet too. Just in case he ever came back.

Chapter Twenty Eight

"I feel like a piece of my soul has loved you since
the beginning of everything.
Maybe were from the same star."

-Emery Allen

Carter

The knock on the door reverberated inside my skull and bounced off the walls of my hollow chest. I hopped back and forth on my feet to keep the buzzing in my bones at bay. I couldn't stop glancing at the driveway, noticing the fact that Penelope's car was gone.

It had been here last night when I climbed onto the roof and knocked on her bedroom window. A knock that had gone unanswered. I could only hope that this morning's knock on the front door wouldn't. I also held out hope that Penelope was home and that Maddie was just borrowing her car as she often did. I hoped I wouldn't have to tear the world apart searching for her, something I should've done the first time she left me.

This time around, oceans wouldn't be enough. Distance, space, and silence wouldn't be enough. I'd find her, and I'd make her tell me to my face she didn't want me anymore. Then, I'd get down on my knees and beg her to change her mind. But God, I hoped I didn't have to.

Heavy footsteps padded down the staircase next to the door, and figure appeared behind the stained glass. It was too tall to be any of the girls. I hoped it was Dan and not Easton. Easton might hit me if Penelope had disclosed all the contents of last night's conversation.

Maybe I did hope it was Easton, actually. Maybe I did hope he'd hit me.

Maybe then I'd be able to focus on the pain he'd cause and not the pain I'd caused Penelope. Not the pain radiating every single inch of my skin and all the atoms in my body. I'd have a reason to hurt somewhere else.

Both relief and disappointment washed over me as Dan opened the door. He immediately sighed, as if he'd already known I'd be the person standing here (as if there was anyone else who'd be standing on his porch at eight o'clock on a Saturday morning, anyone else who'd crushed his daughter's heart the night before). He leaned against the doorway and crossed his arms, studying me for a long, long moment. I briefly thought he may hit me too.

His lips clustered at the corner of his mouth before he nodded to the porch steps behind me. "Let's talk."

I leaned past him, trying to get a glimpse at the top of the staircase, at the hallway behind him, the kitchen. Any glimpse of her. Some kind of confirmation she was at least there. If I knew she was inside, I knew she wouldn't be able to leave without getting past me. I'd at least have a chance. I wouldn't have the patience to sit down and have any kind of conversation with Dan if I didn't know she was inside.

"She isn't here, Carter."

My entire body went slack. My arms hung at my sides limply, as if they weren't connected to anything. My knees nearly gave out as I stumbled backward. Dan looked at me with pity, with apology, maybe a little understanding too. He stepped out the front door and shut it behind him, walking to the steps and sitting down.

"Where is she?" I croaked as I fell next to him, my head dropping between my legs.

He looked down at the watch on his wrist. "Likely somewhere down the I-5 corridor, headed south."

My hands flew to my face. "What?"

"I told her to stay last night. I hoped there was some kind of misunderstanding. I didn't believe that you would react the way you did unless you didn't understand the whole of it." My body was soaked in shame. He huffed. "I woke up about an hour ago and found a note on the kitchen counter. All three of them left. They went together. To L.A. Penelope wanted to move in early. It said she needed *fresh air*." He snorted. "Because I'm sure the air in Los Angeles is much fresher than it is up here."

I flew off the steps and stalked toward the front yard. "Well, we have to call her. They need to stop. They need to come back." I paced, fumbling to get my phone out of my back pocket. "No, I'll go to them. I don't care. They need to stop driving, though."

Dan stood too. "Carter."

The tone in his voice had me halting– pausing.

"Their phones are off. All of them. They wanted uninterrupted time together, that's what Easton wrote in the note they left. I've tried all three of them multiple times. They're not answering. They promised to call when they arrived."

My phone slipped out of my hand and fell into the grass, thudding on the soft ground.

She ran away.

"Please, sit down," Dan pleaded as he motioned to the steps next to him.

Moving on their own, my legs found themselves walking to where he stood before sitting down. I felt outside of my body again. Just watching from above. Because this didn't feel real.

I knew I'd upset her. I knew I said things I shouldn't have. I did not think she'd run away. Not from me. Not again. I tried to mentally prepare myself for the possibility, especially once I saw her car missing from the driveway, but I didn't allow myself to actually believe it.

"I can't believe she ran away from me." My voice broke as I added, "Again." I rubbed my eyes. "Look, you're right. I walked away when I shouldn't have, and even when she was trying to tell me, I wasn't hearing her." I turned to Dan. "You have to believe me. I would never..." My words faded when he picked them up.

"I know," Dan said. "We tried telling her that. Maybe you are two or more alike than you think." He exhaled with a chuckle. "Because she wasn't hearing me either."

I fumbled with my hands as Dan stared at me. I could feel the sorrow in his eyes even when I wasn't looking at him. "I taught her that. The running. It's my fault." He looked away, sighing. "When her mother died, I never even took her back to that apartment. Never let her gather her things. After it was cleaned out, we were given a box of books and a couple of her mother's clothing items. We didn't keep any of Penelope's toys or clothes. We thought it would be better if she just started over. We didn't stop to think there might be sentimental value to any of it. Once we decided to adopt her, I think...I think we almost kind of *wanted* her to forget about her mom. We wanted her to accept us." He shook his head. "That's awful, I know. She's never even opened the box of her mother's things. It's been sitting in the garage for fifteen years. I *let* her run away from her life. I gave her a new one and I tried to show her how much better it would be than her past. I led by example. I showed her that is what you did when you weren't happy. When something bad happened. You run away from it. You never look back. That's all she's ever done. It's all she knows."

I stared down at my hands. I couldn't even begin to unpack the things he was saying. The responsibility he was taking. As if he was trying to convince me not to give up on her. The only instinct roaring in my gut was to go after her. That roaring wouldn't cease until I reached her. "It's not your fault," I found myself saying. "There is no handbook on how to handle a life like hers. Life in general, for that matter. You did your best, and she knows that." I met his gaze. "Trust me. She knows that. So much so that she thinks she has to earn your love. She thinks she doesn't deserve it. Anyone's."

He blinked at me, as if he was expecting anything other than that to come from my mouth. "She said that to you?"

I nodded. "And it's not my place to be telling you on her behalf. But... just make sure she knows. That she knows that she doesn't need to earn the love she's given. I'm sure you've tried. I thought I had made that clear to her too, but apparently, she still doesn't get it." I waved toward the driveway, void of her vehicle. I stood up. "Where's that box of her mother's books?"

Still sitting, Dan looked up at me, shading his eyes with his hand under the morning sun. "Why?"

"I'll take it to her."

He cocked his head, "What do you mean, Carter?"

"I'm going to L.A. I'll leave right now. I'll bring it with me. In case she wants it." I was surprised by the calm in my voice. The finality in my tone. There was no consideration to be had. I'd decided as much the moment I knocked on the front door.

I hadn't even started packing yet. I didn't care. I'd call Dom on my way down, let him know I needed to move in earlier than planned. He'd deal with it. Or, if Penelope rejects me, I'll turn around and drive back here. Then, maybe I'd run away myself. Go to Africa. The pyramids. Somewhere farther. I had no plan beyond her. I didn't want one.

My only instinct was to reach her. That was the only feeling I could focus on. The driving force I had to follow. I needed her, at the very least, to understand that my anger came from a place of misunderstanding, and that she was not to blame for any of it. I'd grovel at her feet and beg her forgiveness if I needed to, but at the end of the day, if she couldn't be with me anymore, I'd probably understand. I just needed her to know that none of it is her fault and how sorry I am that I let her think it was.

Before Dan could give any type of opinion, I said, "I've got to grab a few things and tell my parents. Can you leave the box outside the garage? I'll throw it in my truck when I leave."

He gaped after me, but I jogged back across the street before he could respond.

I stuffed a suitcase and two backpacks with all the clothes I could fit. I stuffed my laptop and my camera into a fourth bag and realized that was about all I had to my name anyhow. I packed everything I had. Everything I needed, anyway.

All I needed except the other half of my soul that was already on her way to my destination.

I ran into my parent's house. I halted in the kitchen where the three of them sat around the dining room table. I told them Penelope left. That I needed to go too. To my surprise, none of them argued with me. They only nodded, Lena and Charlie squeezing me extra hard as they hugged me goodbye. My father advised me to pull over and sleep when I needed to. To drive carefully. To call him when I arrived. I agreed to all of it, and practically sprinted back out the door.

By the time my Bronco was loaded, I noticed the Mason's garage door opening. Dan stood in the driveway with a box in his hands. I jogged over to take it from him. "Do you have the address? Of her apartment?"

He shook his head.

"Okay, it's okay. I'll get it from Macie. I think she has it." I took the box from his hands. "Thank you."

As I turned, he called my name. "Carter, thank you. I– I know you'd never ask. She'd never want you to. But if it makes any difference to you, you *do* have my blessing. You always will." I dipped my head in acknowledgement– in gratitude. "I used to think that God put me in the emergency room that night just so I could find her. So that she could find us, find our family. But I think maybe God put me in the emergency room that night so that she could find you too."

I opened and closed my mouth several times, searching for a response that would never come as his words settled inside me.

He only smiled, as if he understood anyway. He backed into the garage, taking his turn to nod in acknowledgement– in gratitude. I stood there, legs unmoving, as I watched the garage door close.

"And Carter," he said, just as the door lowered past his shoulders. "Tell my children they're all menaces."

I laughed as the door slammed shut, closing us off. I backed up to my truck, setting the box of her mother's books in the back seat.

The third knock of the morning was just as nerve wracking as the first two. Nerve wracking because I'd called Macie twice before deciding to just drive to her apartment. I couldn't leave without knowing where I was going. I filled my truck with gas, even got an oil change and bought some food, trying to pass the time while I waited for her to return the call. I tried calling Penelope too, with no such luck. When Macie didn't answer either time, I decided to just drive to her myself. Since she wasn't answering my calls, and it was before noon on a Saturday, it was safe to assume she might still be sleeping. Macie did not like to be woken up abruptly, or by surprise.

A string of curses greeted me from the other side of the door as she threw it open. She wiped her eyes as she took me in. Her hair was flying in a thousand different directions. She had on a t-shirt that fell to her knees. A groggy, irritated look on her face told me my nerves were warranted.

"What the fuck–"

"Penelope left."

Her hand dropped from the door and flew to her forehead, wiping itself down her tired face. She held the door open wider, motioning me to enter. I'd never been inside her apartment before.

I'd only ever dropped her off here. It was small, but fitting for her. It was a whole mess, covered in empty cardboard boxes and strewn clothes. As if she was meaning to pack up her things but hadn't started.

"What do you mean she left?"

I perched myself on the armrest of her couch. Sighing, I dove into all of the events of the previous twenty-four hours. From Easton's outburst at family dinner, to Penelope and I's fight, to the fact that she literally ran off in the early morning with her siblings and turned off her phone. I tried to dance around the details about what happened at Oxford, I wasn't sure how much Macie knew. She watched me with a focus that I'd only describe as feline until I finished.

"If the bush you're beating around is James, I already know all of that. Did she finally tell you the truth? Is that why you guys fought?"

"Why would she tell you and not me?" I snapped back, an unintentional edge to my voice.

Macie huffed. "You know, I thought about that a lot too. I think it's because I never knew her before. I never saw who she was or what she was like before it happened. I couldn't have known whether or not she changed. When she was hating herself, I still loved her. I didn't love any old version of her, any hope of someone she'd someday become. I loved exactly who she was when I met her, and in her mind, that person was the worst version of herself she'd ever be." Macie's golden eyes were sparkling as she shrugged at me. "It doesn't mean she didn't trust you. She just didn't have faith in herself. She should be forgiven for that."

"I forgave her the minute she walked away from me."

She crossed her arms over her chest. "Well, why the hell are you sitting on my couch then?"

I smirked. "I came over here because I don't have the address to your new apartment. Once you provide me with the information, I'll gladly be on my way."

A grin overtook her face, spreading across her cheeks ear to ear. "You know, I liked you from the moment I met you. I had a feeling about you, and my intuition is never wrong." I flicked my brow at her impatiently, but my face let her know I appreciated her words. "Right, I've got it written down on a notepad in the kitchen."

She floated away on tiptoes before returning seconds later and handing me a post-it note with their address. She opened the door for me once again, wrapping her arms around my shoulders before I made it to the doorway. "Prove to her that she never has to run away again." She stepped back, smiling. "I'll see you *both* next week."

I paused, drumming my thumbs on her door. Her brow furrowed as she wondered why I wasn't moving. I found myself already contemplating all the things I'd say to Penelope once I made it there. As if I didn't have a day's drive to think it through. I thought I had spent the last two months making it clear to her there was nothing she could do that would make me lose faith in her– in us. Hell, I told Maddie I'd be the one to help Penelope bury bodies, and damn if I didn't mean it. It was as if those ten minutes during our argument had taken back all the progress she had made. If my words couldn't make it clear, there was one thing that might. I looked at Macie. "I need your Wi-Fi password."

Before she could answer me, I bolted out her door and to my truck, grabbing my laptop bag before stepping back into her apartment and sitting down at her dining table. She stared at me with confusion as she hesitantly let me connect to her internet.

"What the hell is going on?" she asked as she leaned against her kitchen counter, arms crossed, watching me.

Ignoring her, I opened my computer and found the file I was working on. There were some touches I had meant to add to it, but it'd have to do as it was. I emailed the file to Dom and closed my computer.

I thanked Macie, hugging her again. She blinked at me with puzzled surprise as I shut the door behind me without explaining to her what I was doing in the first place.

As I climbed into my truck, I called Dom. He picked up on the third ring. "I just sent a file to your email. I need you to go get it printed on a forty-by-sixty canvas. It'll be expensive but I'll pay you back. Leave it at the studio and hide the key somewhere so I can get in."

He yawned into the phone. "Whoa. Dude, you are talking a thousand miles a minute."

I grumbled as I repeated myself a second time, slower. "No questions asked, okay? I'll be in L.A. tomorrow. Hopefully not at your place, but maybe, if I need to be. I'll let you know."

"What the hell are you–"

"Dom, promise me you'll get the canvas printed. That you'll leave it at the studio with the key. I need it before tomorrow night."

"Alright, man. Yeah, yeah. I'll go order it right now."

I hung up as I turned on the engine of my truck. Pulling out of Macie's complex, I made a left onto Highway 101.

"A soulmate isn't someone who completes you. No, a soulmate is someone who inspires you to complete yourself."

-Bianca Sparacino

Penelope

Easton had been wrong. He bet that Carter would've shown up at the apartment before we even got there. That he would have flown down and been waiting for us. He hadn't. When we arrived and finally turned on our phones, I had three missed calls from him, but that was it. My father mentioned (in his very angry phone call) that he spoke to Carter yesterday morning. That Carter was upset, but I didn't ask for specifics on what he meant by that. He didn't offer them. Maybe I'd finally pushed Carter to the point where he'd given up. It was the last thing I wanted, but somehow I couldn't pick up the phone and return his call.

I knew he wasn't the type of person to cut me off completely. If he was choosing to end things, he'd tell me. And I couldn't bear the thought that the reason he was calling could be to do exactly that. I'd hang onto him as long as I possibly could, even if that meant ignoring him. There was no logic to any of my decisions. No method to this madness.

I sat on the couch in the tiny living room of my tiny apartment, staring blankly at the tv as Maddie flipped through Netflix. Easton was out getting food. We'd arrived very late last night, or yet, very early this morning. Luckily the apartment was already furnished. We had all stumbled up the stairs, Maddie and I falling asleep in one of the bedrooms and Easton only making it as far as the couch. We spent most of the morning bringing up my few boxes and decorating my bedroom. I was also fortunate in that Macie had been living on her own for a while, and she had everything we'd need as far as stocking the kitchen went. Except, she wouldn't be driving down for another week, so I'd be living off of take-out until then. She'd been very upset when I spoke to her this morning too. Upset that I left Carter. Upset that she couldn't get down here sooner. I told her not to rush. She was already upending her entire life to come live with me, to start over in a new city with practically zero planning. Something I'd never be capable of doing. I wouldn't have her rushing more than she already was because *I* was being unstable.

Once the six boxes I had brought were unpacked and my room was organized, there wasn't much else for us to do. My siblings would be flying out the day after tomorrow, and I knew by then I'd have to call him. I wouldn't be able to sit here by myself for another six days, waiting for Macie, without knowing where Carter and I stood.

Maddie shuffled on the couch, pulling one leg beneath the other and turning to look at me. "You should just call him back. Give him a chance to explain."

I opened my mouth to argue that *he* wasn't the person to be doing the explaining, I was. That I needed to be the one profusely apologizing. That I was terrified that he wouldn't even give me the chance. That he'd end things the second I picked up the phone. That I couldn't even begin to rationalize, or recognize, or entertain the thought of losing him. That it made me numb.

Before I could begin speaking, a knock sounded at the front door. Maddie and I looked at each other. I was sure the house key was on my keychain, and Easton had my car. He shouldn't have been knocking. Maybe his hands were full. I sighed as I stood up and made my way to the door.

Pulling it open, all of that numbness came pouring out of me, pooling on the floor beneath my feet. I began to tremble.

The first thing I noticed were the dark circles under his eyes. They made the hazel of them appear dull, lifeless. The gold highlights that made him look like sunshine had all been smothered out. His curls fell limply in his face, his skin covered in a sheen of moisture. His chest was heaving like he was out of breath. His arm leaned against the doorway as if he needed it for support because he couldn't stand up entirely on his own. His clothes were wrinkled like he'd been wearing them for days. He looked like shit. As bad as someone as beautiful as him could look.

But he was here.

He's here.

"You ran. You fucking ran."

A small, broken, helpless sob cracked from my throat as the whipping wind inside my mind began to whirl. My hand flew to my mouth, trying to keep away the sounds, but failing. I fell into the door for support too.

"You told me to leave."

"Not across state lines, Penelope," he scoffed. "I tried to come to you. I climbed up on your window. I was calling. I thought you were ignoring me."

My shoulders were shaking with my weeping. I could feel the tears streaming down my cheeks and pooling in my hand. I covered my face, unable to look at him. In the brief second I studied his face, I couldn't make out an expression of anything except maybe exhaustion. I wouldn't dare continue to look at him long enough to see his disdain for me. His disappointment.

I felt a pressure on my elbow as I was moved back a step, and I heard shuffling and the door shutting. "I went straight over to your house yesterday morning– the moment I woke up. Your dad told me you were already gone. That you'd slept in Maddie's room the night before, that your phone was off." I felt the warmth of his fingers as they gripped my arm, I felt his breath against my forehead, his heartbeat against my chest. I let myself feel those things because I knew it was possible that I may never feel them again after this conversation. I should have savored them more. I should've savored ever moment I had with him more.

A door shut toward the back of the apartment. It must've been my sister.

He pulled my hands away from my face. I let my eyes fall open, the only thing I could see were his. They were searching mine for something. My face fell between his hands. "Pep," he whispered. "You shut me out. You ran away."

All of my insides began to pretzel at the sound of that nickname on his lips. At the desperation in his tone. The sadness. The hurt. The pain. All of it was caused by me.

My knees began to buckle and I felt myself crumpling toward the floor. He leaned back against the front door and slid down with me, holding onto my arms. I fell between his knees, my body fell into his chest. His arms came around my back, my face in his neck.

"I'm sorry," I cried. "I'm sorry. I'm sorry." He shushed me, drawing circles around my back. Planting kisses into my hair. His breathing was sharp and heavy. I could feel the hard swallows of his throat and I wondered if he was fighting back tears too. "You're here," I sniffled.

He breathed humorously, pushing my hair away from my face and bringing his lips against my ear, "Penelope, I told you I wasn't letting you go again. I told you I go where you go. I told you that I'd always be here."

I shook my head against his shoulder. "You said those things before you knew the truth."

He craned his neck away, bracing my arms and pulling me upward. "Look at me, Pep." I lifted my face out of his neck and rolled it across his shoulder, bringing my face up to his. "That doesn't change a goddamn thing. I'm so sorry for how I reacted." He wasn't crying, but I could see tears brimming behind his eyes. "Please understand, Pep. I didn't...After I got up from that table,

I didn't hear anything. I knew words were being said, but my ears were ringing and I was… I was drowning." I understood him then. "I didn't realize the truth until later that night, after I talked to my dad." His voice broke as the tears spilt over. "God, Penelope. I'm sorry, I'm so sorry." It was his face now falling into my neck. His body is wracking with painful sobs. "I'm sorry it happened." I knew he wasn't referring to our fight anymore. "I'm sorry you were alone. I'm sorry I made you believe you did something wrong."

I shook my head. "We don't have to talk about it right now." We'd talk about it eventually. He deserved to hear the whole story, not second hand from his father, but from me. But right now, it didn't matter. All that mattered was that he was here. "I never should have lied to you, Carter." He pulled back, and I sat up on my knees. His grip around my waist tightened. My neck was wet with a mixture of our tears. He brushed his lips against it, kissing along my jaw. "I was afraid I wasn't good enough for you. I'm still afraid I'm not good enough for you. That I don't deserve you." I sighed. "I was afraid if I told you everything—every ugly thing about me—you'd finally see that I wasn't good enough."

He looked up at me, those golden threads of light beginning to shine in his eyes. "Nothing about you could ever be ugly, Penelope. *Nothing*." His thumb dragged across my cheek, taking my tears—my heartbreak—with it. "I accept every single piece of you. All of your past, all of your future. Every tear, every scar, every wound. There is nothing you should bear alone. Never again. Everything that is yours is also mine. *You* are mine."

My chest cracked open. It filled, and overflowed, and filled again with that golden light. The light that was shining in the color of his eyes. That golden thread that tied me back to earth. "You're here," I whispered. Still unsure if I could believe it. "You're here." I shook my head against his lips. "I didn't think you'd forgive me."

"I'm here. I'm always here." He pressed his lips to mine and then pulled my head into his chest. I wasn't sure how long we stayed there like that before he shrugged up the wall and grabbed my hands, pulling me up with him. "Can we go for a drive?"

"Easton has my car."

He smiled. "I've got my Bronco."

"You drove here?" I asked, stunned. "I– I assumed you flew?"

"I had to drive. I needed my truck. My things. I plan on staying..." He paused, his eyes looking almost fearful. "If you'll have me."

A tearful gasp bubbled from me. "Stay. Stay forever." I dropped my head against his chest, shaking it rapidly. I breathed in the scent of fresh rain and mahogany that still lingered on him. He still smelt good, smelt like him, even though he'd been traveling for almost a full day. Traveling to me. Looking for me. Chasing me after he knew I had run away from him.

"Come on." He opened the front door.

I leaned around the corner toward the hallway that led to the two bedrooms. "I should probably tell Maddie–" One of the doors opened.

"I wasn't eavesdropping or anything, I swear. But, um, you're good. You go. I'll wait here for Easton."

I gave Carter a sidelong glance that told him she'd definitely been eavesdropping.

We bound down the steps to the bottom floor of my apartment building and into his truck. He wouldn't tell me where he was going as he balanced his phone on his lap, using the GPS for directions. The joke was on him because I'd lived in L.A. for one whole day and hadn't left my apartment yet. I wouldn't be able to say where we were going if I was the one navigating myself.

Within fifteen minutes, he pulled up next to the curb in an alleyway behind a set of buildings. We stepped out of his Bronco, and I could just make out the horizon line of the ocean between the two buildings in front of me. The beach was just across the street. Wispy clouds dotted the sky in every shade of pink. Streaks of orange expanded across the world, and I knew the sun was preparing to set somewhere out there.

His hand came to rest on the small of my back. "Pep, I promise I will watch the next thousand sunsets in a row with you, but right now, I have something I want to show you inside."

I looked up at the white-washed building in front of us, accented with blue shutters and doors. "Inside?"

"Yeah, this is the apartment building my dad bought." He stepped up to the door and placed a key in the lock.

"This doesn't look like apartments."

"All the units are on the second and third floors."

I looked up and noticed the balconies on the upper levels. "What's on the first level?"

He chortled as he opened the door. "Just let me show you, Pep."

Through the door was– nothing. A large, empty room. It was spacious, the walls were a shade of white that matched the outside of the building. At the far end were floor-to-ceiling windows that looked out to the beach. People walked and biked right next to them. I could see a volleyball game going on in the sand. The view was spectacular from the windows, almost as if I was outside watching it myself. Three paneled walls stood in the center of the room, each in front of another, seeming to be spaced out strategically.

I had no idea what he was trying to show me.

Grabbing me by the hand, he walked toward the front of the building where the windows were. A door stood to the left of them. On the other side of the door was some kind of counter space, almost looking like it'd be a reception desk of some sort. Which, in theory, could make sense, if I had any inkling to what this space was supposed to be.

Carter walked around the back side of the desk and returned with something in his hands. Something that seemed kind of heavy. He held it upright, covering his chest. I couldn't see it until he bent over and propped it up against the counter.

My hands flew to my mouth in a gasp as he came back to my side. It was a canvas. A *huge* canvas. Almost the size of me. Blues, and greens, and reds covered the canvas in splashes of color, swirling together into something that looked like an oil painting.

Except it wasn't. It couldn't be.

Because it was me.

It was the photo of me laying on my stomach in the water with my head draped over my arms. My hair is wet, swept out of my face and falling down my shoulder. The photo was morphed into something that looked like oil pastel, almost abstract. It was near impossible to tell it was a photo of me. The clearest parts of the painting being the way my eyes reflected off the water in a pure emerald shade, and the contrast of the auburn in my hair to the water beneath it.

"It's me."

I felt his fingers tickle my shoulder as he pulled my hair from behind it. "Yes. I was thinking about how lovely of a painting you'd make, so I created one."

"Carter...It's beautiful." I felt my tears welling again. "How?"

"A new technique I've been trying out. Turning digital photos into traditional art. I guess I've been inspired." His lips rested on the top of my head and I felt him smile. "I'm going to hang it up in here, right above the front desk."

"What is this place supposed to be?"

He wrapped his arms around my shoulders. "I was thinking of opening a photo and art gallery. Highlighting local artists and unique mediums. Focusing on art that is centered around nature. Maybe raise money for charities supporting environmental efforts and ocean conservation." He chuckled into my hair. "I've been thinking about it for a while. It'll be a long time coming because I have no idea what it takes to make it happen, but I'll figure it out."

I whipped around in his arms and looked up at him. His eyes were soft and shining. Sparkling with every color that has ever existed before and will ever exist again. "I think that's perfect." His lips tilted up into *that* grin. "When did you have the time to have that made?" I asked, nodding back towards the canvas.

"I've been working on it for weeks. I finished it a couple of nights ago. I called Dom while I was driving down here and asked him to go get it printed for me and drop it off here. I knew as soon as I reached you, I wanted to bring you here. Show you this. I don't know how else to show you what you're worth to me. You have inspired all of it." One rogue tear fell down my cheek and dripped into my neck. He folded me into his chest, his arms smothering me entirely and in the best way possible. "Pep," he whispered. "You know what my soulmate theory is?"

Before I could ask, he continued, "I don't believe soulmates are two halves of the same thing. Our souls are whole all on their own. Soulmates are two just souls who complement each other– that make each other better. They are built just as much as they are destined. And if we keep going on like this, just believing that the Universe is going to return us to each other every time we drift apart, we're going to fail. We're already failing.

"I need you to trust me. I need you to stop running away. This isn't the last time we'll fight. It's not the last time we'll be tested. You can run from everything else in life, as long as you're running *to* me. I promised you I'd catch you when you fell, and I will. Always. But you've got to promise me you won't run the moment your feet hit the ground."

I pulled back, bringing my hand to rest on his cheek. His eyes were misting, but he wouldn't allow them to spill over as mine now were. "I'm sorry I lied to you. I never should have. But you have to understand where my head was at. When I left Oxford, I *hated* myself. I truly hated myself. If you would've asked me six months ago to tell you one thing about myself I loved, I wouldn't have been able to. I blamed myself for everything." He opened his mouth but I held my hand up to let him know I wasn't finished. "So, when you showed back up in my life, with these memories of me as a completely different person than who I was now, I didn't want you to know the truth. I kept all of it hidden, and I tried to become the person you had known again. The person I thought you could love. I didn't believe that someone like you could ever love the person I thought I had become. I didn't think pure light could love pure dark.

"I never cared about crawling back to my true self until you came back. You made me want that. You made me want to find her. To heal and understand my past, to move forward from it. But it took me so long to get there, and I had already been lying, and the farther I fell into love with you, the harder it was to let go and tell you the truth. I thought you wouldn't see past it. You'd see the person I'd become and you wouldn't be able to believe I could find myself again. I was afraid you'd give up on me."

He swiped his thumbs underneath my eyes. "I wouldn't. I won't. I'm sorry I didn't make that clearer. That I let my emotions get the best of me. That I didn't hold onto that tether when I started drowning." He sighed. "That I let you float away too."

"We both let go," I whispered. "Never again."

"Never again," he promised.

I ran my thumb along his cheek, searching for the words I couldn't find.

They didn't exist. I found the only three that could begin to express the way I felt.

"I love you."

His lips met mine in a kiss that was deep, and soft, and warm. "I love you, Pep."

When he pulled away, I spun back around to look at the canvas again. I squatted down on the ground and ran my hand across my own face. It was smooth, but looked textured. He said it'd taken him weeks to create. I thought about all the late nights he was awake working on it while I was sleeping. The photo he had of me on his computer, and how it was the same one he was creating. I wondered if he, like myself, was so full of all the emotions that came with loving someone so intensely that he just needed to let it spill out. I wondered if this was the product of that.

For the first time, I felt the courage to finally show him the product of all my emotions too.

"We need to go back to my apartment," I said. I stood up and turned back at him.

"Right now?"

I nodded, smiling.

I threw open the door to my apartment to find my siblings standing around the kitchen counter stuffing their faces with Chinese takeout. They both paused mid-bite and stared past me as Carter shut the door behind him.

"I'm going to need you guys to go anywhere else. For a while."

Easton scrunched his nose. "Really, Penelope? *I'm eating*."

I smirked. "Eat somewhere else."

Maddie had already begun to place the food back into the bag and slip on her shoes. Easton scoffed but followed suit. "When can we come back?" she asked.

"An hour."

Carter's arm appeared at my waist, his lips at my cheek. "Better make it two."

"Oh God," Easton muttered.

They gathered their things and headed toward the door. Easton stopped in front of Carter, and I stepped to the side. Easton's face was a hard line, where Carter's looked almost timid. Finally, Easton smirked, and to my disbelief, pulled Carter in for a hug. As he pulled back, Easton slapped Carter's cheek playfully. "I'm not going to get all cliche here, but if you ever pull some stupid shit like that again– if you tell her anything other than how beautiful, and smart, and good she is, I'll kill ya."

I swallowed hard.

Carter only nodded.

Easton stepped past him, and then held back briefly. "You don't need to tell her she's funny. Because she's not. But everything else."

Maddie winked at me as they scurried out the door. I could hear her voice asking if they could go to Disneyland as their steps faded down the stairs.

"You're beautiful, and smart, and good," he whispered in my ear. "But not funny."

I moved to shove him, but before I could, he was scooping his arms under my knees and hoisting me into his chest. My giggles bounced off the walls as he carried me toward my bedroom. I pointed at the room that had become my own, and he nudged the door with his shoulder. Throwing me onto the bed, he began to crawl over me.

"Wait," I said. "I have something for you first."

He backed off the bed and backed up to the door. I leaped and bound to my closet, crawling into the farthest, darkest corner of it. As I stepped out, I noticed Carter looking into the box I'd set on my desk but hadn't unpacked yet. "You've still got my book," he said, holding up his copy of *The Alchemist*.

I held a canvas in my hands that was almost the size of the one he'd shown me in the studio. I held it up against my chest, facing inward so he couldn't see it yet. "You said I could keep it."

He smiled. "I also said if I ever got lost and needed to find myself again, I'd just come find you." He placed it back into the box. "So, I did."

I smiled, but didn't provide a response. Everything I needed to say was held in my hands. I took a deep breath before turning it around and showing it to him.

He tilted his head as his eyes soaked up the canvas. After a moment, his hand found his face as he swayed back a step. "Pep, is that–"

I nodded. "They always reminded me of a jungle. The mixture of all the colors of the earth and how at different times, in different lighting, one color will win over all the others. The gold in them looks like sunlight shining through the leaves of trees."

"The waterfall," he whispered. The waterfall wasn't originally planned. During the sketching phase of the painting, I felt it needed something more. I looked up Carter's portfolio online and found one of the first pictures he'd ever published.

"I recreated the photo from your portfolio."

I set the canvas against my desk and backed up next to him. From farther away, it looks mostly like an eye. The lashes fanning out into the top of the canvas. The skin around it was golden and sun kissed. From a distance, the color of the eye looked like morphing shades of green, brown, and gold. Stepping closer, a picture would begin to form within the eye itself. Ferns, and trees. A rock wall with white water cascading down the center of it, right through the pupil, and pooling at the bottom in the color of pure green. Streams of sunlight filtered in across the face on the canvas, shining into the eye itself.

His eye.

"It's so beautiful, Penelope. I– I don't know what to say."

I grabbed his face. "Don't say anything. It's my way of thanking you. Thank you for helping me find myself again. For reminding me who I am. What I'm worth."

His hands found my face too, closing that gap between us. Pulling away, he whispered against my lips, "I have a confession, Pep."

"What?"

"Your theory about soulmates. About atoms existing in pairs before the Big Bang and finding their way to each other." I pulled back and looked at him. "I googled it, Pep. It's scientifically improbable because atoms didn't exist before the Big Bang. Nothing did."

"Oh," I said. I wasn't sure where he was going with this. I wasn't sure how else to reply.

"But it's okay because I have a better one." He gave me *that* grin. "I think that soulmates are the person who inspires us to become the best version of ourselves, regardless of where they fit into it. Even when it means letting someone go when they need to find themselves. When they need to live without us." He paused, taking a breath. "Selfless love. Our muse. Our *aloha*. That's what we have always been to each other. Since the day we met. That," he waved at the space between us, "*this* is my soulmate theory."

I felt my eyes begin to mist. I thought back to that writing on the bathroom door in London years ago: *atoms are an endless, infinite existence.*

So were he and I.

"Ditto," I said. I was at a complete loss for words, but I knew my smile was saying everything that my mouth was incapable of.

I could see on his face that he knew it too as his mouth feathered against mine, and he kissed me with the force of the sun. The force of the moon– the tides. A kiss that felt like shimmering stars, and rainfall, and golden threads of light.

Five Years Later

Carter

"If you don't hurry, we're going to miss our flight!" she shouted from the living room.

"Pep, we've got two and a half hours before we depart."

"There might be traffic."

"We live fifteen minutes from the airport. We could walk and still make it."

"The Uber is already here and if we aren't out there in five minutes they'll leave," she argued. "And I'll still have to pay!"

I groaned. I overslept and missed *one* flight to Rome, *one* time. She never let it go. Two years ago, she'd gotten an opportunity with *National Geographic* to work in Pompeii. She spent three months in Italy. I'd been there most of the time with her but we had a gallery event I couldn't miss so I had to come back to L.A. for a few weeks while she was gone. My real mistake was going out with Dom the night before I was flying back. I woke up in the hallway outside mine and Penelope's apartment. My phone was dead, and my plane had left an hour before I woke. Penelope never let it go.

Now, she'd demand we be at the airport well before we needed to be. She would insist on packing for me because she thought I'd delay us if I packed for myself. Except, on this specific trip, I *really* needed to pack my own things. Her getting in the way was the true cause for the delay because I had to inconspicuously make her leave the room in order to finish gathering everything I needed. As she rushed me from the other side of our bedroom door, I couldn't help but grin.

I patted the front zipper of my backpack, reminding myself I had what I needed as I swung it over my shoulders and made my way to the front door. She was standing there, hip out, arms crossed. Her *I'm-about-to-throw-a-fit* stance. Her auburn hair was thrown into a knot at the top of her head, her green eyes simmering with beautiful annoyance. My lips found hers in a tug of gravity that was outside of my control. "We'll be perfectly on time, Dr. Mason." I kissed her and whispered, "I love you," as I pulled back.

Her nostrils flared before her face settled. "I love you," she murmured as she swung the front door open. I locked it behind us, falling into step with her as we walked down the hallway and into the stairwell that led to the first floor of the building. The Uber was parked out front, so we had to walk through the gallery to get there.

Macie stood behind the reception desk, furiously typing away at something on her phone. It was a Thursday afternoon in June, so things were slow. Not that I operated the gallery for profit, anyway. Most people came inside to get out of the heat, but stayed to look at the artwork. That alone made it worth it to me, I didn't care if I sold a damn thing.

We did well enough to keep it operating. Anytime we made profit from a show or a particularly large sale, we'd donate it to a different charity. Normally a charity of either the buyer or the artist's choosing.

I stopped briefly at the counter to check-in with Macie and ensure things would be handled while I was away for the next few days. She ran the gallery operations in my absences while the apartment building's operations were handled by Dom. I was away enough that they were used to it, and we'd fallen into a rhythm, but I knew Penelope would want to tell Macie goodbye again anyway.

As Penelope rounded the reception desk, Macie looked at me with raised brows. A silent question. I nodded quickly before Penelope could notice either of our expressions, and Macie shot me back a sparkling smile.

Penelope squatted to her knees in front of Macie. "Bye, Allie. Don't go making any grand appearances until I get back, okay?" She pressed her lips to the swell of Macie's ever-growing belly. Macie was due in about three weeks, and even though we would return in five days, Penelope had been terrified of Macie going into labor while we were gone.

"Oh," Macie scoffed. "I assure you that will not happen. I refuse to give birth to a Gemini. Nope, I'm holding this little sucker in until Cancer season." She rubbed her belly affectionately. "If I had things my way, I'd make her a Leo like her mom." She sighed. "But at least she won't be a Capricorn like her dad. They are *so* incredulous."

Penelope snorted. "Well, maybe you can try planning the next one to ensure they have the astrological sun sign of your choice."

As they bickered amongst themselves about astrology before we said our goodbyes, I couldn't help but pause briefly to take in the piece that hung above the desk. Penelope hated that I hung that painting of her there. It was the first thing anyone saw when they walked through the door. Anytime a customer recognizes her from the painting above the wall and comments on it, she blushes and then later begs me to change it out. And every time, I refuse.

I'd line the entire gallery with canvases of her if I could. In fact, I insisted that she let me take photos of her in every destination we'd ever traveled together. Every place we went. My office that sat behind the front desk had an entire wall filled with photos of her. Photos of her and my mom in Hawaii, her and Maddie in Spain, the two of us in Italy, and Indonesia, and the Oregon Coast. My favorite, a photo of her flipping me off on the beach in Malibu, sat framed at my desk. I kept another copy folded up inside my wallet.

I'd made many of them into artwork too.

Even still, I'd never been able to replace the first piece I ever made. The same piece that had been hanging above the desk since before the gallery was ever opened. No matter how much my skills grow, I'll never move it. It'll always stay there. The reminder of my inspiration.

After all, that's what I named the gallery for. For her. *Muse.*

Penelope

"Good morning, Mahina," he whispered against my shoulder.

"No." I rolled over to face away from him as his laughter vibrated against my skin.

The pure joy Carter felt every time he was back home in Hawaii was one of my favorite things about him. It was almost as if his excitement radiated off of him and went directly into my own bones. I could physically feel the love he had for these islands.

We landed in Oahu yesterday afternoon, and I should've known that by this morning he'd be insisting on waking me up as early as possible. He wanted to soak in every minute. Each moment with his mom, every sunset, and all the sunrises too. I did try to participate, but I was almost positive it couldn't be later than five am. No matter how many years he spent trying to convince me, I'd never be a morning person.

He trailed kisses up the backside of my shoulder until he reached my neck. I felt his teeth at the base of my ear. "You're going to miss it, Pep. You're really not going to want to miss this sunrise."

"Why this one, specifically?" I grumbled into the pillow.

"You'll have to get out there and see for yourself."

I groaned, bracing my arms against the mattress preparing myself to lift off the bed when I felt his hand pin my hips down. I laid flat on my back as his body appeared before me. The gold in his eyes sparkled even in the dark as he smiled down at me. "You're being very contradictory this morning."

That smile formed into a smirk. "I just thought of a better way of waking you." His mouth then found itself starting against my lips and didn't stop until it was somewhere beneath the sheets.

Carter had this secret spot not far from his mom's house that he claimed was the best on the island for watching the sunrise. The cove was rarely deserted, but it was far enough away from the touristy part of the island that it was almost never crowded.

Though this morning we seemed to have gotten lucky because we were the only two here. We walked hand-in-hand through the sand until we found a spot to settle in against a rock. The sky was just beginning to brighten along the eastern horizon, fading from midnight blue to a deep lavender that meshed with the color of the ocean.

I made to sit down when his hand stopped me. "Don't sit yet."

I blinked at him. "Why?"

His smile told me he had something up his sleeve. "Let's take a walk."

He led me toward the rocky embankment that jettied out past the cove. We tiptoed along the rocks, careful of the waves that splashed furiously against them. Once we made it to the end of the jetty, he stopped. Just above us the rocks leveled out to a flatter top, but getting up there would require about ten feet of climbing.

That was where his expression became known. He trusted the ocean wholeheartedly. He fully believed that if he fell off one of these rocks and into the water below, it'd bring him safely back to shore. Maybe not in a literal sense, but he believed that he had both enough skill and enough connection with the ocean that he had nothing to fear. It was a beautiful thing to believe in.

I, however, did not share that sentiment.

I didn't like climbing, especially when falling likely meant my skull being crushed repeatedly against a cliff. I didn't like the slickness of the rocks, either. I'd already been on edge just walking along the jetty. I jumped every time a wave crashed against my ankles, afraid it'd throw off my balance. He must've been reading my expression because he said, "Trust me, Pep."

And I melted just enough that I nodded. He found the lowest place along the rock and hoisted me up so I could grab the upper ledge. I lifted one leg and pulled my upper body over the top. It was not lost on me that Carter had his hands on my ass the entire time. Though if I asked, he'd say he was holding me steady. I had to roll sideways across the top of the rock to get up completely, thankful that movement wasn't witnessed by anyone when Carter then hoisted himself up with seemingly no effort at all.

I rolled my eyes as he sat down next to me, both of us letting our legs dangle off the edge. That midnight blue had completely disappeared from the sky as sparks of orange and pink took its place. I felt Carter's eyes on me and as I turned to him, he said, "Do you remember when I promised I'd be on my knee proposing to you the moment you got your PhD?"

I stared after him for a moment, not wanting to let my brain get ahead of me when it considered where this conversation might lead. I held out my arm and looked down at my wrist as if I was checking a watch. "Sure do. It's been exactly four days, twenty hours, and fifty-seven minutes since I graduated. You really dropped the ball, Edwards."

He snorted as he shook his head. "I want it to be perfect, for whenever it does happen."

I forced my smile not to falter as I felt a small twinge of disappointment. I hadn't truly expected him to propose at my graduation, or even soon after. We were busy. More than that, we were happy– exactly as things were. I just received a full-time position with *National Geographic*, while Carter's begun free-lancing with them himself. We have the art studio to run too. Even if he were to propose, it wasn't as if we had time to plan a wedding. We'd probably end up at City Hall.

Though, I couldn't pretend it wasn't something I was looking forward to. I always tried telling myself I wasn't the kind of girl who cared to get married, but in truth, I only forced myself to think that way because I didn't feel I was worthy of the type of love I knew should come with marriage. And after I found Carter, after I learned to love myself, I realized there was nothing I wanted more. There was nothing I wanted more than to be tied to him forever. Spiritually, physically, and legally, too.

"You could propose to me at the kitchen table, or in the back seat of an Uber, or while I was at the dentist, and it would still be perfect."

He nodded. "I know." He brought his arm up to my face and ran his thumb along my cheek. "But I just always imagined it a certain way. There is something—some place—that reminds me of you. Always has, even in the years I didn't get to be with you. And even though we've already committed to each other for as long as the Universe allows us, I want that place incorporated when I actually put that ring on your finger."

I looked up at him. "What's that place?"

His hand moved from my cheek to the back of my neck as his grip tightened. He brought my head to his and whispered against my lips, "The sunrise on the beach."

My pulse skyrocketed as he closed the gap between us. His lips moved against mine in an unhurried motion. I gave myself into the moment and leaned against his chest, melting into him entirely. When he pulled away, a small brown box was present in the palm of his hand.

"To me, the sun rising against the ocean is the most astounding natural element of the world. It represents new beginnings, opportunities, and fresh starts. It provides hope and beauty and makes me feel completely in awe of the world we live in and all the universe outside of it. It makes me feel overwhelmed with existence itself. It makes me feel grateful for that. For just simply existing, for being able to witness it at all." We both looked out at the sea then. As if it was a canvas that had been splashed with every color imaginable, exploding right before our eyes. The orb of the sun was just starting to hover over the horizon line, shrouding everything in its path with gold. His hand still cupping my cheek, he guided my eyes back to his. "That's how you make me feel, Penelope. You are the moon and stars to me, but you're also the beginning of every new day. You make every moment feel like an endless opportunity. You are hope and beauty, and I am in awe of you. You overwhelm me in a way that I can't describe, and I'll be forever grateful that I get to watch you exist. I never want you to miss the sunrise because these are the only moments that I truly feel I can show you what I see when I look at you. That's how I want you to see yourself."

My throat had closed, choking back all of my tears, but as I watched one spill out of his eye and down his cheek, my own dam broke. I strangled sob ripped from me as I tried to laugh through them. I opened my mouth, trying to tell him how much I love him, but I wasn't able to speak through my sobbing laughter.

Because I love him. *God*, I love him.

His hand moved to his lap and my eyes followed as I watched that little brown box open. An oval-cut emerald ring was cushioned within the box. Encased in a crown of diamonds on a silver band, the ring glimmered in the morning sunlight.

His hands were shaking as he pulled the ring from the box and held it out in front of him. "Will you marry me?" He was blurry through my tears, and my bottom lip was trembling so much that I couldn't speak. I could only nod and hold out my own shaking hand as he slipped the ring onto my left finger. I raised my hand above us as we both watched gemstone dance in the reflection of the sunlight. "I got you an emerald because the color reminds me of your eyes, but if you'd prefer a diamond we can–."

"It's so beautiful," I whispered. "It's perfect." I pulled my gaze from the ring to his eyes. A smile bloomed across his face as he looked after me. "I'll never be able to put into words the way I feel for you, but it's all here," I said, placing my left hand over my chest. "Everything you feel exists inside me too. Loving you is the easiest promise I'll ever make."

He leaned into me as we tasted each other's tears and felt each other's smiles.

It was arguably the most perfect moment I'd ever lived, until he said, "Oh God, your initials are really going to be P.E.E." His laughter was a melody. "I'm so excited to make fun of you for the rest of my life."

"Ass."

He only laughed louder as I rolled my eyes, settling into him. We watched the horizon in silence for some time, though I couldn't stop sneaking glances at the ring. Every time I looked at it, I instinctively got a little closer to him. He brushed his fingers through my hair and would occasionally press his lips against my cheek, or my ear, or the side of my head.

"We should probably go," he whispered long after the sun had fully risen.

"Why?" I asked.

I'd been laying against his chest, so I felt all of it rumble when he laughed. It almost sounded nervous. "Well… I kind of gave our parents the heads up. And… they all flew out. They rented a house about twenty minutes from here. My mom is there too." He looked at me with an expression that was almost sorry. "They're expecting us."

A half hour later we were walking through the front door of a beachfront house that was clearly large enough for both sides of the family. I was practically tackled by our sisters as they begged to look at the ring. Easton was making mock threats to Carter. All the moms were asking how it happened and whether or not it was romantic, and Tom was telling them it couldn't have possibly been since Carter planned it all himself.

When my dad hugged me, he whispered, "When he was nine years old, he asked me if he could marry you and I told him to ask again in twenty years. Here we are, only nineteen later."

My tears flowed again.

Our family was loud and excitable, and in that chaos, I had never felt more grateful. In that moment I realized the only thing I'd truly wanted in my entire life was to feel I belonged. To feel love and comfort, and to find a place to call home. Once I allowed myself to face those needs head on, and allowed myself to believe I deserved them, I somehow found that they had been in front of me the entire time. So maybe it was true after all. When you want something with all your soul, the Universe will work its magic to help you find it.

And when we married a little over a year later in a small, intimate ceremony on the beach of our hometown, we didn't end our vows with, *'til death do us part*, because we already knew that wasn't enough for us. We simply vowed: *In every lifetime.*

Bonus Epilogue

Carter

"Dude, I can't believe you cried. You're such a pussy." Easton handed me a beer as he flopped down into the adirondack chair next to me.

I grabbed the bottle with my freehand, while my other arm wrapped around the waist of my brand new wife. She laid her head against my shoulder, swinging her legs over my knees. Glancing up at me with her emerald-colored eyes, she gave me a soft smile.

Fuck yeah, I cried when I watched her walk down the aisle. It was the most beautiful day the Oregon coast had seen all summer, and the secluded Rockaway Cove we grew up spending our weekends at was nearly deserted, save for our small group of friends and family who attended. Penelope had on a long, flowing white dress, and her new shoulder-length hair was lightly curled. Her freckles sparkled in the sunlight, and her eyes glowed like the moon.

She was the most beautiful thing I'd ever seen, and I'd been waiting for that moment since I was nine-goddamn-years-old. Of course I fucking cried about it.

But I wasn't about to explain that to Easton. Instead, I snorted. "That's not what your sister was saying last night when she was screaming my–"

A throat cleared nearby.

Penelope lifted her head, looking above us before her cheeks flushed crimson. She turned back to me with a glare. I followed her gaze and caught both of our dad's staring down at us. Easton was having a coughing fit nearby as he choked on his drink from his laughter.

"Sorry," I muttered.

"That was so embarrassing," Penelope murmured into my neck.

Dan rolled his eyes at me, while my dad gave me a wink as they both circled the fire pit and took two chairs on the opposite side of Easton, Penelope and I. There were plenty of spots open around the fire roaring in my parent's backyard, but there was no other place I'd rather have her than on my lap.

We booked the honeymoon suite at a beachside hotel not far out of town last night after our reception, but planned to leave for our real honeymoon a day later so we could spend one final night in town with our family before everyone went their own ways. Easton back to Boise; my sister back to New York; and Macie, Dom, Allie, and Penelope's sister, Maddie, would go back to Southern California tomorrow morning. Tonight, everyone gathered at my parent's house for one final dinner before we all dispersed, and Penelope and I left for our three week trip.

I took a sip of my beer as Penelope laid her head back down on my chest and sighed softly, letting her eyes flutter shut.

"Are you guys excited?" my mom asked as she took a seat next to my dad.

When I looked up at her, she was smiling at Penelope, who appeared to be dozing off.

"Yeah," I answered.

"Where to first?" my dad asked.

"London. Then Andalusia, Spain. We'll take a boat across the Strait of Gibraltar, and then spend a few days Tangier and Marakkesh, before flying to Egypt. After that, we'll end the trip in Greece." I smiled down at my wife, running my palm across the backside of her head. "Apparently, Santorini has some kind of museum dedicated to the legends of Atlantis that she really wants to see."

Our honeymoon was planned around ourselves. Our story. Stopping first at the place that Penelope saw that soulmate theory written on the bathroom wall when she was nineteen. Then, following the journey taken in my favorite book. The book I found when I was eighteen and heartbroken over her. Finally, we'd spend some time in an actual honeymoon destination, closing out our trip with lazy days on the beach and letting Penelope investigate her favorite conspiracy.

"Take lots of photos." My mom smiled, eyes the same color as mine crinkling back at me.

I gave her a dead-pan expression.

"I'm so jealous," Dom chimed in as he climbed out of the pool and began to towel off. "When are we taking a honeymoon?" he asked Macie as she walked around the farside of the pool with their daughter in her hands.

"Probably when you stop knocking me up," she said. She stepped up to her husband and he pressed a kiss to Allie's forehead, brushing her dark curls out of her face as she beamed up at him like he hung the moon. Macie seemed to take on the same expression as she smiled at Dom, too. "It's getting close to her bedtime so we're going to head back to our hotel." Macie passed Allie off to Dom as she walked up to Penelope and kissed her forehead. "We love you guys. See you in a couple of weeks."

They made the rounds, saying goodbye to our parents. To our sisters, my stepmom, and Penelope's mom who sat at the dinner table. Dom promised, as he always did, to take care of the gallery until we got back. He raised his daughter's pudgy little arm and waved everyone a final farewell as they exited through the house.

"That gonna heal before you leave?" Dan asked, nodding toward my arm.

I watched a sleepy smile spread across Penelope's mouth as she reached out toward my forearm and turned it over. She skimmed her fingers across the slightly raised skin, now dark beneath the ink. Her wedding ring glinted in the fire light.

"Oh, yeah. It'll be fine."

I'd spent the night of my bachelor party getting a tattoo, though not due to intoxicated spontaneity. It was something I'd been planning for a while. Planning to surprise her with as a wedding gift. Penelope traced the crescent moon, dripping with stars, that now lived beneath the crease of my elbow. She pressed against the sparkles that dotted the space around it, and then traced the script that was written along the crest of the moon: *Mahina*.

A small sketch she'd made on a long haul flight we'd been taking at one point a few years ago. She considered it a doodle on a post-it note. I considered it something so beautiful I wanted to stare at it for the rest of my life. I decided to brand myself with it. With her artwork. With her.

"It's beautiful," she whispered. "I want to get one."

"What do you mean, Pep? You've already got that tattoo of my name on your ass."

My father-in-law glared at me again. I gave him a slow grin and a wink. My dad and Easton both stifled their laughter as Penelope swatted at me.

I pressed my lips against the top of her head as she snuggled back into my chest. Light conversation floated in the air all around us. Between our siblings and our parents. Our dads continued to ask me questions about the gallery, which I'd finally and officially purchased from my father this past spring. He still owned the apartments above it, but the gallery was mine. Ours, now. I talked through the plans I had for the future, but my attention kept being pulled back to the quiet woman in my arms.

As the evening went on, I found myself thanking the Universe for all of it. For our family, for our careers, for the life we get to live together. But every piece of gratitude I had always came back to her. She was every wish I'd ever had, and because of her, all my other dreams came true, too. Everything I'd ever conspired to achieve.

Eventually, Penelope was sleeping against my chest. It was true, some things genuinely never changed. I remember sitting around this exact same firepit twenty years ago, watching her fall asleep in her dad's lap after dinner. I remember feeling something warm inside my gut when I'd watch it happen. Knowing she felt safe, comfortable, and protected. I couldn't comprehend it at the time, but I think that all I really wanted was to make her feel that way myself. Now, as her heavy breaths fell against my neck, I knew that I'd finally found that. I'd finally given her that.

We'd come full circle.

Everyone began to taper off, returning to the house little by little, quietly saying their goodnights and their congratulations. Her dad was the last to rise from his chair. "Do you want to wake her up and take her inside?" he asked, nodding toward the pool house I once lived in.

I shook my head. "No, it's okay. She can sleep here a little longer," I whispered. "I'll carry her inside in a bit."

Dan nodded, squeezing my shoulder as he rounded the chair I was sitting in. "You're always the person I imagined for her, you know," he said as he headed toward the back gate that would lead to his home across the street. He didn't wait for me to respond as he disappeared into the night.

I laid my cheek against the top of her head, watching embers crackle in front of me, savoring the silence. Savoring the warmth of my wife nuzzled against me. Still unbelieving, even after so many years, that we'd finally made it here.

I shifted her in my arms and reached into the pocket of my jeans, pulling out the worn and crumbled piece of paper. I'd memorized my vows easily, given that I'd been preparing them my whole life, but I still had them written down. I'd started writing them years ago, right after we moved in together. I added to them little by little every year that passed.

She didn't know about this piece of paper yet, I was saving it for the last leg of our honeymoon, and I'll give it to her then.

For now, I was content to let her sleep on me. To listen to the fire. To read the words I'd said to her, the words etched into the very threads of my soul, underneath the light of the moon:

When I was seven years old, it was your eyes.

When I was nine, it was your smile.

At thirteen, it was the sound of your laugh and, to be completely honest, the way your t-shirts were a little tighter in the chest than they had been the year before.

At fifteen it was your intelligence– the way you always knew the right answer in class. The way you never made me feel stupid for being wrong.

At eighteen, it was your lips.

At nineteen, it was your determination to follow your dreams, even if it meant you were breaking my heart.

At twenty-three, it was the woman you'd become. Your independence, your strength, and your resilience.

At twenty-four, it was the laugh you make in your sleep. The realization that I'd get to wake up to that—wake up next to you—every day for the rest of my life.

At twenty-six, it was your adventurous spirit when we spent the summer in Europe.

At twenty-eight, it was your artist's soul when you finally let me sell one of your paintings to that cute little coffee shop in Pacific Shores.

Today, it's seeing you in a white dress, looking more beautiful than my mind ever would've been capable of imagining you. Today, I'm just as intrigued by your eyes, enraptured by your smile, and enamored by your laugh as I was when I was a kid. I have just as big of a crush on you now as I did as a teenager. I'm just as intoxicated by your lips as I was when I kissed you for the very first time. Just as desperate for you as I've always been.

Every piece of you that's been given to me throughout our lives I cherish as much right now as I did the day you handed them to me. The only thing that changes is the depth in which I fall in love with you. Everyday I'm blown away by you. I'm amazed by you. I'm eternally grateful for the powers that be who allowed us to find each other as children. The powers that brought us back together after all those years apart. Because each day you gift me with a new piece of you to love.

People may think that's impossible, they may say that it's been twenty years and there couldn't possibly be anything more for me to learn about you, but everyday you show me something new. You give me another reason to thank the Universe for you. Another soulmate theory to believe in. Another reason to believe that the sun and the moon and the stars aligned just for the two of us.

Because our lives could've gone in a lot of different directions. And while I never would've imagined the route we ended up taking, I've known with certainty, since the very moment those big green eyes looked into mine for the first time, that we'd be standing right here someday.

And as I look at you now, the girl of my dreams who became the center of my Universe, I know for certain that we'll be standing right here again in every realm, every dimension, and every lifetime that comes next.

That's what I'll promise you, Penelope. That I'll love you beyond this life. No matter what, my soul will find yours– every single time.

Keep reading for a sneak peek at Macie & Dom's story:

The Fate Philosophy

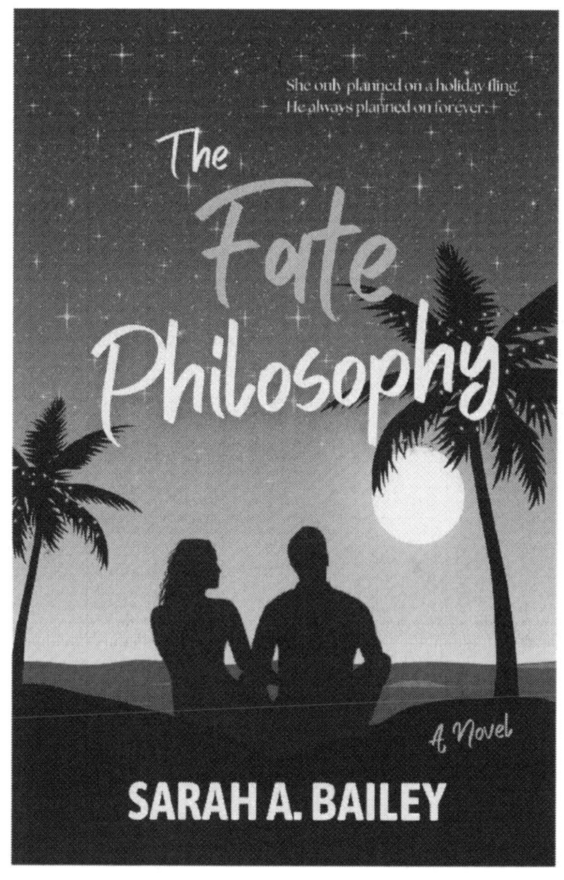

She only planned on a holiday fling
He always planned on forever.

Available November 1, 2023

April

Dominic

The air was musky with the scent of sweating bodies and lack of oxygen.

It was so packed that I could hardly make out my surroundings, but I could see enough to tell the dance floor was to my right, and the bar behind it. A spiral staircase in front of me led to an upper level that overlooked the floor and was littered with leather couches. That must've been what Carter meant when he said they were upstairs.

I chuckled to myself as I took the steps two at a time. I tried time and again the last couple of years to get Carter to try going out with me when he came to visit, and I failed every damn time. I don't doubt that one bat of Penelope's eyelashes had him agreeing to coming to a stuffy place like this. Although I hadn't seen her in a few years, the Penelope I knew would've hated this too.

It made me wonder how they actually ended up here.

Spending twenty years of your life around someone gives you a keen awareness of their presence, so it took me no time at all to locate my best friend. He was standing at the back of the upper level, leaned over the railing with his eyes intently watching something below him. I came to stand beside him without saying a word.

We didn't greet each other that way. Never had. We don't hug, and we don't say goodbye, either. We rarely answer the phone with a greeting, choosing instead to jump directly into the conversation at hand. We'd never been taught to live without each other. In the entirety of our childhood, I could count on one hand, probably, how many times I went more than twenty-four hours without seeing Carter. So when we ultimately became separated in our adulthood, we didn't really know how those things worked.

I looked at him, he nodded in acknowledgment to my presence, but he didn't turn away from where his stare was. His brow was scrunched in concentration– or frustration, sometimes it was hard to tell. By the tightness of his jaw and the clear grind of his teeth, I guessed at the latter. I followed his gaze and was snagged by a deep red ponytail swinging back and forth.

Ah. Okay. Frustration, then.

It had been years since I'd seen that expression, so I didn't recognize it immediately. Everything began to click into place as we both watched Penelope twirl on the dance floor, her hands slowly sliding up her torso in a seductive way that was clearly a message. I spent so many years watching that expression on his face, wanting to smack it off him. Begging him to do something about his incessant, painful, and seemingly (to only him) unrequited love.

When he told me he was going on a trip with her, I thought it meant something different.

But I guess we're back to square one.

God, they're fucking annoying.

It made sense to me now why he was here, though. If Penelope walked up to me wearing that good-for-nothing shirt and asked me to endure ear-drum decimating, shitty dance music and the smell of alcohol induced body odor, I'd say yes too.

I could've sworn she didn't have boobs like that the last time I saw her.

"Stop."

Another thing about being friends with someone your entire life is a keen awareness of their thoughts too, apparently. I laughed. "He speaks."

He took a long slug from the beer bottle in his hand and looked at me from the corner of his eye. "Hey."

"What are you doing, dumbass?"

"I don't fucking know." He shook his head. "She asked me to dance and I said I had to wait for you."

"Glad to know we've gone back in time ten years and you're using me as an emotional blockade again."

"I locked up, dude. I don't know what's wrong with me."

We both looked back down at the dance floor just in time to catch her glance up at us too. I grinned, waving at her. Her eyes darted away, pretending she hadn't been looking.

"Why are we here?"

"Honestly, not where I'd like to be. I doubt Pep would, either. But Macie wanted to come." Right. Penelope's friend or something.

"You all came because she told you to?"

Carter chuckled. "She can be a commanding presence." He shrugged. "She planned the trip, she's entertaining to watch, so we endure."

"She sounds...interesting."

Carter nodded. "She is. She's the blonde down there with a red dress on. Curly hair."

I scanned the crowd, my curiosity growing by the second to get my eyes on this girl. Before I could find her, I noticed some buzzcut douche bag pressing up behind Penelope and whispering in her ear.

"Better unlock yourself and go get your gir–" I turned to face Carter but realized he was already gone. I laughed to myself.

I followed Carter down the stairs just in case things turned physical and he needed me. I highly doubted it. That wasn't his thing. But if the guy said something derogatory or threatening to or about Penelope, he may start swinging.

Halfway down the staircase, I looked out to the dance floor again, doing a double take as I finally spotted her. My feet stopped working. I paused right there on the stairs, nearly tumbling down them at the abrupt halt in my steps that had the rest of my body swaying.

Her head was tilted upward, the harsh lights of the night club shining down on her smooth skin. The smile that graced her cheeks was carefree and blissful. Curls fell down between her shoulder blades and swayed side to side in time with her hips.

Her hips.

She was petite. Thin. But her hips were round. Lush. They were the kind of hips that would look best wrapped around my face. Her body was tight and small. Her fucking dress clung to every curve perfectly. It stopped mid thigh, showing off her flawless legs, and the halter top that tied around her long neck complimented the shape of her body. She moved in perfect time with the music, and was given all the space she needed despite being directly in the middle of the dance floor. People all around watched her. Some with admiration, some with lust, others with jealousy. I found myself wanting to pummel the men who licked their lips and raised their brows with every movement she made, and I hadn't even spoken a word to her. I knew they were wondering how those movements looked without clothes on, because I was wondering too.

With every swing of her hips, her dress glittered in the lights. She outshined everything around her. There weren't any spotlights on that dance floor but there might as well have been. Right on her. She demanded to be seen. Her movements were effortless and fluid, as if she was made for this moment. Made to be the center of attention. Made to bring the world to its knees. Her dress shimmered with each roll of her body, and her smile shined like the brightest star in the night sky. Everything about her sparkled. Like a fucking beacon, calling to me.

My feet began moving again. Not toward Carter. He was on his own now. No, my feet began moving toward her. Desperate to see her up close. To see if she's real. I stumbled down the rest of the stairs, thanking luck or fate or God when I noticed her move to the edge of the dance floor.

She seemed to be in search of something. Her eyes were wide...maybe panicked? They settled to my left and she let out what looked to be a sigh of relief. I followed her line of sight and found our friends huddled close together, whispering in each other's ears. Buzzcut was nowhere to be found. Macie must've been so entranced in the music and her dancing that she lost track of Penelope, and began to panic when she couldn't find her. I was able to take a deeper look at her face as her features relaxed. Her eyes were a bright, yet deep, hazel color. Her round cheeks were flushed and glowing, her pouty lips pursed as she panted through them. Beautiful. She was deliriously beautiful and I couldn't stop walking toward her. As my body reached hers, she turned to me. Her eyebrows narrowed as she took me in. Her arms crossed against her chest as she waited for me to say something.

Say something, idiot.

My mouth dropped open, and those brows of hers raised. A small smirk appeared at the corner of her mouth as she looked me up and down. Starting at my feet, her eyes slowly dragged up the length of my body, lingering on my arms and shoulders before reaching my face. They flared just enough that I knew she liked what she saw. Yet, just as quickly, they settled.

"Stop drooling, Dominic."

I felt my eyebrows rocket into my hairline, my mouth drop open in surprise. Not only does she know who I am, but she unabashedly acknowledged my failure at subtly checking her out.

"You know who I am?"

Her lips twitched, her own failure in attempting to look bored and unaffected. "I had a general description of what you look like and I knew you'd be meeting us here." She shrugged. "I couldn't imagine why any other stranger would be sniffing me out like a bloodhound." *She saw me coming?* She flicked a brow. "Although, I'm not sure what you need from me, either."

Everything, I found myself wanting to say.

I inched closer to her on instinct. Despite the fact that the building smelled like sweating bodies and cheap perfume, Macie smelled delicious. Like vanilla and something more– something warm and spiced. Cinnamon, maybe. I fought the urge to lean even closer to her and breathe her in. An oasis in a desert of bodies. She smelled fucking decadent.

Pulling myself together, I craned my head to the left. "I came down to help out, but it appears my assistance is no longer needed." We both turned our heads as we watched Penelope lead Carter to the dance floor.

I shot Penelope with an exaggerated smile and waved again. She gave me an accusing eye roll but waved back. As I turned to Macie, her eyes were positively glowing with equal parts mischief and delight. As if she was elated to see the two of them holding hands.

A grin spread across my mouth. *I think I'm going to like her.*

She looked back at me, lingering longer than before. She nibbled on her bottom lip as her gaze snagged on my chest and stayed there just a moment too long. Once her eyes found my face again, I smiled at her. She glanced away quickly, as if it would stop me from noticing that she had clearly been checking me out too.

I was already enticed by this game we'd begun playing.

"I like your dress," I said.

She crossed her arms and picked at her nails. "I know."

"Do you want to dance?"

She shrugged nonchalantly. "Not sure I should dance with someone who's been known to make out with my best friend."

"I–what?" *What the fuck is she talking about?*

Of all the reactions I expected her to have to that question, that was not one of them. Only a few minutes in and this girl was throwing me off my game completely. She was entirely unpredictable. As if you never knew what would come out of her mouth next.

It was intriguing. It made me want to see what other words I could pull from her.

"You were Penelope's first kiss, no?"

Oh. *Oh.* A cackle escaped my mouth. "Like, a hundred years ago, and I'm not sure I'd call it making out." I shook my head, hiding a smile. "But say that again when Carter's around, will you?"

Her head fell back as she laughed, and I thought it may just be the most musical sound I'd ever heard. She uncrossed her arms and swiped at her dress, straightening out the hem that fell along her thigh. As I followed her movements, my eyes caught there. She glanced up to me and as she sucked in a swift breath, I knew my gaze was burning through her. I licked my lips. I was normally much better at hiding my attraction to a woman. I wasn't one to put myself on display so desperately.

But Macie was an abnormality. She made me feel like one too.

"So...dance?" I found myself asking again. Uncaring if it sounded like a plea.

I could count the minutes I've known her on one hand, and yet I knew with absolutely certainty that I'd crawl on hot coals for the opportunity to feel her skin.

She bit her lip again.

"Probably not a good idea." She pointed at the upper level of the club. "My boyfriend is upstairs."

Disappointment flooded me. "Shit. I'm sorry. Nobody told me."

She shook her head, a coy smile still on her face. "No, it's okay. I mean, at least you ask before groping. Most men here don't."

I frowned. "Fuck that." I nodded back toward the floor. "You dance, and if a hand touches you I'll remove it, yeah?"

Her blush was instant as she dropped her eyes to the floor. Finally, some kind of reaction.

I realized that she hadn't said no either time. She couldn't say yes, though. Not when she was here with another man. And I couldn't blame her for that because nothing about the way I would touch her would be considered platonic.

When she looked back at me, that blush was gone. As if a mask of cool indifference covered her features. "I'm entirely capable of shoving away scrubby-ass men on my own, but if you need an excuse to continue ogling me, be my guest," she chimed. There was a playful glitter in her eyes that told me that was exactly what she wanted me to do, even if she couldn't say it outloud.

I raised one brow at her, a silent understanding. I knew what she wanted, and I'd give her exactly that. Her eyes flared before she flipped her hair behind her shoulder and spun around, sauntering back toward the dance floor, her beautiful ass swaying with every step.

Fuck. Fuck. Fuck.

A boyfriend? Upstairs? While she's down here *alone*? I was out here offering to stand guard so men didn't touch her against her will when she had a man who wasn't even paying attention? I blew out a frustrated breath and stepped into the mosh pit of bodies. I moved around enough to give the illusion that I was dancing, but truthfully, I was only standing. Staring at her.

She was an enigma. I didn't know her but I could tell already that she'd be unlike any other person I've ever met before. I could tell already that I'd never meet someone like her again. There was some kind of current flowing between us, some pull I had to her from the moment I saw her.

I couldn't tell if she felt too. Her body language, the way her eyes glittered just a bit brighter when she looked into my own, that blush and her coy smile, the sound of her laugh; all things that made me think she did. At the same time, her chilly demeanor and snarky attitude made me think she didn't feel anything at all. I could tell her mouth got her in trouble sometimes.

I already loved that about her, I think.

In an artificial world, Macie seems real.

Maybe she's hiding her reaction to me because it makes her feel guilty. It can be hard to recognize an instant attraction to a person when you're already in love with someone else.

I rubbed at my chest, hating the tension it built when I thought about the fact that she is, indeed, in love with someone else. Probably, anyway. I didn't know enough about her to know she even had a boyfriend, let alone how long they'd been together or how serious they were. But I did know that Macie lives in Brighton Bay, which likely means her boyfriend lives there too. If he made this trip with her, they're at least serious to travel together.

But the way her eyes lingered on my body, the way her face lit up when I asked her to dance. That meant something. She saw something. At least enough to make her curious. To make her attracted to me. And maybe I couldn't do anything about that, at least not right now, but it was enough to mean that in some universe, I may have a chance.

A while later, she reached me again. Panting and out of breath, she let me know she needed a break and was going to head upstairs to check on Jeremy.

Jeremy. What the fuck kind of name is Jeremy?

I nodded as she bit down on her lip again, redness rising to her cheeks.

Fuck. That look on her face is going to ruin me.

"Do you want to come with me?" She glanced behind her. "It looks like Carter is...preoccupied."

I laughed. "Yeah, sure."

I followed her through the sea of bodies and up the staircase. I let her walk in front of me to be gentlemanly, but also because it gave me a great view of her ass, and I had to take what I could get at this point.

"Why is he up here all by himself?" I asked as we reached the top level.

She paused. "Oh, um, he just doesn't like clubs, really." She said it hesitantly, as if she was embarrassed.

I found myself understanding, because I don't like clubs either. But if she was mine, I'd never send her downstairs on her own. I'd never make her dance by herself. I'd never sulk alone, knowing I had a beautiful woman who was forcing herself to have fun without me. I'd dance with her. I'd be trying to make her laugh. I'd try to give her everything she wanted in life. Even if that was musty clubs and blaring music.

She shouldn't be embarrassed that her man wasn't giving her that. He should. He should be embarrassed that he attained one of the most compelling women I'd ever met, and he's not cherishing every millisecond he gets to spend with her. He's a blind, stupid fool.

She should be downright angry.

We made our way to the back corner where Carter had been standing earlier. I noticed for the first time a red-headed man sunk into the leather couch with a phone screen brightening his features. He was completely oblivious to the world around him. I hadn't even seen him when I walked in. He had no reaction to Macie's reappearance until she was standing in front of him with a hand on her hip for several seconds. He typed something into his phone before finally locking it and looking up at her.

"Hey, babe," he said in a monotone voice that was anything but affectionate.

"Hey. This is Dom, Carter's friend. Dom, this is Jeremy."

I reached out to shake his hand, flashing him my most charming, salesman smile. He returned it with one that was bland in comparison. I knew Macie could see it too. His grip was weak, and he didn't move over to make room for Macie, so she was forced to crawl over his lap to the empty spot next to him.

And while I understood the urge to make that woman crawl, to have her in my lap and her body against mine, that wasn't why Jeremy didn't move. He just didn't care.

It annoyed me. Everything about him annoyed me.

I asked them how they met. They'd both gone to college in Portland before landing jobs at the same school. Jeremy was from Seattle, and when I asked him about that, his face lit up slightly. Not about his girlfriend or their relationship. Not when I asked about their life together. He hardly responded. When I asked him about his own past, though, he smiled. He began talking, and didn't seem to want to stop.

Finally, I urged the conversation back to Macie. Asking her how she was liking L.A. She gushed about the sunshine, the beaches. She talked about all the reality TV stars she wanted to find, admitting reluctantly that reality television was her guilty pleasure. She seemed to emphasize the word *guilty*. She seemed surprised when I told her there was nothing to be guilty or embarrassed about. Jeremy rolled his eyes at that. I laughed when I pulled out the list of restaurants I had saved in my phone that I knew were frequented by celebrities. She was enamored by it.

I'd made that list when I first moved here because Allie loved the same shows. She was supposed to come and see me, so I planned out an itinerary that would hopefully help her catch a glimpse of a few of the people she liked most. The same thing Macie was doing now. Allie never made it out to visit, but I hadn't had it in me to delete that list. When Macie began talking about the same things Allie loved, something tugged at me. A feeling that was familiar and warm and welcoming.

So, I took that list of restaurants and gave them to Macie instead.

As we talked, everything around us seemed to fade, except that warm and welcoming feeling. That only grew stronger as she talked about all the trips down to L.A. she would have to make once Penelope moved. All the things she wanted to do and see. We began talking about traveling, all the places we wanted to go in the world. How we'd both been bungee jumping and ziplining, but eventually wanted to try skydiving. She spoke of her favorite foods and her favorite music. Literally jumping up and down with excitement when I agreed with her that Oreos are the superior cookie.

Jeremy had grabbed her arm and told her to calm down.

Her face fell. I found myself clamping my jaw shut to avoid snapping at him.

Because when Macie jumped with excitement over something as miniscule as cookies, it reminded me that there were people out there—people like Macie—who believed in savoring even the smallest moments of joy. I didn't know her well, but I could tell that Macie was the type of person who appreciated every breath she took, and who wanted to live as fully as she could before she took her last one. In sad moments, she'd be able to make those around her laugh. She'd always be a light in darkness. She was what this world needed more of.

And the fool next to her was trying to dim her. Snuff her out.

The more she spoke, the brighter she seemed to shine. The world blurred until she was the only light within it. The center of all my focus. All my attention. Nothing she said was boring. Even when she was talking about the fact that she bought the dress she was wearing on a discount– she spoke with so much excitement, so much animation, that I couldn't help but feel intrigued. She was a shooting star, a flash of blinding brightness in a life that had become so dark.

She came out of nowhere, knocking the wind from me, and I knew she'd leave me with sparkles in her wake.

I decided then that I could play the long game. I decided that if fate ever did me a favor and allowed this woman to cross my path again, I'd make her mine.

Acknowledgments

Wow, okay. Well, to be honest, I wasn't initially going to write up acknowledgments for this novel. I suffer from this little, annoying thing called imposter syndrome, and I've spent a lot of time telling myself that as a self-publishing indie writer releasing their debut book, I didn't deserve to have an acknowledgments page. That was reserved for big, successful authors.

Except, acknowledgments aren't for me. They're for all the people who've told me time and time again that my stories are worth telling, especially when I wasn't capable of telling myself those things; and for the people who helped me produce this piece of artwork that you've just finished reading.

First and foremost I'd like to acknowledge my husband, Bubs, for just generally being the greatest human being I've ever met in my entire life. The day I said "I think I want to start writing" you did not hesitate when you filled up my water bottle, gave me a cup of coffee, sat me down at my computer and told me to get to work. I think at the time you saw it as an opportunity to play uninterrupted video games, but the moment you read the first chapter I ever wrote, you smiled at me and said, "Yep. This is it. This is your *thing*." Ever since, the words of love, encouragement, and pride have not stopped flowing from your mouth, not for one second. For that, and so many reasons outside of it, I'll never stop being grateful for you. I can write hundreds of thousands of words about love, but none of them could come close to summing up the way I feel about you.

I want to extend my deepest gratitude for my friends Jasmine, Chey, Steph, and Joc for always hyping me up and making me feel like I'm not totally embarrassing myself on the internet. For always listening to my way-too-long voice memo rants, for looking at my reels before I post them, for the daily check-ins, the proofreads, and the "can you just look at this chapter?" or "can I use your Canva log in?" or "I'm sending you my newsletter, can you make sure I don't sound stupid?" For helping me make sense of the wild world that is self-publishing romance. I love you endlessly and I'm so glad to have found you.

I want to thank my life-long best friends, Julie, Kes, Lauren, and Lilly for their endless support. Not just in this book, but in literally everything I've done in my life since the age of thirteen. Even the dumb stuff. Like when I throw chocolate milk across your bedroom in a fit of rage, or convince myself I saw a ghost standing at the foot of your bed in the middle of the night, or when I'd make you lie for me about a sleepover so I could sneak out and go hang out with boys in high school. No matter how questionable my decisions or embarrassing my moments, you've always had my back. You four have been my biggest cheerleaders and my most shameless fans. My day-one homies. I love you so much and I can't wait to ride bikes with you someday soon.

My parents, for raising me to have a voice, and teaching me how to have the courage to use it. My mom for being deliriously enthusiastic in every venture I've ever taken. For thinking every single thing I do, or think, or say is really cool, even when it's not. My dad for being a dreamer, and making me witness all of the work that goes into following those dreams, so I could understand what it took for me to make my dreams come true too. Also, for being an extremely dramatic storyteller by nature, and for passing that trait onto me.

My very first beta readers, Kaycee and Brenna, for looking past the many, many grammatical errors in the earliest drafts of this novel and seeing the story beneath. For believing in that story and giving me the courage to move forward with it. For helping it become the book we read today.

My editor, Jacelyn, for helping me fix those grammatical errors and develop this into the best possible version of the book that it could be.

My cover designer, Gemma, for taking my extremely poor stock photo, clipart mess of a what-the-hell-is-this mock up and turning it into this beautiful design we see now.

My ARC readers, who got excited about this story before ever even reading it. For all your early reviews, your posts, and your love. The Book Community is hands down the best place to be. The endless positivity, support for Indie Authors, and universal love for books is truly a blessing to be a part of.

And of course, everyone else who has picked up this book since it was published. You are responsible for helping my dreams come true and I'm so grateful that there are people out there in the world who want to read silly little words I put on paper. I love you so much and I hope I get to keep doing this forever because of you.

About The Author

Sarah fell in love with reading as a child. She quickly learned that books can take her to all the places she always dreamed of going, and allow her to live endless lifetimes in the one she was given.

Sarah believes a good romance novel can make even the darkest days a little bit brighter. She believes in love stories readers can root for, the kind that will make even the skeptics believe in all that cheesy stuff like soulmates. She aims to produce stories that readers can pick up, and regardless of what's weighing them down in life, feel a little lighter when they finish.

Sarah was born in California and raised in Southern Oregon, and still considers herself a Pacific Northwest gal at heart; right down to being a coffee snob, collecting hydro flasks, adamantly believing in Sasquatch, and feeling like rain-drenched forests are a form of therapy. Sarah now resides in Arizona with her husband, Mike, and their dog-baby, Rue. When she's not writing, she's likely reading, and if she's not reading, odds are she's out searching for a decent cup of coffee, or a rainy pine forest.

Become a newsletter subscriber to learn more about what Sarah has coming next, and receive exclusive access to bonus content, early ARC sign ups, and more!
sarahabaileyauthor.com/newsletter

Connect with Sarah on social media:
@sarahabaileyauthor